Naughty Marigold

Best Wishes

Lois Fenn

Dedicated to all the people I love and have ever loved.

Naughty Marigold

Lois Fenn

Crow's Nest Books

First published in 2019 by Crow's Nest Books
18 Westgate, Ruskington, Lincs, NG34 9ES
www.loisfenn.co.uk

Distributed by Lightning Source
The right of Lois Fenn to be identified as the author of the work has been
asserted herein in accordance with the Copyright, Designs and Patents
Act 1988.

British Library Cataloguing in Publication Data
A catalogue record for this book is available from the British Library

ISBN 978-0-9542884-4-0

Typeset by Amolibros, Milverton, Somerset
http://www.amolibros.co.uk
This book production has been managed by Amolibros
Printed and bound by Lightning Source

THE AUTHOR: Lois Fenn is a retired school teacher with two sons and two daughters, six grandchildren, eleven great grandchildren and two great-great grandchildren. As well as writing novels she likes to spend time composing and illustrating poetry, gardening, learning to play the guitar and maintaining her country cottage. She has enjoyed sharing her wartime experiences, as an evacuee from Hull during the Second World War, with many groups of people around Lincolnshire.

Previous novels written by Lois Fenn:
The Magic Mooncat
Cobwebs in Time
Edge of Square Nine

The Magic Mooncat won the David St John Thomas prize for Best Fiction 2003/2004

All three novels were endorsed by Ann Widdecombe and are known collectively as *The Lincolnshire Trilogy*.

Of *The Magic Mooncat*

'The *Magic Mooncat* convincingly evokes the innocence and the ignorance of a past age.'

Ann Widdecombe

The Magic Mooncat won the David St John Thomas prize for Best Fiction 2003/2004

Of *Cobwebs in Time*

'Holds one's attention from beginning to end...a superb sequel to *The Magic Mooncat*...such depth of feeling bringing the characters to life.'

Sue Hodge

Of *Edge of Square Nine*

'For those who first met Hannah in *The Magic Mooncat,* it will be intriguing to find her now in the moral maze of modern living. Most people will recognise their own journeys from Square Nine.'

Ann Widdecombe

www.loisfenn.co.uk

Acknowledgements

As always, I have had the support of my family and friends.

My daughters, Lisa McGregor, and Karen Smith, and my sister Jacqueline Kemp have contributed to this novel with their ideas for the exterior and interior of Crystal House, sharing with me the enjoyment of creative writing. I have appreciated advice on computer technology from my son-in-law Fred McGregor and my grandchildren Vicky and James.

Thanks to Jane Tatam of Amolibros for editing and typesetting and advice and friendship, and to my guitar teacher, Gary Moir, for teaching me to play 'Somewhere over the Rainbow' which I have shared with Caroline!

Chapter One

This scene had taken place many times in Caroline Thorston's imagination, her brain taking on the attributes of a time machine, it seemed as she visualised his funeral with changing backgrounds, the seasons passing by. But in spite of her vivid imaginings, his life had continued year after interminable year. Now, at last, his funeral day was a reality; drearily autumnal, the air damp with a drizzle of rain and with the afternoon light fading towards a premature dusk.

In reality, she knew this area of the cemetery well. Once or twice a week, she used it as a short cut to the high street, following the pathways, reading the epitaphs on the gravestones and enjoying being removed temporarily from the great unhappiness of her married life. She prolonged her meanderings, pondering on the once physicality of the occupants of the graves, using names and ages to give fuel to her fertile imaging. Where had they lived? What had been their occupations? Sometimes her questions were answered. Large ornate gravestones indicated the roles played in life, particularly of those who had served the community. Some names showed a progression of births and deaths in rapid succession: a still-born buried with a mother, or an earlier sibling; a husband and wife united in death. She read the inscriptions each time, although after a while, their names and their life spans were as familiar to her as those of her acquaintances in the present time. She considered some names to represent homeliness and good nature, whilst other names, sounding unusual and cryptic to her senses, formed an image of lean and mean.

The trees, planted at the turn of the twentieth century, had been allowed to mature; her favourites being the magnificent horse chestnuts with their red 'candles' of blossom in the springtime, and now, in the autumn, the fascinating glimpses of their brown shiny fruits bursting through the green spiky casings. The children would be here soon, she mused, throwing sticks to knock them to the ground and exclaiming excitedly as they filled their pockets with the pristine conkers. Each year she would retrieve some ready-to-be-harvested on the ground, kicking her feet through the brown, crinkly leaves. It was widely claimed that conkers placed in the wardrobe would keep away moths, and scattered near entrances, repel spiders. She had no idea of the validity of this country remedy, but continued to repeat the act year after year, and had never been troubled with the ravages of clothes moths in the wardrobe although the spiders did not seem to have knowledge of this country remedy, frightening her with their sudden runs across the living-room carpet.

So, what was his viewpoint now? Had he ever collected conkers when he was a boy? Indeed, was he ever a boy, she wondered? He had never spoken of his childhood, in all of the years she had known him. Her mouth twisted at the idea of him as a playful child. Now, she allowed her vision to travel up the trunk of the tree close by the open grave. Initially, she was distracted by the texture of the bark, her eyes taking in the detail of the rough surface, followed by a desire to trace the details into her brain as though she were making a pencil sketch.

A sudden gust of wind rustling the leaves and fanning wisps of hair across her cheek, drew her concentration back to her question. She brushed her fingers across her face in an effort to control the wayward strands and drawing attention to herself. Her fellow mourners were staring through the rain, from under their umbrellas. Did they think that she was brushing away a tear? As if, she thought! So, was he looking down on the scene from up there? Had he stood silently listening to the description of his life, brief as were the details, earlier in the church nearby and then led the way to the waiting grave? She shivered. Eyes stared. He had listed the order of service; the prayers and hymns, yet to her knowledge he had no religious convictions.

Did he approve of her new black coat? Did he appreciate how long she had taken to select it, knowing that she would not choose to wear it again and begrudging the cost of it in the period of uncertainty preceding the reading of his will? But then would he care? She wore it for their approval. Did he ever care what she did, or thought, or felt?

She stared at the coffin as it was lowered into the grave. He was there! She drew her breath in sharply. He was there! Of course, he was there! He was inside the oak box that he had chosen from the catalogue many years ago, when he could still settle his mind to such things. There had been no discussion about this either. As with all areas of his life, she was not consulted. It was only after his death that she was aware of his wishes. He had decided to go for the most expensive coffin in the catalogue, with its ornate brass fittings and the brass plate later to bear his name.

This grave was his chosen place, wasn't it? He wanted to have his name carved on his gravestone as witness to his life and scorned any suggestion of cremation, almost cowering away from anonymity, she thought. He had no desire to be separated from his body and to allow his spirit to soar above the treetops. He had scoffed at such ideas; calling her an idiot to believe in eternity. He did not believe in the survival of the spirit, and after all, she thought, was not belief in eternity a crucial part of the whole business of being? We are what we think we are. She had always believed that. So, had his attitude rendered him spiritually powerless? Was she free from his critical gaze forever?

It was raining hard now, and the hazy autumn sunshine, that had filtered through the trees earlier that day, was now masked by grey clouds gathering over the cemetery and adding to the gloominess of the ceremony. Caroline glanced along the rows of mourners lining each side of the open grave, sheltering under an array of black umbrellas and listening to the voice of the vicar levelling into a drone of ritual incantation. She guessed that each one of them was impatient to escape from the steady, and chilling, drizzle of rain, to the comfort of the local hotel, noted for its generous supplies of savouries and desserts, and excellent coffee, and later, as their attention moved to lighter more personal topics, no doubt pronouncing it 'a good funeral.'

He would be pleased about that, she thought, the bitterness of her thoughts registering in the dryness of her mouth.

She shuffled uneasily, wondering if her last thoughts had escaped from her brain into audible sounds, but the watching faces remained impassive in the dull light and the ceremony drew to an end with the final words directing his soul to rest in peace. It was her turn now, apparently, to bring it all to an end. She dutifully gathered up some soil and dropped it on to the coffin lid. Traditionally, from the loving widow, it should have been flowers, a single rose perhaps. She shrugged and turned away.

Time moved on slowly after this. Her feet ached in the tightness of black narrow pointed-toed shoes, which she vowed never to wear again, along with the black coat, destined for the charity shop. The path through the cemetery to the waiting cars no longer appealed with its borders of neatly cut grass and variety of trees. She stared straight ahead, walking alone and then travelled alone to the hotel, sitting stiffly in the back of the funeral car and looking neither to the left nor to the right, unaware of a small gathering of voyeurs, curious townsfolk, at the cemetery gate.

Jenny Alford had given up trying to keep dry under the shelter of the trees, fringing the boundary of the cemetery. It had been overcast when she had set off, and she was cursing herself now for leaving her umbrella in the boot of her car. She squinted through the rivulets of water escaping from the strands of hair on her forehead. It was like looking at a scene from a film, she thought. A mystery kind of drama. Yet, she herself had been part of that drama three times a week for the last two years.

She had recently reached her fifty-second birthday and was in the throes of the menopause, with the accompanying hot flushes and a spasmodic menstrual cycle that wearied her with its effects on her hormones; her energy levels dropping down almost to a state of exhaustion for days on end. She waged war at infrequent interludes against the gathering of fat on her midriff, trying the latest fad, and giving up each time after a few weeks. However, in spite of all of the indignities she suffered as a middle-aged woman of single status, she took a pride in her ability to support herself, and to keep a car on the road, after her escape from the acrimony of an ill-fated relationship. She counted herself as fortunate that she had never committed herself to marriage, but on many occasions during the passing years, had experienced the vulnerability of being a single mother.

Her employer, Mrs Thorston, looked thin and decidedly black in her funeral rig-out, she thought, like a thin black twig, liable to snap at any moment. She had been at breaking point for months she mused; run ragged by that husband of hers. I bet she is glad to be on her own, playing the role of the grieving widow, and concealing her feelings behind that narrow black veil attached to her hat. It seemed that she was the only person, amongst those standing around the grave, who was dressed entirely in black, complete with the obligatory hat and gloves of someone of her class. There was no mistaking that she was the chief mourner. But then was she the only mourner? Were the others merely paying lip service?

Oh well, Jenny thought, that was the end of another chapter, and now what? Each day of her time spent at the house during the last two years began with picking up a list of instructions on her arrival. They were always placed carefully it seemed, on the worktop nearest to the kitchen door and, mostly, her services were required for general cleaning. But occasionally she would be requested to do some laundry work, applying washing to the machine or tackling a pile of ironing; not a favourite job. In spite of that, she looked forward to working in such elegant surroundings. The only people, apart from her employers, who she bumped into every now and again, were the window cleaner and the gardener. She was aware, from occasional overheard remarks between husband and wife, that a certain Mrs Wilson came at five o'clock each day to cook an evening meal, but their paths had never crossed. That woman would be wondering about her job now, she guessed. But then Mrs Thorston would still want to eat. She did not seem like the domesticated kind of person. One of the idle rich, Jenny mused, thinking of her daughter's description of her earlier that day.

She squinted through the rain. Apparently, the service was at an end. She watched her employer walking slowly away from the grave and struggling to get into the back seat of the funeral car. I bet she's relieved, she thought again. I would be. He was stark staring mad by the sound of him. He scared me, she mused and I did not have to go near him. He should have been in a secure place, locked up. But then perhaps she loved him. Perhaps things had once been different. Perhaps she had married him for his money. Their kind had arranged marriages like the Royals. Look how they turned out.

So, what now? The question was back in her mind. It was not her only job; she did dog walking and evening work, but it was the most highly paid, and she relied heavily on the money she received each week from Mrs Thorston. Not that she had given any indication of no longer requiring a 'daily'. In fact, she had not announced the death of her husband personally to Jenny, and the list of jobs accompanied by her wages had been on the worktop last week, as usual, with no sign of her employer. Her daughter had read the notice in the local newspaper of his death and of the date and time of his funeral at the local church.

She assumed that Mrs Thorston was married to him, she thought, as she watched the bedraggled mourners making their way back along the cemetery path. Well, she was known as Mrs Thorston. Was it all his own money, she wondered, or was she already a woman of means when she married him? He used to have a business in the town. She knew someone who had worked there as a typist, but she had no idea what kind of business it was. She might well be wealthy without his money and would not care about his business connections. But then what if she was now celebrating rather than bemoaning his fate? Still, that did not mean that she would inherit everything. Thoughts and arguments flitted backwards and forwards in her mind. She turned away now and walked along the pavement avoiding the deepening puddles in the uneven surface. Before she had reached the carpark at the local supermarket, the funeral car drove past, and she watched as it pulled in to the space at the side of the George Inn a hundred yards or so along the high street, and Caroline Thorston carefully stepped out onto the pavement.

Caroline knew that all of the mourners, present at the funeral, were now expecting her to acknowledge them for attending, and she dutifully stood in the foyer of the George Inn, shaking hands and mouthing words of thanks. She had lifted the narrow veil from over her eyes and had layered it on the top of her black felt hat. The former kind of disguise, now no longer concealed the shadows under her eyes and her wan features, and she had a sense of increased vulnerability. She needed to use the ladies' room, and by this time she had a sharp pain in the centre of her spine, combining with the fullness of her bladder. She gripped her stomach muscles hard, at the same time forcing out the words of acknowledgement expected by this company of strangers. At last she could retire for a while and sought out the door marked 'ladies' along the corridor at the rear of the premises.

'Thank God!' she exclaimed. She stared at her face in the mirror as she washed her hands. Good grief, she thought, I look like a dishevelled little mouse. He had often described her as mousey in the latter years of their marriage, she recalled, and she had never made any attempt to alter the colour of her hair, or to use heavily tinted make-up. It had all seemed pointless. She had no desire to be attractive to him, and who else was there? Her light brown hair, once her pride and joy, was fading into greyness at the temples, and her eyes had begun to droop and wrinkle with anxiety rather than with laughter lines. Now, in the emptiness of 'the ladies', it seemed that even her thoughts were echoing. She shivered in the chilling, clinical kind of atmosphere of the cramped room; white-tiled and smelling strongly of bleach; her shoulder muscles tensing and her pale lips pouting at her reflection. The sudden realisation that at last she was truly free, and able to be who she wanted to be, uplifted her for a moment, but then the entrance of two women, talking about the latest soap scandal, threw her thoughts back into isolation rather than freedom.

Two hours later she had returned to that sense of isolation in the house where she had spent the last ten years of her life, and ironically now to the freedom she had so long craved for. She spoke to the cat but the returning plaintive sounds and the rearing up into a begging pose, only reminded her that her pet was hungry. 'It's not time yet!'

Her voice was harsh against the ensuing silence, and again that sense of loneliness was overwhelming; not as some may suppose because of the death of my husband, she thought. No, she had always been lonely, hadn't she? It was a lifetime of loneliness. So, what is different now, she asked herself?

She went out into the garden, unable to tolerate the feeling of imprisonment indoors; even though the man she had always regarded as her prison warder was dead and buried. The rain that had fallen locally in unwelcome showers during the burial procedure in the cemetery was now draining from the foliage here and soaking into the small patches of soil still unencumbered by summer growth, or into places where the hoe had scraped away the recent invasion of chickweed and dandelions in her last rather vague attempt to bring some order.

Her mind now dwelt on that gathering of people; mostly strangers to her. He still owned shares in the commercial and retailing development business, but she was not familiar with many of the members of staff who had dutifully attended his funeral. Equally, most of them were not acquainted with her, and later, at the wake, she had entertained the feeling that they regarded *her* as a kind of spectre at the feast. She recalled how his secretary, Pamela somebody or other (her name was of no importance) was making little comments under the cover of her gloved hand. Her sallow-faced companion kept nodding as they both looked in her direction. In an unguarded moment one of them voiced the words 'rather running to seed'. The words were recognisable for everyone as a sudden lull in conversation dropped the level to a quiet hum. She knew that she was the target of this verbal barb, as the hasty covering of the mouth of one and the glance in her direction of the other, followed by muffled laughter, was, as she ruefully described it to herself, 'a dead giveaway'.

She wandered around the garden now, breaking off seed heads here and there and clutching them in her fingers. However, most of them were unidentifiable, and somehow, it did not seem to matter; man-named but not man-made, she thought. The importance was, that they, apparently like her, had all run to seed. She giggled hysterically, recalling the very thin lady at the funeral with her frizzy white hair whom she had likened to a dandelion; one puff and she would be lost in time forever like the childhood ritual.

She returned to the back door, with her posy of seed heads, suddenly feeling vulnerable in the failing light. A chill was creeping up her spine, and the first thing she did as she closed the door behind her was to reach out and turn up the thermostat on the boiler. She automatically set the temperature at seventeen degrees, and then carefully quarter-filled the kettle ready to make a hot drink. She perched on the high kitchen stool, as usual aware of its hardness, but her body not yet in tune with her mind and still accepting his rules. However, as she rested her elbows on the breakfast bar, listening to the familiar drone of the electric kettle in action, her eyes focused on the boiler thermostat. Why was she shivering? Why had she let herself be so controlled?

Yet still she hesitated, allowing only her mind to reach out to freedom from his tyranny. It was very hard to break the rules, and she automatically turned her head in anticipation of rebuke, catching sight of her face in the mirror on the opposite wall, and being startled by her own pale reflection. She reached forward again and turned the thermostat control towards eighteen, and then twenty. This act of defiance seemed to be the catalyst for her escape from her prisoner-like state. It was as though doors were opening wide and new landscapes were coming into view.

Her imagination was one place where he had never been able to enter.

'But I did allow him to darken my dreams,' she murmured.

Talking out loud was not unusual for her. She had begun to do it as his illness had trapped her more and more into the solitude of her own company. Now, the sound of her voice reminded her that she could say and do whatever she liked, and the first thing actually to do, she decided, was to rid the house of his presence, beginning with his clothes. She knew that it would be hard to do this. Not for any emotive reasons; any connectivity. There were just so many of them.

Being brought up through those years of 'make do and mend', he saw little reason to discard a garment with some wear left in it, even if it was considered to be no longer fashionable, and an array of suits, each in turn being given an airing at business or civic events, were sponged, brushed and re-hung back into their allotted place in his large mahogany wardrobes, together with his jackets and his shirts of similar vintage. Of course, there were those for best; top quality suits in their plastic protectors that barely saw the light of day. He always envisaged some kind of honour being bestowed on him as a local benefactor to the town.

What did he give, she remembered asking him once? His reply was a blow across her head. She shrugged her shoulders at the memory. Her head stayed intact, his did not. She giggled nervously at her kind of joke as she remembered that it was not so long after that incident, that he had started forgetting things, and the dementia had begun to creep in.

With such resentment of both the physical and the mental pain he had inflicted on her on numerous occasions, she had no qualms at the removal of his personal possessions from the house. Her unwillingness lay in the actual handling of them, and half an hour later armed with plastic gloves and bags she opened each drawer of the tallboy in his bedroom and gathered up the contents stuffing everything into the black bin bags as quickly as she could. Next, she slid the suits and jackets off their hangers in the large mahogany wardrobe, and unceremoniously crammed them into the waiting bags. The sight of his shoes, with the shoe trees in place were somehow a reminder of his cruel obsessive nature, and her skin prickled as a bin bag fell forward emptying some rolled-up pairs of socks across the floor.

'You can't haunt me!' she yelled hysterically. 'You did not believe in life after death, and it only works if you do.'

She repeated this sentiment a number of times, both mentally and verbally, during the next hour as if trying to convince herself of its validity. He had been dead for three weeks, and although he died in his own bed, and death was expected, there had been some discussion of an inquest. She had tried to continue as though everything was the same. In fact, nothing had changed except the hired nurses were no longer in attendance. The household maintenance continued, and she had made no effort to alter her routine. But as the circumstances of his death were accepted as above suspicion and an expected death was pronounced, the final documentation recording his death was completed, and his presence in her life began to wane. Of course, during those weeks before his funeral, she was no longer wakened each morning by the sounds of his harsh voice berating his nurse, or demanding his first drink, or his toiletry needs. Yet in spite of this, his presence seemed to remain, clinging to the general articles around which everyday activities depended. She visualised his lips touching the rims of the cups; lips that twisted into sarcasm and hurtfulness at her expense.

She fancied that she could hear his voice through the sounds made by the boiler, or the washing machine; stupid cow, stupid cow. She told herself that she was imagining things, and that he was still driving her mad, and now, turning away from the opened wardrobe, she sank down onto the bare mattress and cried; too exhausted to care that it was his bed, and the site of his most recent agonies. She stayed there for over an hour, until her limbs became stiffened by their stillness, and she struggled to her feet, casting a backward glance at the black plastic bags propped up against the skirting board as she left the room.

She had already decided to put the house on the market and find somewhere smaller and easier to maintain. It was described as a detached family house when her husband had purchased it ten years previously with its four large bedrooms and two box rooms, a large lounge, separate dining room and spacious well-equipped kitchen, all set in a half acre of land on the outskirts of a small market town in the heart of Lincolnshire.

She was surprised that she had been the sole beneficiary of his will, and at first was begrudgingly grateful for his apparent concern for her future. But on contemplation during the long hours of each night since his death, she began to realise that, through the twisting of his mind, and his conviction that he owned her, he wanted her to remain intact with all of his other possessions; one of his shackles, assuming that she would continue in her role as the obedient wife. As her train of thought concerning his intentions for her after his death took root, she was reminded of his love of ancient history and of how he admired the Egyptian rulers with their practice of taking their possessions to the grave. Did this include their household; their servants and possibly their wives?

She remembered from his comments on a television programme, a number of years ago, that he was in full approval of the Indian practice of suttee where the wife was expected to follow her husband into death on the funeral pyre. Arrogant pig! Yet, he did not believe in life after death, did he? It was really all about everyone remembering his life on earth.

She had smiled at the idea of him now turning in his grave and in a sudden gesture of vulgarity and boldness, quite alien to her in normal circumstances, she had yelled into the darkness, 'I'll make you turn! I'll make you bloody spin around!'

She spent the next three hours of the night trying to sleep, finally turning the light on and reading for a while until her head ached, and then wandering downstairs to make a drink.

'This is ridiculous,' she said to her reflection in the hall mirror. It seemed that he was tormenting her now more than ever. Over the years she had tried to ignore his criticism and had locked herself away in a prison of her own thoughts or had spent hours in the rambling back garden hoeing and planting in the spring and early summer, and dead-heading the roses, tidying the perennials in the border and cutting the grass during the remaining months of fine weather.

He had no interest in the back of the house, she recalled, as she sipped her hot chocolate. Apparently, no one of any standing saw that. His concern lay in keeping up appearances, and he had hired a man to keep the bricked forecourt in a pristine condition with a regular application of weed killer and jet washing. He had considered me incapable of doing anything really, she thought. Not that she did not appreciate having someone to do the cleaning. She had never used a vacuum cleaner in her life, and the thought of cleaning bathrooms and toilets made her shudder. All that was left to the cleaning woman. What was she called. Oh, of course! Mrs Alford, she mouthed. She would still need her. There was so much to do.

She frowned at the memory of his violence towards the cook two months before his death. He had accused her of stealing. That lady had walked out vowing never to set foot in the place again but then his lack of appetite no longer justified employing a cook and she herself had become indifferent to food apart from a bowl of cereal at breakfast and soup and a sandwich in the evening. He would not have appreciated my efforts anyway, she thought. Not that she could blame him for that. She smiled triumphantly recalling her attempts, in earlier days, to produce even a two-course meal, and hoping that it would give him indigestion. It was always a relief when he told her to telephone for 'a Chinese' or an 'Indian'. Even at breakfast time he had blamed her for his repeated attacks of pain in his gut. 'I think you are trying to poison me.'

His words repeated themselves in her brain now, and she remembered how the injustice of his criticism had angered her so much one evening that she had thought it would serve him right if she did poison him. Since the death of her parents she wanted to get rid of all of the people in her life who had endeavoured to make it a misery. Her mind had focused on the can of weed killer that was stored in the garden shed awaiting the next brick cleaning treatment. She visualised herself adding it to his nightly bedtime drink, and how he would suffer as he had made her suffer. Now, such thoughts had begun to haunt her, and reminded her that she must clear the garden shed at the first opportunity. Weed killer must have no place in her new life.

She made her way back up the steep staircase, hanging on to the banister in her state of weariness, and lurching in through the bedroom door. She switched on the radio, with no regard for the programme and its content and eventually drifted into an uneasy sleep for a few hours.

A burst of music returned her to a conscious state and she kicked the covers away, for a moment or two trying to cling on to a disturbing dream, but then giving up and coming face to face with reality. Suddenly, she remembered that it was Mrs Alford's day for doing the bedrooms. 'I should have told her that her services were not needed today,' she moaned, her voice merging with the Radio Four commentary. She looked at the clock, screwing up her eyes in an attempt to focus on the position of the hour hand. It was pointing past nine, and she jumped up in a panic and staggered across the room.

She always felt inadequate when she measured herself against the efficiency of Mrs Alford, yet that lady seemed pleasant enough she thought; simply doing her job, with no axe to grind. There was just something about her. She was what her mother would have described as vulgar; working class, probably with no aspirations other than downing a large gin and producing a succession of babies, all who increased the burden for respectable members of society. She could hear her mother saying it now. She could see her face, an indelible imprint on her mind; mean, twisting into contempt and spite. Her attitude towards anyone she considered to be beneath her had made a deep impression on Caroline's young mind in those early years of her life, and still, thoughtlessly, she retained this attitude towards the so-called working class.

She struggled to put some fresh clothes on, and gave her hair a quick brush, patting it down against her head again with her fingers, in an effort to make it presentable outside of the bedroom. Such a beginning to the day without the invigoration of a shower was already throwing her into a state of depression and when the ringing of the backdoor bell sounded some ten minutes later, the face she presented to Mrs Alford was what one might expect of a recently bereaved woman.

Jenny Alford was no stranger to the atmosphere in this establishment. 'You could cut it with a knife,' was her favourite pronouncement when discussing her employers with her daughter.

But then she had expected Caroline to be different now. He was finally laid to rest in the cemetery, and she was free at last, presumably with all that insane bastard's money. God, I would be dancing a jig, she thought as she took off her anorak and hung it on the peg in the hall. As always, she felt ashamed of her shabby coat, its grubby appearance made more apparent by the grandness of the surrounding furnishings. There was no list of duties on the work top, and she stood waiting for instructions, aware of the tightness in her chest. She had struggled to breathe during the early hours that morning and needed to use her spray. Her developing asthmatic condition was not something that she wished to broadcast. Dust could not be the enemy of a hired home help she reasoned, and she had begun to bleed again after a space of two months with no sign of menstruation. It was such an effort to get out of bed, but she needed this job and again was worrying about her future employment. The next words uttered by her employer seemed to establish her fears.

'I'm sorry. I didn't really need you today. I have been sorting stuff out. I'll pay you of course. Would you like a drink and then you can get off home?' Caroline was dabbing at her nose with a tissue and sniffing.

'Oh, bless you! Everybody seems to have got this cold. It couldn't have helped yesterday standing in all that rain. I saw the gathering across the cemetery. It was a good turnout, I must say.'

Jenny hesitated, taking Caroline's disapproving frown as an unwillingness to agree.

'Sorry Mrs Thorston. There's nothing good about a funeral is there? But it always seems to rain for a burial. Wouldn't do for me. I've told them all. Cremation, that's what I want.'

Caroline sighed, and reached for the kettle. Her face had set into deeper lines, the tension spreading from the eyebrows to the corners of her pale lips, and Jenny Alford, recognising her employer's vulnerability, kept control of the situation.

'Here, you sit down,' she directed, 'and I will make you a coffee. That is what I am here for, isn't it? But I will join you, thanks a lot. I don't really feel so well myself. I know you expected it. Folks think that makes it OK but when it comes to it, it is still a shock. Did many of your relations attend the funeral or were they all his? I've never heard you talk about them much. Not that there has been much time for chatter. Me always being so busy.'

She was not deterred by the silence that followed her questions. She had a feeling of power now. Suddenly, Mrs Thorston was the victim, and she herself was intent on 'finding things out', as she would describe it, busying herself making the coffee. What was she sorting; paperwork, his possessions, her things? Why did she not want help? Has she sacked me or is it just for today? Perhaps he had left everything to someone else. But then they had no family from what she could gather. There were no photographs around and in all the months she had been coming here, there had been no talk or sign of relations. Perhaps there was nothing left in the piggy bank, she thought. It must have cost a lot with all those medical expenses. She assumed that he did not rely on the National Health Service doctors, and those nurses were not from social services. Perhaps he had to pay for a previous relationship with a family involved. There were so many complicated relationships these days.

Now, Caroline sipped slowly at the steaming coffee. In spite of her reservations about her companion, Mrs Alford, after all, was another woman and therefore in this time of need, an ally; someone who would listen to her and perhaps offer some advice on where to take the bags of clothes. In spite of her loathing of him, it would not seem right to put them in the dustbin. What would the bin collectors think? Besides, she reasoned, there were too many bags and what about the suits and overcoats?

She broke the silence.

'I need to dispose of some bags. Do you think anyone would be glad of them?'

'What? Do you mean bin bags? Do you mean his clothes?'

Caroline nodded, and gave her coffee another stirring. She could feel the colour rising in her pale cheeks, and Jenny Alford, a woman not described as quick on the uptake by her friends and family yet criticised by them for her compassion without prejudice, leaned forward to give her employer's arm a reassuring squeeze, followed by a scraping back of her chair ready to retreat from such familiarity.

'Don't you worry,' she said. 'It must be so upsetting for you. I'll take them to the charity shop. I'll do that instead of the bedrooms, shall I? Then I can stay for the rest of the day if you like. I don't mind doing something different to normal. I'll load everything up in my car. It will save you getting your car out and it won't take me long. Unless you want to go of course. Or do you want to sell anything?' She stopped, taking in a deep breath, and waited for a reply.

Her employer's vigorous shaking of the head at the idea of profiting from the disposal of the clothes and then nodding and mouthing, 'Yes please' at the suggestion of needing some help, were reassuring, and Jenny's spirits lifted. She was heavily in debt this month, paying off one credit card with another. She was hopeful of finding a good outlet for the suits and jackets and in any case, she desperately needed to keep this job.

'There's no rush is there? Well not for me at any rate. I can stay on. There's nothing pressing today. You look done in. Are the bags upstairs? I'll get them down and you have another coffee and put your feet up. You'll make yourself ill, you know. Just you tell me what you want doing, if you need any help that is.'

She stopped talking, taking another deep breath as the wheeziness was back, and reached forward to refill the kettle, suddenly sensing hostility and realising that she was stepping out of line.

'I'm sorry Mrs Thorston. Me and my chatter! I'll leave you in peace. I just hate to see you looking so miserable. I'll vac the lounge while you decide what to do.'

Caroline watched her leaving the kitchen and that uneasiness was back. She was feeling more inadequate now in spite of seemingly having an ally. This woman, who had rarely spoken in the past, was now probing into her privacy. She could still feel the pressure of her fingers on her arm. Oh well, she thought. I'll get her to sort out the clothes and then I will manage without her until I find somewhere else to live. Or perhaps I'll go on a world cruise. That idea comforted her and she returned briefly to a favourite daydream of sunshine and sea and sand.

Half an hour later, Jenny Alford loaded the bags of clothes into the boot of her old car, aware of the gaze of her employer at the lounge window. That lady had taken little or no persuasion to stay at home and leave the charity-shop run to her employee. Jenny waved as she pulled away, smiling at the success of her ploy to profit from this so-called act of charity. She turned in at the next road, coming to a halt at a convenient stopping place, and got out of the car. She knew that there were some items of clothing far too good for the charity shop. A so-called 'Nearly New' shop that had recently opened up at the far end of the High Street would welcome the addition of suits and jackets. She had heard that they paid a fair price and assumed that it was not a place her employer would visit. She carefully folded three pairs of trousers, two overcoats and three jackets, putting them to one side in the boot, alongside the two suits in their protective plastic sleeves, and rummaged in the bin bags, pulling out shirts and unravelling ties. There was little wear in some of them, and a great deal of wear in others. Her nimble fingers quickly sorted them into two piles; one for the charity shop and the other to complement the suits.

She ignored the bag containing his shoes. She was superstitious about shoes. They seemed to be far more personal; each crease registering a significant step. Dead men's shoes! She shuddered. However, she fished out a few cotton vests and tee shirts, and bundled them into the corner of the boot. Her brother ran a back-street car cleaning service and was glad of old rags to get the worst of the dirt from car exteriors. 'How have the mighty fallen,' she sniggered, recalling how Mr Thorston had threatened to give her the sack when she was taking an unscheduled break. He had come into the lounge and found her sitting on the settee.

How dare I, she asked herself now, visualising his face twisting in anger? That was a few months ago before he became totally bed bound. Private nursing care was established from that time on and his room was out of bounds. Not that she had any desire for contact with him or any information regarding his state of health. He had no sympathy for her shortness of breath on that particular day, she remembered. Instead, he had implied that she should stop smoking. It was on the tip of her tongue to tell him that she did not have bad habits like he did, but she needed this job and, in any case, she liked Caroline Thorston.

She toyed with the idea of treating herself to a coffee before she returned. She had deposited bags of clothes first to the nearly new shop, and then the nearest charity shop. She had thirty-five pounds more in her purse now than when the day had begun, but her expectations had been higher. Snotty cow, that shopkeeper, she fumed inwardly. OK so they were not in, what did she say, a pristine condition – that was it. Jenny had never heard the word 'pristine' before, but from the woman's comments about coffee stains or worse, she guessed that it meant that dry cleaning was necessary. 'We can't all be bloody pristine,' she muttered as she sank back into the car seat and switched on the engine.

As she drove back along the main road leading away from the

shops, she cast her mind back to Mrs Thorston. She had been working there for over two years now yet she knew very little of the family. Indeed, she thought, there did not seem to be a family. She knew that her employer was named Caroline. She had seen it occasionally on envelopes delivered by the postman, which she gathered up from the hall floor and put on the small table next to the ornate coat stand, during her morning cleaning sessions. But usually, the envelopes were addressed to him; R B Thorston Esq. Business letters in long buff envelopes. She could not remember many square white ones that could have been greetings cards; not even at Christmas. She was recalling now how even the regular mail seemed to diminish in quantity as he became increasingly bed-bound, with the inevitable leaflets advertising goods and services sliding through the letter box unsolicited.

When she arrived back at the house, she went around to the back door as usual. It was standing open and she glanced across the patio, catching sight of her employer beyond the lawn, in the act of digging a hole. She was about to call out but stopped and watched as Caroline laid down the spade and walked along to the garden shed. Moments later, she emerged, carrying some kind of container. Jenny dodged behind a potted tree on the patio slabs, reaching in her pocket for her mobile phone. She felt that something was not normal, and she had got into the habit of using her phone camera ever since the time that she had been advised to photograph any evidence of her ex-partner, Trev's, personal extravagancies when she was claiming monetary support for her daughter. She had done this a few years ago, when Sherry needed a sports kit for school. She discovered that he planned to share a meal with his latest 'little bit on the side', as he called the brassy blond who looked the same age as her daughter Sherry. It was truly a slap-up meal, and yet he was claiming poverty. The social services woman had taken her side then. There was no way he could deny it, and he had been forced to pay off some of the arrears.

Now, she peered out from behind the foliage. Caroline was holding up the container in the act of dropping it into the hole and in the same instance Jenny's mobile phone camera was put into action in video mode.

Chapter Two

'It is weed-killer, isn't it? Look. You can see the side of a "w" and then "k-i-l".'

Jenny Alford pointed to the brief video imagery on her phone, putting the action on hold. Her daughter Sherry peered at it.

'Could be, I suppose. God, Mother, your phone went out with the ark. Isn't it time you upgraded it? But why would she be burying a can of weed killer? Why not put it in the bin? And why did she wait until you were out of the way?'

'I don't know. Unless she thinks it's dangerous. They do tell us not to put chemicals in when it's going to landfill, don't they?'

'So, she put it in the land in her garden! That doesn't make sense either. You don't think she poisoned her bloke, do you? Now that would make sense.' Sherry giggled and puffed at her 'roll up', blowing the smoke out across the kitchen.

Jenny shrugged. 'It seems like a strange thing to do don't you think, when she is in the middle of clearing out his clothes? And why wait until I was out of the way?'

'What did he die of?' Sherry stubbed out her cigarette on her plate; stirring in the ashes amongst the biscuit crumbs. 'I know you said you hadn't seen him for a while. A lot of medical care or something, wasn't it?'

'I really don't know. I heard him shouting his head off. He had a foul temper even before he became ill. I tried to keep out of his way. He threatened to sack me for having a break. I had a cold and my breathing was bad. Why she stayed with him God only knows. Still, I suppose she was having an easy life.' Jenny shook her head as if in disbelief. 'She had a roof over her head,' she continued, 'and there was plenty of cash you know. She didn't have to do anything around the house, did she? I've been doing it for over two years. I don't know about the cooking. Someone used to do an evening meal and I remember hearing they had a full-time housekeeper at one time. Apparently, she left suddenly. Still, there is only so much flesh and blood can bear if he made her life hell. We all know what that is like.'

She stood up scraping the chair legs on the dingy vinyl tiles and gathered up the mugs and plates. 'Can't you use an ashtray? What do you think my kitchen is? A midden? Anyway, it wouldn't be the first time, would it? You know. Poisoning a husband. Did you watch that programme on tele the other week? It was about women poisoners in the Victorian years. It said that these are the stories of the ones who got found out, but poison was a favourite way to get shut of somebody and many cases must have gone undiscovered Of course the bodies had to be exhumed. He was buried.'

'Who was?'

'Mr Thorston! Her hubby! It wasn't a cremation. If she had poisoned him, she would have had him cremated, wouldn't she? I read the announcement in the *Journal*, and then I walked across to the far side of the cemetery. Got a good view from there. Bloody awful day, yesterday, wasn't it? I don't think it stopped raining for long.'

'So, Miss Marple! Are you on the case then? I would rather go to bingo this after. Do you fancy it? Did she pay you by the way?'

She went into the small area that separated the bedroom and bathroom from the general living space to get her coat from off the peg, and Jenny seized the moment to reach for her handbag and to push it to the back of the worktop behind a half-eaten loaf of bread and the electric toaster. She could visualise the bank notes in payment for the 'nearly new clothes', hidden away in the zipped pocket inside. With that addition to her income, she had not reminded her employer of her wages, worrying about getting finished there and leaving herself with an excuse to return on her usual Tuesday of the next week.

So, she could now truthfully reply that she had not been paid. 'I will get it next week I expect,' she said as her daughter re-appeared. 'I don't want to press her. I have the feeling that she is going to give me the push. She didn't know I was back you know. I crept around to the front again and sat in the car out of sight and had some crisps. When I went around again there was no sign of her in the garden and there she was, sat in the kitchen just staring out of the window. I told her it was all done and I would be back on Tuesday or earlier if she needed any extra help. She just nodded and waved her hand at me. She looked a bit strange really. In a kind of a trance or something, I didn't like to press her. So, I'm a bit strapped for cash at the moment.'

'Really! And when was that news then? You're always stony broke. I don't know why you don't ditch these jobs and get down to the benefit office. I bet you could qualify with all the complaints you have. It's no good talking to you, though, is it? You're not even listening, are you? I'll leave you to your fantasies then and don't forget you owe me for your bingo when that rich old cow pays you and just you stick to your diet. I've lost another five pounds.' Sherry's voice echoed in the small kitchen as she finally took a breath.

Jenny sighed as the door slammed. The speed with which her daughter could speak never ceased to amaze her. That was the third time she had reminded her of that loan, she thought. What about all the times she had helped her out? And did she have to shout. Noisy little cow, she thought. Anyone would think I was deaf or daft. She stroked her hand over her stomach. It wasn't bad. It was normal to spread a bit after the change. She'd read that in a magazine. Apparently, it was all about hormones. She had had a super figure when she was Sherry's age. These kids don't know the half of it, she thought. And all this talk of upgrading phones. Where did that fit in with her daughter's benefits? Along with her new all-singing, all-dancing television, she thought, her mouth twisting in criticism at Sherry's attitude towards life.

'Anyway,' she announced to the parrot, 'she can wait for her money and I'm going to enjoy my treat. And if you promise not to tell, you can have some of it.'

She unfastened the top button of her jeans and slid down the zip.

'God that's better,' she exclaimed. 'Now for the bra.' She struggled to undo the hooks, sighing with relief as the tightness around her breasts was released. 'Bloody bras crucify women,' she said to her pet. 'You don't know how lucky you are not to be trussed up like a chicken. Men don't know they are born.' She giggled at the idea of Polly being trussed up. What a tiny meal she would make!

In spite of the release of physical tension, she was finding it difficult to take a deep breath. The smoke from her daughter's last cigarette still drifted against the ceiling, and she thought of her employer's elegant house with its high ceilings and clean air and sighed with frustration over the unfairness of life. This cramped space went under the name of social housing. It could hardly be called a house. Merely a collection of small spaces each with a purpose to help with survival. The living room housed a settee and a coffee table. A small television crouched in one corner on a stand with a shelf underneath to store the controller and any current magazines or circulars, and in another corner the bird cage obscured part of the view through a netted window. The tiny kitchen, situated beyond a white door discoloured by age and neglect, housed the basic utilities; a stainless-steel sink, a fridge-freezer and a washing machine along one side under a frosted glass window and an electric oven with a gas hob on the opposite wall, with an oblong of worktop; sufficient space for a small microwave oven. The blue table, with its Formica top, and accompanying two plastic seated chairs, was as old as her relationship, bought from a door to door salesman for a few shillings a week for ever; or so it had seemed at the time.

She made herself a cup of coffee and then opened the fridge, reaching into the back of the top shelf and drawing out a paper bag containing a vanilla slice; thick custard sandwiched between flaky-pastry, and the top heavily coated with sticky icing sugar. It was her favourite dessert and she decided that, together with the milky coffee, it would see her through until tea-time. She chose to relax on the settee in her tiny living room, and slowly pressed her teeth into the flaky pastry, licking away the custard before it descended on to the plate and ignoring the stickiness of the icing sugar, already transferring itself onto her fingers. To hell with the calories, she thought. Did that

Mrs Thorston care about calories? She wouldn't have to, would she? She could afford to have plastic surgery. Anyway, she was already stick thin. If I had her money I could be stick thin and get rid of these, she reasoned, patting first her chest and then her bulging stomach.

She savoured the taste until the last of the sweetness had slid down her throat giving her a sense of wellbeing and then she relaxed back on the sofa with a sigh of contentment and turned on the television. As she stared at the screen, her thoughts returned to her employer. 'She ought to be enjoying life, poor cow,' she muttered. 'I'll take her some cream cakes next week.' She closed her eyes and during the next half an hour, her body slid into a blissful sleep state. A sudden burst of laughter from a contestant in a television quiz show woke her with a start, and she struggled up from the sofa and returned to the kitchen, rinsing her fingers in the washing-up water and feeling that life was not so bad now that she had some money for the weekend. As long as our Sherry doesn't get wind of it, she thought.

Caroline had watched with mixed feelings as Jenny Alford had disappeared down the drive. There was something about the woman that she mistrusted and yet to be fair, she thought, she had been very helpful. Yet it was that sudden burst of familiarity. 'Give them an inch and they'll take a mile.' Her mother's words of advice echoed in her head. She had never actually communicated much with Mrs Alford before, beyond making the occasional request to do a special task. And that was once in a blue moon, she thought. There was always a list of jobs for her to do and on a Friday her wages were placed in an envelope on the kitchen dresser. She could be relied on to be thorough. That was one good thing about her.

'I didn't give her any wages, did I?' she said out loud. Oh well. It was not long until Tuesday. She would have to wait. Her thoughts returned to earlier events. Clearing out clothes had never been a part of the 'daily's' weekly chores simply because nothing had ever been thrown away before. Perhaps she had not gone to the charity shop. Perhaps she had kept them for her husband. Did she have a husband? Caroline had no idea of her home life. Did she have a family? It was pretty obvious that she did not have much money, although she did have a car. Well, of sorts. She certainly was not starving, but then perhaps she filled up on bread and chips. From what she had heard, the working-class people often did, or perhaps she feasted on take-aways. She could certainly do to lose some weight, she mused.

'Oh well!' she mouthed patting her flat stomach and running her hands down her hips. The woman was a god-send at the moment with her local knowledge and in spite of her working-class attitude. She would keep her on for the time being. If she put the house on the market, there would be a lot to do to make it presentable for would-be purchasers. 'Better the devil you know,' she muttered. There could be a few trips to the charity shops before she had finished getting him out of her life, and she had no intention of humiliating herself by associating with such places and being recognised by past employees at the engineering works.

The weekend passed by with little activity for Caroline. She meandered, as she would describe it, designating various items to various piles in an effort to bring some minimal feel to the place. According to Mrs Alford, people liked the minimal thing these days. Possessions had been his thing, she thought. But not any possessions. They had to be investments.

She gave up re-organising the house quite early on Saturday, spending some time in the supermarket and trying to drum up an appetite for a meal. Now that the private nursing care team were no longer needed, she was relying on herself to prepare food. They had made sure that he was well looked after, and she had always been included with a tray set for her in the dining room, after he had become bed bound. She knew that she could well afford to keep some extra staff on for all of her requirements, but the association with her husband pinned her memories to his illness and she decided that she could survive on ready meals stored in the freezer and easily microwavable.

The usual evening television drama satisfied her need to fantasise. It was a complication of crime scenes leading to a super sleuth solving all the riddles. She had watched the weekly episode and, for an hour, it took her mind off her own problems. Sometimes, she drifted into moments of sleep, and struggled to follow the plot, but her awareness of her solitude now had sharpened her mind, allowing her to fantasise. As the credits appeared on the screen, she sank back into her chair, taking in a deep breath. She could relate to the leading character in the drama, who was a woman of substance surrounded by grasping relatives. Not that I am bothered with relatives, Caroline thought, but the wealth was real enough, and no doubt she was in danger of being exploited.

However, she was ready for her bed by the time the programme had ended and slept soundly, waking up some eight hours later, energised and more resigned to return to the chores she had abandoned on the previous day. It was eight o'clock, and she switched on the radio, picking up on the latest news and weather forecast. The warmth of the bed, and the drone from the radio gripped her senses. But then the sound of children going to school and of the dust cart making its noisy way along the streets wakened her thoroughly into a working week.

So much was going on in her mind, and now she knew that this had to be her new start. This was a new week, a new time when everything that had gone before was gone forever. She must not dwell on the past. All the repressed energy over the greater part of her married life was now seeking to escape, albeit with some hesitation, but the act of ridding the house of his personal possessions had propelled her mind into action. Mr Carter, their solicitor, or as he kept reminding her, Brad, was urging her to come to terms with her monetary situation. She knew that it all had to be done, and that she had no knowledge of investments; stocks and shares and the like. All she wanted was money in the bank, a bank card and a cheque book. She had no desire to have any form of 'on line' banking, she declared, on the grounds that she would be in danger of the rest of the world invading her privacy and stealing her money, but the truth was that she was totally ignorant of anything to do with computers, learning about the prevalence and threat of cyber-crime from a recent programme on the television. The nearest she got to modern technology was in the ownership of a mobile phone that she used purely as a traditional phone, carried around in her handbag during the last few years for times of emergency involving his care. Text messaging was a mystery to her. After all, she had no one to text message, and the phone remained dormant in her handbag, switched off for the main part now that she was a single woman again.

She understood money on a monthly basis. He had paid her an allowance each month to cover the cost of running the household in as much as she organised the shopping and the cleaning. She paid Mrs Alford weekly, and the window cleaner every fortnight, and took responsibility for the regular shopping trips for food. Give him his due, she thought, as she carefully folded her clothes fresh from the tumbler drier, he gave her a generous allowance. But then he expected me to live up to his image. It had not been pleasurable for most of the time. She had not enjoyed buying new clothes, agonising over whether he would approve or whether she would have to return them and choose ones he would like. In fact, during the last year she had bought nothing. These days she felt comfortable in jeans and a casual acrylic top with the addition of an old chunky 'woolly' when the temperature became too low on inclement days.

There would be no need for that now, she thought, giving a little giggle and visualising him checking the meter and totting up how much gas was being used. The house felt so different; warm and cheery. Did she really want to move and leave her garden behind? She could always dig up all the plants and take them with her. She shrugged. 'Stop wasting time,' she muttered. His sudden decline at the age of sixty-two had heightened her awareness of the speed in which life could change. At a stroke! The expression came into her mind, as she recalled the day when it happened. That first major sign that something was wrong. She had accepted his mood swings and violent outbursts as a normal part of his personality. She could not remember him ever being placid, but according to his doctor, dementia had been on the cards for a number of years, and the stroke was a prelude to greater and greater mood swings and delusions.

The sound of the telephone ringing in the lounge startled her, causing a lurching feeling to travel across her chest as she hurried across the room.

'Hello,' she gasped into the receiver.

'You sound out of breath. Sorry, did I disturb you? Are you OK? Brad here.'

'Oh! Hello Mr er Brad.' Caroline repeated her Hello, trying to repress her feelings of panic, and attempting to sound like the confident and matter-of-fact person she longed to be. She felt the tears pricking at the backs of her eyes and blinked, screwing up her face in an effort to gain control of this dreadful feeling of panic.

'You sound tired.' The solicitor's voice had that soothing quality she knew he used when speaking to clients. She had witnessed him in action on the occasions when he had visited the house. Yet, she longed to be drawn in to that comforting world, and the tears now ran down her cheeks. She breathed in sharply, at the same time dragging her fingers across her face and merging the tears into the dryness of her skin. All those years of repressing her emotions had left their mark, and now she spoke slowly with apparent control assuring him that she was fine and that he must be psychic, as she was on the point of ringing him.

She did not hear his response. The actions of Peggy the cat suddenly caught her attention. The little creature had stopped part way through the act of washing herself and now leant back, one leg poised in the air, her eyes fixed and staring. What was she looking at? Caroline followed the line of her vision to the half-opened lounge door, and she felt the goose pimples rising on her arms and neck. 'Just a moment,' she gasped into the phone. She went over to the door, opening it wide, and looked into the hall, allowing her gaze to travel up the steep staircase. The signs of emptiness and the stillness first reassured her, and then sent shivers down her spine.

Peggy now had resumed her vigorous actions of cleaning herself, and Caroline returned to the phone feeling rather foolish, her arms prickling with goose pimples. 'Sorry about that,' she murmured. 'The cat decided to jump up on the worktop. You know what cats are like. So, when is it best for me to come and see you?'

'It's all pretty straightforward, but probate is never easy. Your husband did you a huge favour leaving everything to you. But we still have to jump through all the hoops.'

She pretended to consult her diary, even going through the actions of turning pages in the air and confirming that Wednesday at two o'clock would be fine.

'Oh, my God! I'm going crazy. I must get out of here,' she exclaimed after replacing the phone. She spread her fingers through her hair, clawing the strands outwards and pulling against her scalp. The tension spread down through her shoulders joining the pain lurking in the pit of her stomach. The cat had now curled up on the doormat and a stillness filled the house, threatening rather than reassuring. She was convinced that 'he' was there checking up on her and on his money. The cat was aware. Cats were like that. She had read that somewhere.

She knew that there was a great deal of paperwork to get through, and, she would willingly leave it in the solicitor's capable hands, but as executor she had to sign the various legal documents. What if she declined? What if she said that she did not want his money? Would he leave her alone or would he haunt her for ever? She sighed. It was going to take weeks. That Brad Carter had said as much.

Ten minutes later she was walking along the avenue, a scarf tied tightly around her head and her coat collar turned up to shield her throat from the cold wind. Her feet, it seemed, were intent, at first, on following their usual route through the cemetery, but then her eyes looked beyond the gates to the beginnings of the narrow high street. She fought against the urge to look up the path between the gravestones, cursing herself for being so impulsive and not taking the car out of the garage. She walked quickly, her gaze fixed on a row of shops at the far end beyond the supermarket. She did not recall seeing them before. 'Nearly New'. The shop sign caught her attention. Was it an antique shop? Perhaps she could get some advice on all the clutter he had accumulated over the years.

She was disappointed to find the shop window space was hung with clothes and a sign in one corner proclaiming that top prices were paid for good quality clothes. She was turning away, when the navy suit displayed on a mannequin caught her eye. It was his best suit! She knew that immediately. He had boasted of the unusual buttons and the midnight blue satin lining, now showing where a flap had been deliberately pinned back to attract attention. There was no visible price tag on it and she guessed that it was given pride of place to draw potential buyers into the shop.

She hesitated, wondering whether to go inside and see what else of his was for sale, and at what prices. But then did she really want to draw attention to herself or re-acquaint herself with his clothes? She looked behind her to see if she was being observed. Would any of his colleagues recognise the suit? Would they gossip about her greediness in selling his clothes and with all that money! She could almost hear their raised voices at some coffee morning or during office tea breaks. Those two gossiping at the wake. 'Fancy, she has got his clothes for sale.' 'Really! With all that money. Greedy cow!' She turned back quickly, stumbling on the kerb and began to walk briskly up to the next bend in the road, fixing her gaze on the large supermarket sited at the trading centre built on the edge of the town. Yet still her thoughts dwelt on the suit and she frowned, recalling the deceit of her employee.

No wonder she was so eager to help. She must be rubbing her hands now and telling her husband of her good fortune. Did she have a husband? She had asked herself that question before and was still no wiser. It wasn't the money, was it, for goodness sake, she thought. It was just the deceit of it all. She herself had no desire to profit from his clothes. The thought of it made her shudder. The image of the suit on the mannequin began to merge with her memory of him standing in front of the cheval mirror in his dressing room and it suddenly seemed that he was re-incarnated with a plastic featureless head of a dummy; brought back from the dead. She began to wonder where the rest of the bundles of clothes had ended up. Somehow, it had not occurred to her that she might see them again. They were good quality after all, in spite of the fact that they were old. Men of his age did not cling to fashion and no doubt someone in the town would have an eye for a bargain or perhaps a benefit scrounger, as her mother had described people on welfare, would swagger around to the local pub, showing off the unusual details on the jacket.

She wandered around the supermarket filling a basket with an assortment of foodstuffs, her arm beginning to ache, and later with two carrier bags dragging down her shoulders, she trudged back to the house. The last stretch of road was a challenge. This was not something she ever did without taking the car, and she staggered up the drive and struggled to fit the key in the lock. She stared dispassionately at the groceries as she emptied the carrier bags. It had seemed like a good idea to keep her strength up with a variety of fruit and vegetables but now she had no appetite for anything except a strong cup of coffee and a biscuit.

Later, as she huddled in bed under the covers, her eyes remaining open yet seeing only blackness, her body still ached with tension. Eventually, after over an hour of willing herself to fall asleep, she gave up on the whole idea of it and reached out to turn on the light and the radio. Familiar music blared out.

'Oh God,' she moaned. 'It's always the shipping forecast.' She had listened to it so many times in the past, falling asleep during an earlier programme and unerringly waking up to the monotonous tones of the shipping forecaster's voice. Sometimes she turned down the volume, waiting for it to finish, and straining to hear the sounds of the national anthem, but usually she suffered all the way through, glad of any noise. Now, she listened, visualising the map of the British Isles as the radio voice travelled around the coastline, mentioning place names and using descriptions of weather conditions so familiar to her yet still incomprehensible. He was at Cape Wrath. Not far to go now. She screwed her thoughts up in an attempt to visualise Cape Wrath. It reminded her of a book she had in her childhood. Giant Land. Giant Two Heads could have lived at Cape Wrath or was it where Little Tim set sail in the giant's tricorn hat?

She gave a sudden shudder. That book used to fill her with terrors, yet she could not stop studying the black and white engravings with the strange occupants of Giant Land. She hated the sea. The thought of all the strange creatures moving around in the blackness below the surface made her cringe. A giant crab in the story had filled her head with visions of monsters, and a film depicting the terror of a giant squid, its tentacles writhing across the deck of a ship and watched during her childhood, had put horror pictures in her head for months afterwards.

Two bad channel crossings in later life had imprinted themselves on her memory. The boat had tipped and tilted and, on both occasions, she had fought and lost against nausea and fear. The channel tunnel would have been a favoured option for her, rather than a sea crossing, but he would not hear of it. Sea sickness was not part of his agenda he had once declared. 'Arrogant swine,' she mouthed into the surrounding, subdued lighting, remembering his words. It did not matter that she was trapped in the toilet area with the sounds of other people experiencing sickness adding to her own suffering. These yearly crossings during what she supposed could be described as normal days of their marriage were in no way connected to holidays. He had no desire to share his leisure time with her. His business meetings spending two or three days at a time in hotels in different locations satisfied his need to travel and the channel crossings were purely to stock up his wine cellar and to buy a selection of cheeses from the French supermarkets. He directed her to sort out the cheeses, she remembered, in readiness for those dreadful cheese and wine parties when he entertained his cronies and their wives, all intent on so called one-up-man-ship.

As she stared up at the ceiling, noticing a spider making its way along the flaking surface, she recalled their pretence at sniffing and tasting the wines, and the behind the hand comments as their eyes moved around the furnishings and ornaments. Now here I am, she thought, miles away from all of that lifestyle, and still lost at sea in the middle of the shipping news. She gave a nervous little giggle, realising that even in this agonising, she was making a huge drama out of it all, yet somehow taking strength from it.

She had done this as a child, she recalled, smuggling a torch upstairs at bedtime, projecting the beam around the bedroom or under the covers, pretending that she was in a different world. What a lonely little rich girl of Schoolgirl Annuals she was, packed off to boarding school during term time and left in the care of the au pair during the holidays. She had known she was adopted from the early years of her schooling. In fact, she could recall the exact day, Friday the thirteenth of May, when she had become aware of her own history. She visualised the jeering face of Stephany Staid. Hers was a name she would never forget. She was the class bully and her spiteful ways blighted the life of anyone of a timid nature.

'Caroline Pearson! That's not your real name.'

'Of course, it is.' Caroline remembered her words so clearly. She was struggling to translate an English passage into French. It was always a major task for her that way around, whereas French to English allowed for some guess work, easy with her fertile imagination that coloured not only foreign languages in her life.

'They're not your real mum and dad. You were adopted. Probably found on a door step. So there! It's common knowledge my mum says.'

Apparently, she had not wasted any time in telling everyone in the class that she had overheard her parents discussing it.

Caroline could remember that day not with anguish, but with a strange kind of relief that a huge puzzle had been solved. Now threads of memories began to weave together into tangible thoughts. She had always felt different. She was an only child but there were aunts and uncles and cousins. They all seemed to be related in both looks and personalities. No one ever said that she had a look of the Pearsons or the Greenways. Well, once or twice perhaps. 'You can see where she has come from,' somebody once said. How quickly it was denied by her mother. She did not understand why but now she knew. How could she look like her mother who wasn't her mother, after all? Admittedly, she was tall and thin like her adoptive mother. But there the resemblance ended, light brown hair and hazel eyes rather than the fair hair and blue eyes. She could have been related to the man she called father for her hair colouring. He was tall and thin, but apart from physical characteristics, she had never had a sense of belonging.

As the day progressed, it had begun to make sense and lend rein to her fantasies. Somehow, it was like a gate swinging open into a whole new landscape, no longer imprisoning her into a seemingly allotted space. Her origins, apparently, apart from the strange door step scenario, could now be under her own control; how she herself supposed them to be and ripe for development. By late afternoon, she had already confounded Stephany's spiteful intentions by rejoicing in her new-found state.

Later, when she wove her stories in her enchanted world, she would refer to her adoptive parents as her pretend parents. They were pretending to be her mother and father, and she was pretending to be their daughter. This belief allowed her the freedom to be whoever she fancied with a variety of possible parents and relations. Of course, she still had everyday relations; people she called aunties and uncles, yet she had no feelings for them.

Her mother was upset when she was told of Stephany's spiteful words but angered by Caroline's apparent indifference and her change of attitude.

'Be grateful,' she had yelled. 'You could have still been in a children's home if we had not rescued you. Left to cry on your own you were. Not wanted! We have given you everything, even our name.'

Caroline's thoughts had returned to those words on innumerable occasions, particularly when she was feeling sorry for herself as she was now. Sometimes this fact of abandonment saddened her. Her real mother did not want her and had left her to cry or perhaps die in the cold. Her birthday was on the fifteenth of October, or so they said. How did they know if she was found abandoned? She had asked this question, but no one ever answered and she had decided that she would prefer to be a September child. She liked words beginning with 's'. But then she would remind herself that she could be whoever she pleased, and it became a new game for her to present varied versions of her origin to her companion Marigold, a rag-bodied doll with a pot head.

A noise drew her attention away from the past and back to the confines of the room. The spider was no longer on the ceiling. She sat up, straining her eyes in the dim lamp light and scanning the surface of the duvet. The strains of the national anthem signified the end of the shipping news and she twisted the radio knob, turning down the volume. Her throat had become dry with anxiety. She reached for her dressing gown draped over the foot board of the bed and gave it a vigorous shaking. Sleep was out of the question until she had made sure that the spider was not anywhere in her vicinity. He had scoffed at her fears, she remembered, on one occasion actually holding up a large spider by one leg and dangling it in front of her. In spite of her hysterical reaction, she was most upset to witness his cruelty, as he pulled off each leg and tossed the dismembered body into the fire. He ought to have been burnt not buried, she thought, memories of his burial escaping and adding to her disquiet. Perhaps if he had been cremated, he would not be able to haunt her like he was doing; reminding her of all the ways he had upset her; tormented her, the swine, the pig, the monster!

It was impossible to sleep. She was back to hating him and resenting everyone in her past. If only I had my daughter to care about me, she suddenly thought. If only, if only. Her thoughts echoed in her head. That was all like a forgotten dream, or rather a part of her life that had no substance now. She tried to push these thoughts away, back into what seemed in the most part like a figment of her imagination; some bright adventure she had experienced in her childhood. It seemed that it had happened to someone else. That 'she' of a different life.

But it was there now. It stayed with her as she went down the steep staircase, her bare feet cautiously judging the gradient as they always did. Now, the kitchen re-illuminated, looked strange. The stillness of the night it seemed, had the house in its grip. She shivered, feeling the hair rising on her arms under the fluffiness of her dressing gown. Leaving the rest of the downstairs rooms in darkness, she closed the kitchen door and filled a mug with milk. The sound of the microwave going through its programmed two minutes occupied her mind briefly but moments later, as she sat sipping the hot chocolate, her thoughts returned to her daughter.

'Daddy's friend!' Her mouth twisted with emotion. She stared into the past, seeing his thin, expressive face and pale grey eyes. She had been so attracted to David Dreighton. That was not an act of badness, was it? They, her parents, had made it bad. It was like reading a newly opened book; on the first page of an exciting story and not knowing what to expect. Indeed, with no thought of expectations, only of living in the present. She recalled the excitement of those stolen hours, turning back the pages of time; their secret meetings; the lies, the little looks that fell between them when he came to visit her parents. He had devised a code in his 'game'. She knew that when he cleared his throat he was telling her that he loved her, and when he clicked his fingers and thumbs together in a seemingly empty gesture, he was telling her that he would love her to be sitting on his knee, enjoying the closeness of her body against his, and, as the relationship deepened, the touching of his ear lobe meant that he was yearning for physical intercourse. He had described it graphically to her as part of his secret message, and she had known exactly what he meant, her body aching with memories of those sensations. The list grew as the weeks went by, and during their secret meetings when he met her outside school and took her to his little hideaway, as he called it, in a small rural settlement a few miles away, they play-acted episodes in the supposed lives of the lord and lady of the manor. She would have done anything for him. It was the first time, indeed the only time, she mused, that she had cared so much for anyone. That was true at that time in the relationship, but then of course not the only time. Her mind was back with her daughter. During that brief period of knowing April, her baby had become the essence of love and life. She was the little princess that they had imagined in their play acting. They would all be together in the castle of her dreams, he had declared.

How they had torn down her magic world! How they had tarnished her secret love with words of condemnation. They could never know her pain. She still loved him and wanted to be with him for ever. Their frustration lay in the fact that termination was impossible. She was six months pregnant before her secret was out. Indeed, during those early months she had no idea herself, such was her ignorance. She was always thin, like now, she thought, absently running her hand over her stomach. He had assured her that no harm would ever come to her, and she trusted him with her life; body and soul. Did he know that she was pregnant? Should not he have guessed the outcome of his passion? That first act of submission had happened on her eighteenth birthday. It had seemed like the supreme sacrifice; a tumbling down into a world of pure emotion. He was omnipotent in her eyes; a stolen deity. From that time on, she was overwhelmed with the desire to surrender herself to him and she could still feel that intense passion and emotion all these years later, her skin prickling and her pulse quickening at those memories of their forbidden secret love. She sighed, recalling how, initially, she had worried over the change in her menstrual cycle yet was too embarrassed to talk about it. But then it had become a fantasy in her mind. Part of a fairy story where she was the heroine under a magic spell.

She had met his wife on a number of occasions at shared social evenings where business was mixed with pleasure, and had cast her, in her secret drama, as hard and unfeeling. She had judged everything she could about her on a negative scale, from her heavy breasts to her severe haircut and her loud voice. Indeed, Caroline ignored the tenderness in her expression as she looked at her husband, failing to recognise his returning affection. She had supposed that he was as able at play-acting as she was herself, taking pleasure in the role. How wrong I was, she now thought. I was just a part of his little fantasy in his day-to-day routine.

Yet she still loved him, didn't she? If he came back into her life now, she would follow him to the end of the world. But was it the relationship; the physical attraction? Or was it symbolic of her defiance, her rebellion, her desire to escape? Her life seemed to be made up of escapes; stumbling through one crisis after another like a nightmare. Like walking through a field of craters; a battle ground, falling in and climbing out, and falling in again. This last crater had been the deepest ever, and now she had climbed out, she was determined to leave this scene of war forever.

To this day, she had no idea what had immediately happened after the discovery of her pregnancy. Of course, she had realised since, that it would not have been advantageous for anyone to make it public knowledge. As far as she knew, his marriage did not suffer, and, although he never came to the house again, there did not seem to have been any acrimony. The old-school-tie, she thought. It was always there in the midst of business and public affairs. You scratch my back and I'll scratch yours. How she hated it all, and yet she was free of it now. Or was she? How could she banish the memories of hatred and duplicity embedded in her memory?

She stood up and put her mug in the sink, turning on the cold tap and jetting water onto the chocolate dregs. 'So, why am I thinking about it then? Why can't I be the woman I want to be?' Her voice sounded strange and hollow against the gurgling of the water in the plug hole.

'You are looking for your daughter.' She answered herself silently. Am I? Is that possible? How old would April be now? Was she called April? She had called her that because she was born in April. Was she registered in that name? They had known each other for three weeks before she was taken away for adoption. That had been the end of a chapter of deceit and a return to her life with her adoptive parents. It was a long time ago; so long that it seemed to be in someone else's lifetime. In fact, her supposed good fortune at meeting and marrying one of the wealthiest men in her father's acquaintance had banished any desire for motherhood firmly into the out-tray as he would say. She was a possession alongside his gold watch and cuff links; a pretty young woman to wear on his sleeve. The agony of child birth had stayed fresh in her mind. She had read since of women who talked about a kind of amnesia; all pain forgotten until the next time, but the lack of sympathy from her mother, and the grim face of the midwife, middle-aged and prejudiced, still coloured her memories.

That then was the continuation of her servitude from dutiful daughter to dutiful wife. She was at their mercy with no freedom of choice. She regarded herself as a prisoner. The Lady of Shalott, bewitched in the tower. Behave as we say or die. The curse has come upon me! So, she had conformed. Her Sir Lancelot was banished. She played their parts now, becoming word perfect. But that was not really me was it, she asked herself? It was as though she had just awakened from a long sleep. A time filled with the unreality of dreams and nightmares; sleep walking; not conscious of the choices she had made or could have made. Her fiftieth birthday had come and gone during the previous year. He was no longer capable of rational thought, not knowing or caring what day or even what year it was, she remembered. It seemed of little consequence to her as well, and now here she was approaching her fifty-first year feeling more lost than ever in days filled with freedom. How ironical is that she mused? Perhaps her Sir Lancelot was old and grey, or perhaps dead, in spirit alongside King Arthur, her lord and master, both rotting away on Avalon. The magic was gone; the bewitchment, the servitude, the pretence, all gathered up into the past. 'Just leave it there,' she whispered.

Chapter Three

She spent the remainder of the night in front of the television, uncomfortably settled on the sofa, and woke up to the early morning programme of bright voices heralding a new day. She was in no mood to welcome anything. In spite of her earlier protestations about leaving the past behind, she wanted to return to her dream. He had been there. The love of her life. She had been in this strange house with old Victorian style furniture, and she had followed him through room after room, always with other people blocking her way. He had spoken of the secret room where they could meet in their dreams. She remembered that. It was not a dream. It was part of their make-believe all those years ago. But now that room never materialised. Or if it did, there was never a way in to it. She could still feel the passion and the aching for contact; the frustration of being prevented from speaking to him, yet such emotions were fleeting and thinning away moments after she had woken to the stark reality of her single status.

Her throat was dry and her back ached. For a few moments, she had no sense of time. Daylight had not yet penetrated the heavy, navy blue, velvet curtains and the light, from the electric lamp on the side table, still illuminated the room. She screwed up her eyes to focus on the face of the grandfather clock. Its chiming mechanism no longer functioned; a blessing indeed, but according to her late husband it was devalued, and had been on his list of jobs to be done for a long time. 'Stop thinking about him, for God's sake,' she muttered. 'What's the time?' She could just make out, between screwed-up eyes, that it was well beyond eight o'clock. 'Oh, Mrs Alford again!'

That lady as always was punctual. Bad time-keeping was not one of her faults, and she was eager to make a good impression and to keep her job. She arrived at nine o'clock, ready to make a clean sweep as she described it to her employer, her round face breaking into a grin and exposing a row of white even teeth. 'Is there anything else for the charity shop or the tip? I don't mind going again if you are still sorting things. The house doesn't look bad and first things first. That is what I always say.'

Indeed, you do, thought Caroline. Should she mention the Nearly New shop and the suit on display? Perhaps not. To be fair, she recalled, the woman had suggested that they could be saleable, and she herself had declared little interest. She could have said something about the shop, perhaps, on her return, but then if she was short of money-well. Caroline shrugged in reply and shook her head.

'By the way. Before I forget. I didn't pay you for last week, did I? I will give you the full amount even though you only came on one day. That wasn't your fault obviously. I will need help for a while, but I may sell up and go abroad. I really don't know yet. The whole place could do with a good clear-out. Would you be able to help in getting things up to scratch for the saleroom? A good lick and polish before I get valuations?'

Jenny Alford nodded, her heart sinking at the thought of this job coming to an end. Still, if she played her cards right, she thought, she could spin it out a bit. There was a hell of a lot of stuff in this house to be given a good wash and polish she reasoned, and she would enjoy it. In spite of back-street raising, she had an eye for beautiful workmanship and a longing to own valuable things.

As she set to with a tin of silver polish and a cloth on a collection of spoons, she glanced across at her employer, who was opening and closing drawers in a tall chest and itemising the contents carefully in a hard-backed notebook. Jenny found this to be an aggravation, even though she reasoned that it was a good idea to make an inventory of the contents of the chest. With her innate feelings of inadequacy as one of the serving classes, it seemed like a criticism; a distrust of her. She rubbed harder at the spoon and allowed her eyes to wander across the room towards the window. There was a big world out there; one she longed to discover. She was already better off with the sale of his clothes. Was this an opportunity to get herself out of debt? She was sure that her employer had no idea of values or indeed of what lay hidden in the drawers and cupboards in the many rooms of this house. It seemed that she was correct in her assumptions. As each drawer was opened, her employer made comments or little gasps registering pleasure or condemnation. They had no break for coffee and soon a lengthy list of collectables; cutlery, larger tableware and silver works of art in the form of figurines and decorated trinket boxes had filled three pages of a hard-backed notepad.

'Most of these have not seen the light of day for years,' Caroline commented.

Jenny grunted and shook her head. She glanced across at the old wall clock ticking the seconds away. 'It's time I wasn't here, Mrs Thorston. I have a doctor's appointment at one-ten.'

'Oh, have you? Nothing serious, is it? I will need a lot of help. I was going to suggest that you come every day, but don't worry if you have problems.'

Oh hell, Jenny thought. Why did I say that? It was just that she had worked longer than her agreed time, and she was always being taking advantage of, according to her daughter Sherry.

'Oh no. Just woman's stuff you know,' she lied. 'The fifties aren't good, are they?' Jenny winked in what could be described as a conspiratorial way, and then shook her head as if in a denial of intended familiarity. 'Of course, I can come every day. It's a pleasure to clean such lovely things.'

After the sound of Mrs Alford's ancient car engine no longer fractured the air, Caroline went out into the back garden and sat down on the rustic bench. It was a favourite place; a hiding place, partly enclosed by tall growing, wayward Kerria Japonica still bearing a second showing of yellow blossom in this mild autumn. The recent deluges had promoted the growth of long grass and weeds. It was beginning to feel like a waste land and ordinarily would have prompted a desire to restore order. However, Caroline was content to sit amongst it, breathing in the cool air and watching a blackbird foraging in the leaf debris that was already gathering in the paths and amongst the summer bedding.

Her breath extended into a long sigh. She tutted to herself and straightened her back, aware of the tension and pain in her muscles around her kidneys. Lack of exercise, she thought, or was it the result of carrying those heavy bags of shopping? The cleaning woman was right. The 'fifties' were not a good place to be.

The prospect of spending long hours in the house with all of his stuff suddenly appalled her. Did she really care what it was worth? There was plenty of money in her bank account or would be once the solicitor had organised it all. Just get rid of his ill-gotten gains and get the hell out of here. That thought began to take root, and the sound of the telephone ringing, motivated her legs to return to the house, all physical pain forgotten and with a sense of relief already forming in her troubled mind.

It was the solicitor.

'Brad here,' he announced.

'I was just thinking of you,' she gasped, her breathing unsteady, with her dash to answer the kitchen telephone.

'Great minds and all that, as they say.'

He laughed at his pronouncement, and Caroline visualised his head tipping to one side, his heavy brows furrowing with his action. 'I had you on my mind after I had notice of a coming auction in the town. It could be a good outlet for a lot of the small stuff in your late husband's collection. I know that you want to down-size as they say. Would you like me to cast an eye over some of it and get the ball rolling? I do know one or two experts in the field. It can all be listed officially at the same time, so two birds with one stone so to speak.'

Caroline nodded into the telephone, irritated by his triteness. In any case, he left little space for her to answer, concluding with the assurance that he would always have her best welfare at heart, after all the years of connection to the family, and to give him a ring when she had decided which items to dispose of. 'But don't let the grass grow under our feet,' were his parting words.

Have it all, she wanted to say. Sell the lot! None of it meant anything to her. The house felt like a mausoleum now. Well it always had hadn't it, she decided. Really, her few personal possessions were what mattered. Forget about the fancy clothes and jewellery she had been obliged to wear when she accompanied him to some of his business functions. Books and music were what mattered to her. In the latter years, she had listened to a wide range of music on her portable radio, with her ear phones firmly in place, shutting out the intrusion of his manic demands on her time. This was her only journey into modern technology, knowing nothing of computers, merely possessing a basic 'pay as you go' mobile phone, in case of emergencies. She had arrived at this house with a few boxes of personal belongings and her books and guitar. Her guitar was hidden away in her bedroom cupboard. He did not like the sound of her playing it. She had to admit that it was a struggle but it had given her immense pleasure in those days in between losing her child and becoming a married woman. In a strange way, its shape and contact had been so comforting like a companion. But these days, even that relationship had gone, and her fingers were as stiff as pokers; her description. The notes of music, in her early tutors, now seemed like a foreign language to her; black dots rambling along the lines, their names and values forgotten. The memory of it 'stirred my soul' was how, in an unguarded moment, she later described it to Brad. He had smiled and patted her hand. His action irritated her, not only by its familiarity, but by that kind of amused patronage. The little woman, bless her, kind of sentiment, she fumed.

Experts from the auction house under the instructions of Bradleigh Carter and Co, Solicitors or as she described him, 'my late husband's adviser', arrived at the house and catalogued a host of silver items with basic current valuations. Apparently silver objects had been her husband's forte and in the current climate were highly valued for their base metal worth as much as their desirability as works of art. However, his gold coins and nuggets were stored in his bank vaults, representing true currency. Caroline gasped when Brad Carter produced the facts and figures of this solid evidence of his wealth.

As the day of the auction drew near, Caroline became enlivened by her thoughts, not only of the decreasing of his possessions in her life, but also of the future increase in her bank balance. Until now, in spite of the fact that she was the sole beneficiary of his worldly goods, she still looked upon the bank account in the name of Caroline Thorston as the only one that was truly hers. Of course, she argued with herself, it had always been his money, his allowance to her, but she considered that she had earnt it like a paid companion, rather than in the role of wife and partner.

She arrived at the auction rooms in good time and remained in her car in the car park waiting for the opening of the door at the front of the building. She was not in a hurry to get a good seat as were the people already queuing at the door, having left their cars in the car park or arriving by foot. Some of the cars, she noticed, were by their appearance, owned by the better-off in society. Well shod, he would have called such people. He knew most makes and vintages of cars, whereas she admired the colours, staying loyal to her ignorance; a failing that had always prompted a sarcastic comment from him, she recalled. To be fair, he made sure that her car was top of the market, with her personalised number plate. But then, he was showing her off like a possession. She shrugged at the memory and smiled. His lips were well and truly sealed. Were they not? It was all about her opinions now, and very soon, all about her increasing future bank balance.

The doors were open and the waiting people shuffled forward eager to get a seat near to the front. Caroline watched them, studying their appearances, and feeling superior for the first time in her life in the midst of a crowd. They wanted what she owned. She tossed back her head and grinned with the anticipation of witnessing their greed in action.

It was the policy of the auctioneers to save the best until last, with perhaps some small items with less value displayed for sale in the catalogue, to whet the appetite and keep up the interest. The viewing time on the previous day had roused a great deal of public interest. Most people knew of the Thorston empire as it was known locally, but very few recognised the thin-faced woman, a headscarf tied tightly around her head, allowing only wisps of her greying hair to escape.

Of course, Caroline was familiar with many of the items on sale that had been vigorously polished by Jenny, and later identified and valued by her solicitor and his experts. However, items from other sources attracted her, and she was tempted to bid for them. Once or twice, she raised her hand but was relieved to be out bid, reproaching herself for her stupidity. But then a mystery box, as the auctioneer described it, caught her attention. His assistant held up a doll in one hand, and a jigsaw puzzle in the other. 'Books and puzzles. Toys sundry, A box full here. Any offers? Any grandmothers wanting to treat a little girl, or a little boy?' he added.

Caroline stared hard at the doll. The size and shape looked very familiar. She waved her hand. 'Here,' she called. 'Five pounds.'

People turned to stare. Such an item was so out of place in this sale. 'Charity shop stuff!' she heard a woman behind her comment. 'It's never worth a fiver.'

'Any advance on five? A bargain madam, I am sure some little girl will be happy or is it a grandson?'

Caroline held up the card with her number on it. They would have no idea what the sight of that doll had done to her. It was identical to her dear Marigold. Suddenly, it seemed, she had been restored to her childhood; an existence, pre-Mrs Thorston, and the strength of new resolve flooded into her.

Time passed slowly by, culminating in a lengthy wait for the solicitor, now in the role of her business adviser, to reckon up the sales and other facts and figures with the auctioneering house. Apparently, it had been a good day for the sale of silver items, and the shaking of hands was executed with great enthusiasm on all sides. Brad gave her hand a squeeze as he congratulated her on her success, with a promise to be in touch and keep her up to date with the latest developments. She watched him drive away, still aware of the pressure of his fingers against her hand. His skin was damp. Was it with excitement, she wondered? His face was flushed, and his glasses were balanced on the tip of his nose, giving him a mildly eccentric look. Did he have some kind of deal with them, or were his charges to her increased by his endeavours in the market? She really did not care all that much, she told herself, clutching her purchase under her arm.

The public car park was empty now, save for her car looking lonely and forlorn. 'You look like I feel,' she muttered, guiltily half turning to see if anyone was close behind, witnessing the outward expression of her thoughts. The box was awkward to carry, and she kept one hand firmly over the contents, not allowing the doll to escape her grip. Brad had smiled at the sight of her clutching the box. She guessed that the 'little woman' kind of thoughts were in his head. Was that an improvement on the 'stupid cow' label that 'he' used to pin on her?

She opened the boot of the car and put the box inside, her hand still clutching the doll. 'You can come with me,' she murmured. She drove home with the shabby little doll propped against the back of the passenger seat and secured in its position by the pressure of her handbag resting on its legs to prevent it from falling forward. The remaining contents were of little interest to her, and when she arrived home she pushed the box underneath the kitchen table. Perhaps Mrs Alford will know someone who likes puzzles, she thought. However, the idea that she would be ridiculed somehow for her rather childish impulses encouraged her later to empty the box with the intention of putting the contents into the recycling bin. The final item filled the space at the bottom of the box. It was hard to remove and appeared to be much more substantial than the boxes of games and the jigsaw puzzles. She could feel the texture of leather as she struggled to extricate it. Her sense of touch indicated that it was an album of some kind, with ridges of pages enclosed in the leather binding. How curious this was! She reached in the knife drawer for a pair of scissors. It was hard on her fingers, as she cut down through the cardboard sides, and she sank back on to the kitchen chair, pushing back the flaps and exposing the rather shabby, brown leather album. Already, her mind was visualising the contents. Was it a scrapbook? Cigarette cards perhaps. What did it have to do with a child?

She could smell it. What was the smell? Leather and age, she decided. She opened the cover, aware that this action had been done many times before. This was well loved. She knew that without anyone telling her. 'A photograph album!' she exclaimed, as the first page revealed two sepia photographs of a young woman. She shook her head in disbelief at the thought that anyone would sell a photograph album of this apparent antiquity. As she turned the pages, old and young were revealed in varying poses, and at a number of locations it seemed. But who were all these people? Why was the album discarded in this box? Didn't they care? Perhaps it was found in the attic, left behind by previous tenants. She had read of such finds. Usually it was an item of furniture, or some books or rarely a valuable antique.

Caroline was fascinated as she turned page after page, recognising the faces from those on previous pages, as they aged from childhood to maturity. There appeared to be three generations. It would seem that the two images on the first page were of the matriarch of the family, and sepia was followed by black and white, and black and white by colour on the following pages as the years had passed by.

All thoughts of the auction and the resulting increase to her bank balance, left her mind. She spent the rest of the afternoon turning the pages of the album, backwards and forwards, noticing family likenesses and giving names to the ones she admired, or characteristics to those who she surmised were argumentative or gentle or charismatic, or like she herself used to be, shy and withdrawn.

She was feeling surprisingly hungry by the time the light began to fade and she switched on the television in the kitchen in time for the evening news, and made a plate of cheese sandwiches, and a mug of drinking chocolate. 'Well it's food, isn't it?' she said to her cat. 'Go on then. I know you can smell the cheese.' She cut off a thick slice and dropped it on the floor. 'Disgusting habits, and I don't care!'

She imagined that Mrs Alford was there with her. She would laugh, wouldn't she? What would Brad Carter think? He would probably wrinkle his nose slightly as though there was a bad smell. She noticed he did that when Mrs Alford was in his way. What would they both think of the photograph album?

Later, as she watched her favourite 'soap' on the television, her thoughts kept returning to the album. Did she ought to make some enquiries as to who owned it? Was it a house clearance of little consequence to the people who were doing it? That old lady was a grandmother. She could have been my grandmother, she thought.

If she was, then who was the daughter? Which one would be my mother? Were the younger images of brothers and sisters, or had she been an only child with a number of cousins? That would be less complicated, wouldn't it? Yes. She was an only child with aunts and uncles and cousins. But where were they all now? Well the older ones had died and the cousins had gone to Australia and America. All she had left were these photographs and her memories of childhood. The album had been in her mother's possession until she died ten years previously. Hadn't it?

Was that long enough she wondered, already caught up in her fantasy? Yes. No one knew anything about her, ten years earlier. Her adoptive parents had died a few years before she had moved to this house with her husband, and she had never developed any close friendships. She had no idea who she really was and her childhood fantasising had continued into adulthood. Now that she could put faces to her make believe, her mind readily began to weave her past. They needed names, and as she watched the drama that followed the soaps, she noted the names of the characters and studied the cast list as it panned down the screen. She returned to the album with a pen and a sheet of paper, and identified the photographs, carefully considering names that seemed appropriate.

The grandmother became Elizabeth Mary. One daughter was Alexandria, and the other was Felicity. Alexandria was my mum, she decided. What a regal name and how good-looking she was. There was a lack of males in the album. Still, she had never known her grandfather, had she? She imagined that he was killed in the Second World War and her father's likeness had been removed from the family album after he had an affair with an actress and a divorce followed. She remembered very little of him, being only a toddler at the time. Her mother had never re-married. Once was enough she maintained. Caroline knew where she was coming from!

She studied the photographs until her eyes ached with tiredness, having identified most of the characters with their fictitious names. She had gone through this exercise so many times during her childhood, giving herself an assortment of relatives; fat thin, tall short, old young, rich poor. What was needed now, she decided was the addition of photographs of herself at various stages. That would have to wait until tomorrow when she had time to make spaces on some of the pages by the removal of groups, or of those people who she now regarded as distant relations, of little consequence in the family tree.

Later, in the comparative seclusion of her bedroom, she began to make comparisons with her adoptive parents. She had not thought of them for years. Occasionally, after their funerals, she had recalled certain events linked with dates on the calendar. She remembered now their twenty-fifth wedding anniversary not long after the birth of her baby. They had always seemed to be so old. Yet they must have only been married for about six years when they adopted her. Thinking about it now, that was a strange thing to do. Obviously, there were problems on one side or the other. There was never any talk of having a baby of their own. But why would they take in a kind of changeling, someone else's reject? At their level, money-wise, surely, they could have adopted a better class of child.

She had been abandoned by some 'nobody' it seemed. Her adoptive mother had always had contempt for her birth mother, blaming my bad behaviour, she mused, on my doubtful heritage. Perhaps their circumstances had changed. Perhaps they had acquired their wealth through good luck or inheritance. They must have had a different outlook on life then, she guessed. But then she could never remember any loving contact. She had a nanny apparently in the infant years, and then a lonely childhood with little contact with other children outside of school hours, and a succession of au pair girls during one year, until she went to boarding school.

It was a shock when the road accident happened, even though she had dreamed quite vividly of such an event. She had wished death on them many times in her unhappy childhood and then following the birth of her baby and their subsequent actions organising the adoption. How she had cursed them.

"Lizzie Borden took an axe. Gave her mother forty whacks." The words chanted in her head. She had memorised them at school when an American girl, Charlene somebody or other, she recalled, had used them during a skipping game. Forty skips were required without tangling the rope. It was called pepper speed, referring to the 'salt, vinegar, mustard, pepper' challenge when no breaks were allowed in the final rhythm. To do forty skips at such a speed without tangling the rope was never achieved to her knowledge; certainly not by her. Skipping rhymes were in common usage during her childhood, and she had forgotten most of them, but this one had stayed firmly embedded in her memory. She remembered how, according to Charlene, Lizzie Borden had been a real person and was accused of murdering her parents. She had chanted the words, substituting her own name. It fitted. 'Caroline Pearson took an axe…' Her cheeks flushed now with the guilt of it all. Be careful what you wish for. Who said that? Some wise person.

Yet she could still remember how disappointed she was that they were dead. Disappointment, not grief. She wanted to do it. She wanted to be responsible. Lizzie Borden. Lizzie Borden. It had been in her head like a series of images on a screen. Click, click, click! Whack, whack, whack! But that imaging had become obsolete, and now her thoughts drifted briefly back to her desires to end her husband's life. But would any amount of fantasising negate the cruelty inflicted on her?

She supposed that she would have grieved if she had been of their flesh and blood. Would she though, she wondered? Is grief and love an automatic emotion between parents and children? Does flesh and blood come into it? What did April think about her? Could she ever love her real mother automatically, or was she captivated by an imposter? Would she grieve for her foster mother come what may?

Jenny could not wait to tell her daughter about the auction. She described how she had deliberately left it until the last minute before the sale began; standing at the back of the room. She could see her employer sitting about halfway along.

'I recognised that headscarf,' she told Sherry. 'It's the one she gardens in. I think she was kind of incognito as the saying goes. Most of the stuff on sale was from her house. I recognised it. I felt really good about how I had polished it and brought it up to scratch. I bet it put the value up. Some of those little figurines went for a small fortune. I ought to get some commission on it.'

'You, get commission? As if! You ought to have smuggled some out in your bag. She wouldn't have noticed I bet. You could have off-loaded it on to Uncle Mike's mate. He can soon lose stuff in the crowd, no questions asked.'

'That solicitor bloke keeps hanging around. I don't like the way he touches her. She doesn't either. It's pretty obvious what he's up to.'

'Well get in there first then mother! Honestly! Do I have to spell it out to you?'

'Oh, you think you are so clever. Well I am telling you there's more than one way to skin a cat.'

'Well, get skinning then! You'll soon miss your chance and she'll be up and gone. Then you'll be sorry. Cats or no cats.'

Chapter Four

Caroline woke from a disturbing dream where crowds of people invaded her privacy, all demanding to buy her possessions, or claiming to be her relations. The faces in the photograph album seemed familiar already and she felt that they were haunting her. Were they dead or still living? What kind of demands could they make on her? This was a new kind of imaging in her dreaming state and she felt oppressed by the wealth that surrounded her rather than liberated by the freedom such assets could give her in her new way of life, away from his control.

She found herself wandering, still half asleep, back into the kitchen with the intention of making the inevitable milky drinking chocolate. The sight of the box of puzzles under the table reminded her of the little doll. She must be feeling lonely in a strange house, she thought, then giggled at her childishness. She had left her in the living room, resting in the armchair nearest to the door. Of course, she could not possibly be Marigold. What, after…what would it be, she mused, forty-four years? Nothing so fragile could last that long. But then, by its style, it would seem to be from that era. She stirred in some chocolate slowly when the microwave released the latest mug of milk, dissolving a generous level of sugar. This was not conducive to her well-being. She was eating far too many cakes and biscuits, and three spoons of sugar was too much She knew that without being told. But then there was no one to witness her bad habits. Her mind was still back in its sleepy state and drifting readily into the past;

the contents of the photograph album and the resulting fantasies, encouraging her to turn back the years.

She struggled to her feet and went into the living room, turning on the light switch, and looking across to the arm chair where she had propped up the doll on the previous night. She had noticed that a shoe was missing. Marigold was always losing a shoe. Always the left one, she remembered. This was the left one! She sat back on the opposite chair and closed her eyes, her thoughts drifting into memories of her childhood. She had no idea where Marigold had come from or why her mother appeared to despise the little doll. She had never known life without her. She appeared in photographs from Caroline being very small; little more than a toddler, and she recalled how her mother had complained of the dirtiness of the cloth body, and the blue striped dress, and of how the pot head with its frizzy orange matted hair was a sure magnet for germs. Yes, she remembered her using the word 'magnet', because she could not understand the connection. Once, her mother had threatened to put Marigold into the washing machine or worse still, the dustbin.

'Please Mummy, don't put her in the dustbin. She'll be frightened. It's smelly in the dustbin, and she doesn't like the dark. I will be good. I promise, Mummy. You can smack me but don't put Marigold in the bin.'

Caroline remembered that conversation as though it was yesterday. She had been so caught up in her imagination, weaving fantasies with her imaginary friends. Only Marigold was real to her in this world of make-believe, and so powerful was the story that she had ignored the demands of her own bladder. A drawing-room cushion became the casualty. She remembered trying to hide it under the sofa along with her wet pants. The cushion it seemed was more important than anything else. Her mother had noticed its absence and saw the corner tassel of it protruding out. And then I had blamed Marigold; betrayed her! How could I?

'I didn't do it, Mummy. It was Marigold. She is so naughty. I told her not to hide the cushion. Naughty Marigold.' Her words seemed to echo in her memory, and Caroline still felt the tension in her throat, all these years later. Looking back now, she remembered how she was always blaming Marigold. 'Don't lock me in the cupboard. Put Marigold in the cupboard. Naughty Marigold.' Sadly, she remembered the sequence of the events which were to follow.

She recalled that a few weeks later it was her eighth birthday. In her parents' walk of life, occasions were all about keeping up appearances. So, what's changed, she thought? She was excited of course. This was her special day and she was wide awake early, anticipating the importance of being eight years old. It was like climbing a ladder, she reasoned and this next rung must bring changes and excitement. She thought about her favourite board game, Snakes and Ladders. She admired the shapes and colours of the snakes in spite of the fact that landing on a square where the head gaped, its tongue waving, meant a descent to some lines further down. But then, how exciting was the climb up a ladder, and the promise of reaching the hundredth square before anyone else. Usually 'anyone else' was Marigold, or a strange little mouse knitted by some well-meaning relative who of course was not a relative after all.

She had to feel different somehow, and she waited impatiently, visualising the blowing out of the eight candles on her cake, and the silent wish she would be expected to make. She knew it had to be a secret, otherwise it would not come true, and she guarded it in the back of her brain where she visualised a special place for secrets. Even so, she was sorely tempted to share it with Marigold.

She could not bring to mind now what her wish had been. There had been so many wishes since. Perhaps on that day she wanted to be the star and wanted everyone to love her.

In fact, she did not remember much that preceded the magician's performance. He had arrived earlier clutching a large top hat and carrying an old suitcase. She would never forget what he looked like. She knew that he was different and accepted his strangely dishevelled appearance as customary in his magical way of life. His hair hung down beyond his ears, and his long nose dominated his face. He was ushered into the kitchen to share sandwiches with the cook and kitchen maid. Of course, she was not supposed to see him, she guessed. Childhood was full of things one was not supposed to know. He was the big surprise, but it was already common knowledge that the tea party was to be followed by magic tricks. Apparently, Melanie Peasgood had 'had him' at her birthday party. However, apart from hearsay, he was an unknown quantity for Caroline. She had not been well enough after her bout of measles to accept Melanie's invitation.

They had the usual games; pass the parcel, pinning the tail on the donkey, and then musical chairs. The excitement was rising, threatening a riot of shoving and screaming, and the final game of statues, where everyone had to stay perfectly still, was designed to be the prelude to the high light of the afternoon.

The magician appeared from the hall resplendent now in the top hat and a voluminous black cloak. The latter said garment was draped around his shoulders and hanging down his arms, allowing only his hands to be visible. He seemed to have a heavy sun tan that ended on his jaw line, and his eyebrows were dark and sinister with obvious eyebrow pencilling. He introduced himself as the Great Majesto and began to produce playing cards from under the cloth draped over the large box on the coffee table, even though he had shaken the cloth first and shown his audience that nothing was there, and then he reached forward to the children on the front row making them giggle and squirm as he plucked pennies from behind their ears. He took off his top hat and rummaged inside, producing a tiny black kitten, clutching it by the loose skin at the back of its head and holding it up for the children to see. There were the usual 'aghs and oohs' accompanied by the squeaks of the frightened kitten; its green eyes pulled sideways into squints by the magician's grip. Just as quickly as it appeared, it disappeared back into the hat. Caroline felt sad for the little creature and gave a little 'Oh' of disapproval.

She recalled how he leaned forward giving her a toothy grin.

'Now for my finale,' he had announced.

She remembered wondering what a finale could be. He had pointed to her and she had shrunk back, suddenly shy.

'Don't be frightened,' he said, his lips curling back to reveal gaps between his yellowing teeth.

She could visualise him now. He became the bogie man in her future dreams.

'Now my dear. You have a dolly that will be able to help me with my next bit of magic. I can see it sitting next to you. Would you like to bring it to me, duckie?'

'No. Marigold wouldn't like to be in some magic. She would be frightened.' She remembered how she had tightened her grip on her doll.

Some of the children laughed at the idea, and the magician joined in with their laughter.

Caroline blushed with embarrassment. She looked across at her mother. She was shaking her head and tutting.

'Perhaps somebody else has a doll.' The magician looked around. There was silence, and he turned back to Caroline, his head tilted to one side in a pleading posture.

'It won't take long, dear. I am sure you will be very pleased with this magic.'

'Go on, Caroline. Stop being such a chicken.'

That was Melissa's voice. Caroline was goaded into action and moments later Marigold was pushed down into the top hat, her legs sticking out for all to see. Already, she had lost her left shoe. It dropped onto the floor near to the magician's table. No one else seemed to have noticed. That was to be the only evidence of the little doll's long stay with Caroline. With a loud 'Hey Presto' the magician pushed his hand into the hat and drew out a doll with long blond curls and a smart dress and jacket. She was like a fashion model.

'A Happy Birthday,' he yelled, stretching his arm forward to give Caroline her present.

Everyone clapped.

Caroline stared, her face flushing. She turned to look at her mother, who mouthed, 'Happy Birthday,' and applauded with the children and the magician. Of course, she applauded, Caroline thought now! She wanted to get rid of Marigold. It was an obsession with her. But why? It couldn't have been that the doll was old, could it? In her memories of her adoptive mother, there always seemed to be aggravation, and yet, one would think that she wanted a child. Otherwise, why would she adopt me?

She recalled how she begged and pleaded, 'Can I have Marigold back now please?'

'This is Marigold,' the magician had replied. 'New for old. Isn't that amazing? I wish someone could do some magic on me. What a lucky little birthday girl you are.'

All the memories of that day came flooding back as though it was taking place right now. Caroline could feel the pain, and tears flooded her eyes and escaped down her cheeks. She wiped them away, tasting the salty bitterness at the corners of her mouth.

'Marigold,' she said to the doll. 'Could you be my Marigold? But then where have you been all these years?'

At the tender age of eight years, she had believed that the magician could magic her doll away, and change her into a brand, new version with clean long hair and new clothes, but then she had retrieved the shoe from under the table after everyone had gone home and puzzled over the fact that her new Marigold had two shoes. How could that be? The new Marigold would have had only one shoe, wouldn't she? It had always been a mystery and she had kept the shoe for a long time. Now, of course, she knew the truth. Such magic was impossible. Obviously, it was a special top hat with a false crown, and the box must have concealed not only the kitten, but the new doll, and later, her Marigold. She remembered how the magician had shown them the empty hat, somehow allowing for his trickery and sleight of hand.

She had that shoe for years, she remembered. She had hidden it somewhere out of sight of her mother. She tried now to bring it to mind. Did it match the shoe that this doll was wearing? She was sure now that it did. She picked up the doll and examined the dress and the knitted cardigan. She held it to her face. It was Marigold! She could smell her Marigold! She could remember the feel of that little body against her skin. She was aware of the stubby little foot dirty with age, suddenly recalling how she had hidden the shoe at the back of the cupboard where she stored her toys. But that was in a different life time; even in a different town. So much had happened since then. She had gone to boarding school. Her parents had moved to a different house and her possessions had been packed and unpacked a number of times, with new things replacing old things as the years went by.

What did she have in those teenage years? Very little, she thought. Life still seemed to be about essentials in those days long after rationing had ceased. Shortages and hardship had indoctrinated a way of thinking in the older generation, even for those who were fortunate enough to live in areas away from the chaos of re-development, and high-rise flats and where old traditions persisted.

She suddenly recalled the attic in the rambling old house where a box containing her school books and stationery was stored. The pencil-case! That was it! That was where she had hidden Marigold's shoe! She could actually visualise the shoe now, pushed into the corner of the zipped-up canvas container along with a metal pencil sharpener. She could not believe how she had forgotten about that. But so much had happened. So much grief had dulled her brain. Yet how incredible was the memory process to store an image of a childhood hiding place for such a long time.

In the next instance, her excitement plummeted into a mood of despair and disparagement.

'Who am I kidding?' she asked the little doll. Of course, it would all be gone, she thought, and there must have been hundreds of these dolls manufactured with identical clothes.

Yet, it seemed that her brain, having set out on this retracing of past memories, was now committed to a journey of discovery. Now she could remember the size and nature of the box. It had previously stored some kind of household or garden chemicals. It was in the cupboard under the stairs where she spent many hours in punishment for bad behaviour. The odour had long since left her senses but the memory of its presence lingered on. There were text books, a pad of water colour paper and a tin of well used paints; some favourite novels; that was it, *Jane Eyre*, *Pride and Prejudice*; of course, *Alice in Wonderland*! Her memory zig-zagged into that Wonderland of Alice's dream. The sleepy dormouse and his treacle well.

Did her father know how long she was locked in the cupboard? Would he have cared? What would she have done to him? Off with his head! She giggled. The Red Queen would sort him out. But then who was the Queen? Was she her mother, or was the Duchess her mother? Their cook was not like the one in Alice. She was called Mrs North; a fat jolly lady who loved food, and was always testing her recipes, eating large helpings herself. However, like the cook in the story she did like pepper, and the kitchen maid used to sneeze loudly at times, but there was no baby changing into a pig. Was that magic? No. The magic story she enjoyed was The Wizard of Oz. Mrs North read it to her sometimes and in Caroline's memory she was like the good witch, tapping on the cupboard door before she opened it wide enough to hand in a biscuit or a buttered scone hot from the oven and spread with a layer of jam, her fat face beaming reassurances. But then she got the sack and was never seen again. Did she get the sack because of me, Caroline wondered? Was it because I had jam on my mouth? Did I betray her?

Yes! It definitely was that box from the cupboard that had been used, and she was sure that it was in the loft. She could remember now how he had carried it up, commenting on her meagre possessions. She had put her 'O' levels certificates in it and the little pouch with her swimming medal for life saving. Fancy, me getting a medal! She giggled and shuddered at the idea of her saving someone from drowning. She nearly drowned getting the medal! Swimming seemed to be in someone else's lifetime. But then, what about the pencil case? Did that still exist or was it part of her earlier childhood replaced later by something more sophisticated?

She could not remember throwing these things away. She would go up in the morning when Jenny was here. The space under the roof was extensive but would require a ladder to gain access. She was too afraid of heights to venture up there on her own. But then should she risk not finding the shoe in the pencil case, or even not finding the pencil case itself? Would it be more sensible to leave things in the past?

'What do you think, Marigold?'

She sat the doll back on the cushion and yawned, suddenly tiring of this mental journey into her own past. There was so much to think about and her brain could not cope with reminiscing plus all of the recent fabrication with the photograph album. For many years, she had simply accepted the daily routine of being Mrs Thorston. Now she was reinventing her life; not only with someone else's memories in the photograph album but struggling to bring her own memories back to mind. She returned to her bedroom, knowing that she would be so tired if she did not get some more sleep, yet unable to escape from her thoughts. She had slept on her own for many years and that had been no problem. It had been such a relief to escape from his snoring and his desires which lessened as the years progressed. Wandering back into past memories had suddenly revived her recollection of how he would consult his diary to check on her cycle, expecting her to be as methodical in her habits as he was. Even so, he would double-check. 'No complications?' he would ask. Many times, she was tempted to say that there were his so named 'complications' but she feared his anger more than she despised his attempts at satisfying his sexual urges. She screwed up her face now in memory of it all. She had tolerated his clumsy brutish actions knowing that it would be very short-lived, with no desire to please her. It was rape, she thought bitterly; once a month and part of his timetable like a board meeting. She recalled how she had discovered that he made an entry in his diary each month after the event. She had no knowledge of this habit until he had reached a stage in his dementia when he was not really aware of who she was or indeed of who he was. She had come across an old diary amongst his possessions and had not understood the coded entries until he had included an extra comment in one particular month. She giggled hysterically. It was like Bletchley Park breaking the codes. Various symbols were used, apparently recording his levels of sexual prowess, she remembered. Whatever could have happened when the overall grade was C minus?

Bastard! The word fell from her lips so easily. She had heard it so many times in the past. He used to call her that. But it seemed to apply to her for all of her life. She could remember her foster mother calling her that when she pushed her into the cupboard and locked the door. 'Little Bastard!' She remembered yelling back that she would find her real mother one day and that she would love her.

She did not know what a bastard was until she looked the word up in the dictionary. She was older then, but she remembered struggling with the spelling and the meanings. 'A person born of parents not married…a despicable person…vile…'

Her mother had used that word again when April was born.

'Like mother like daughter,' she had said. 'But what should we have expected from a bastard? No one will want you now. We will have to pay someone to marry you.'

How much did they pay, Caroline wondered? Did they auction her off? Was she spruced up like the silverware or was her future husband so repulsive to the rest of the world that they got a lucky break? He certainly never mentioned her illegitimate child. Why had her mother turned against her? Was I such a great disappointment to her, she asked herself, or was she so caught up in the rules of society that she had no choice in her actions? She had certainly left her imprint on me, she thought, her bitterness now clouding her expectations of discovering the box in the attic. She left the drawing room without a backward glance at the shabby little doll.

Chapter Five

'Now you just be careful! I wish you would let me go up there.' Jenny was genuinely concerned for the welfare of her employer.

Caroline half turned, her face showing by the frown and the pressure of her lips one against the other, the fear she had of heights, even though, at this stage, she was only a few rungs above the level of the landing. The trap door in the ceiling was hanging with cobwebs, invoking images of spiders waiting to drop on to one's head with the initial upward thrust.

'Just keep hold of the ladder,' she ordered. 'You don't know what I am looking for. I will recognise this box immediately.'

She reached up to push her free hand against the trapdoor and was relieved when it pivoted upwards and tilted back revealing the dark roof space. Suddenly, she became enlivened by the idea that this was a special place. This resurgence of child-like thoughts of secret passages and magic happenings quickened her pulse, and she no longer gasped with fear.

She grasped the edge of the opening with her right hand and half -turned to call down to her companion. 'Can you come up behind me now and pass me the torch? I don't know how much is floor-boarded up here. I'm sure he had workmen to do it when we first came but I don't think he would have actually come up. There may be nothing to see except cobwebs.'

Jenny reached up with the torch and they both clung to the sides of the ladder as it creaked.

Moments later there was a loud yell.

'Wow! There's loads of stuff up here, Jenny. It's like something out of a mystery novel.'

Jenny experienced a surge of emotion not only reflecting the excitement of her employer, but by the fact that Caroline had used her Christian name. This familiarity after years of having little recognition except as an employee was somehow like a taste of sweetness in the bitterness of her everyday life. The sounds of her employer's footsteps on the floor boards of the attic were reassuring and she waited for further commands.

'I knew it would be here. Isn't it amazing after all these years? Mrs Alford! Are you still there? Can you come up to the top and grab hold of this box? Be careful. It isn't heavy. Just awkward.'

Jenny reached up and struggled to support the brown cardboard box as Caroline dragged it over the hatch space. In the dim light coming from the bulb further along the landing ceiling, she could make out the name Caroline Pearson written in black capital letters on the base and the shapes of the letters became stored in her memory together with a miscellany of facts and figures for future referral. The only way to accommodate the descent without harming herself, seemed to be by supporting the box on her head using her left hand, and hanging onto the side of the ladder with her right hand. This was easier than it looked as it seemed by the weight of it to contain very little.

Nevertheless, she was relieved to be back to the safety of the landing floor, her feet sinking into the thickness of the carpet. Now, in the full light of the sunshine coming in through the landing window, she could study the old cardboard box, becoming aware of a musty odour suggesting antiquity and something indefinable.

Caroline was descending the stepladder, her face flushed with exertion and excitement. She nipped her nose between her finger and thumb and grinned broadly. 'You can still smell it, can't you?' she exclaimed. 'Fancy! After all these years! I can manage now, Mrs Alford. Although I think I could do with a coffee. The dust up there is inches thick and my throat is really dry. There are a lot of boxes containing goodness knows what. A job for a strong man or two I think.'

She stood rubbing her hands together and staring ahead, in obvious expectation, it seemed, of her employee fulfilling her next duty. Jenny sighed and turned to make her way down to the kitchen. Her few moments of being treated as an equal were somehow swept away like the dust on the mysterious box, and once more she experienced those feelings of inadequacy that dogged her life. A sudden pain dragged in her stomach reminding her of her latest fear of cervical cancer. A friend of hers recently had a smear test and was warned of possible suspect cells. Jenny had looked it up on her computer as soon she had got back home, and it seemed that she had all the symptoms.

She heard Caroline following behind her, and she turned before she reached the kitchen door in time to see her employer going into the lounge carrying the box. Apparently, she was not invited to share in the inspection of the contents. As she stood by the worktop spooning coffee granules into the beakers, she tried to envisage what could be so important to risk climbing up into that dusty attic with its creaking boards and spiders' webs. She assumed that it must be of great value, her mind back on the antique sale and the numerous items still waiting to be cleaned and catalogued. Or could it be a bundle of letters hidden away? Could Mrs Thorston have dark secrets? That thought enlivened her, and she giggled to herself. Whatever it was, there was little weight there in the box, and that strange smell! Perhaps her employer would talk about it later over the coffee, or was she herself not included in this early coffee break and expected to continue with her weekly cleaning chores? 'Of course! Why do I ask?' she muttered.

Caroline was sitting in the armchair nearest to the bay window, the box still unopened on the floor at her feet, when Jenny walked in with the tray bearing two beakers of coffee and a plate of chocolate biscuits.

'I thought we deserved some nourishment as well after our adventure with the ladder,' she said with contrived brightness. 'This packet was opened. They will go soft.'

'Not for me Mrs Alford. Just the coffee. Tell me. Is the window cleaner due today? It could be a good idea for all the insides to be done. I am sure he leaves them streaky and blames it on the insides being dirty. I am not in the mood for more sorting today. I know it has to be done, but perhaps we could start again next week. So, do the windows and then you can get off home.'

Over an hour later Jenny rapped on the closed door of the lounge. 'I am going now,' she called. After waiting for a few seconds, she opened the door and looked in. Her employer was still sitting on the chair, now with her head drooping in sleep and with the unopened box at her feet. Jenny tutted and shrugged her shoulders. So, what was all that about, she fumed silently. Getting me to risk an injury and being so secretive. Sherry was right, she thought. Their kind of people don't want to know us. And why was she asleep? Goodness me! She wants to do what I do and then she would be tired. She just uses me. Oh well. What's sauce for the goose.

Caroline opened her eyes at the sound of the door latch clicking into place. She was so impatient to open the box yet dreading the disappointment if her memory had deceived her. Either way it was not a time to share with anyone else. It had to be the right box. The musty smell had overpowered her senses and taken her memory back to those days when she was still a gauche, innocent schoolgirl. Days when her worries were caused by the threat of bullying. But then for a few moments up in the confining darkness of the loft, her earlier childhood fears had surfaced, taking her breath away in rising panic. In that moment, as she detected the musty smell of the box, she was mentally back in the under-stairs cupboard which housed, amongst other things, a malodorous box containing garden fertiliser, and she was locked in with it all to repent of some naughtiness. It just took seconds of time to recall the horror of spiders and beetles with only that pale glimmer of light showing through the crack in the hinged door. She remembered numerous occasions, of crying and begging to be let out; of sometimes gripping her legs to avoid the inevitable wet pants and the consequent threat of more punishment. She had called out to God, to Jesus, to Father Christmas to help her, but she knew that her punishment was measured by a set rule of time. Ten minutes for each crime she committed. How long those ten minutes were, as she strained her ears, listening for the sound of her mother's footsteps. She could not stand up in the confined space and the fear of what lived in the bare floor boards added to her hysterical cries. Marigold comforted her if she was part of the punishment, but then if she had blamed Marigold, she was tormented by fears of her precious companion being put in the dustbin. She remembered now how she would tighten herself up into a kind of ball, listening for sounds of the world outside of her prison. Sometimes she heard the front door bell ring and wondered if she would be released early and hurried off out of sight into the kitchen.

Later on, until she was bathed and put to bed, she could smell the fertiliser. It seemed to cling to her clothes and her skin. It would never have entered her head that the memory of that musty smell would have guided her to the box in the loft all these years later. But it had been instant recall today. What did she do that was so terrible? She had often asked herself this at times when, in later years, her husband was punishing her; no longer being locked in but rather locked out she reasoned.

She heard the sound of Jenny's car engine revving, and the crash of the gears. Poor woman. She had been so helpful today. The pain of loneliness was back. That was nearly as bad as imprisonment. Bad feelings, yet even so, mild in comparison to those of her teenage years; those years that followed on from her late childhood. Now, once again, self-pity moved her memories back to her youth; to the ecstasy and the heartbreak; her body used and cast aside. Was a paedophile the real definition of her lover? Even though she was eighteen years old, she still had the mind of a child, didn't she? Her all-consuming innocence had totally clouded her judgement. Yet, she hated that word paedophile used so readily these days in the cases of sex scandals. It almost gave the abuser some standing; in fact, some purpose. This kind of person was defined in the dictionary, as though he or she was part of the fabric of life and therefore allowed to exist. No. April's father was not part of that. He was a soul mate and under different circumstances she would have shared her whole life with him. Her daughter was the only good thing at the end of it all, but then like Marigold, she was taken away and a respectable marriage was put in her place like the brand-new doll coming out of the magician's hat. Well, she mused, I have got rid of yet another abuser, and now if I find the shoe in this box, I will have turned the clock back even further. First Marigold and then who knows, perhaps I will find April, my daughter.

She reached down to the box, pulling at the yellowing sticky tape sealing the flaps in place. Screwed up newspaper filled most of the space inside. She unravelled it and smoothed it out looking for signs of its age. Through the yellowing of the paper she could make out the year, 1979. She was sixteen years old. It was the right box! Her heart was thumping in her chest as she pulled out the packing paper. There were her 'O' level certificates, and her two subject books, *Jane Eyre* and *Pride and Prejudice* together with that treasured copy of *Alice in Wonderland* and the little square box containing her life-saving medal, all nestling together, like good companions, she fancied. There was no need to open the little box. She could visualise the contents as clearly now as on the day it was presented to her at the end of term Speech Day. The images of teachers and pupils came readily to mind, and for a moment or two she was back to those school days, agonising over examination results and dreading failure. She cleared her throat and inhaled sharply. It seemed that only some screwed up newspaper remained, but as she grasped it, she was aware of another object underneath. It was the pencil case. Her heart thumped, and her cheeks became hot with both excitement and apprehension. She squeezed against the fabric, identifying first a fountain pen, then a pair of compasses and a six-inch ruler, seeing those familiar objects in her mind's eye and searching her memory to identify them.

'For goodness sake!' she exclaimed. 'Just open it.'

She pushed her fingers into the end. No, just pencil shavings. 'Ah' she gasped. 'The pencil sharpener.' Then her mouth dried in the next moment, as she identified the shape and texture of Marigold's shoe in the exact hiding place of earlier recollection.

But was it the same? Did it match? She pushed the contents of the box on to the floor and went over to the other armchair at the side of the fireplace squeezing the shoe in her hand. The doll was hidden from sight under a cushion away from prying eyes. She represented memories of a private world locked up in the past and was not to be shared. Caroline giggled nervously as the drama unfolded. She had a sudden recall of Cinderella trying on the slipper, but hers was glass. This one was pink and green felt and almost a perfect match. The colours were a little brighter than those on the one which was still intact, but Marigold could have been played with over the years and become shabbier and faded. It fitted perfectly, as she knew that it would. A little loose perhaps, but then the sock was missing as well. But what if after all of this journey into the past she was not Marigold? Would it matter, she wondered? Of course, it would, she told herself. It would be like losing a favourite book and replacing it with a second-hand copy from a bookshop or a charity shop. She had to find out why this doll was in a box of games and puzzles and who owned the photograph album.

The song 'Little boxes,' came into her mind. She used to sing it and wonder what it was like to live in a little box. The idea scared her, reminding her of the under-the-staircase cupboard, and yet she longed for a hiding place when she was at boarding school, she recalled. She picked up the copy of *Jane Eyre* that had been hidden for such a long time in this box. It was a favourite story of an orphan sent away to boarding school. She identified with Jane at the time of her eighteenth birthday believing that she had found her Mr Rochester. How wrong she was! The bad thoughts were back and now she was remembering how a day or two later after that eighth birthday party when Marigold had disappeared, she had deliberately smashed the glass in a frame displaying a likeness of her adoptive mother and had stabbed the eyes in the exposed photograph with a sharp pointed knife that she had taken from the kitchen drawer. Her muscles tensed with the memory, and she was mentally caught up in the violence. Had I wished I could harm her? Yes. She could feel those murderous intentions. They were still there. She still wanted to punish her for her part in stealing Marigold, and later April.

"Lizzie Borden took an axe. She gave her mother forty whacks."

She shivered, and her arms prickled with goose pimples underneath her cardigan sleeves. How strange that no one ever seemed to miss that frame and photograph. She had smuggled it out into the dustbin, her guilty secret moving away into the anonymity of the refuse collection cart, two days later. Yet, she still owned the guilt.

It was here lurking in the back of her mind all these years later, and Marigold was part of it, staring up fixedly at her from the armchair and sharing her bad memories. Of course, the doll was Marigold! She was a kindred spirit; here in the present yet part of the past.

'What a carry on! Do you mean to tell me that she went to all that trouble to get up there and making you risk life and limb just to get a box? You could have been crippled for life!'

Sherry stubbed her cigarette out impatiently on the tea plate and glared at her mother.

'It wasn't heavy and it wasn't all that far up. It just seems it when you look down the steep stairs behind you from the landing. She didn't need much help. Mind you, it did pong. Like something had died in it!'

'So, what was in it then? Not dead husband parts! I knew someone who had a skull in a box under the bed. It was something to do with his studies and he had bought it from somewhere. It had soil inside it! It must have been dug up! Can you imagine your skull ending up under a student's bed in a grotty bed-sit?'

Jenny shrugged. Nothing her daughter said these days made much impression on her, but she continued with her own musings all the same. 'I don't know,' she said. 'She was being very secretive. She sent me into the kitchen to make her a coffee, and when I got back with it she was sitting in the armchair staring into space. In fact, she might have been asleep. I did notice a name written on it in black felt tip pen when she lowered it down. The box was pretty old, so I guess it was her maiden name. Caroline Pearson. Not very posh sounding, is it? I would have thought she had a double-barrelled name. Mine sounds posher.'

'Do you think she is losing the plot?'

'No, nothing like that. But she did buy a box of puzzles and things at the sale. She bid a fiver and no one else wanted it. She could have got it for a quid. It was so out of place amongst all that stuff, although there was a lot of rubbish from a house clearance. It could have been part of that. Some folks are so greedy.'

'So, you are no wiser then about the box in the attic?'

Jenny sighed and stood up scraping her chair across the floor.

'Oh, I have no idea,' she muttered, glaring at her daughter who was lighting another cigarette and she wafted the smoke away from her face. 'There are a lot of boxes up there from the sounds of it. She is going to need help to get them down and it won't be me, I can tell you. She could end up like Miss Haversham, couldn't she?'

'Miss who? Is that another of your weird employers?' Sherry pressed her lips around the cigarette as she picked up her bag, pushing the crumpled packet and the lighter into the front compartment.

'No! You know! That woman in Dickens who was jilted and lived on her own in her wedding dress with the table set out and her cake gone all rotten. You saw the film! Oh, never mind!'

'Sounds crazy!' Sherry shrugged and, turning to go, could not resist one last attempt to solve the mystery.

'Doesn't she ever mention a family? She must have bought those puzzles for a child. Perhaps she is a grandmother, and he didn't want any kids around the place. She's weird, you know. I wish you would do yourself some favours before she gives you the push.'

On the following day, Jenny looked across the room to where a doll sat in the armchair.

'I used to have a doll like that, Mrs Thorston,' she remarked. 'Well not exactly like that, but it had a pot head and a rag body. They used to be all the rage didn't they, before the ones came along that can do everything? Are you doing it up for a granddaughter? I still have things put away from my daughter being little. She doesn't want any children though. It must be nice to have grandchildren.'

Caroline grunted in response. She seemed intent on itemising the contents of the china cabinet, which filled the space to the left of the chimney breast. 'Sorry. Oh, the doll. That's Marigold. I have just got her out of the cupboard. She's very old. Brad er Mr Carter is organising a sale of china ware and fine arts. Perhaps some water colours. We seem to have them all over the house. Some of it I will hang on to because I like water colours, and some of the art nouveau, but I think my husband inherited most of it from his mother, and I never did like her taste. No doubt it is worth a lot of money. But then money isn't everything, is it?'

Jenny shook her head and rubbed even harder at the application of wax on the sideboard. She loved the graining in the wood and the way the polishing brought out the richness of the colours. If this was mine, she thought, I would polish it every day.

An hour later, she was in the kitchen preparing the mid-morning break. The kitchen waste bin needed emptying and she went out onto the back patio, breathing in the fresh autumn air, glad to be away from the depressing atmosphere and the long silences. The dustbin was full and as she pushed down the contents to make a space for the kitchen bag, she noticed the cardboard box that had come to light on the previous day. The odour from it was unmistakable, and somehow added to the air of melancholy in this household. There was something deeply troubling her employer, and she longed to console her in a woman to woman role, she reasoned, and not for financial gain. Her own daughter Sherry was like the devil, trying to push her into acts of dishonesty. She had enjoyed moments of intimacy with Mrs Thorston, but now it seemed that they were back to square one and she was merely the hired help.

It was as if her thoughts had travelled ahead of her into the living room, for as she struggled to carry the tray to the coffee table, Caroline said, 'Oh Jenny careful! Let me help you.'

Jenny felt the warmth spreading through her and she smiled and muttered her thank you.

'So? How's your family then?' Caroline continued, 'You said you have a daughter but no grandchildren as yet. I have been looking through my old album which has just come to light. It's all about family trees these days, isn't it? Not that I know anything about computers. Do you?'

'No, not me,' Jenny lied. Admitting to owning anything that could imply wealth would not create the impression of neediness. Sherry's advice about looking after number one hovered in her mind. 'You must be joking,' she continued. 'I haven't got time or the money for that kind of thing. My daughter is never off it and as for Facebook, well! Goodness knows why they want to tell somebody what they are doing all the time. My brother is doing the family tree. Now that is worthwhile. Apparently, we have Irish and Welsh blood!'

'Oh really. So, what's Facebook then? I have never heard of it. Is it something to do with make-up?'

Jenny giggled and shook her head. 'It's a bit like using text messaging but they all share each other's news and gossip. I like to keep my news to myself but that's how we were brought up, isn't it? My mother used to say, "A still tongue in a wise head".'

Caroline smiled. 'Mine used to say that. I was always being hushed up. That wasn't good either, was it? But I think it has gone too much the other way now and programmes on the television shock me. Which reminds me. Did you watch that programme about tracing a lost daughter? It is amazing what they can do these days. Like I said, I'll have to show you my family album some time. But I must get on. Brad is coming over later today to talk about the sale of some of this china and art stuff. Can you help me to put it all on the dining room table before you go?'

Jenny nodded and gulped down the dregs of her coffee. She decided in that moment that she would not tell her daughter Sherry anything about the day. The mystery of the contents of the box was solved. It was a photograph album hidden away in the loft after all and really, the only question was why was it hidden away? Didn't he approve of her relatives? Perhaps she was ashamed of them. And why did it matter now? It was all becoming a drama and her skin prickled with excitement.

Caroline watched the old car pulling away from the house. She liked Jenny, in spite of her working-class image. There was something about her, she thought. Perhaps it was her appreciation of the finer things of life. No doubt 'he' had despised her. In fact, she could not remember him ever acknowledging her. 'She's a damn sight better than your lot,' she muttered. She looked at the clock. Brad was due in just under two hours. Everything was arranged on the table for him to catalogue. Her thoughts returned to the album and her plans to remove some photographs here and there and put in images of herself when she was growing up. She had found her old album in the back of her bedroom cupboard, together with an assortment of photographs stored in an envelope and taken in the early years of her marriage. She did not need 'him' to be in her family album, or any of those taken of her foster parents. They would play no part in the life she wished to present to her daughter April.

She went upstairs, taking the doll with her. Brad would be asking questions and she was not prepared to answer them. She closed the bedroom door on her secret and turned towards the airing cupboard opening the door and feeling under a folded fleecy blanket on the top shelf. The recently acquired album from the sale room was as familiar to her now as if it had always been her possession. She put it on the bed, allowing space to prop pillows behind her head and for her to sit cross-legged on top of the duvet.

She turned the pages slowly, familiarising herself with the images. She reasoned that she herself would have belonged half way through the sequence during her early years, and then in the later pages, she would have been a teenager. The next task was to remove some of them to create spaces for her own photographs. She had five that seemed compatible regarding the aging of the actual photographic paper and the style of dress of the subjects. She hoped they would blend in.

She carefully removed an image of a young man, and then a family group taken from some distance and out of focus, resulting in blurred details. There were names scribbled on the back of the family group, faded and difficult to read. By their style of dress, she guessed that the photograph had been taken at a time when she herself would have been very young. The third photograph that caught her eye was of a man wearing a top hat, and obviously posing for the camera. She looked more closely at it as she removed it, and then turned it over to see whether there was a clue to this man's identity. Her eyes widened and she gasped. There, clearly written were the words 'The Great Majesto'.

The mystery was unravelling. Obviously, the photograph album together with the puzzles and Marigold, came from the house of the magician, or from someone in his family. He must have taken Marigold back with him after her eighth birthday party, no doubt at her mother's request, and kept her for his own children to play with. So, where had he lived? Presumably it was local to where her parents lived at that time. It would be unlikely that he had a car in those days. Probably he had arrived on a bicycle, or did he have an old van? As she cast her mind back, she had vague recollections of a door slamming and seeing him drive away, although the disappearance of Marigold had ruined her party, reducing her to tears, and she had been sent to bed in disgrace as soon as the other children went home. She had cried every night for weeks on end and had abandoned the new doll under her bed.

She turned the pages of the album, searching for more clues, but the image of the magician never occurred again. Perhaps it was just a photograph of him at a children's party. Perhaps he did not live with these people; was no relation in fact. That idea satisfied her for a moment, but then that would negate her new belief proving that Marigold was who she seemed to be; the genuine article, and why would his image be in a family album if he was merely an entertainer at a party?

Dare she still claim that this was her family album? If she found April would her deception be exposed? What if April lived nearby? What if she knew this family? What if in the worst scenario, she was adopted by this family after she had been taken away from Caroline? Oh! She was being ridiculous now, she chided. It was all becoming very complicated, and her delicious fantasising was becoming a nightmare.

The sound of the door-bell ringing startled her. She looked at the bedside clock. 'Oh hell!' she exclaimed. 'I can do without you today, Mr Carter!'

She ran her fingers through her hair and patted some colour into her cheeks, stumbling on the last step of the stairs and almost falling against the front door in her haste. She could see the outline of the solicitor through the stained glass, and struggled to turn the key with a muttered, 'Hang on!'

'Goodness me!' Brad Carter exclaimed. 'Are you all right? I don't usually have that effect on people.' He giggled, exposing uneven teeth, and Caroline nodded, turning away.

'You made me jump, that's all. Come in. I'll make coffee.'

Caroline felt her body panicking and her heart quickened its beat. She frowned, impatient with her reactions. It's fear, she reasoned. I don't want another man in my house. They had all betrayed her. Besides, he was not her type.

'The stuff is all there ready on the dining table. Mrs Alford has been very helpful,' she gabbled.

'Can you trust her? Her sort is on the make you know. Give 'em an inch and they'll take a mile.'

'She's not like that. Actually, you'd be surprised. She has a nose for quality and gives me good advice.'

Brad grunted and raised one eyebrow.

'He' used to do that, she thought. Was it an omen?

'Really?' he continued. 'Perhaps she can give me some advice. Only joking of course. She is probably fine, but I can remember we had a succession of cleaners, and my mother had to sack them one after the other. Being let loose in a big house with little supervision is a big temptation. Especially when most of them are on the fiddle with benefits. I don't suppose you would miss the odd item and that is what they rely on.'

'Are your parents still alive then?' Caroline had no desire to discuss her staff arrangements. After all, she reasoned to herself, she was his employer and she knew little about him, even though he had been working for her husband for many years. What was to stop him from cheating and stealing?

'What? Oh no. I am on my own like you. I rattle around in a big old house which needs a great deal of attention. I inherited it with all its problems, but I would lose a lot if I sold it in its present state. It would be the same with your house. They can be a bit of a millstone you know.'

Caroline was aware that he would like her to respond. It was obvious that he knew all about the Thorston wealth, and that she needed him to put everything in order, yet she felt that his interest was straying outside of business affairs. She decided to encourage him in his personal disclosures rather than in hers.

'Are you an only child then?' she asked. 'It's not easy is it having doting parents? They expect so much of one.'

'I know what you mean! My father expected me to be top in all my exams. I hated boarding school. I was hopeless at sport. Why does everyone have to be good at sport particularly rugby?' He shook his head and wrinkled his nose.

It was quite red, she noticed. Was he a heavy drinker?

She laughed obligingly. 'I was pretty useless,' she replied. 'I was terrified of the hockey ball coming towards me and I couldn't run for toffee. I nearly drowned getting a bronze life-saving medal.'

'My mother cared of course,' he continued. 'But she wasn't allowed to have much say in things. You have never had children, have you? I noticed you bought that box of puzzles and the doll. Did Mr Thorston have young relations?' He put his head on one side encouraging a reply. There had been no indication of demands on the will from any other family members, and he was relieved that it was all relatively straightforward, even though such claims could lead to the increasing of his bank balance in lengthy drawn out legal procedures.

Caroline shook her head. 'No. We didn't want children,' she replied. 'So, shall we get on with fixing reserves and things? There are a lot of interesting pieces of fine china, and some water colours. I am very tempted to keep some of them, but it would be best to start with a clean slate. On with the new as they say.'

'Indeed,' Brad replied, patting her on the hand.

'So? Did you get your hands on anything then? No of course you didn't. I wish I worked there.' Sherry was making her daily visit to her mother's after her bingo session.

'So? Did you lose at bingo again then?'

'Yes. I bloody did and don't sound so smug. At least I try to better myself.'

Jenny rolled her eyes in mock disbelief. 'He was going this afternoon,' she said.

'Am I a mind reader or something? Who's he?'

'Brad Carter, the solicitor. I don't think he likes me.'

'Brad Carter? Well, you know where he lives, don't you? That big old place at the back of the supermarket. It must have been devalued when they built that shopping area, although I expect his parents made a quid or two from the sale of the land. So, swings and roundabouts I guess. That's just reminded me of something Old Maggie next door said. You know how she rambles on about the past. Apparently, she used to cook for that Carter family a long time ago. Well, she got the sack. She reckons that no one lasted for more than a month in that house, and it was all his fault. Your solicitor bloke I mean. Maggie has some right tales to tell of him. She thinks that he was such a spoilt, bored brat that he used to make up stories and get people into trouble. She reckons he bats for the other side, if you get my gist. She is a right card is Maggie. She must be ninety if she's a day.' Sherry rummaged in her bag for her cigarettes. 'I bet he is after that Caroline woman's money,' she continued. 'I wouldn't trust him. How do you know he isn't shoving things in his briefcase when she isn't looking? You could get the blame. Like I said, he was always getting people into trouble. A leopard doesn't change its spots. The next thing you know she will be giving you your marching orders.'

Jenny shrugged. She found it difficult to keep up with the conversation. She really did not want to discuss her life with her daughter, yet she had no one else in whom to confide. Caroline had been so different today, but then as Sherry always maintained, it was us and them, and never the twain shall meet. Was that Brad bloke after Caroline as Sherry said? According to Sherry's ancient friend he was not interested in women. How did she know? Some people just loved to gossip. But then, at his age was he interested in sex at all? Should she try to warn Caroline? How could she do that without causing offence? It was not her place to be so familiar. Perhaps, she could ask her advice about something. Appeal to her superiority in matters of, say, dress sense. Perhaps she could suggest that Caroline helped to choose a rig-out for a wedding. It wouldn't be a lie. An invitation had arrived in the post that morning, and she had no idea what she was going to wear. She was sure that Caroline would be flattered and must need to get away from that house. Perhaps they could go on a shopping trip.

'Mother! I'm talking to you! Are you in cloud cuckoo land? Just think on!'

Caroline washed her hands, applying layer after layer of creamy soap from the dispenser. Brad had grasped both of her hands and squeezed them, followed by 'Well done! That's another lot ready for the sale room.'

She was appalled at her reaction, allowing her hands to remain in his, and enjoying the sensation of the physical contact. Her legs had weakened, and she knew that she would not have resisted if he had pulled her closer and the contact between them had extended down from her breasts to her stomach and beyond. It was a physical sensation she had never experienced with her husband. He did not show any affection; merely made demands on her for his own gratification.

She allowed the hot water to run between her fingers. She was reminded again of his diaries. She had found one amongst some books on the previous day and discovered from the entries that his marking system in the early years of their marriage had extended beyond his experiences as a husband. It seemed that she had been competing with a series of sexual partners, probably on business trips, and all of them, apparently, by their grades, exceeding her in his marking system. He was paying them but using her. It was rape every time, she told herself now, and yet here she was experiencing a kind of forbidden pleasure at the hands of another man. Was she re-living those moments of excitement as an eighteen-year-old girl?

She stared at her reflection in the mirror, visualising herself as that immature young woman in that overwhelming grip of first love. She shuddered with revulsion, now suddenly likening herself to a pathetic, trapped creature in the power of a predator.

Later, as she watched Brad Carter drive away towards the heavy wrought-iron gates, she returned to the comparisons she had been making. Her lover was still there in her life through her teenage memories. The reminiscing; the overwhelming desire to find her daughter; all tangling her mind into tight knots of regrets and fears, alongside the excitement of the freedom and the means to follow her dreams. Yet, she had loved him, hadn't she? And, in the years that followed, she recalled how she had relived the moments of passion; feelings so lacking in her relationship with her husband. She imagined meeting with him again. She visualised him seeking her out to tell her that his marriage was over, or that his wife had died and at last he was free to be with her. She had planned on ridding herself of her husband, imagining all the ways he could change his life or change hers. Yet, she knew that Robert would never divorce her. That would go against his pride. And why should he do that? He was free to choose his company when he wanted to within the protection and respectability of marriage. He could die of course, but he seemed to be in good health. Later, when he did fall ill, she had suffered with remorse and guilt and had panicked at the thought of having the freedom to live with her lover; that Mr Rochester of her youthful desires.

She went upstairs to the bedroom. Marigold was staring across towards the window, her matted hair revealing bald patches on her head.

'You are my constant star, Marigold,' Caroline said to her. 'All these years you have been hidden from me, yet you were my first love. Perhaps I do have a granddaughter, who could love you. April will be thirty-four now. She has been hiding away like you.'

Perhaps, she is looking for me, she thought, like the woman in the television programme. Perhaps, all I have to do is join up the dots.

She went back down the stairs and opened the French windows, revealing the patio and the wildness of the back garden. My grandchildren would love to play out here, she thought. But how would she ever find them? And what if there weren't any children? What if April hated her for giving her up? What if her daughter was living a dangerous kind of life, a weak person who took drugs and went out drinking every night? What set of circumstances, what complications, was she inviting into her life? Should she write to the television programme producers and rely on experts to make decisions? They must have to do a lot of research before someone's private life was exposed. What if none of it was true and it was all done by actors? Would the public ever know? Anyway, what would she write? Was she prepared to disclose the circumstances of the illegitimate birth? 'Washing your dirty linen in public.' That was her adoptive mother's voice in her head. So, where could she get advice? Brad would know, of course. He seemed to know everything about the law and had to trace claimants if no will materialised. He had talked about such happenings and commented that she was lucky that her husband had been so organised with his affairs. But then she did not wish to be beholden to Brad in any way. She watched the clouds blowing across the sky, greying in the gathering of water vapour and reaching those already heavy with threatening rain. She took some deep breaths of the cool air. There was no way that she could encourage a relationship with Brad after his familiarity today. No man would ever pull her strings again she decided.

Chapter Six

It was Friday, the last day of the week, but a very long day for Jenny. It was always late in the evening before she could relax at home in front of the television, or with her favourite current paperback. Caroline also was needing a break from the seemingly unending task of clearing the house of his possessions. They were in the library taking books from the shelves. Jenny was dusting each one and Caroline was flicking through pages and deciding on future values and possible venues. She had no idea of their worth and had invited a book dealer to the house early in the next week. There was little urgency in this endeavour. Brad had sounded apathetic about the value of old books. It was not his forte, he explained, and many of the encyclopaedic tomes had long since gone out of fashion with advancing technology. He talked about checking availability and second-hand prices on the internet. 'You could google them,' he said. Caroline had no idea what he meant by googling.

She thought about the word now. 'What is googling?' she asked turning towards Jenny, who was attempting to control a sudden sneezing fit.

'Sorry! This dust is getting to me! Google is a website on the internet. You type something in and it comes up with all the information. Don't ask me how it works or how it knows all this stuff.'

'So, for example, if I put this book title on, it would tell me all about it.'

'I think so. I suppose it depends on how old it is and whether people still read it. I really don't know. My brother is the whiz kid in our family.'

'Oh. I remember you saying that he was doing the family tree. Is that all about birth certificates and the census?'

'Yes. Apparently, we have gentry on one side. Fancy that. We don't know whose blood we have in our veins, do we?'

Caroline looked up and was about to comment when the sound of the phone ringing could be heard from across the hall. As she hurried from the room, leaving the door wide open in her haste, Jenny thought for a moment of the way time stood still in this house. Even the phone system was still not modernised in that it depended on a main line connection with no cordless phones to take from room to room if necessary. She doubted whether Caroline had any idea of the convenience of a cordless system. Had she got a mobile phone? She had never seen her using one. She visualised her now standing in the hall, leaning against the small, so called, telephone table.

She heard her employer say, 'Hello, who am I speaking to?' And then a silence as the caller was presumably giving details. Caroline's voice sounded strange Jenny thought, as though she was pretending to be someone else. 'No, just some puzzles and a doll. That was all,' she heard her say. 'No, no photograph album. I was attracted to the doll. I used to have one similar to that and I thought my grandchild would like it. You don't wish me to return it, do you? I have kind of promised it to her. Oh, that's good then. Well I hope you find the photograph album. I would be very upset if I mislaid mine. Goodbye'

Jenny's face registered curiosity as Caroline re-entered the library and Caroline, in her confusion, felt obliged to explain.

'Fancy!' she exclaimed. 'That was someone who thought she had sold her family photograph album by mistake. Apparently, they had had a house clearance company in and some things were packed together in boxes with no regard for their values. The auction company has told them that I bought a box at the sale. You know, the one with puzzles and games in it. How awful for them to lose an album!'

Jenny nodded in agreement. 'Perhaps they will find it in a strange place like you did in the old box in the loft. I was so pleased that you remembered where it was. It must have puzzled you for years.'

'Oh yes, that's right. I must show you it sometime, now that it has come to light. There is so much up in that loft but I think we will have to get someone in. I daren't go back up there and you can't, can you?'

Jenny shook her head. 'No. I'm not paid danger money.' She grinned, but Caroline knew that it was not a joke. But then, why should she, she reasoned? Her mother would have ordered one of the staff to do it. Well, I am not my mother, she told herself, and in any case, she was not my mother. She was not anyone's mother, was she?

That thought restored her sense of well-being and she left her recent guilt behind saying enthusiastically that today would be a good day to look at the album.

'I am sick of these dusty old books,' she said. 'Let's leave it until next week when the expert arrives.' She giggled and pushed her hair back away from her face in a gesture which Jenny found appealingly vulnerable.

'It's not much fun looking at photos on one's own, is it?' she continued. 'See if you can spot the family likenesses. I am usually useless at that. People seem to change from day to day. I'll just go and fetch it.'

Jenny watched her hurrying from the library and then heard her footsteps on the stairs, followed by the creaking of hinges as a door was opened. The only door that she could visualise at the top of the stairs was the one giving access to the clothes airing space near to the hot water cylinder. Why would she put the album in there after retrieving it from the attic? She returned to her previous contemplations about the attic and its mysterious contents and waited for Caroline to put the rather shabby, brown, leather-bound album on the table.

'So, let's start at the beginning,' Caroline said. 'This handsome lady was my great-grandmother. She was called Sarah and lived to be nearly ninety I was told, although I do not recall having seen her. I expect I was a baby during her last years. And this is my grandmother on my mother's side. Apparently, she played the violin, and gave lessons to swell the coffers. There are no photographs of my grandfather. I believe that he was killed in the war and he left her as a young widow to look after my mother and her brother. If he had lived, no doubt there would have been more children. I am not sure who some of these others were. Cousins I expect. And this was my mother Alexandria. She was very good-looking don't you think? She also played the violin but married well and so she did not have to earn money. The marriage didn't last and she must have got a good settlement. I was an only child and was able to go to boarding school and had lots of attention really. But lots of loneliness as well. That's me, look, when I was about seven, I think. That was taken in the garden. I had a private teacher then. Ah, and here's me in my tennis rig-out. I must have been about twelve there.'

Jenny studied the photographs, commenting on different characters, and, apparent family likenesses. As the pages were turned, with the passing of time evident in the fashions of dress and hair styles, and in the advancing maturity of the images, she began to feel that some of the scenes and characters were familiar to her. She had a vague recall of episodes in her childhood when she lived in a village a few miles distant.

'Where was that one taken?' she asked, pointing to a group photograph outside of a church. 'It reminds me of somewhere I used to live when I was a child.'

Caroline hesitated, and looked more closely at the photograph. 'Oh, I'm not sure,' she replied. 'I was away so much. I don't know some of these people. I was only home for holidays and then quite often we went away. Anyway, we'd better get on.'

She stood up, closing the album and pushing it to one side of the table. Jenny stared at the cover for a moment or two, her lips pursed as if she wanted to make further comments, but then stood up and looked away, aware once more of her role as an employee and the feeling that she was overstepping the mark.

Later on, and back in her own surroundings, Jenny put some milk in the microwave in readiness for her coffee. She was tired yet knew that her day's work was nowhere near at an end. It was not a favourite day of her week. She was employed on two evenings a week by an elderly lady, who expected a cooked meal, and her house cleaned from top to bottom before she was helped into her bed. Following on from her work at Caroline Thorston's house or her weekly shopping trip for a bed ridden old neighbour it was hard work for Jenny and on Mondays and Fridays, she collapsed into bed, too exhausted to catch up on the soaps. There was nothing enjoyable about these evenings of her week with her elderly employer. It seemed, the old lady could be described as querulous; not Jenny's choice of word but, apparently, a local opinion of her, and she repeated this sentiment in her own words to her daughter who had arrived soon after she had prepared her milk in the microwave: 'She is a miserable bossy old cow, and I feel like giving her the miss,' she said.

'Well, her money is as good as anyone else's,' Sherry commented. 'She's not picking on you in particular. That's the way she is. And you really don't know how long your day job is going to last. That Mrs Thorston could put the house up for sale and go on a cruise or something. Have you thought about that? No, knowing you! So, what have you been doing today then?'

Jenny weakened in her resolve to keep her private life away from the curiosity of her daughter. 'We were sorting books ready for a dealer coming,' she replied. 'There are shelves and shelves of them, and the dust is still choking me.' She noisily cleared her throat and gave her nose a good blow before continuing. 'She had a phone call about a box of items at that sale. Do you remember I told you that she bought a box containing puzzles and I think that old doll was part of the lot. You know, the old doll she keeps moving around. Did I tell you about that? Well, apparently, someone has lost a photograph album and wondered if it had been left in the box by accident. I heard Caroline say that there was no album in the box but she was really red in the face when she came back into the library. Then she suggested that we could have a break and look at her photos. Do you remember I told you that I helped her to get a box out of the loft and it seemed to be all about her family album? Anyway, we had a look. It was very battered looking. I would have to get a new one, but posh kind of people like old things, don't they? I mean, I do, if they are beautiful. But this one looks as though it has been in the dustbin. God knows what is up in that loft.'

'So, what about it then? Why is it such a big deal? Is she still going on about family trees? Do you think she is going loop the loop?'

'No. Hang on a minute! You are so impatient! No. The strange thing is, I felt that I knew some of those people. I recognised the church. It was definitely in the village where we lived when I was a child. She must be about the same age as me, but I don't remember her. I know she said once that she went to boarding school, so perhaps they didn't mix in the village, but even so some of those faces looked familiar.'

'Oh well, Mother. It's all keeping you amused. You know what I think about it. You'll be sorry you haven't got more out of it when she gives you the push. Has the mystery grandchild turned up yet or is that all in her head as well?'

'Actually, I think she is just interested in family trees. I told her Mike was doing ours and she talked about that television programme where people trace relatives. She got those puzzles, didn't she, and that doll? There is something mysterious about her life and I mean to find out.'

Sherry left her mother to get ready for her evening job, and Jenny sank back into the chair and closed her eyes. She could not get the photographs out of her mind. She knew those people. It was a long time ago but they were definitely in her childhood. Suddenly she was back in her memory to the time when she had her eighth birthday, and the face of a local man came into her mental vision. He had come with his magic tricks. He wore a black cloak and had a black top hat. Who was he? The Great Majesto! Of course! It was all coming back. He lived in a big house at the other end of the village near to the church. She remembered now. It was the church in the photograph in Caroline Thorston's album. How strange, but then what did that prove? Well nothing really, she mused. Just that she had been right in her recognition of the village scenes, but the likelihood of mixing with Caroline's family would have been as remote as it was now. But then, wait a bit, that woman who Caroline said was her mother, did have connections with the magician. She could visualise them now walking down the village street arm in arm on their way back from church and she had wondered if he could really make things disappear. She remembered ducking behind a tree and waiting until they had passed by. Goodness me, she thought. What had kept that in her mind? Fear I suppose she said to herself. So, was the magician, actually Caroline Thorston's father? But then she had said that they were divorced and she had a good settlement. He would have had a good living wouldn't he and not have been a child entertainer? In any case, wouldn't there be a photograph of him in the early days, or was he wiped out of the family memory? She was sure that there had been boys in that house. So why would Caroline say that she was an only child? What was she trying to hide? Or was it her own memory playing tricks on her and was she confusing it with a different place?

Chapter Seven

Caroline was tired of the constant cataloguing of her husband's possessions and of the dustiness of the drawers and cupboards in his office. Brad queried every certificate and record of purchase. It was becoming a nightmare and she could not see an end to it. She wanted to escape into the sunshine of the late autumn days, but the nights were drawing in and sudden drops in the temperature threatened worse to come.

Brad suggested that she would benefit from a change in surroundings, adding that he was overdue for a break, and she guessed that he was hinting at her keeping company with him. She nodded and said that a holiday was a good idea. She even, momentarily, considered responding to his innuendoes before reproaching herself. How desperate am I, she thought? Men were totally out of her equation.

'Well, it gives us both something to think about,' Brad said, as he bundled together his papers and reached for his briefcase.

Caroline watched his car pulling away from the gate. He was a decent man, she thought but too much like her husband to envisage spending a holiday with him. In any case, what were his intentions? She knew that he lived on his own and apparently had never married. He had tried to make physical contact but then, after all, it was polite to shake hands. So, what alternatives did she have? Would she enjoy going off on her own? She shook her head. Loneliness in a strange place would be unbearable. She could always have a companion, like the young woman destined to be the second Mrs de Winter in *Rebecca*, she thought. She had just finished reading that famous novel, having found it amongst the piles of books waiting for collection, and had likened herself to the young companion rather than to the odious, rich woman who was employing her. But, of course, it would have to be the other way around in my case wouldn't it, she mused, in as much as she would be the employer? She could advertise for someone to accompany her and organise a holiday. Would she dare to do that? Her mother had employed an au pair girl to look after things in the school holidays. She was nice, Caroline remembered. Perhaps Mrs Alford could find out for her. Perhaps such services were available on the internet.

Later that morning, she brought up the subject whilst Jenny was doing some ironing. They had decided to have a good clearance of clothes in the dressing room where Caroline had accumulated years of fashionable evening dresses and day dresses, as well as twin sets popular in previous decades and sensible skirts for afternoon wear. Some would benefit from a wash, whilst others needed an airing outside the confines of the cupboard, or a sponging and ironing.

'You've got some beautiful clothes, Mrs Thorston,' Jenny remarked, running her fingers across the heavy brocade of a royal blue evening dress. 'It would be a pity to give these away. There's a shop in the town that pays good prices.'

'I don't think I want to do that. You know, now I think about it, perhaps some of them would fit you. You look to be about the same size as me. Perhaps a little broader, but I used to have more weight on me. I have shed a few pounds over the last few years, with all the stress of my husband's illness.'

Jenny looked up from the ironing, her eyes suddenly bright with anticipation. 'It would be good to have something smart to wear for a family wedding. I got an invitation the other day, and it has been worrying me.'

'So, that's a good a reason for sorting out my wardrobe. I am so pleased I can help you. Actually, I have been thinking of taking a break, and would like to get some casual holiday clothes. Where do you think I should go for a holiday? I would like to travel abroad. He never would.' Not with me, she nearly said.

'Well, I have always wanted to go to Italy and see the sights in Rome and Florence and then go down to Sorrento and the Amalfi coast. It was in that film wasn't it about those gold thieves? And then there's Capri. You know! Where Gracie Fields lived.' Jenny stared across the room, holding the iron above the bodice of the dress, poised in her visualisation of a world unknown to her except from images on the screen.

Caroline stared at the plump features of her employee. The colour had come into her pale cheeks and her eyes shone with enthusiasm.

'Goodness me,' she laughed. 'You know a lot about it.'

'I saw it on our Sherry's tablet. She was looking something up about some celeb. I just wanted to see the sights. Oh, and there's Pompeii and Mount Vesuvius. I forgot about those. Yes. That's the place to go.'

'Shall we go then?' Caroline asked. 'You can be my companion and do things for me in return for the holiday. You would still be working for me, wouldn't you? Do you think you could find out about it?' She hesitated and then shook her head as if in denial. 'But then you lead a busy life, don't you? I expect it would be too much for you. Don't worry. Perhaps Brad will know. It was just an idea.'

Jenny stared, struck temporarily dumb by this bombshell. Her face, flushed previously with enthusiasm, was now paling with the shock caused by her employer's words. 'Oh, no…no,' she stuttered. 'No, I would love to go. That would be amazing. You wouldn't have to worry about anything. I could get it all booked. We would need to fly. Are you OK flying? I have never flown but I've heard that it takes forever on a coach. Could someone get us to the airport? Perhaps my daughter could take us. Or do you want to drive there?'

'Hey, slow down! That's no problem. We'll just order a taxi. So, why can't we go to the travel agency on the high street and get it all booked? We don't need any help do we? Come on. Get your coat, Jenny. We'll do all this clearing out later and have a real reason for sorting clothes.'

It was as though life and time were on their side. The streets were strangely empty of traffic. All the traffic lights were green, and a parking space, close to the travel agent's, seemed to be waiting for their arrival. They were met with enthusiasm by the young woman at the desk. Apparently, trade was not brisk, at this time of the year. The children were back at school and most people had booked their autumn holidays well in advance.

'Italy?' She said the word as though it was an unknown destination, Jenny thought.

'Yes, that's right,' Caroline replied. 'Do you have availability now? We would be flying of course and would like to get in as much as possible before the weather changes. Rome, Capri, the Amalfi coast, Pompeii. You know, the usual.'

Jenny giggled, changing it into a cough, and grabbing for a tissue in her coat pocket. Caroline was putting on the style as they used to say.

'Is this with your husband? Would you want a twin room?'

'We'll have one each shall we, Jenny? Then we can spread out.'

'Oh sorry. I didn't realise you were together.' The woman looked from one to the other.

She returned to the computer and went onto a search programme for availability. 'Sorry,' she said. 'Italy has been so popular this year. It's almost the end of the season. There's this country of course. Here's one with availability and it's down to half. That's lucky!' she exclaimed. 'A cancellation has just come up in a couple of weeks for North Wales. Not singles I'm afraid. But then they are never brilliant. So, two double rooms for seven days. Could you manage that? The pick-up point is on the high street. It is a well organised trip with included excursions. We have good feedbacks and if you look on the internet you can get some idea on the hotels, etc. But I would advise you take my word for this as it will soon be snapped up.'

'Internet?' Caroline turned to Jenny.

'It'll be on Google. Our Sherry will know.'

'Oh well. It all sounds splendid. Book us in then.' Caroline searched in her handbag for her purse. 'You will need some kind of deposit I expect.'

'The total amount is required now. Sorry but it is a late booking,' the young woman said.

'Of course! I'll use my card, shall I? '

It all seemed so easy and Jenny was out of breath with holding it. Her cheeks were flushed with excitement and her legs were shaking.

The details would arrive soon, they were told, and they left the agent's and returned to the car without saying one more word until Caroline navigated the drive. 'Sorry it wasn't Italy,' she said. 'Perhaps next time. I don't know whether I can be that daring at the moment. To be truthful, I have never flown and there is still so much to do. Snowdon will have to be a substitute for Vesuvius.'

Jenny wanted to say that she had never had a proper holiday in her adult life, but she did not want to put any doubts into her employer's head about her capabilities as a companion.

An hour later she almost ran up the stairs leading to her third-level two-bedroomed flat. She was usually flagging by this time, and very often the lift was not working as was the case today. However, she did not consider this a physical hardship, being quite nimble, apart from her problems with asthma which were more often than not triggered by stress. In any case, by using the stairs, she could avoid reading the graffiti on the walls of the lift that appalled her with their vulgarity. She had heard someone describe the crude words and symbols as missiles, invading the mind and scarring the sensibilities. These words used by this rather well-to-do-looking man with whom she had shared the lift one day, had stuck in her head and she had repeated them to Sherry. Her daughter had laughed and said that he must be that posh toff who hung around with the 'drugee' on the top floor.

Jenny agreed with his pronouncement, even though she would not have chosen those words to describe the effect that such vulgarity had on her, but the pain was real enough and the memory of it continued to impinge on her senses.

What would Sherry think of their holiday plans? Should she tell her? Perhaps not. She would say something to spoil it knowing her.

In spite of her burst of energy, she was out of breath by the time she reached her landing, a covered way with a view of the concreted area below that provided spaces for parking. She always had her latch key ready to slide into the lock. This was not a safe place to linger, being a public pathway where an opportunist could snatch a bag or issue threats, particularly when the light was fading, or in the dark when electric light bulbs failed or had been stolen. However, today, Jenny felt the urge to stand and lean against the safety barrier and shout her good news to the whole block. She stared out across to level three on the next high rise building where washing fluttered on a line strung across the landing. 'I'm off on my holidays,' she whispered.

She turned the key in the lock and opened the door. She could smell the stale fish and chip odour, a reminder of her meal on the previous night, coming from the plastic bag hanging on a hook near to the sink in her kitchen awaiting transfer to the bin. A chip had escaped from the screwed-up paper on to the floor and was providing a meal for a number of blue bottles buzzing relentlessly in the stale air.

'Oh, for God's sake!' she screamed. 'I only sprayed all this yesterday!'

'What do you expect if you leave food around! I bet you clean up after her ladyship, don't you? And all for a pittance. Still, it's your life.' Sherry was close on her heels.

Jenny spun around, her face twisting with aggravation. 'You made me jump, you stupid cow. I wish you wouldn't creep around.'

She wanted to defend Caroline, but at the same time she suppressed her excitement about the planned holiday, knowing that her daughter would scoff at such an arrangement, and call her a fool to be taken in by such promises. However, as she put the mugs of coffee on the table and wafted her hand through the cloud of cigarette smoke already drifting across the narrow space in her kitchen, she had the urge to boast.

'I am going to Wales,' she said in a quiet, measured kind of way. 'In a fortnight's time, for seven days.'

'Wales! Did you say Wales? How can you afford that? Have you won it or something?'

'No. I am going with Mrs Thorston. We booked it this afternoon. She has never been there before as her husband wouldn't ever take her on holiday. He just went on business trips.'

'Ah! So, you are going as her luggage carrier and general dog's body, are you? You know, like in these dramas on the tele where the staff have to go along to do the ironing, and pack and unpack. I don't suppose you will have a holiday. She won't want to be seen with the likes of you when she is mixing with the toffs.' Sherry drew on her cigarette and then blew a mouthful of smoke slowly out through pursed lips.

Jenny stared at her and then shrugged her shoulders. 'Anything's better than this rat hole,' she said.

Sherry chattered on about the argument she had had with the benefits woman who, apparently, was trying to reduce her rent allowance.

'What does she think I am going to do? Sleep in the street! I have got enough problems without having her going on.'

Get a job, Jenny thought, then reproached herself for her criticism. Sherry had tried, and she did have problems with migraines. She would not see her daughter on the streets but memories of her living at home during those turbulent teenage years before the breakdown of her own relationship were still raw. She could see now that those teenage tantrums caused many of the outbreaks of the violent behaviour of her partner and his increasing alcohol dependency.

After Sherry had drunk her coffee and polluted the air again before making a noisy exit, Jenny sank back into her shabby armchair by the gas fire. She turned the control, igniting one panel of gas, and sipped at the remains of her coffee. She should not have told her, she thought. She had known how the criticism and spitefulness would follow her announcement, so why did she do it? 'I am an idiot,' she said out loud. But then who else would she tell? The crazy old woman who wanted her house cleaned for a pittance, or the young woman at the check-out? As if they cared. It did not change the fact that she was going to Wales on a coach and was going to stay in a hotel. Of course, Caroline Thorston would need help. She was not doing it for nothing, was she? But then it did seem that she was wanting company as well as help. Oh well. Jenny shrugged her shoulders and leant nearer to the fire, a shiver suddenly travelling up her spine.

She allowed her mind to wander back to previous holidays of her youth, spent camping or on school trips staying at youth hostels. She had never stayed in a hotel and now she was going to have a room to herself. Would it have an en-suite, she wondered? She watched programmes on the television where couples insisted on en-suite facilities in the bedrooms of houses that they were viewing for a possible purchase. They always had huge budgets and appeared to be living on a different planet to the one she inhabited.

The thought of money led her mind back to her own finances. She was self-employed and time off was a luxury she could not afford. Presumably, Caroline was treating the holiday in lieu of wages. She had said that, hadn't she? What did she actually say? She sat up, panic flooding her mind. She would need pocket money, wouldn't she? And the bills would still need paying. The rent had gone up last month and she was struggling to pay the electricity bill. Seven days away from home would mean cancelling three evening sessions with old Mrs Bagley. She was well named The Miserable Old Bag she thought bitterly. She wouldn't take kindly to doing without. But then whatever her personality, her money was as good as anyone else's, and perhaps she would find someone else to clean her pokey little house. You couldn't blame her, could you? There were plenty of people out there needing extra cash. Perhaps Sherry would do her a favour and fill the gap, although she would want most of the fee. Probably, knowing her, all of it. Still, it would secure the job. She would have to talk nicely to her and treat her to a packet of cigarettes. But the price of them! What a waste of money! Jenny was back with her criticism of her daughter and her blatant claims on the welfare system.

She closed her eyes and drew in her breath, her mind sinking into despair. The excitement of the last hour dissipating into the vagueness of a dream; a fantasy.

It was Friday again and Jenny was anticipating the day with mixed feelings. She had become so critical of her own abilities to cope with change that the excited reaction to the future holiday plans had become a tangled worry of 'what ifs' in her mind. Her worries about paying the bills, as well as having spare cash for pocket money during those seven days in Wales, now weighed so heavily on her mind that she had spent all of her spare time during the last few days in looking at 'help wanted' in the columns of the local paper or in shop windows, or on super market boards where free advertising was sanctioned. What was she prepared to do? She had questioned herself before she set off. Housework of course, dog walking? Yes, she could do that. Gardening…decorating? She could use a paint brush. How about baby-sitting? That wouldn't be a problem, she thought. She had two weeks to raise some cash.

She arrived at Caroline Thorston's house with added worries. The car was loath to start and she guessed that the battery needed charging. It was not holding the charge and really needed replacing. She had hoped that it would keep functioning long enough to reach the next MOT. This seemed to be the final blow.

She recognised the solicitor's car in the driveway and brought her car shuddering to a halt a few feet behind. She smiled wryly at the idea of him being blocked in if he wanted to leave first. How would he feel at having her jump leads fastened to the engine of his black leather-seated vintage Rover?

Caroline greeted her at the back door. 'Good morning Mrs Alford,' she said. 'Could you continue with the ironing and the bed linen needs changing. There is a small amount of washing to be done and then, if there is time, the oven needs cleaning. I have a lot of paper work to sort with my solicitor so try not to disturb us. Of course, we will need coffee at eleven as usual.'

Jenny struggled to erect the ironing board and plugged in the iron. This was not a favourite job; she much preferred cleaning. However, she had to be quiet it seemed, although the washing machine was noisy. The door to the sitting room was slightly ajar and she could hear his voice quite clearly.

'That's a sudden change of plans, isn't it? So, you will be away for the next sale then? Wales is a long way to go at the moment with so much to do. You are not going on your own, are you?'

Jenny strained her ears to hear the response, but Caroline's voice was lost with the scraping of chair legs across the floor.

'You are taking Mrs Alford? What, the cleaning woman? Do you think that is wise? Has she been before?'

Jenny held the iron aloft, turning her left ear towards the doorway.

'No. But the travel agents give clear directions and I can always ask. As my mother said to me constantly, 'You have a tongue in your head, well use it.'

'So Mrs Alford will still be in your employment presumably, and will sort out luggage, etcetera, and your requirements each day. You really can't expect much from someone of her breeding, can you?'

'Of course not,' Jenny heard her employer reply. 'No doubt she will be able to occupy herself in her free time.'

The colour flooded into Jenny's cheeks and then drained away, leaving a pallor accentuating the dark circles under her eyes. She bit her lip in an effort to control the tears which were welling up in her eyes. She felt so betrayed, and her daughter's words came back to her, as they had done frequently during the last few days. Sherry was right. Sherry was always right about that lot as she called them. She was going to be a dog's body. Someone to make sure her ladyship had her clothes pressed, and all her requirements; general gofers as her daughter described the serving classes. In return, she would not have any money for a week and her other jobs would be in jeopardy. She had suggested to her daughter that it would be a big help if she could keep things going and had offered half of her wages in return, but Sherry was not keen on the idea. 'Someone will shop me,' she had said. 'Then I will have all my benefits stopped. You know I am not allowed to work.'

The voices of her employer and the solicitor had faded into an occasional comment about items of sale, it seemed. Jenny methodically ironed and folded each item, placing them on a pile ready for the airing cupboard. She was relieved when the clothes basket was emptied and she carefully gathered up the ironed clothes and carried them up to the first-floor landing. The airing cupboard door was slightly ajar, and she pushed her foot in the gap pulling it towards her, preparing to off load the pile of clothes onto the shelf. However, the available airing space was taken up with what she immediately recognised as the old photograph album. An envelope was sticking out from the side. She carefully moved the album across to one side and deposited the pile of ironing. There was no sound from downstairs. Again, Jenny was wondering why this album was in the airing cupboard. It was as though it needed to be hidden. She opened the envelope and examined the contents. There were three photographs of Mrs Thorston. She could recognise her likenesses in spite of the obvious passage of the years since they had been taken. She looked at the backs of them for dates, and found instead, brief instructions as to apparently on which page they belonged in the album. She opened the album, turning to the relevant pages and discovering that photographs had already been removed to create spaces. Opening a separate envelope revealed some other old photographs. Jenny gasped as she looked at the image of a man in a top hat. She had instant recall. He was The Great Majesto of her childhood days. The man she had earlier visualised walking with the lady on the village street close to the church. The scribbled, faint pencilled letters on the back of the photograph confirmed his identity. How curious, she thought. So, this was not her family album. It must be the missing one. The album belonging to the person who had rung up earlier. But why had she lied on the telephone? As she stared more closely at the photograph of the magician, she became aware of irregular marks in the surface. She held it up towards a shaft of sunlight that was coming in through the landing window, realising that each eye in the photograph of the magician had been stabbed through by some sharp implement. She shivered. Why would anyone do that?

She replaced the album in the cupboard, back where she had found it, with the photographs returned inside the envelope, but now with the pile of freshly laundered clothes underneath it. Would Mrs Thorston realise that she had seen it there? Or would she have so little regard for affairs of the household that she would not give it a second thought? She must be concerned though and feeling guilty about denial.

Jenny returned to the kitchen. It was time for their coffee break. She had no need to ask. He preferred black with one sugar, and she liked half milk and half water with two sugars. The customary digestive biscuits completed the ritual and she coughed and said, 'Coffee madam,' before entering the drawing room.

'Thank you, Mrs Alford. You timed that well. We won't be much longer sorting out these sale items. Do you have to rush off?

Apparently, some of the big furniture from the study could do with a good clean. Another sale is coming up soon.'

There was still an hour and a half left before she completed her morning's work and Jenny was puzzled. She nodded looking for a clue into the reason for this request, but her employer had returned her attentions to the solicitor.

She went upstairs to change the sheets and pillow cases on Caroline's bed. The other rooms were in need of fresh air and she opened the windows and drew back the curtains. Honestly, she thought, this house really does get more and more like that Miss Haversham's. Talk about living in the past. Well, she would soon be in the clutches of that Brad bloke and serves her right. All these people with their airs and graces. I'm just the cleaner and here to work. Well, she wouldn't go to Wales now even if that rich old cow offered her double wages.

'Jenny, could you move your car? Mr Carter is going now.' That was Caroline's voice on the stairs.

Jenny giggled nervously. She was visualising the choking noise coming from her dying car battery and anticipating his impatience as she offered him her starting leads.

A half an hour later he drove away, his face red with impatience. He was not good at working out the comings and goings of the car engine as he would describe it and to make matters worse, it seemed that this cleaning woman was some kind of an expert.

Caroline could not stop giggling as he pulled away. 'Oh dear, Jenny,' she said. 'You have not improved his day. I spoilt it somewhat by telling him that we are going to Wales. Come on. Let's start planning for our holiday.'

She ran ahead of Jenny around to the back of the house and into the garden. 'What a wonderful day,' she exclaimed. 'Fresh air! That's what we need.'

Jenny walked slowly along the path to join her. Caroline had no idea of the extent of her problems. That Brad knew of course. He would be turning the knife no doubt. What would she do if I explain, she wondered. Oh well. It was all becoming impossible. She had no choice now. Anyway, she thought, she was only there to work. Like

Sherry said, and Mrs Thorston, who had just made it obvious to that odious solicitor, that she would not want the company of a working-class woman like her. She would only be there for her convenience; a shadow in the background like the servants in Downton Abbey

Caroline was patting her hand on the bench seat. 'Come and sit down, Jenny. You have done enough work for one day.'

'I thought you wanted me to do some extra hours. I don't mind.'

'No. I only said that to put him off the scent. I don't want you to work. I want to talk about our holiday.'

'I don't think I can go,' Jenny blurted out, her lips pressing together hard in denial.

Caroline leaned forward, her eyes widening with the impact the words suddenly made. 'Why not?' she asked.

Jenny hesitated, then rushed headlong into the response she had rehearsed for the last few days. It was a list of financial reasons, beginning with her inability to pay her way if she took a holiday. A holiday in lieu of wages did not pay her rent or her utility bills, she explained, and then she would lose her other jobs which she relied on, if she absented herself for a week.

'Oh, goodness me!' Caroline exclaimed. 'How stupid of me. Of course, you have bills to pay. Well, that's no problem. I will give you your wages as usual and that is nothing to do with the holiday.'

'That's very good of you, Mrs Thorston, but what about the other jobs I do?'

'Do you want to do them? Would you be miserable if you didn't do them?'

Jenny shook her head.

'Well, I'll put up your wages and you can work some extra time for me when we get back. How's that? So, let's talk about our holiday. I have found a book all about Wales, so that's a good place to start. We have got to know where we are going and what to look for. I am sure you are much better than me at finding your way about. And you had better start calling me Caroline.'

Brad stared out of the window of his gloomy Victorian house onto

the rear of the supermarket car park. He preferred this view in spite of the fact that the back windows of the house looked out over a wide expanse of cultivated land, with lawns and well stocked borders, a summer house and greenhouse, all within the confines of an old, six-feet high, red brick wall. His parents had sold a large area of the land at the front of the house at a time when family finances were being threatened and the supermarket was in need of space. Consequently, the ornate, arched front door now opened directly from the public footpath leading to the car park of the newer development and all signs of a driveway were lost forever.

He had not understood at the time that his parents had spent a lot of money on his private schooling. Indeed, he did not consider it an advantage, having suffered years of bullying and abuse at the public school where he had boarded for ten years of his childhood. He hated sport, and wanted to hide away and read, but rarely escaped from being made to look feeble and at the receiving end of physical and mental anguish. He had often thought since he had reached adulthood that *Tom Brown's Schooldays* was based on such an establishment, with all the fagging and abuse from the older boys. He remembered how the new boys were lined up, and he had been so afraid as he stood there, stripped bare and shivering with cold. He had been picked out, 'chosen' by a boy called Harry Bodwell. He recalled how he had changed the name to Bodewell, giggling to himself that nothing about him would bode well. However, his cleverness was no defence against the cruelty and abuse which followed. He cried himself to sleep every night, dreading to feel the covers being pulled back, and curling up tightly, drawing his knees to his chin against the threats against his boyhood.

In the end, it was his delicate state that saved him. He fell ill during the summer term before his fourteenth birthday in August and was sent home to recover. His mother would not allow him to return when he begged her to support him. He could not disclose the full extent of the abuse he had suffered, but surely, she must have understood. Still, he often wondered in later years. His father had no sympathy. He was a bully until the day he died, and no doubt was one of the bullies during his own school days. He had declared that his son must return and finish his education. It would make a man of him. God! How I hated him, he thought. His mother had intervened, bless her. It must have taken a lot of courage to do it. He adored her. He knew from overheard conversations that she was a victim of her husband's strong opinions, and he did his best to protect her, setting himself up as some kind of vigilante, spying on the staff and reporting anyone who he suspected of being dishonest or insubordinate. He wondered at the time of his return home, how his mother could have won the argument, until the day she was left as a widow, and she told him that she had inherited the property from her parents together with, originally, a healthy bank balance.

He held his father responsible for all of the family unhappiness; his bad habits of drinking and smoking leading to his early death and leaving large holes in the family fortune. Since then he often bemoaned the loss of the frontage of his property, blaming his father for what he described as 'an act of sacrilege'. However, the rear of the property, with its regular maintenance by a local odd jobbing gardener, was a constant reminder of happier days, with picnics on the lawn and servants bringing out fresh supplies of lemonade and cucumber sandwiches. Yet, such memories also jagged his mind into feelings of bitterness and recriminations. Elizabeth had thrown her diamond ring at him out there and had flounced off forever. Since then she had appeared in his dreams, sometimes a pretty, carefree girl; her long, blond hair streaming down her back and falling into ringlets. Golden memories. But then there were the times when she plagued his mind with her hatefulness, her face twisting with spite.

He recalled how he had spent hours searching for the ring in the flower bed, breaking down the autumn blossoms of dahlias and asters. He had never found it, and now the value of it left bitterness in his mind. Such bitterness sullied the previous happiness of summer days when they walked under the trees or lounged on the banks of the sunken garden. She was the love of his life, and he vowed never to give his heart to anyone again. No one would ever replace his mother, but he was lonely and frustrated with lack of money. He knew that he had had a lucky escape. Elizabeth would have spent all he had; loving the pop scene and wearing the latest fashions with little or no regard for the cost. She hated his taste in classical music. Yet, in spite of their conflicting interests, he loved her, and had no desire to fall in love again.

It was thirty-one years ago this month since she had thrown the ring into the flower bed. He transferred the date, September 26th, each year into his new diary, and went into a kind of mourning for the whole of the day. It was not necessary to cancel appointments; he never made any on that date, no matter how urgent the occasion. His excuse was that he was sick, and he had no qualms about not communicating. He was lovesick. This day was the major one of many rituals and he drew comfort from the belief that he was safe within their grip.

But now, as he stared out of the window at the people with their bags of shopping, making their way to their cars, he was thinking of Caroline Thorston. She was so rich. She doesn't realise it, he thought. Oh, my God, what he could do with all that money. It would enable him to have work done on his house and then to sell it at a top market valuation. He could leave his bitter memories behind and retire to a life of sunshine and leisure. He thought about what she had said today before he had left. Did he have any desire to keep her company? Not really, he mused. She was all right as women went but could he spend more than a few hours with her without his thoughts returning to his lost Elizabeth? But then that cleaner woman was out for the main chance, he mused. How could Caroline trust her? She could so easily steal small items. Probably had done already, he guessed. There was so much in that house, so far uncatalogued. Mr Thorston had certainly been a hoarder and money had been no object. Greed had ruled his desires. And now here was this money-grabbing woman accompanying Caroline on holiday. He could not believe Caroline's foolishness. She had pointed to a book on the table. What was the title? A woman's name? He couldn't remember, but, apparently, it was about a rich woman travelling with a companion. Just what age was she living in for God's sake?

He decided to telephone her at the earliest opportunity and arrange another meeting. He had an appointment with a client that evening and he reasoned that she would not welcome a visit at a later hour.

He had to play this game carefully. Somehow, she had to feel some gratitude for his actions. Perhaps he could introduce her to a different level in society. More gentility and less of the hard business mentality of her husband's circle of friends and colleagues. She appeared to be so vulnerable and a target for every rogue in the neighbourhood. Yet, he knew very few people on that level himself. Socialising was not his strong point, and after his mother died, he had hidden himself away during those times not spent with clients, spending long hours on his own at weekends.

He held the phone in his hand, staring at the keypad. Hers was one of a number of names on the 'T' list in the phone book details. He decided to move it to 'C' and tapped in the letters to spell 'Caroline'. No other number occupied the 'C' list. That made her seem special, and he smiled to himself. So, what would he say to her if he rang her now? Would he have the courage to invite her here to his house? He could offer her advice on her holiday. He remembered Wales well from his younger days. It would not have changed much. In fact, come to think about it, he had a folder of tourist information. He remembered seeing it the other day when he was searching for something else in his store cupboard in the back bedroom. The sight of it had prompted him to clear out a lot of his old papers, but then he had pushed that thought to the back of his mind along with his plans for getting the roof repaired.

He needed to warn her about the likes of that cleaner woman. He frowned at the memory of her rusting, broken-down car, and the dirty interior with its strange odours. His hands had felt polluted by handling the sticky jump leads coiled up amongst a pile of old rags in the boot. As soon as he arrived back in his house, he had applied two layers of antiseptic cleansing gel to his hands and sprayed his throat with a concoction promising to be a barrier to the influenza virus; He was a firm believer in alternative medicines, and his medicine cupboard was full of pills and potions. There would seem to be little danger of contracting influenza in the late summer, but he had always been a 'belt and braces' kind of man, according to some of his acquaintances, and a hypochondriac to others.

Now he paced up and down the corridor, waiting for the sound of the front door bell. Why couldn't people be punctual, he fumed? When his client arrived, he hurried through a bundle of legal documents, excusing his obvious impatience with the pretext of a tiresome headache, as he described it. He did not care excessively about the bad impression he was giving. The client was a shopkeeper, supposedly in the antiques business, but, in reality a second-hand dealer of anything with a profit margin. Bradleigh Carter despised the common tradesmen, as had his father before him, but they were bread and butter. But then would his father have approved of his growing list of malcontents in the so-called matrimonial stakes. They were mostly female clients, scheming, manipulative sluts, he ranted inside his head. They were looking for compensation or so they claimed, but they were very loath to compensate him in return for his hard work. Occasionally, a badly done to husband would appear on his doorstep, and he took great delight in arranging the best divorce settlement he could, going the complete mile, and even ending up with a slim profit margin. 'How was that then, Elizabeth?' he would say as he closed down his computer for the night and poured himself a large brandy.

As he closed the door behind his client, he glanced at his watch. checking the time with the grandfather clock in the hall on his way to the lounge. He always did this with time. It was one of a number of rituals beginning with the bedside clock when he awoke together with his mobile phone and followed by the kitchen clock and the large wall clock in the lounge after his breakfast. It was an obsessive need to double check the passage of time, a habit that had followed him from his school days when he was in constant fear of being late for his classes.

Now, he stared at the ornate clock on the wall above the settee. Eight forty-five, he mouthed, checking with his watch. She would be sitting on her own after her evening meal, he guessed. He tracked down the list of television channels. Would she watch the soaps? He decided in the negative. *Coronation Street* was not her scene. So, go on then, he mouthed. He pressed the phone book button on his phone and panned down to her number. It was ringing. What was he going to say?

He panicked, ready to end the call, but she was answering and he gasped, 'Hello Mrs Thorston. I have just discovered a load of info on Wales. Shall I bring it round, or did you say that you were going out? Perhaps you could call around and pick it up. I have got quite a busy week ahead.'

He stopped talking and waited for her to answer, cursing himself for his confusion. His ears were burning, another habit that had begun in his youth and which had caused amusement with his peers.

'You only just caught me in,' she was saying. 'I was just on my way out to the supermarket. Actually, I have run out of tea, and I can't function without it in the morning. It's like a drug.' She laughed, and Brad smiled in relief at her seemingly casual reply.

'That's virtually on my doorstep,' he said. 'I never worry about running out. One good thing about living at the back of a twenty-four-hour supermarket. So, I will see you shortly, then. I will get this file ready and watch out for you at the back door.'

He could not believe his good fortune. Then the panic set in and he checked the time with his watch and then with the clock on the wall. Did she like wine or would it be tea? Or was that just at breakfast time? He put a bottle of white in the cooler and got out two of his mother's best wine glasses from the china cabinet. His heart was beating fast and he had to stand still and control his breathing. After a few minutes, he had calmed down and went to the small bedroom to seek out the folder labelled 'The Mountains and Valleys of Wales', before positioning himself close to the large sash window, in the back corridor, where he had a view of the supermarket car park. The public pathway was visible through the closely meshed net curtain, but with no light on in the corridor, he could stand and watch, unseen by the pedestrians on their way to and from the carpark.

Caroline was in no hurry to put on her coat and find her handbag. She was really not in the mood to venture out again, but she knew that there was a strong possibility of her being awake in the early hours of the next morning, and she could not function without a cup of tea. It had become an established habit during the last few years when she lay awake listening to his loud shouts and curses, alternating with the rasping sounds of heavy snoring. Now, of course, it would seem that she could stay in bed and catch up on lack of sleep, but recently with all the organisation of his possessions involving outside agents like Mr Carter and Mrs Alford, together with visits to see the bank manager to change all details of ownership and liabilities, she was more tired than ever.

The excitement of her initial plans and that great sense of freedom they gave to her, were settling now into a mixture of doubts and fears; her old enemies. Did she really want this adventure? Wouldn't it be simpler to get the garden tidied up and stay in the kind of clothing she had worn during the last few years; sensible, comfortable. Could she really enjoy the companionship of a woman who spent her time cleaning up other people's dust and dirt? Could she sit opposite her at the breakfast table or hold polite conversation at the dinner table?

She sighed. It was all done and dusted, as her mother would say. She stood up and went into the hall, reaching for her jacket and checking in her handbag for her keys. Her car was in the garage, and she tensed against the creaking sound of the automatic door lifting, as she pressed the key pad. The noise reminded her of Jenny's engine attempting to fire up, and of Brad Carter's face twisting in disgust at the state of the ancient car. Poor Jenny! She had as much right to the good things of life as he did. Suddenly, her thoughts were back on track. They would enjoy this holiday. After all, why should everyone conform? I'll be me and she can be her, and Brad Carter can be as obsessive as her husband had been without any strings, she told herself. He was not going to become involved in her personal life.

A half an hour later she left the supermarket with a packet of tea bags and several food items that had taken her fancy and headed towards the rear of the car park. She knew where he lived but had never actually been inside his property. Her husband had mentioned it in connection with his business dealings, and she remembered him saying that it had been ruined by the sale of the front garden and driveway. Now, she sought out the entrance, carefully managing the steep front step, and climbing up to an elegant Georgian front door, the large brass knob of which was within the grasp of any passerby, and finding herself uncharacteristically in tune with her late husband's opinions. She rang the bell and glanced at the window, discerning a movement beyond the nets. In the next moment, the door was opened, the bottom edge scraping on the tiled floor. She was aware of cooking odours mixed with the musty kind of smell she associated with dampness.

The solicitor was greeting her as though she was a long-lost friend, she thought. He grasped her hand and guided her over the threshold.

'Watch that ridge,' he said. 'There has been a little subsidence at the front since it was all altered.' His expression had changed she noticed. The smile had changed to a frown, and his hand had tightened on hers.

She pulled her hand free, aware of the stickiness of his skin, and stepped forward allowing him space to close the heavy door behind her. For a moment, she panicked, stifled by the heavy atmosphere in this old house, and a feeling of entrapment as the door clicked back into place blocking the outside world away.

'I mustn't be long,' she said. 'I'll just pick up the info on Wales, and then I must dash.'

'There's no need to rush on my account. I have had a tedious client harassing me for the last hour and I am looking forward to sitting quietly with a glass of wine. I find that is the best thing to help one to unwind. It would be so nice to share it with someone who is not trying to pick my brains and bore me with their trivial problems.'

'Well I am afraid that is what I usually do, isn't it? My life seems to be all problems at the moment.' Caroline bit her lip. She immediately regretted her words, recognising them as an invitation for consolation.

He rose to the occasion as she knew that he would, and propelled her into the large drawing room, his hand firmly resting in the small of her back. She moved quickly, her body instinctively wishing to escape contact, and sank down into the nearest armchair. He stood in front of her, his hands now behind his back. 'I am sure you have time to share a glass of wine with me. What time is it?'

He looked at his watch and then at the large wall clock to confirm the time. 'Ten passed nine. A long time to go before our bedtime.'

He giggled. Caroline stared at him. He was like a little boy, she thought, and was remembering her husband's comments about his sheltered life under the dominance of an overbearing mother. That was one thing she had in common with Brad she supposed, a small spark of sympathy suddenly lighting up in her head.

'Oh, just one then. I rarely indulge.'

As she gulped down the cool, sweet liquid, Caroline had to admit to herself that it was a pleasant experience. Her husband had always preferred red wine, declaring it to have the full body of the grape. Red wine invariably gave her a headache, and she associated all alcohol with a lack of well-being at the end of the day. Now, it was a necessity it seemed, to escape from this entrapment. But he was filling up her glass as she looked at the tourist information and leaflets depicting scenes of Snowdonian splendour.

She began to experience a floating sensation, her eyes finding it difficult to focus on the words and pictures.

'It all looks amazing,' she murmured.

'It would be so good for you to have some guidance,' he was saying. 'If you had mentioned it before, I could have accompanied you. None of these places are good for women travelling alone.'

'It's hardly New York, is it?'

'Well, wherever, it's a big world. There is no shortage of opportunists. But then, you will have your cleaner to protect you, I suppose.' His thin lips grimaced in a twisted smile. 'When are you going, by the way?'

'Next week. September 20th, I think. Is that a Monday?'

Caroline gulped down the wine and closed her eyes. She felt overwhelmingly tired. She struggled to stand up, then sank back down into the chair. His voice seemed to have distanced itself from her and she strained to hear his next words. He was mumbling about some occasion on the 26th. She nodded in agreement, not wishing to appear weak or disagreeable. He had refilled her glass and was now proposing a toast to their continued friendship.

'Are you all right? Come on outside. You need some fresh air. I have got all the lights on. It looks so lovely at this time of night and only me to see it.'

Caroline tried to reply, her head feeling strangely light.

❄

She opened her eyes, screwing them up momentarily against the light that was entering through the pale blue flowered curtains, but then sitting up startled by their unfamiliar colour and pattern. She stared around in the half light of early morning seeing, first, a large chest of drawers and then an ornate dressing table with triple mirrors reflecting other parts of the room. She turned her head to locate the door. It was slightly ajar, and she stared at it, straining to hear any sounds coming from beyond it. She could not remember entering this room. She must still be in his house she reasoned, and it must be early morning. There were no sounds coming from outside other than the twittering of sparrows welcoming the dawn. She looked at her watch. It was nearly six o'clock in the morning! Had she spent the night with him? Where was he now? Her thoughts shocked her into action and she jumped out of the bed, curling her toes against the coldness of the wooden floor and trod carefully towards the window, pulling back the curtains to reveal a view of a large lawn with borders, where late flowering asters and chrysanthemums competed with tall, seeding fennel, and patches of ornamental grasses. She allowed her eyes to wander around, appreciating the beauty of it all in this early light, but then jerking back into the horror of her present dilemma.

She returned to the bed, sitting on the edge and staring at her reflection in the dressing table mirror. 'You look terrible,' she whispered, running her fingers through her hair, and smoothing her hands down the creases in her skirt. Her instinct was to get out of this house as quickly as possible, but how could she do that without his involvement. He would have the key no doubt. She could not imagine him leaving it in the lock, and in any case, how could she ever face him again if she left without an explanation or apology? She returned to the window, watching the birds in their early search for food, and listening for sounds of his awakening, her head throbbing with the latent effects of the wine and the stress caused by her present dilemma.

Brad, in his bedroom across the landing, had heard her moving about and also was debating as to the best way to deal with this situation. He had done his best, he reasoned, remembering how she had suddenly staggered and was sinking to the ground outside on the terrace. The cold air had had the opposite effect to what he had intended, and she was losing consciousness. He had panicked and struggled to get her back inside and onto the sofa, shouting at her and gripping her arms in a futile attempt to arouse her. Then he had sat for a long time studying her condition, checking her breathing every few minutes, and feeling her pulse. He considered a number of times over the next two hours whether to call for help, but then what about his reputation? How could he explain that he had given her too much wine? But he hadn't done it deliberately had he for God's sake, he thought angrily? She was so unworldly. He had come to the conclusion that she would just have to sleep it off. Anyway, he had done his best hadn't he, carrying her up the stairs and putting her into his mother's bed? He reasoned that she would be very afraid if she had woken up on a chair and in any case, he needed to rest his weary body and stretch out on his bed. She was the guilty one, wasn't she? She did not have to drink the wine so fast that it knocked her out. He had lain awake listening for most of the night and had eventually decided to unlock the bedroom door. Initially, it had seemed like a good idea to lock her in, afraid that she might wander in her sleep. The noisy click of the lock echoed in the silence, and he tiptoed back to his room, standing by the window and staring out across the lawn. The birds were singing their dawn chorus in the half light and sounds of early-morning delivery vehicles drifted around from the front of the house.

His thoughts were back to that dreadful time when he had discovered his mother's inert body. Her death had moved in alongside of his recurring dreams of rejection and abuse from Elizabeth. He was devastated by the loss. She was everything he cherished; loving him with no judgement, no condemnation of his weaknesses. After his father had died, they became so in tune that he had no desire to seek out another companion. But then on that dreadful morning, he had found her apparently asleep, but on further investigation, not breathing. He sat by the bedside for a long time. Now, he had little recognition of for how long, but he recalled how his joints and muscles had begun to stiffen and ache and such discomfort had propelled him into action.

The weeks that followed promoted other times of anguish; nightmares and conscious fears, and realisations that he was on his own. It was an unexpected death in as much as she had not recently been assessed by a doctor. He had argued that her health had been failing for a long time and she was over the age of eighty, still an inquest was ordered. He agonised over the questions and the answers he would give. She had wished for cremation, but he could not entertain the idea of her body being reduced to ashes and now he visited her grave every week in a strict pattern of behaviour come rain or shine.

He could not bear to change her room, and the bed was as she had left it, with her favourite duvet cover and pillow cases. He had agonised over depositing Caroline's limp body under that duvet and seeing her hair spread out on the pillow, but it was his only option other than giving up his bed, and he reasoned that Caroline would suspect the worst of him if he did that.

His awareness leapt back into the present day, hearing sounds of movement closer to him. She was walking past his bedroom door. He heard the click of the bathroom latch and then sounds of running water. He needed to speak to her before she attempted to leave the house. He would give her the opportunity to apologise, and reassurances that their relationship had not been harmed by her behaviour. He dressed quickly, stepping silently down the staircase and into the kitchen, where he filled up the kettle.

In spite of his soft tread, Caroline was aware of his movements, and drawn by the steady drone of the kettle heating up, she found her way into the kitchen. They both began to speak at the same time and then both apologised with 'Sorry'.

Caroline giggled nervously. 'You will be giving me a bad name,' she said.

Brad frowned. It was not her name at stake, he thought. 'I think you need a strong coffee and then you had better rescue your car. You must learn not to drink so fast or perhaps not drink at all. You really had me worried, and I could not leave you on the chair. It was pretty obvious that you were out for the count as they say.'

Caroline nodded. She felt guilty at causing him so much

inconvenience yet wanted to accuse him of having ulterior motives. She remembered his previous reaction to her decision to go on her proposed trip with Jenny, and a cup of coffee would have sufficed. His plan had failed! She felt triumphant in spite of her embarrassment, and her face began to recover, the muscles tightening in her cheeks and her eyes brightening with resolve.

Ten minutes later she left his house with a polite thank-you and no backward looks. To her relief, her car appeared to be unmolested and with no threatening penalty issued for parking longer than was allowed. That briefly restored her faith in humanity. No one seemed to be about at this time of the morning in spite of the fact that it was a twenty-four-hour opening store. She drove along that familiar route to her house with a stiffening resolve to make her own decisions and not to lose faith in her convictions. Bradleigh Carter was her employee. She paid him for his services and she was in charge.

Her house, which she had often compared to a prison in past unhappy days, now appeared as a sanctuary and she flung open the door, taking in deep breaths of the familiar scents. She could not wait to remove all vestiges of his house, and ran into the bathroom, turning on the bath taps and preparing for the luxury of a long hot scented bath. Minutes later, as she lay there staring at the ceiling, she cast her mind back to the previous evening. She could bear to do this now in the safety of her own home. Yet she could remember nothing beyond the third glass of wine. She realised now that she had drunk the sweet liquid down in gulps. She had been nervous, and her throat had been dry. She had become a victim again, she thought. He was the predator. How easily I fall into the trap, she mused.

Chapter Eight

Sherry could not wait to spread gossip. She always spent hours looking at the daily Face Book offerings, enjoying the trite contributions of like-minded individuals, all seeming to have an abundance of time to waste. However, on this occasion, she had no need of other people's use of modern technology. The evidence of scandal had presented itself to her through the normal process of observation.

She banged on her mother's door impatiently stamping her feet, and then rattling the letter box.

'Come on, Mother,' she yelled.

Jenny, alerted by the urgency in her voice and the rarity of being addressed as 'Mother' pulled her dressing gown around herself, covering her bare flesh. She was halfway through shaving her legs in an attempt to live up to the promised new clothes, and, already, had cut into a roughened area of her skin where it was difficult to control the angle of the razor, and blood was trickling down in a bright red rivulet.

Her daughter, her cheeks pink with the effort of climbing the three flights of stairs, pushed her way past her anxious mother, with no apparent signs of a major problem.

'Just you wait to hear what I've got to tell you. You'll never guess what your precious Mrs Thorston has been up to.' She did not give her mother space to guess but continued in the same high-pitched dramatic voice. 'She only spent the night with that creepy solicitor.

It's all over Facebook this morning. I couldn't wait to tell everybody. It isn't often that I get so many "likes".'

'I don't believe you. She can't stand him.' Jenny had sat down, clutching her dressing gown around her bare legs and trying to conceal the line of blood now beginning to circumnavigate her right ankle.

'Well then, what was her car doing there all night then?' Sherry's voice had taken on the ranting characteristics of a child with the typical 'so there' echoing from the past. 'I saw it parked in the supermarket carpark at around eleven. I had run out of fags and couldn't face waking up this morning without one. It's the only thing that gets me going.'

'Well, that's not "all night" is it?'

'Hang on! So, I woke up early and decided to see if she was still there, and there was her car all on its own in the car park.'

'She's not the only one with a blue Mini Cooper.'

'She is, with that number plate. CATH 22N. That had me confused until I remembered that she is called Caroline Thorston. There aren't many of them around. New Minis I mean.' Sherry grinned, triumphant in her revelations.

Jenny refused to be convinced, although she was morbidly enlivened by her daughter's news. Old habits die hard, and she had grown up with local and sensational gossip somehow brightening a dull day.

'You don't know the circumstances though, do you? She may have left it there if it wouldn't start. She may have just gone to the shop and then had to get a lift back or something.'

'Hold your horses Mother! I saw her. I saw her. Just as I was turning to go back home, his door opened, and she came out into the street. I didn't get a good shot of that, as by the time I had got my phone out, she was running back to her car. I just managed to catch the tail end of it but if you zoom right in you can make out that number plate.'

She pushed her phone under her mother's nose. Jenny peered at the small screen. She did not demand proof. Her daughter was no fool when it came to gossip. She shook her head and sighed.

'It's not very kind is it to spread such stories? There might be a perfectly good reason for her to be in his house. He is dealing with her husband's affairs. What has it got to do with anyone else anyway? How would you like it if everyone kept up a running commentary about your comings and goings?'

'Come off it, Mum. It's hardly gone viral has it?'

'What does that mean? I wish you would stop being caught up in all this gossip. I hate all this tittle tattle. Just because she has got money and lives in a big house, it does not mean to say that she can't have relationships without it being all over Facebook. You are as bad as these goblins who cause trouble for everybody.'

'Goblins! Goblins! Do you mean Trolls?'

Sherry choked on her cigarette smoke, and her mother turned away half in confusion for getting it wrong but then the other half of her thoughts consoling herself because she had got it wrong.

'Viral means putting it on the internet so that anyone in the world can see it. It could be read by hundreds or thousands or even millions. Everybody does it. But I only have about fifty odd people on my "friends' page" who can read it.' She wagged her fingers in the air to denote the apostrophes, causing yet another jerk of aggravation in her mother's mind. 'That's no big deal, is it?' she continued. 'It's just a bit of a laugh. Trolls make up stories about someone they don't like. And put fake news on.' She frowned and sighed at the same time. 'Just thought it would amuse you, that's all.'

Minutes later, Jenny winced at her noisy exit. In spite of her condemnation of the use and abuse of the modern media, she was now feeling very disturbed by her daughter's revelations. She had planned to spend the morning in sorting out her basic clothes, and then Caroline had invited her over to try on some dresses perhaps suitable for her to wear on holiday. As she sat staring out of her window across to the next block of high rise flats, the doubts she had already experienced, were returning, and she was recalling how her employer had made light of her role in the arrangements. After all, it was no huge concession for her to pass on her unwanted clothes. They were destined for the charity shop. But then, she had offered to give me holiday pay and increase my wages, she reasoned. Did that not mean that she cared? But then that was no big deal, either. It was all for her convenience, wasn't it? She just wanted somebody to give her a hand with everything. She had so much money that it would not affect her in the slightest. Jenny suddenly shuddered at the idea of him touching Caroline, and perhaps both of them giggling over the incident with her flat car battery, or the common way she spoke. How could she share his bed?

She went into her bedroom where she had piled up clothes in two heaps. The enthusiasm to organise her preparation for the holiday had left her. Instead, she pushed one crumpled heap onto the floor and flopped down into the empty space, a feeling of deep gloom descending on her. As she lay there, her mind was now determined to dwell on her life in a huge wave of self-pity. 'Men!' she exclaimed out loud, and then pressed the side of her face hard into the pillow. She could see the face of her ex-partner so clearly in her mind's eye. Good-looking. Yes, she would give him that. Charming as well. He had wooed her with his musical abilities, playing love songs and singing to her. 'Smoke gets in your eyes'. Yes, that was a favourite. But that was as far as the goodness went. He began to hate her when she became pregnant. He did not want to share her and resented her periods of sickness and tiredness. The sexual act became a torture for her, as he demanded his rights. She desperately needed her sleep after she had given birth to their daughter, and he despised both her and their child. He replaced her father with his cruelty and with his contempt of women. She had been raped by both of them. She turned over onto her stomach, her mind battling against those memories of early childhood when she had begged her mother not to leave her. She had listened from her bedroom to the sounds of violence; the crashing of ornaments on to the floor, and her mother's screams. If silence followed, she would strain to hear any indication of what must be taking place. Had he killed her? Had she run away? Was he coming upstairs to prolong the anguish? Was it her turn next?

She rolled over and stared at the ceiling. She had vowed never again to visualise his abuse of her, and yet how easily the memories slipped back into her present-day consciousness. How could Caroline let that Brad touch her? Once more, her mind had shifted into the present and her daughter's gossip. But why should she care so much? Because I love her, she suddenly thought. It was like a huge wave sweeping over her. The constant repression. The desperation to conform. The memories of idolising an older girl at school. The relief of the normality of giving birth, yet the revulsion of contact with her husband. She loved Caroline Thorston and despised Brad Carter, not because he belittled her, she reasoned, but because he was a man and he was competing for the affection of the love of her life. It was as though everything had jumped into place, she thought, as she stared up at the ceiling. Her body had become very hot, and she put her hands over her cheeks, her fingers massaging and smoothing away the sudden heat.

But then the surge of emotions, so exciting and reassuring in their resolution quickly dissipated, and she sat up, swinging her feet back down on to the floor.

Now she was ashamed of her feelings of happiness. The discovery of her true self, the sexual connotations, suddenly appalled her. She could never tell anyone how she felt. The sexual act had always been indescribable in her childhood language; just an incoherent dread of listening for his tread on the stairs and to the creaking of the door opening. She was too frightened to utter a sound and too ashamed to tell anyone else of his unspeakable crime. She endured the sexual act after she and her partner had moved in together, feeling duty bound to please him; assuring herself that this was something no woman really wanted and was only the means of having a child. She had wanted a baby. She wanted to be everything her parents had not been, and here she was now professing her love for another woman. How low could she stoop? What would Sherry think of her? What would the world think of her?

For a few seconds, she experienced a feeling of tenderness towards her daughter, but then the irritability, the condemnation returned. Sherry did not have a good word to say about Caroline. But then she had nothing but contempt for the men who had come and gone in her life. Perhaps it was hereditary, she thought. Did her own parents have a good relationship when they were younger? Why did her mother condone such violence? She must have known how he had abused his daughter. Now, here she was criticising her own daughter. She often wondered how Sherry would react if she told her about the abuse that she had suffered in her life. She thinks she knows everything, she mused. But then did she herself know everything about Sherry's life? Everyone had secrets. Of course, there was no need for a daughter to know anything about her mother's past or her present. And as for the future, she thought, that was a page waiting to be turned. She smiled at the idea of her life as a storybook, a fairy tale with a happy ever after, and her spirits rose.

She completed the onerous task of shaving her legs, carefully avoiding the previous damage where the bleeding had stopped. Then she switched on the curling tongs and got dressed, enjoying running her fingers down the smoothness of her legs. Each time she made the effort to spend time on her appearance she vowed to make it a regular event, but then tiredness, or a feeling of despair with the futility of her life, negated her resolutions. Now, as she wound each strand of hair into a ringlet, staring in the mirror, and studying the lines of tension that were deepening between her brows and at the corners of her mouth, she made a fresh resolution to give herself more time in the day for self-improvement.

He used to say that she scrubbed up well. The description did not please her in her thirties, but now she clutched at the memory. 'You do scrub up well,' she said to her reflection. An application of the tinted foundation cream that she had found in the bathroom cabinet and the dab of blusher on her cheekbones had given her a healthier look. Was it too much? She stared anxiously into the mirror. 'No, you look good,' she told herself. She applied a layer of red onto her lips, then pursing them into a kissing mode and giggling. She ran her fingers through her hair. She was greying at the temples. Her hair had always been her crowning glory according to her mother; a thick deep brown mantle cascading down her back, or in thick pigtails secured by ribbons during school hours. She would not say that now, Jenny thought. That was the next thing to do and she scribbled 'hair rinse' on her shopping list.

By the time that she reached Caroline's house, her feelings of confidence were diminishing. The car, as usual had been loath to start, and now, her chest was tight with the stress of struggling with the charger and the anxiety of keeping her employer waiting. She glanced in the driving mirror as she pulled up in the driveway. Her face was now very red from the exertion, together with the applied blusher. She rubbed her cheeks in an effort to remove the make-up, only adding to the redness, as more blood rushed to the surface of her skin. The dampness in the air already was causing her hair to become limp, and she sighed as she reached back for her handbag.

'Goodness me! You look hot and bothered,' Caroline exclaimed. Have you had car trouble again? You must get that fixed.'

'It's not worth spending any money on it. The MOT is due soon and I think I will be back on my bike, or the bus. Might do me good.' Jenny grinned, her face settling back into its normal colour.

The next hour was occupied in sorting through the piles of clothes, some considered to be suitable for Jenny for the holiday and later on for the wedding. No mention was made of Caroline's overnight stay at Brad Carter's house, strengthening Jenny's suspicions of there being something to hide. But then she wouldn't expect me to know anything about it would she, she mused? Caroline must feel so protected from the threat of gossip in the world outside of her privileged life. As she carefully folded the items of clothing that she had chosen, she envisaged the possible social networking springing from this gossip and wondered if Brad Carter was feeling threatened. She knew that he had a social site for business purposes. She had looked at his profile and had giggled at the photograph of him in his youth. The modern world was full of vanity, and as for the 'selfies'. Me here, me there, me everywhere, she thought. It did not stop there, did it? Her daughter had such an axe to grind against those better off than herself, and apparently the people, with whom she associated, thrived on the hate mail they read and wrote; wicked acts so prevalent these days.

Sherry was nicknamed 'Blather Mouth' when she was a child, Jenny recalled. In the past, she herself had learnt to change the subject if her daughter came into the room, and her friends were used to the disjointed conversations with her over the telephone. Already, she was regretting discussing recent affairs with her, but then the feelings of despair had clouded her judgement. Now, she vowed to keep her plans to herself and not to be drawn in to her daughter's gossip. It might be wise to bribe Sherry with one or two of these items of clothing, although she was in danger of losing her figure with the amount of booze she could knock back. Silly little cow! Possibly none of these would fit her.

'Penny for your thoughts.' Caroline's voice broke into her contemplations. 'You have ironed that blouse three times I think. By the way, I meant to ask you. Have you ever had your hair tinted?'

'I used to put a rinse through it occasionally, but not lately. I am going grey. I noticed this morning.'

'Me as well. I will make us an appointment each. I haven't been for ages. It didn't really seem to matter.'

'It was hard for you seeing him so ill and I don't suppose you went anywhere for a long time.'

Caroline sighed and looked away. Jenny noticed the black circles under her eyes and wanted to touch her hand.

'Actually, it was a relief not to go anywhere,' Caroline suddenly said. 'He used to leave me sitting on my own and joined his friends. I longed for the evening to end and even then he ignored me.'

The colour had flooded into her pale cheeks, enhancing rather than marring her appearance.

Jenny longed to give her a hug.

'You look tired,' she said instead. 'Are you not sleeping very well?'

'I had a bad night. Actually, you'll never believe this. I ended up sleeping in Brad Carter's house.' She gave an embarrassed kind of giggle.

Jenny stared, taken off her guard, yet her curiosity was barely on hold.

'It was not what it seemed. I didn't want to be there. I had run out of tea, and he rang me just before I was setting off for the shop. I can't bear it if I wake up in the night and can't have a cup of tea. He lives just at the back of the supermarket, you know.'

Jenny nodded. 'Yeah, yeah.'

'He said he had a lot of information on Wales and if I called in he would give it to me. But obviously, he wanted to make it more than that. He had a bottle of wine cooling and two glasses on the table. I don't know about you, but I am not a drinker. One glass of wine goes to my head. I just wanted to get home and I gulped it down. He immediately filled the glass again. I was already feeling woozy and panicked, I think. Anyway, I gulped it down again, impatient to leave. But then he insisted on showing me what the back garden was like. It was pretty with lights hidden in the flower beds and shrubbery but the cold air added to my confusion and before I knew what was happening, he had filled my glass again.'

'Goodness me! What a carry on. He was trying to get you drunk, wasn't he? So, what happened then?'

'I don't know. I woke up in this strange bedroom. It was just getting light and I could hear the birds singing so I knew I was at the back. The front is the road to the car park. But I was on my own.'

'That must have been a relief. So, where was he?'

'I don't know. In his bedroom I expect. I think I was in his mother's room. It was all there, it seemed, as she had left it. Honestly, all I could think of was Norman Bates in *Psycho*.'

'How creepy! Oh, look. I am all goose pimples!'

'I had to go to the bathroom. I could see it along the corridor. The whole house is like something out of a novel.' Caroline was back to visualising Manderley, the house in the story entitled *Rebecca*, and momentarily imagined herself to be Mrs de Winter wandering along dark corridors escaping from Mrs Danvers the sinister housekeeper. She looked away, staring at the window.

Jenny followed her gaze observing how the rain was beginning to patter against the glass and waited impatiently for the revelations to continue. Then, she herself broke the silence.

'So, was he up then?'

Caroline jerked her head back in the direction of her companion, Mrs Danvers pushed back into her dream world.

'Oh, yes he was,' she said. 'He was in the kitchen, making a cup of tea for me, and I drank it as quickly as I could and got out of there. He said that I had collapsed and he didn't know what to do, so he carried me upstairs and put me on his mother's bed. I was completely dressed. I don't remember anything about it but I'm sure he didn't do anything untoward if you know what I mean. I would have known, don't you think? Even so, how can I look him in the eye again?'

'I bet he is regretting giving you that wine. If I were you, I would take advantage of it all. Make him grovel. Make him do plenty for you.'

Caroline nodded. In that moment, they were both on the same wavelength.

Jenny drove home in a much better frame of mind. She re-lived her employer's ordeal, visualising each scenario as though she was watching a film with aspects of the interior of the house based on Caroline's vague descriptions. Poor thing! She was so unworldly. Should she tell Sherry that her gossip was unfounded? Or would Sherry seize on the true events and blow them out of all proportion on Facebook? It would please her to make a laughing stock of Caroline. Best to leave it to settle down. Another scandal would soon hit the headlines. At least Caroline could have chalked up some brownie points, she reasoned with a wry smile, and none of them would notice the bond growing between herself and her employer. As Sherry had surmised, everyone would think that she was only going on this holiday to look after the daily chores.

The next two weeks passed by so quickly and suddenly it seemed that after all the shopping trips and visits to the beautician for aroma therapy, waxing, hair colouring and nail sessions as Jenny called them during the second week, there couldn't possibly be anything else to do.

They sat in the kitchen sharing their late morning coffee break, with the travel documents spread out on the table top.

'It's a shame that we are not going to Italy, isn't it?' Caroline said, regarding her artificial cerise-coloured fingernails. Since she had had them done yesterday, she felt at arm's length with the world, hardly daring to even hold a cup, yet such an indulgence warranted more than North Wales in her expectations. 'What time do we leave tomorrow?'

Jenny giggled hysterically. 'You have asked me that ten times,' she spluttered. 'Don't worry. I will set your alarm and I have my phone app on.'

They had decided that it would be advisable for Jenny to spend the night at Caroline's house, as her car had finally made its last journey, breaking down on the town bypass and being transported away to a garage and destined it seemed by the shaking of heads, for the breaker's yard.

Jenny tried not to let this news of the death of her car depress her, and, as she told her daughter when she telephoned to say her farewells, she was living each day as if there was no tomorrow. Sherry, true to form, encouraged her mother to get everything she could whilst her luck held out, implying that a journey in a coach would be long enough to get on each other's nerves, never mind the days spent on excursions.

'I bet they are all old people,' she giggled, and Jenny could visualise her mimicking the old woman who lived in the flat next door, hunching up her back, and screwing her face into a frown.

'There could be some young ones,' she protested. 'Daughters with mothers you know. Anyway, the excursions sound adventurous, and I can't wait to get into the hotel and see my room. It will have an en-suite. I have looked on the internet and it all looks fabulous. Anyway, I don't care what you say. You are only jealous.'

'Jealous of sharing a holiday with that posh cow. She'll have you waiting on her hand and foot. You'll see.'

Jenny pushed her phone into her bag. The doubts she was having concerning the role that she would be expected to play in this holiday, were back in her mind. She had indeed found the hotel location on the internet site and read the comments made by previous holiday makers. 'Do not stay on the third floor.' 'Our shower did not work, and the meals were worse than school dinners.' 'Wonderful service, and the meals were fresh and tasty.' 'We had a wonderful week and would recommend this hotel to anybody.' 'Room 101. Never again!' Now, her daughter's spiteful remarks were beginning to hit home, and she walked back into the house to re-join her employer, her feet dragging in the gravelled path.

Chapter Nine

The next day began for them with the buzzing of the alarm, and they had little time for conversation or misgivings, although, in any case, Caroline was not a morning person, and made little effort to be sociable at such an early hour.

They were at the designated bus stop twenty minutes early, and Jenny had long since given up on communicating, although she was very used to making an early start in her everyday working life. Caroline stamped her feet on the uneven surface where the remnants of a recent heavy rain shower were seeping into the cracks. She was feeling very vulnerable at this early hour, exposed to all the threats of a world of trades people and labourers Not her kind of people. She glanced at Jenny. She was looking cheerful and comfortable, she thought. But then her life always began at this early time, when everyone was rushing out to earn a living.

'Are you in the queue?' Caroline turned around at the sound of a shrill voice and came face to face with a rather large woman. Before she could remark that it was not really a queue, the woman turned away to address a small man struggling with a large suitcase.

'Oh, for goodness sake, Ernie!' she yelled. 'He's not used to a bit of hard work. Spends too much time watching footie on the tele. Typical man.' She grinned, baring her ill-fitting dentures.

'She's packed the kitchen sink.' Ernie grimaced and gave a rueful smile in Caroline's direction, before dropping the offending case, narrowly missing Jenny's feet.

'For goodness sake! Excuse my hubby! I spend my life doing it. He's one big excuse after another.'

Jenny also grinned in response at the miscreant hubby and cast a knowing look at her travelling companion. Caroline returned the gesture with a sigh and turned away.

'Here she comes,' yelled Mrs Ernie. 'You see, we only just made it.' She nodded in the direction of her husband, shaking her head and tutting at the same time.

The coach pulled up at the stop and the driver came slowly down the steps studying a clip board. 'Should be five,' he remarked. 'There's always somebody.'

He raised the panel in the side of the coach and pushed the cases into place amongst a variety of large and smaller items of luggage, wincing at the weight of the Mrs Ernie case, and glaring at Caroline.

'That's not mine,' she protested. 'Mine's the black leather.'

The driver grunted. He ticked their names off on his list and indicated for them to mount the steps.

Already the coach was almost full. Most of the passengers were settled in their allotted places, having begun their journeys at a much earlier hour and apparently, there were only two more pick up stops before the drive up north to the main coach station. After a further wait of ten minutes, the missing passenger arrived, and the driver secured the luggage door and climbed back into his seat. Everyone stared at the lone traveller as he stumbled along to the end of the coach.

He mouthed, 'Sorry,' several times, with no sign of remorse on his face. He had the kind of face that did not seem capable of concern, Caroline thought, as she watched him make his way towards the rear vacant seat. It seemed that he was picking up on her thoughts, giving her a big grin, and shaking his head as if in denial of the trouble he was causing in the eyes of his fellow passengers.

'Wow! Have I got all the back seat to myself? That's lucky. I only booked a couple of days ago and what a bargain. It's been a bit of a rush though. I'm Harry by the way.'

He appeared to be addressing the world in general, but he stared directly at Caroline, and she felt the colour rushing to her cheeks.

'In any case, we have to change again don't we,' he continued, 'to get our proper travel seats? This is just the feeder I understand. I am off to Wales eventually!'

'Llandudno?' Jenny queried. 'So are we.'

Caroline's jaded spirits rose with the knowledge of an obviously more cultured fellow traveller, and she half-turned to give a hasty appraisal of his dark good looks. In his mid-fifties, she guessed. Quite an improvement on Ernie.

At first, the level of chatter in the coach was audible, and comments were made about scenery and points of interest, but gradually the enthusiasm waned and lack of sleep or boredom with the dullness of these early hours, induced a state of drowsiness amongst both old and younger travellers alike.

At last, they reached the interchange station and Caroline and Jenny shuffled along the coach behind a queue of people. Their lateness in booking had resulted in them being allocated seats at the end of the coach like Harry, and by the time they reached the steps, they were desperate to locate the promised facilities of this break in their journey. The driver had enthused about a variety of 'eats and drinks', and plenty of space to unwind, but at first, it seemed like a place of total confusion, with people wandering in all directions, clutching travel documents, and with anxiety and fatigue already showing in their tensed faces and sagging bodies. Many of them were well past their prime, and Jenny sighed, remembering her daughter's words.

After a considerable wait and two cups of coffee later, whilst all the luggage was transferred to the relevant coaches for holiday destinations, they responded to the voice over the loud speaker advising them to make their way to bay 10 to join their travelling companions for Llandudno.

An argument was in progress over seat numbers.

'There's always somebody, isn't there?' a large, red faced woman mouthed. 'You would think it was the end of the world if we sat in the wrong seats.'

'I am not getting up again. You'll have to sit there until we have a break. Does it really matter?'

'Look! It says here in black and white. We should be in 27 and 28. We asked for the driver's side. You are 29 and 30.'

'Well, I am not moving. My legs are killing me.'

Caroline sighed, and shook her head as if in disbelief that people could be so unreasonable. She turned to look at Jenny, who was craning her neck to see what was causing the delay. The angle of her jaw line showed the tension across her face. Gosh, she was looking very tired. Poor Jenny, she thought. Her companion really needed this break. In fact, she mused, she needed a complete change in her lifestyle. Caroline straightened her shoulders and took in a deep breath of air. In that moment, she vowed that this was going to be the beginning of a new way of life for both of them.

Harry was again in the long seat behind them, apparently with no one to share it.

'Well, we were lucky here then,' he exclaimed. 'Was yours a late booking?'

Before either Caroline or Jenny could answer, the conversation was interrupted by the strong northern-accented voice of the driver.

'Welcome to "Happy Days" holiday tours. I am your driver for the week and will be at the hotel when I am not driving, so if there are any problems you can seek me out, so to speak. We can't guarantee the weather, but we can promise a wonderful holiday come rain or shine. How about a bit of Cliff to get us in the holiday mood?'

Jenny sighed as the sound of the familiar voice singing 'We're all going on a summer holiday' drifted down the coach; the vocals almost masked by the awkward couple, who were still complaining about being in the wrong seats. Suddenly, it seemed that a shaft of gloom penetrated her mind, breaking across its horizon of high expectations. She glanced sideways at her companion. Caroline had closed her eyes, and Jenny wanted to hold her hand and to comfort her. Harry, behind them, was humming along with Cliff, and his energy and presence seemed to both threaten and yet excite her.

The hotel looked huge, spreading along the side of the esplanade, with rows of windows like eyes, Jenny thought, all with views of the sandy beach and the sea. Already, the steep steps up to the main entrance were proving to be a challenge for some.

The queue for the room keys was the last straw for the exhausted travellers. At last, Jenny clutched the key marked 232 and looked for the main staircase. Apparently, there was only one lift, and everyone was being advised to use the stairs whilst the luggage was taken up to the rooms. She sighed, shuffling into a queue of elderly people, some of whom already were back in their grumbling mode. She turned to seek out the whereabouts of her employer. Caroline was in conversation with a middle-aged man who seemed to have an air of authority, Jenny thought. She waited, straining her ears to hear their words above the chatter of fellow travellers. 'That will be more to my liking, thank you. Could you amend my details? I will get back to you if I have any problems,' Caroline was saying.

Jenny watched as the man nodded and pointed to a sign above a door to the left of the reception area. Suites 1 to 6. So, they were not to be neighbours after all. Oh well, she thought. What did she expect? At the end of the day, nothing changed. The staff always ended up in the attic.

Caroline was waving to her. Jenny ignored her and continued to stumble along on the heels of a large woman who was grasping a formidable looking walking stick in her right hand. The staircase was steep, with landing after landing, until the signs indicating room numbers had progressed beyond the first two hundred. She was gasping for breath when she reached the corridor where a board above a doorway listed rooms 220 to 232. There was an air of depression now, accentuated by the shabbiness of the paintwork and the strips of black tape crisscrossing the carpet runner, where the constant tread of feet had worn it threadbare.

Apparently, Room 232 was at the end of this corridor, and in spite of her laboured breathing and her disappointment at being on the third floor, she experienced excitement as she reached it and turned the key in the lock. It was the first time she had stayed in a hotel, and she opened the door slowly and peered around the gap. Twin beds occupied most of the room, leaving limited space to access the wardrobe and the dressing table. The window was tall and narrow, with heavily patterned curtains hanging lop-sided on each side, and with a view of the back of the hotel grounds, where delivery vehicles could park for unloading, and the necessary outbuildings housed equipment and electrical cabling it seemed. Jenny studied this vista for a moment or two, as she caught her breath.

Then she sighed deeply and sank down on to the nearest bed. It would have been so good to have a view of the sea. It was years since she had actually seen the sea. Ten, she mused. Or was it twelve. It was on a day trip to Bridlington with him. The sea was the only good memory. She looked around, noticing a door half opened next to the wardrobe. She was curious to experience the luxury of en-suite facilities, and eased her aching back into an upright position, stumbling on the uneven floor. Each footstep produced a creaking groan in protest she thought and she envisioned her future possible discomfort if she made this small journey in the dead of night.

However, she had little time to investigate the facilities in the dark little room beyond, for a sudden knocking on the bedroom door made her jump back in alarm. 'Who is it?' she croaked, trying to clear her throat,

'It's me. Caroline. Honestly! You went up those stairs nineteen to the dozen. We are not staying up here. Come on. I have got a suite on the ground floor at the front.'

Jenny opened the door to find Caroline with her hands clutching her waistline and breathing heavily. They began to giggle and linking arms almost broke into a run in their efforts to leave Room 232 behind.

'My room was 286. Miles away at the other end. I noticed a sign describing upgraded rooms, so I asked the manager. It is only another ten pounds a day.'

'That's not bad, I suppose. Is that for both of us?'

Caroline did not answer. She was leading the way down the long flight of stairs, avoiding an elderly couple who were stopping on each step on the way up, to catch their breaths.

'Over there,' Caroline directed.

The crowd had dispersed now and Jenny glanced across at the reception desk as Caroline waved to the manager.

'Do you fancy him?' she asked, turning away to giggle again. She wanted Caroline to deny any feeling of attraction and was happy to hear her companion say that he was obviously too full of his own importance.

Moments later they were both exclaiming with joy on entering through a door at the end of a short, deep carpeted corridor. The view through the large bay window was of the esplanade, leading to golden sands and blue sea. The walls were covered in cream wallpaper, and the gold coloured curtains swept elegantly down to the floor. The counterpanes on each of the two single beds were in a fabric matching the curtains, and the carpet was a pleasant mossy green.

'Don't worry. It's a suite. We can have a room each. OK?' Caroline nodded in the direction of a door halfway along the wall opposite to the beds. 'I knew you would prefer it rather than sharing, and to be honest, so would I. I am so used to my own privacy and I guess you are too. But we can watch the television or sit and chat in here, can't we, if we have any time to pass before our meals?'

Jenny's happiness now knew no bounds. She could not wait to text message Sherry and send her some photographs via her phone.

The cases had been delivered by the porter, and Caroline was suggesting that they should unpack.

'We'll do mine first,' she said. 'Just pop yours into your room.'

Jenny opened the door leading into a second bedroom. It was small, with a tiny window high in the wall for ventilation. More like a cupboard, she thought. Obviously, it was for a child. A single bed was pushed against the wall, and a narrow wardrobe and a chest of drawers were positioned along the opposite wall, leaving little space to walk around. There did not appear to be washing or toileting facilities. She could not control the sigh escaping from her tensed lungs. It would have been better in Room 232, she thought. At least she would have had her own en-suite.

'Oh well,' Caroline said, stepping in behind her, 'I thought it was too good to be true. It looks like we are sharing most things after all. But then we are actually sleeping in separate rooms so you won't hear me if I snore. I don't know if I do. Do you?'

'I am on my own these days, so I have no idea how I sleep. My partner used to say that I did, but I don't know how he knew. He was always flat out after a belly full of beer, and I was glad when he found someone else.'

Caroline giggled, and sank down onto a bed. 'We have not had much luck with men in our lives, have we? We had separate rooms for years. Even so, I could hear him snoring all over the house. I used to have the radio on full volume and fall asleep during the shipping forecast most nights. I won't do that here, but I may have the light on for hours so we can keep the door closed, and I won't disturb you.'

'There's one good thing. The floors in here seem pretty solid.' Jenny stamped her feet up and down. 'The floor boards creaked terribly on that third floor. Somebody put that on that hotel website. Apparently, they didn't get a wink of sleep!'

'You and your websites! Let's forget about our old lives and kind of re-invent ourselves.' Caroline was back in the realms of fantasy with Daphne de Maurier's Mrs de Winter, and Manderley in mind. She sank back and closed her eyes, her hair ruffled against the pillow, and Jenny longed to cuddle against her and share her visions of the future.

Instead, she stood for a moment, lost in her own small world of fantasy, knowing nothing of her companion's flights of fancy. But then she was overcome by the need to be organised. It was not her nature to dream. She went into the small adjoining room and began to unpack her case, carefully hanging up her three dresses for evening wear, and neatly folding sweaters and jeans to be housed on the top shelf of the wardrobe. She had indulged in some new cosmetics and a bottle of her favourite perfume. She glanced around for an electricity point where she could plug in her curling tongs, but it seemed by the absence of such facilities, that this would not be considered a requirement of an accompanying child. In any case, there was no mirror where she could study her image as she manipulated the tongs. She sighed. Her place in life, it seemed, was always to be pushed further and further back in the queue. In fact, she was at the end of the queue more often than not, she mused. How good it must feel, to be the Queen, or Caroline Thorston for that matter. But then was the Queen happy? Caroline certainly was not.

'Are you wanting a shower? I think we should leave things until later. I'm having a lick and a promise tonight. We've got half an hour before dinner.' Caroline's voice sounded shrill, Jenny thought, as though it was squeezing through the crack in the door. It was her bossy voice. The one she used when giving orders. She had not spoken to her like that for some time. Perhaps she was tired.

'OK. I'm just going to freshen up. I'll have a shower before I go to bed. But my hair's a mess. I need to plug in my tongs if you are not using the sockets. I don't appear to have any.'

She pushed open the door waving her curling tongs, the cable dangling down in front of her legs.

'They reckon hair is a woman's crowning glory. Mine's falling out. You don't know how lucky you are to have a natural wave.' Her voice tailed off and she stopped and stared. Caroline was standing in the doorway of the en suite in only her bra and pants. Her vulnerability was apparent in the sudden flushing of her cheeks, and the hasty grabbing of her dressing gown from off the bed.

'Won't be long,' she gabbled. 'There are two sockets on the wall for the kettle and tele. Unplug one of those.'

Jenny studied her face in the mirror, as she carefully wound each strand of hair. The chestnut rinse suited her, she thought. There was not a sign of a grey hair at the moment, but no doubt she would soon be back with her middle-aged look. She cleaned her face with a wet wipe, and re-applied her makeup, pursing her lips and accentuating her 'cupid's bow' with some magenta lip colour.

Caroline opened the door a little way and peered around. 'Oh, you haven't changed yet.'

'No. I thought we were not going to bother tonight. This top and trousers will be fine. I don't suppose many people go to a great effort.'

'Oh well. I had to get out of those clothes. They were sticking to me. This is such a comfy rig out.'

How does she do it? Jenny asked herself. It was not just the cost of things. She always seemed to look like a million dollars even in her everyday clothes. But then this was really something. The skirt hugged her figure as though it had been tailor made for her, and the stylish jacket with the ornate buttons partly covered a cream round-necked blouse.

'That looks amazing,' Jenny gasped. 'Have you just bought it?'

'No. It's quite old actually. I thought it would do for tonight. Like you said, I don't suppose anyone will be dressing up.'

'Perhaps I ought to make an effort.'

'No. You look fine.'

Caroline sat at the dressing table and applied a layer of cream on her face, and carefully pencilled in her eyebrows. She brushed her hair, patting it into its natural waves as it rested on her shoulders and Jenny leant forward to push a wayward strand into place, looking into her employer's face as it was reflected in the dressing table mirror. For a brief moment, their eyes met, before Caroline stood up, pushing the chair back. Jenny backed away, suddenly overcome again with that overwhelming desire to make physical contact with her companion.

There was a queue of people waiting at the door leading into the dining room. Jenny could see Mrs Ernie as she had named the woman with the henpecked husband of earlier acquaintance. Her mouth was already in top gear, as Sherry would say. Snatches of conversation drifted along the queue. 'You ought to see our shower. We have complained but I don't suppose they will do anything.' 'Our wardrobe door won't shut properly.' 'You should be so lucky. We haven't even got a wardrobe.' What room are you in then?' '101'

Jenny suppressed a giggle. Not the dreaded 101.

'Why are we waiting?'

Somebody had broken into song, and there was a loud shriek of laughter from Mrs Ernie.

Jenny looked at Caroline. Her mouth was set in a tight line, and she stared fixedly at the dining-room door as though willing it to open.

'Hurray!' A cheer rose from the waiting holiday makers.

The queue moved along slowly as table numbers were allocated. 'This is your table for all of your meals,' a young woman told them as she escorted them towards a line of tables at the side of the room. Caroline sighed, with relief, Jenny guessed. They were well away from the noisy ones in the queue.

They had settled down into the chairs facing each other and were both admiring the view of the esplanade.

'This is good, isn't it? What a lucky escape!' Jenny giggled.

'But look,' Caroline retorted. 'This table is set for three. I hope they haven't made a mistake.'

The waitress was back, her foreign accent indicating an Eastern European homeland.

'Would you like to join these ladies, sir?'

Jenny looked beyond her to the man of previous acquaintance on the coach. She gave a quick glance at her companion. Caroline was smiling sweetly, too sweetly she thought.

'We meet again. What a relief to be on this side and with you. I'm not playing gooseberry, am I?' Harry grinned as he pulled out the chair and squeezed in next to Caroline.

Caroline was taken off her guard by his words and went into a hasty denial, reverting to the formality of her upbringing.

'Not at all,' she said. 'Actually, I was recently widowed, and this is my housekeeper Mrs Alford.'

'Actually, it's Jenny.' Jenny glared at Caroline.

Harry turned to acknowledge Jenny, but then his eyes quickly turned back to Caroline.

'Join the club,' he said. 'I am without a partner as well. I bet he wishes he was.' He nodded in the direction of Mrs Ernie and her husband.

'He's called Ernie.' Jenny giggled.

'Really! He doesn't drive the fastest milk cart in the west, does he? No way, I guess. If he did, he would have escaped long since.' He grinned broadly at his little joke, then picked up the menu. Jenny was still giggling, but Caroline had apparently missed the point and was staring out of the window towards the rocky promontory known as The Great Orme.

Jenny studied her blank expression and concluded that such vulgarity must have escaped her in her younger days. She was still annoyed over Caroline's description of her. 'Mrs Alford, my housekeeper'! Why could she not relax and join the human race, she mused? That bastard of a husband had a lot to answer for. In fact, my bloke did as well. He could be just as charming as their present male companion, who was now regaling them with tales of his recent exploits in Italy. But get him on the empty end of a bottle of whisky at throwing out time, she recalled, and he qualified for the biggest bastard ever.

They continued eating mostly in silence now, concentrating on each stage of the meal, with brief comments on the service or the merits of each course. Jenny agonised over the formality of it all, afraid to warrant Caroline's demeaning description of her by using the wrong knife or fork. Occasionally, she sensed an apology in her employer's glances, but she was in no mood to capitulate.

By the time that they reached the coffee stage, they were in no hurry to escape to their rooms, and eagerly sought out the delicacy of the chocolate in fancy gold wrapping foil, resting in each saucer, and already melting into sweet stickiness. Such a simple little luxury was appealing, away from the mundanity of everyday life.

'It's a free day tomorrow,' Harry said, carefully wiping his fingers and dabbing at his mouth with his napkin. 'No planned and paid for excursions. The Great Orme is the place to be if the weather permits. It's quite a walk up there, but there is a tram. I am going to order a taxi from here in the morning for the first leg. There's no point in being worn out before one starts. Conserve the energy at our age for the good bits. That's my philosophy.'

'Mine too,' Caroline agreed. 'It all depends on the weather, doesn't it?'

'I'll check it out later and let you know. I haven't got a wi-fi connection yet, have you?'

Jenny was pleased to note Caroline's blank expression and answered for her.

'No. I've got to sort it. Apparently, it is only available in the lounge area,' she replied.

'We can always get the forecast on the news,' Caroline interjected. 'We should be able to escape from those wretched things when we are on holiday.'

'I do agree with you, but unfortunately it is not easy these days. There is always somebody demanding one's time. So, are you up for it then, weather permitting? We can share a taxi. So, round about tennish then? Would that give you time to get organised?'

Before Jenny could reply, Caroline was nodding.

Jenny looked from one to the other. It was as though she was not part of this arrangement. What would they say if she said that it was not really her thing, she wondered? Probably nothing. Perhaps just give a shrug and turn away to continue their conversation.

She followed behind them as they made their way out of the dining room.

'They can't wait to get going on the bingo,' Harry said, nodding in the direction of Ernie's group. 'A fate worse than death.'

Jenny saw Caroline's nod of agreement and heard her little giggle. Of course, it would be drinks on the terrace for them. She pressed her lips together and narrowed her eyes. Well, she thought, I am going to have some fun. At least Mrs Ernie and her fellow diners were enjoying life by the sudden sound of their raucous laughter. She saw Caroline's shoulders hunch at the loudness and decided that she could always be a vulgar thorn in her side the following day. 'My housekeeper' indeed. Just who the hell did she think she was?

She waited whilst Caroline unlocked the door. That was another thing, she thought. There was only one key. What if she wanted to get into the room on her own?

'I am going to see what the entertainment is like,' she said, as Caroline sank down into the armchair. 'Are you coming with me, or do you fancy an early night?'

She knew what the answer would be but wanted to add to her sense of grievance by demanding negativity.

Caroline obliged, shaking her head. 'I will be quite happy to put my feet up and watch a bit of tele,' she replied. 'But you go. I know you like your bingo. Goodness knows what the entertainer will be like. It's not really my scene.'

'I might as well get the free drinks we're allowed, and he looks good from his photo on that poster in the entrance. Mind you, it could have been taken years ago. He may be earning a bit of cash in his retirement.' Jenny shrugged her shoulders. 'But, what the hell. So, shall I take the key in case you nod off?'

'No, I may need to have a wander. I will still be awake when you come back.'

Jenny sighed. Where did she intend to wander? Was she meeting up with Harry? He had said something to her as he turned to go up the stairs. She recalled that Caroline had nodded.

Jenny was used to bingo sessions on her own. Occasionally, she went with Sherry, but then that could end up with her paying for the last books of tickets; her daughter pleading poverty. Usually, the numbered pages were companionship enough; that immediate ownership, that promise of good fortune. This would be a low return of course, she mused. Not like last week at the club. It had been a 'national link' game with a huge prize of over five thousand. She had needed one number, and she recalled how her back was wet with sweat and how the numbers glazed under her hard stare. 'Another day, another dollar,' she heard someone say, and repeated the words now as she found an empty table and looked around. Already, Mr and Mrs Ernie were in a prime position with a good view of the machine, which flashed up each number. Jenny could remember the days when the numbers were picked out of a drum and read out by the caller. Now, the screen was a double-check, but for most people it was eyes down and ears open for the sound of the caller's voice and markers ready. The regulars responded to the calls, familiar with the ritual of rhymes and innuendoes. Eighty-eight, two fat ladies, twenty-two, two little ducks. 'Quack, Quack,' came the response. 'Sweet sixteen and never been kissed.' Mrs Ernie shouted out, 'Those were the days.' Jenny guessed that she always made that response. Ernie was sniggering into his beer.

'Be quiet! I can't hear what he is saying,' someone called.

The caller repeated the number followed by 'Twenty-one, the key of the door.'

How Caroline would have hated this, Jenny thought, smiling at their loudness and antics. She stared at the numbers, automatically marking them off along the rows. The reward was hardly worth the effort, but everyone went through the ritual as though it was vital for the continued turning of the planet, she mused.

'House'. The cry echoed around the room. It jolted everyone out of their transfixed postures and the inevitable protests followed. 'I only needed one more.' 'I was waiting and waiting for twenty-six.'

'That was the one I needed.' 'Oh, well, we would have shared it. No big deal, is it?' 'No, it's just a bit of fun.'

Jenny looked across at Mrs Ernie. It was a matter of life and death for her, she thought.

A depression had fallen over the room like a damp cloth, and the bingo caller rallied his audience with the promise of another full house, and a doubling-up of the prize on the last page. He was a past master at these sessions. This was his time of power, and he relied on the likes of Mrs Ernie to add to the atmosphere and the drama.

Jenny recognised him, not as an individual, but as a part of her lifestyle. Each scenario had its clown, its financial expert, its villain, its heart throb. Her partner was all of them, she mused. But at the end of the day, he was worthless. She watched the caller as he checked the winning line, noticing the shabbiness of his jeans and the overly long hair straggling in the nape of his neck. That Harry was the direct opposite. Well turned out, her mother would have said. But that did not mean anything either. They were all males.

She drained her glass and went to the bar to get a refill taking her bingo book with her. She marked off the numbers, leaning her elbow on the hard surface. It did not seem to matter whether she won or lost. She sighed. This holiday had taken away the joy of possible good fortune. She did not need money. Caroline was taking care of everything.

Caroline had decided to catch up on the world news. Not that she cared at the moment, but it was a well ingrained habit of her everyday life. Someone analysing her pattern of living would have surmised that she needed established habits to both pad out her days or to give her the reassurance of being a woman of the world.

She was relieved when Jenny decided to head off in the direction of the ballroom and bar. Solitude was both established and acceptable in her existence and a constant demand on her opinions was eroding her sense of well-being.

She watched the news channel, depressed by the latest reports of terrorist activity, and the evidence of male dominance in the rowdy street scenes. Some news reporters were women, but she sensed in them a high presence of male genetic imprint, and once again decided that it was a man's world, with the dice heavily loaded against women.

Harry seemed like a nice guy, she mused. But then they were barely acquainted. She frowned, remembering how she had reacted to his suggestion that she and Jenny were a kind of item. What did he say? Playing gooseberry? She knew that she had upset Jenny by describing her as the housekeeper. The rich employer in Rebecca had treated her travelling companion like that, she thought. The hired help, the general dog's body. But it was his implication of a relationship. Playing gooseberry! That was what had triggered her response. She sighed. If we were sisters, or mother and daughter it would be fine in the public eye, she mused. But two friends. That could be something else. She mentally backed away from her companion and cast her mind forward to the next day when there would be safety in numbers.

Suddenly, the room surrounded her in its loneliness. She needed to be outside of her reflections. She walked across to the window and looked along the esplanade. It was a fine evening, and people were exercising, in an effort perhaps to help to digest the substantial dinner, before settling in for the night. The tide was out, exposing a deep expanse of sand, and the horizon was becoming blurred in the failing light. Bulbs, strung along the front, twinkled dimly in the fading light, with the promise of increasing brightness, pointing on to the Great Orme and the pier.

She had not entertained any intention of leaving the room again, but Jenny had irritated her by the petulant tone of her voice. This was her room and her key. She was not going to be dictated to. As if in denial, she suddenly decided that she would have a stroll not outside in the chill of the evening air, but around inside the hotel.

There was a deserted feel about the corridor outside of her room, isolating her in her fears, but then the door opposite swung open allowing two elderly ladies access to the toilets, and to her, the noise of music and chatter escaping from the entertainments lounge. As she walked past the two ladies, she gathered from their excited comments that they had enjoyed the bingo and that the entertainer would soon be arriving, and that they had better find the toilets before they showed themselves up. They were giggling. Silly old fools, Caroline muttered. She was back with her thoughts of the suffragettes, a recent novel of those times fresh in her mind. What hope was there with an incontinent, bingo-crazed sisterhood?

'Just going to look at the notice board. We will catch you up.'

Caroline followed the voice of a woman walking ahead of her. Harry had mentioned the notice board. She waited by the window, staring through the shadows into the hotel parking area. Once the woman had moved away, she put on her glasses and began to read the schedule for the Happy Days coach trips.

> Tuesday…free day.
> Wednesday…Snowdonia and the Ugly House, with coastal views on the way home.
> Thursday…Betws-y-Coed and surrounding area
> Friday…Free day
> Saturday…Snowdon peak by train (Weather permitting)
> Sunday…Return home

She felt reassured by the apparent surety of the timetable. She needed to be organised; carried along by the schedule. Everything was in its place, waiting to be discovered, day after day, come rain or come shine. The people who were dependant on the tourist industry followed a close pattern; getting up, going through the motions, going to bed. Perhaps they would envy her. She had so much freedom, she mused. So, why was she feeling so trapped? She could do whatever she liked.

'A penny for them.'

She jumped in alarm at the sound of Harry's voice behind her.

'Oh. Oh. Just thinking how lucky we are to be getting such good weather,' she stammered.

'Aren't we just? I'm going to take advantage of this last hour of dusk with a stroll. I am told that the next turn off is a little shopping centre which may be useful. Apparently, we are a good step away from the main centre. Do you fancy exploring?'

'Just get my coat.' Caroline turned sharply away from his gaze. She could feel the colour rising in her cheeks.

'Don't rush. I'll meet you on the steps outside reception.'

Caroline did rush; caught up in a panic of excitement and apprehension. She gave a quick glance in the mirror and flicked her fingers through her hair. The blond streaks caught the light and she thought how young she looked with her hair combed back loosely from her face, rather than in the bondage of a hair band. That had been Jenny's doing, she thought, her mind flitting back to her companion.

'I mustn't be long,' she said to Harry as she joined him on the hotel steps. 'We only seem to have got one key, because it's a suite rather than two rooms. We did book separate rooms, but they were pretty awful, and I was offered a so-called suite as the only upgrade they had. It is really a family room, with a small room adjoining. It just gives Jenny that bit of privacy. She is quite reserved.' She was aware of her speech galloping into a gabble. As if acknowledging her nervousness, and reassuring her that all would be well, Harry put his arm across her back, and guided her down the steps.

Caroline's skin tingled under his touch. 'Wow!' she exclaimed. 'What a view there is along the coast. That must be the pier all lit up and look how stark the Great Orme looks against the sunset. I can't wait to get up there tomorrow.'

'Is your housekeeper OK with our plans? She seemed a little impatient I thought. Perhaps she would rather have the day off to do her own thing.'

'Oh no. Jenny is really excited to see what's on offer. She has had a hard life and doesn't get many breaks.'

Caroline stepped away from the protection of his arm. Suddenly, his intimacy was threatening rather than reassuring. 'I mustn't be long,' she said briskly, her voice harsh now, with her feelings of discomfort. 'The wind is getting up and we can soon feel chilly. There is little protection along this front is there?'

'Just a quick stroll then. I want to see if there is a chemist's near-by. I have come without my hay fever tablets and my sun-cream. It was such a rush, and I am sure that the shower soaps and shampoos in the hotel will be the cheapest of cheap. Terribly drying for the skin.'

Caroline relaxed in this evidence of his insecurities. What would Jenny have to say about male hypochondria, she wondered, and how many times had she witnessed it herself? Her memories took her back momentarily to the bathroom she had shared for years with her late husband. As his life advanced, he had run out of space in the medicine cabinet, pills and potions piling up on the shelf, promising an elixir of life.

The shopping area was quite basic; two sides of a short road leading off from the promenade. There was a chemist's shop, still open, but the small supermarket, and a cluster of gift and craft shops were closed until ten o'clock the next day. Caroline window-shopped whilst Harry made a bee-line for the chemist's. He emerged five minutes later with a carrier bag full of a variety of pills and potions it seemed, together with a purple bottle of shower lotion and a shampoo, which he described as amazing for thickening the hair.

'You should try it. They do one for women as well.'

Caroline laughed. 'My hair is thick enough, thank you.'

'Oh, gosh. I didn't mean that you need it. I just get carried away with all these things. There is so much out there. There is no reason for anyone to look ugly these days. Unless, of course you are an Ernie with a dreadful wife. I don't know how these people survive with their lifestyle. Bingo keeps them going I suppose. I wonder what the entertainment was like. I expect your housekeeper will fill you in.'

When Caroline made no response, he lapsed into silence, and they concentrated on walking against the sudden chill of cold air. Caroline was feeling somewhat deflated. It was not because of the change in temperature, although that had stiffened her muscles against the cold. What am I doing with this strange man, she thought? Her brain supplied an answer. She was allowing herself to be manipulated again. He had already commandeered the next day. She could not wait to get back in the company of Jenny. She quickened her pace and turned up to mount the hotel steps well ahead of her escort.

Jenny had left the hotel ballroom before the end of the act. The guitarist/comedian was good but obviously geared up to this 'end

144

of season' aging audience, and his humorous quips did nothing for her. She opted for an early night, perhaps sharing a television programme, or the ten o'clock news, with Caroline. After repeated knocking on their room door, anxiety was followed by impatience, and a resuming of anxiety again, when there was no response.

There must be more than one key for this room. She retraced her steps to the reception desk in an increasing state of agitation, and was tapping her fingers impatiently on the counter, after ringing the bell for attention, when she heard her name being called. She turned around to see Caroline hurrying through the entrance door with Harry hard on her heels.

'I'm so sorry, Jenny. We went to find some shops just around the corner. I had a headache and needed to dose myself and I bumped into Harry here. There are some nice gift shops and an art and craft one you would like.'

Jenny watched her companion's face flushing and felt her own sense of power rising. She knew that Caroline had come well prepared for all aches and pains, and a headache cure had been high on the list. She glanced at the face of her adversary in this threesome. In the harsh light of the decorated, gilded chandelier, he looked pale and puny in his tightly fitting trousers, and trendy bomber jacket. A con man, she thought. Oh Caroline! Don't fall into yet another trap.

'Ten o'clock then,' Harry called, as he made for the lift.

The lift was engaged, and after waiting in vain for a few minutes, Harry Bainer turned to the steep Victorian staircase and slowly made his way up to the third floor. He was in an attic room, described as a double by the booking clerk over the telephone call of the previous day, but as he had to squeeze around the foot of the bed, and had problems opening the door into the en-suite, when he got changed for dinner, he decided that it was more like a single room. However, he was not unduly concerned about this. He had slept in far worse situations, and if he was reading the signals right, his dining companion was definitely what he would describe as a woman of substance, although she would not have liked or even deserved for that matter, the description of elderly and infirm. Where had that come from? He must have mistaken what Brad Carter had told him. He guessed that she was in her fifties and seemed to be very fit. Her housekeeper, Jenny, could be a stumbling block, but she herself was definitely a very interested party, he mused. Her reaction to his query as to whether they were an item, said it all. Caroline Thorston was certainly in the market for some pampering. Even her name spelled class. She had pointed out her expensive looking leather suitcase in the foyer to her companion, and he had read her name and address, pretending to locate his cheap canvas holdall amongst the assortment of luggage waiting to be carried up to the rooms by the porters.

The brief instructions he had received from Brad Carter had confused him initially. Usually he had to dish the dirt on some woman who was what Carter described as a gold digger. He gave the impression that he was saving some honest, God-fearing man from being totally ripped off. This one had a personal connection. It had all been so last minute, finding a vacancy at this late hour, and making hurried arrangements, and then looking for an old woman with a kind of carer. Had he actually described her as old or was it middle-aged? He did not remember a Christian name. It was all so clandestine as though they were in the middle of a detective novel. Well, he was no Sherlock Holmes and the promised fee came minus the cost of the holiday. Pocket money really. Anyway, he was to report each day to Carter, on her actions and make sure that she was not being targeted by some 'scumbag' after her money. That did not have to include him, he reasoned. He was protecting her money. But what was the game being played by the housekeeper? A wannabe lesbian if ever he saw one. It seemed to be a middle-aged thing. A disenchantment with one's own gender. He had seen it before. He sniggered. It was pretty obvious that Caroline Thorston would not be interested. The normal vibes were there in spite of her reserve. She was just asking for it, he mused. He had heard on the grapevine that Carter had been crossed in love and kept a shrine to his mother in that big ugly old house at the back of the supermarket.

Well, he thought, it was all going to plan even though there had been no plan. He could not believe his good fortune to be seated at their table for meals. He decided that it must be a sign that his luck was changing. 'About bloody time,' he muttered as he struggled to turn the key in the lock. He sank down onto the unyielding mattress and looked in his wallet, finding forty-five pounds in notes. His jeans pockets' loose change amounted to another three pounds sixty-five. He would offer to pay for the taxi. It could not be more than a fiver, and with a bit of luck, she would pay for the tram ride and hopefully a cup of coffee each when they reached the top of the Great Orme. He carefully folded the two twenty-pound notes and slotted them behind his driving licence. Carter had promised more to come. He did not trust him, but he had always paid up in the past, hadn't he, and had a reputation for twisting the law to suit his wealthy clients. Two can twist. How about it being his turn to play a double game?

Oh dear, he mouthed, I have come without my debit card. He said the words again, out loud, looking at his reflection in the dressing-table mirror. It had worked with that ugly bitch in Nottingham last month. Would it work with Caroline Thorston? They would have to lose that Jenny woman somehow. He had five days to weave his web. He lay back, resting his head on the pillow. What would he be this time? The explorer one usually worked well. She had listened to his imagined Italian wanderings, relayed carefully from a recent television programme. He had better stay away from anything academic, he mused. She seemed to be pretty smart. But somehow, in spite of her air of good breeding and her apparent expensive taste in clothes, he felt that he could impress her with his stories of travel in exotic places. She appeared to be very unworldly. Actually, he had never left the British Isles. This was his first visit to Wales. Scotland had always seemed a mile too far and he firmly believed that Ireland was for the Irish. It was a big win on the horses, and then the phone call from Carter, that had persuaded him to seek his fortune elsewhere, and with a bag full of smart new clothes restoring his confidence, he hoped that the next few days would work out to be to his advantage.

'He's a fast mover, don't you think?' Jenny's pronouncement bridged the awkward silence, as Caroline carefully closed the door behind them, and put the key on the bedside cabinet next to her bed.

'Just being sociable I suppose,' she muttered, her voice fading as she drew the curtains across cutting out the view of the coloured lights along the esplanade.

'More than sociable, if you ask me. A real wolf in wolf's clothing. Are we going to go along with his plans tomorrow?'

'Well, it will be a good day to discover the local sights, wouldn't it? There's no harm in sharing a taxi. That makes good sense. He is probably lonely. I don't get a bad feeling about him. He seems to be well educated.'

Jenny shrugged her shoulders and muttered, 'Whatever.'

'You use the bathroom first. I am going to look at these brochures. There is one all about the Bronze Age copper mines on the Great Orme. Then we should try to catch up on sleep.'

Jenny frowned. Caroline was back in the driving seat. What if I don't want to go to bed yet, she thought. Again, the memory of the room in the attic appeared in a more favourable light. So, the view from the window was dismal, and the room sadly in need of refurbishment, but it would have been her space to watch the television and sit up until the early hours if she so wished.

Chapter Ten

Breakfast time with the late arrival of Harry was rather a silent affair. Jenny had been awake from the early hours and had become stiffened from a long period of imprisonment in the narrow bed in the annex with its confining space and lack of stimulus. She had ventured out of this small room once to use the en-suite facility, creeping past Caroline and carefully opening and closing doors. Her employer was sleeping like a baby, she had mused, as she huddled back under the duvet. She was glad of that. She certainly deserved it after all those trying years. She was reproaching herself now for her bitter thoughts. It was not Caroline's fault that the room was small, was it, she asked herself. She had done her best to please. Still, she did not have to be manipulated by that Harry whatever his name was. He had not gone that far, had he, with his disclosures? They really knew very little about him.

Caroline was wiping her mouth carefully with her paper tissue.

'I enjoyed that. Harry is going to be in a rush if he does not arrive soon.'

Jenny nodded. 'Are we still going if he has not booked a taxi? The sky looks a bit gloomy.'

Caroline did not answer. She was waving her hand in the direction of the breakfast bar. Jenny looked behind her to see Harry striding across the room, carrying a bowl of cereals in one hand and a cup and saucer in the other.

'Sorry! Whoops, sorry.' He dodged around people vacating their tables; chairs scraping and plates and cutlery balancing on the arms of the waiters as they wasted no time in clearing away breakfast ready for preparation for the next meal.

Caroline is welcoming him like an old friend, Jenny thought, seeing how her face had lifted out of its set lines, and her lips parted revealing her small evenly spaced teeth.

'Sorry I'm late,' Harry gasped. 'Wow! What a rush! I went to get a paper from those shops we saw last night and got caught up in such a drama. While I was waiting at the counter, an old man collapsed in front of me and we had to call for an ambulance. Did you hear the siren? I did all the right things. My training in Africa served me well.'

'Goodness me,' Caroline gasped. 'Was he all right then? It was a good job you were there. Look, you don't have to stick to the plans, if you would rather unwind a bit. Did you book a taxi?'

'Oh no probs.' Harry shook his head as he vigorously stirred his coffee and then began to attack the bowl of cornflakes. 'I have ordered it for ten o'clock. I thought that would give you ladies time to get sorted.'

'That's fine then. Thank you. We'll meet you on the steps.' Caroline gave her mouth a final dab with the tissue and pushed back her chair.

She had never looked at me, Jenny thought. Neither of them did. Am I bloody invisible or something? What a liar! That was the sort of thing her brother would do. She had seen him in action with his wild stories of heroics. Training in Africa! No way!

She followed behind Caroline, wanting to repeat her opinions out loud, but knowing that it was not the right time. He would betray himself, she thought. What did her mother used to say? 'Give a man enough rope.' Well, he had the rest of the day to complete the saying and perhaps by tomorrow Caroline would have sussed him out for the con man that he was.

The taxi driver was punctual, giving only moments for Harry to ingratiate himself any further. He opened the back door for Caroline, and Jenny clambered in after her.

'All right at the front, mate?' he asked, and the driver nodded.

Jenny studied the back of him, noticing how his hair looked greasy and badly cut. His head was nodding and moving from side to side, as he engaged in conversation with the driver, and she was reminded of the plastic dogs people had in the backs of their cars, nodding away in endless communication, it seemed, with the passengers in vehicles following from behind.

It was a relatively close distance to the foot of the Great Orme by car, the uphill gradient being of little consequence.

'That was quick!' Caroline exclaimed.

The driver grinned. 'It will still cost you a fiver,' he said.

'Oh of course, We are not complaining.'

Harry had stepped out into the street, and Caroline reached into her handbag for the fare. Jenny narrowed her eyes and glared at Harry as she reached the pavement. He grinned and shrugged his shoulders.

'I'll sort out the return,' he said. 'Look, there's a tram waiting to go up if we hurry.'

They joined the queue one behind the other, each one proffering a five-pound note.

'We will need to get off at the halfway station,' Caroline directed. 'We may as well visit the mines first.'

Her companions did not argue with the note of authority in her voice. Jenny was pleased for Caroline to take charge, although she would have preferred Harry to have gone on in his separate way leaving her to enjoy her employer's company with no competition.

The views were spectacular in the light of the morning, the threatening mists already melting away into a clear blue sky. Jenny could not take her eyes away from the steep rocky ledges as they climbed steadily upwards. Caroline was reading out the history of the tramway from a tourist guide she had collected from the hotel rack.

'Construction began in 1901,' she read, 'and it was completed with the upper section in 1903. After thirty years there was a tragedy. A tramcar broke loose and a child was killed and several people were injured. But we are assured that it is very safe now.'

'Phew, that's a relief, laughed Harry, mopping his brow in a theatrical way, and raising a giggle from a small grey-haired lady who was clinging to the edge of the seat.

A silence descended over the carriage, apart from the sound of the grating and clicking of the coaches in their function of climbing the steep and rocky hillside, and the passengers stared out of the windows, caught up in their own impressions of the vista, or their minds wandering into earlier events of the day. Some were studying their phones, picking up on the latest social networking or taking photographs of the view or of each other, or of themselves.

The driver's voice brought their attention back to the comparative urgency of the present moment.

'Change at the halfway point, ladies and gentleman and either follow the path to the mines or wait for the next tram which will take you to the summit. The path to the mines is downhill going. A bit harder coming back. But then there are beautiful views and the weather forecast is brilliant. There are refreshments and a welcome sit down at the top So, as they say in America, 'Have a good day!'

'Are you going to see the mines, Harry?' Caroline asked. 'We are getting off here.'

'Oh yes. I'll tag along. According to the write-up it is unmissable.'

Nobody has asked me, Jenny thought. Of course, he was tagging along! She found herself walking behind them as they left the halfway station, and began to follow the narrow, well-trodden pathway down to a cluster of buildings and signs of excavation and rocky outcrops.

Caroline offered a twenty-pound note, requesting two tickets, and Jenny was pleased to see Harry scrabbling in his trouser pocket for loose change. They were directed towards a large container for the purpose of selecting a hard hat. Jenny did not question this. It seemed like part of charade somehow, and they laughed over their choices: Caroline and Harry selecting green ones and Jenny choosing bright orange.

'We certainly won't lose you!' Harry exclaimed, and Caroline shared his reaction.

'Snap!' she giggled as she fastened the strap under her chin.

The walls of the building were covered in boards displaying information and maps. A skilled artist, it seemed, had used historical facts to depict what the working conditions would have been like for the Bronze Age people, and Harry and Jenny dutifully followed this tourist route, stopping as Caroline read out the information.

'Uncovered in 1987 in a scheme to landscape an area of the Great Orme, one of the most astounding archaeological discoveries of recent times…Dating back 4,000 years to the Bronze Age, they change our views about the ancient people of Britain and their civilised and structured society 2,000 years before the Roman invasion…Over the past thirty years, mining engineers, cavers and archaeologists have been slowly uncovering more tunnels and large areas of the surface landscape to reveal, what is now thought to be the largest prehistoric mine so far discovered in the world.'

Harry was showing signs of impatience, Jenny thought, taking her gaze away from the wall charts and covertly studying him. Why doesn't he just clear off? His hands were in his pockets now and he shuffled his feet one to the other. She guessed that he wanted Caroline to shut up. Would he have told his wife to shut up? Did he have a wife? What was his game?

Caroline was oblivious, it seemed, to the increasing restlessness of her companions, and continued to pause at each display, pointing at and commenting on the stages of exploration and discovery.

An open door ahead seemed to beckon, and they followed the route, Caroline reading the final message board to make sure that they had securely fastened their hard hats as the tunnels were narrow and low.

Jenny's breath quickened. She was not anticipating any restrictions. In fact, she did not know what to expect. She could not imagine the public being given the freedom to put themselves in danger and had viewed the photographs of the exploration with a certain sense of detachment from any danger to herself.

'Caroline,' she whispered, shaking her employer's arm, 'I am not going in a narrow tunnel. I won't be able to breathe. I'll wait somewhere.'

'Oh, that's a shame,' Harry said. 'It's a good job I'm here, isn't it? Don't worry. I'll take good care of her.'

'I can take care of myself,' Caroline retorted. 'Didn't you realise, Jenny, before I got the tickets? Oh well, I expect you can take in all the views and your orange hat suits you. You will have to find out where the exit is and join us later.'

Jenny watched them making their way to the tunnel entrance.

There was no way that she would go in there. She heard someone telling their friends that there was no turning back and how it went deeper and deeper into the ground. She turned away and began to follow the narrow path along the lines of excavation. She rested her hands on a metal barrier and looked down into an excavated pit with narrow tunnels here and there, and for a while, in the warm sunshine, she had a sense of history, her mind wandering back to the illustrations in the information building, and the details read out by Caroline. It was hard to imagine what life was like for these people four thousand years ago, and yet the same sun shone down on them, and it rained, and tides came in and went out.

She sat down on a large boulder at the side of the path, and leant her back against the rocky bank, closing her eyes. The worn surfaces had become warm in the heat of the morning sun, and the orange hard hat, still fastened securely with the band around her neck, formed a stout barrier between her skull and the weathered rock face. In spite of Harry, this was an amazing adventure, she mused as she drifted into sleep.

'Here she is!'

Caroline's voice penetrated her dreams. Jenny opened her eyes, squinting in the bright sunlight.

'We've been looking everywhere for you.' Harry was standing with one arm around Caroline's waist. 'I had to push her up the last bit.'

Caroline pulled away from his grasp but laughed all the same, Jenny noticed, getting to her feet, brushing her hand down the creases in her cotton T-shirt, and straightening the hard hat that was now pressed over to one side and digging into her cheek.

'You missed an incredible experience,' Harry said. 'Didn't she, Caroline?' They were walking along in front of her now, and she struggled to remove the hard hat, putting it on a rocky boulder at the side of the path.

The path grew steeper before it levelled out near to the tram halfway station, and Jenny sought out her inhaler, breathing the chemicals down into her lungs. At that moment Caroline turned to check that she was keeping up, and Jenny felt reassured by her look of concern.

'Slow down, Harry. Jenny is having problems with this hill. I am struggling as well,' she added.

But then her words were not necessary, were they? It was as though Caroline was feeling obliged to explain. After all, this man was of no consequence in their lives.

They walked on in silence, Caroline dropping back to keep in step with Jenny, obliging Harry to walk ahead at his faster pace.

'Was it worth seeing then?' Jenny asked.

Caroline described how the narrow passages went down and down, and how claustrophobic it must have been for the poor people who spent a good part of their lives chiselling into the rock with only the light from primitive oil lamps.

'They found skeletons down there,' she said. 'They were of young children. Can you imagine it?'

'Well, I suppose it wasn't so long ago since children worked in factories, was it? Or got pushed up chimneys.' Jenny smiled, her body revived now, and her spirits soaring once more as she found herself back in step with her beloved Caroline.

They were relieved to find the tram waiting for them at the end of the building housing the power source, and with more information along the walls. No one was dawdling at this point, as the tram was due to leave. They climbed aboard and made their way to the empty seats at the rear. The excited chatter that had accompanied the grinding and rattling of the first part of the journey had subsided to occasional short comments, as the passengers stared out across the green hillside set against a clear blue sky.

It was not long before a building came into view, and as they drew closer they could recognise it as the refreshment area described in the brochure. Harry signalled to Caroline from his position further down the tram, pretending to be holding a cup and making a 'T' sign with his fingers.

Was he offering to get the drinks in, Jenny wondered? Or was he wheeling his way back into Caroline's good books so that she would splash the cash again.

They followed the line of sightseers along the path to the large building. The sight of the tables and chairs through the open doorway were a welcome sight. It was midday and the temperature already rising. Throats were dry from the exertion; most people unused to the steep gradients and the abundance of fresh sea air.

Caroline led the way to a table by a large window where the blue of the cloudless sky and the fresh green of the hillside were like a work of art, Jenny thought, caught in a white shabby frame, as the light became hazy on the horizon.

'Sorry, I'm hogging the best chair.' Caroline sank down into a leather armchair, leaving the comparatively naked tubular metal chairs for her companions. Jenny sat down opposite to her, and they both stared expectantly at their male companion.

'What are you having then, ladies? Hot or cold?'

'Cappuccino for me,' Caroline replied. 'Same for you, Jenny?'

Jenny nodded and smiled, trying to suppress a giggle. They were back on the same side it seemed; batting for the females.

'Oh look! They do scones with cream and jam. Shall we share one, Jenny? That will be wonderful, thanks Harry. I am feeling really peckish after all our wanderings.'

'You are sure you don't want one each?'

Harry's sarcasm backfired on him as Caroline smiled and nodded at the idea. 'Oh yes, what a treat!'

She pressed her knee against Jenny's under the table, and Jenny's grin widened. 'Can't wait,' she said.

Jenny became absorbed in her favourite occupation of people-watching, noticing how, more often than not, the women stood in the queues organising the plates of food and the requests for beverages, whilst their male counterparts guarded the tables and chairs. Harry was standing his ground in the midst of them, turning his head and shrugging his shoulders in silent protest.

'Did you get any sugar?' Jenny enquired, as at last he staggered to their table and lowered the tray on to the table.

'What did your last servant die from? Oh, but then that is your job, isn't it?' Harry grinned and headed back to the counter.

Caroline gave Jenny a disapproving stare and then they both fell into silent contemplation as they sipped at the hot drinks and carefully shared the cream and jam onto the freshly baked scones.

Harry downed his fizzy fruit drink in several gulps and stared across towards the door.

'Excuse me,' he said. 'Nature calls.'

Caroline nodded, waiting for him to go out of earshot. 'I think he needs a smoke. He's probably regretting hanging around with us.'

'Typical male,' Jenny said.

'Well, actually he is rather nice really. A bit shy I think. He seems to be quite knowledgeable. He was telling me about his adventures in Egypt when we were looking for you, and how claustrophobic it was to go into the pyramid. I don't think he is well heeled, even so. Did it all on a shoe string. I'll pay for the taxi back.'

'Really,' Jenny said, shaking her head, and looking away out of the window. Grey clouds were moving across the blue sky now, blotting out the sunlight, and she knotted her fingers down against the palms of her hands, and sighed.

Harry, it seemed, was intent on getting his money's worth of fresh air, as he described it a half an hour later, striding off over the hillside, and leaving the two friends to walk slowly up the steep inclines to the summit, and then make their way down again to the tram terminus. He was nowhere to be seen as they boarded the tram and Jenny relaxed, although part of her mind fixed on how he was avoiding paying his share for the taxi on the return journey.

'Do you fancy a stroll along the pier? At least it is flat and there are plenty of seats. Harry seems to have abandoned us. We don't want to go back yet, do we?' Caroline tugged at Jenny's sleeve, as they stood up to leave the tram.

'Whatever,' Anything, Jenny thought, to lose that creep Harry.

The pier was catering for family entertainment it seemed, and they concentrated on dodging pushchairs and ice creams until the space ahead became more inviting in the open vista and the fresh air.

A gaily painted structure about thirty yards ahead caught Caroline's eye and she tugged at Jenny's arm and pointed. As they drew closer, they could make out the words Gypsy Marie Louise. Her name was written in a bold black script, and underneath was the description 'clairevoyant extraordinaire' in an artistic flowing of curves and loops.

Caroline stopped walking and stared at the canvas flap.

Jenny giggled. 'Come on,' she ordered. She tugged at Caroline's arm. 'A fortune teller! I bet it'll cost you a fortune.'

The canvas flap opened, revealing the head and shoulders of a seemingly middle-aged woman, her face heavily coated in a layer of theatrical makeup, giving her a swarthy Eastern look, and her eyes dark with liner, and accentuated with green eye shadow. A hand, bedecked with gold bejewelled rings, came through the fold; the index finger beckoning for them to come in.

Jenny drew back, tugging at Caroline's sleeve, and no longer giggling. 'Come on,' she repeated. 'I need another coffee. Look, there's a snack bar up there.'

'I'll meet you there. How long will I be with a reading?' Caroline stared at the face of the fortune teller, noticing the blackness of her eyes, and experiencing a shiver of apprehension and fear in the same moment.

Jenny let go of her friend's sleeve but continued to frown and shake her head in protest. She wished Harry was back on the scene.

Then the gypsy pulled back the curtain, and Caroline stepped into another world; an in-between world between the past and the future, away from the jostling holiday makers and the protection of her friend.

She followed the direction of the pointing finger and sat down on a cane chair, drawing her legs under an old, wobbly table draped with a red velvet cloth. 'Marie-Louise. Palm readings £5.00. Palm and crystal £10,' the folded card on the table advised. The shabbiness of the interior was in sharp contrast to the gypsy's flamboyant dress, but as she carefully lighted the candles, the atmosphere became both intimate yet mysterious.

Without waiting for an affirmation of Caroline's preferred service, the woman said, 'I think both palm and crystal. I do like the money in advance, dear.'

Caroline fumbled in her handbag, her cheeks flushing in her confusion, and drew a ten-pound note out of her purse. She was panicking now; regretting her impulsive decision, and her feet pressed hard into the ground ready for flight.

The woman grasped the note and in a quick, obviously well practised action, she pushed it down into the cleavage of her breasts, out of sight under the folds of the rich brocade.

Caroline frowned, her mind distracted by the action. Who would be handling that note next, she wondered? 'A day in the life of a penny.' She remembered having to write an essay about that at junior school. He hated handling money, she recalled. 'You don't know where it has been.' His words flitted through her brain.

'Come on, dear. Your hands please.'

Caroline obeyed the command, turning her hands palms upward. The woman stared and traced a finger along the deep lines. She muttered, 'Ah! Very interesting. That's strange. We shall see.'

'What can you see then?'

Her heart was beating faster than normal, and her feet were still pressing hard into the ground. She was never comfortable with physical contact; aware of skin texture and perspiration. She gave a slight shudder and made to withdraw her hands.

'Very dark. Very dark thoughts. You liked skipping when you were young.'

The gypsy stared at Caroline, narrowing her eyes and tipping her head to one side 'Sticks and stones. Just sticks and stones can break your bones. Little words from childhood. Not your fault. All very dark. Very dark in the cupboard. Let's try the crystal ball.'

Lizzie Borden! Lizzie Borden! Skipping rhyme! Oh my God, she knows! Caroline stared wildly at the gypsy, her breathing uneven, and her heart racing.

The fortune teller released her grip on Caroline's hand, and drew the crystal ball towards her across the table. Placing her hands around it, she gazed into the cloudy depths.

'I see. Your mother,' she waggled two fingers in the air, 'was your aunt, wasn't she?'

Caroline shook her head. 'No relation,' she said.

'Ah. You didn't know, yet you had a look of her. More like your father though. Saving the family name perhaps. Your mother is Bella. All right let's get it right, Isabelle. A twin sister. Her twin sister. Twins get complicated. They share everything. Even their men. I suppose it is all the same. One gene pool. This is so dark. A crystal? Oh, I see. A crystal house in the crystal ball. They are playing tricks on me. Where? Past or future? Oh, it's gone. Sorry dear. So dark. So dark.'

She relinquished her grip on the crystal ball and drew back in her chair.

'That's it dear. You must follow the clues. Crystal House in the north I think.'

'But I don't understand,' Caroline said. 'You say my adoptive mother was related to me after all. Why didn't I know?'

'Dark secrets are hidden away. There is often only a glimmer of light. It shone out in the ball. Your hands show your destiny, but I cannot read them yet.'

She blew out the candles and stood up.

'Take care my dear,' she said.

Caroline struggled to her feet. Her legs had become stiff with the hardness of the chair and the tension in her muscles. Now, in this windowless cabin, a lack of air stifled her, and she pushed against the rickety table in a panic to escape back to the comparative normality of the pier. Her eyes were no longer focusing on the strange features of the gypsy. She was also looking into time; the under-stairs cupboard, the name calling, the theft of her child, the repeating of history. It all made sense. She was being punished for her mother's sins. Crystal House! A dark place.

She pushed her way through the canvas flap, screwing up her eyes against the brightness of the sun. Jenny was sitting on a seat further along the pier, her gaze directed across the bay towards their hotel, and the Little Orme, a smaller rocky promontory in the distance. She turned as Caroline reached her, immediately aware of the distress signs; the deep frown, the drooping of the mouth, the unsteadiness of her gait.

'Sit down,' she exclaimed. 'You look as though you have seen a ghost. I bet she has given you a load of rubbish. I remember one who cursed me at the door when I wouldn't buy anything. Just forget about her whatever she said.'

Caroline knew that she could not explain to Jenny the revelations concerning her past, or the future action advised by the gypsy. As far as her cleaning lady was concerned, her parents and relations were in the old photograph album she had bought at the sale. Her vivid imaginings about her ancestors were tangling into a huge web of deceit.

She tried to cast it from her mind, obeying Jenny's directions to look at this or regard the view or to notice the changing sky indicating rain on its way.

'Shall we get a taxi back? It's really coming in dark. Look at the horizon now. It's like a mist rolling in.' Jenny pulled anxiously at Caroline's sleeve.

'I wonder where Harry got to. He was going to organise it.'

'Dream on,' Jenny muttered. She took out her phone and located the taxi details,

'Thank you. Five minutes. Yes. End of pier. Two ladies. We will wait by the bus stop.'

Caroline stared vaguely ahead, following Jenny's brisk footsteps back towards the street.

Harry was punctual for the evening meal, and at first offered no explanation for his disappearance. He considered the instructions given by Brad Carter, when he had a made a phone call from the pier after observing the two ladies standing near the gypsy's booth. Apparently, he was to listen to their conversation and ask leading questions.

What the hell were leading questions, he wondered? The guy was living on another planet. He spent too much time on his own. What did he think the housekeeper was going to do? Persuade her employer to part with a load of cash and then make a run for it. What! In a seaside town in North Wales.

'Are you ladies planning any more trips this year? I get itchy feet, but I expect you like to settle down for the winter.'

'Not really,' Caroline replied. 'I have a great deal to do in getting my house ready for selling. It is far too big for me now, and there is a large garden at the rear of the property getting totally neglected. I will be needing a gardener. The one we used to have only knew how to use weed killer. Do you live locally? I don't suppose you know of anybody.'

'Don't look at me!' Harry laughed. 'Don't you know, Jenny? That's more your strata of society, isn't it?'

Jenny gave him a long look, her eyes narrowing, and Harry grinned.

The puddings arrived, and the three of them carefully spooned up the crumbling meringue nests with their fruit and cream fillings.

'So, did you go on the pier then? I saw you heading that way. I was further down the tram. Just caught it and could not keep up with you. It looked a bit hectic for me on the pier. I can't stand all these kids running everywhere.' Harry directed his question at Caroline. He wondered if she would mention the fortune teller. He had not actually seen her going into the gypsy's booth, as Jenny was hovering and he kept well out of sight. They were nowhere to be seen when he came out of hiding.

Caroline merely nodded in his direction, turning towards her companion. 'Are we ready, Jenny? We have had an exhausting day. It calls for an early night, I think.'

Jenny needed no prompting and gave a final wipe to her mouth with her napkin before pushing back her chair and standing up.

'No bingo tonight then?' Harry was determined to have the last word.

Jenny shrugged. 'Apparently not,' she muttered.

They made their way around the tables to the doorway leading into the entrance hall. Jenny was desperate to know what had upset her employer. She had hardly strung more than a few words together since they had travelled back in the taxi, striding ahead up the hotel steps, and noisily slamming the bathroom door behind her after they had gained entry into their shared suite of rooms.

Now, with Caroline once more in the bathroom, she sank down into the basket-work chair by the window and looked out across the sea. The threatened sea fret had lifted and the sun shone low on the horizon, casting a red glow over the calm waters of the bay. There were a few people out walking off their evening meal; couples arm in arm, striding in unison, complete, intact in their relationships.

She shivered, not with cold, but rather with a sense of disquiet. She wanted to rush off on a great adventure. She wanted to laugh and scream on a rollercoaster. She wanted to be swept off her feet. She heard Caroline crying in the bathroom. Little croaking, choking sounds. Oh God, she thought. What am I doing with my life? This was my great adventure, and here I am just tagging along as usual. That Harry had knocked the final nail in, implying that she would know where to find a gardener. I know my place. Who said that in a comedy sketch? Well, it was true, wasn't it? Caroline regarded her as a servant, even though she had been very generous. She was still using her as some kind of protection from the dangers of life outside of her home, rather than a loving friend. The couples walking along the esplanade were what people called items. She had never been an item. She had always felt singular. Why was Caroline crying for goodness sake? She struggled to her feet, her legs cramped with her low position on the basket chair.

'Caroline. I need the lav. Will you be long?'

'Can you go to the public one. I am not feeling good. It is just around the corner along the corridor.'

Jenny waited for a few seconds, hoping for further enlightenment so that she could give some comfort, but then not sure where the comfort would lie.

'Can I get you something? Do you want a drink? Tell me what's the matter. Has that Harry upset you? He's a lying toad. I have seen his type before. All mouth and trousers as my mother used to say. Typical male.'

She heard the click of the lock, and seconds later Caroline's face appeared around the door. She had removed her make-up, and in the harsh light escaping with her from the shower room, she looked ghastly, Jenny thought. She wanted to wrap her arms around her and protect her from whatever had come into her life.

Caroline sank down on to her bed. 'I can't tell you,' she gasped. 'It has to be a secret. I can't tell anyone.'

'It's that gypsy, isn't it? You've not been the same since you had that reading. Did she predict something horrible like that you are going to die or something? I could see she was rubbish.'

163

'I can't tell you. There are so many bad memories and so many lies. It's best you don't know. Anyway, the toilet is all yours. I am going to bed. Go to bingo if you like.'

She peeled off her sweater and jeans, struggled with her brassiere and pushed her arms into her nightgown.

Jenny longed to help her but was afraid of the strangeness in her face; the wildness in her eyes and the tight compression of her lips.

'Well, if you are sure that I can't help. Perhaps you have got over tired. We did do a lot, and neither of us is super fit. Try to have a good dream. Think of something nice.'

Caroline nodded. A picture of her mother – her aunt – was in her head. It was the photograph with holes stabbed through it. The one she had taken out of the broken frame, attacked with a point of a knife and later hidden in the dustbin. And he was in her head also. So, was he her father? The gypsy said that they shared everything. Twins share everything. How could 'she' live with him knowing that he had seduced her twin sister. Couldn't she conceive? Was that what the gypsy had said? Twins share everything. She narrowed her eyes, drawing her brows together in a deep frown. 'For God's sake,' she muttered. All these men in her life. One big betrayal!

"When she saw what she had done, she gave her father forty-one."

She had never included him before, had she? Although…she knew that the American girl had done so when she chanted the skipping rhyme. Lizzie Borden was accused of the murder of both of her parents. He had never been on my hit list, she mused. She did not see much of him. So, who did she take after? Bernice, her late adoptive mother or Isabelle – Bella, the gypsy had called her, now locked up in a strange house? Both, if they were identical twins? Somebody once had said she was like her mother. She remembered wanting to deny it. But then she could remember someone else describing her as a Pearson. She tried to picture her father, if after all he was her father. It was so difficult to get a whole picture. Bit by bit – he had dark hair greying at the temples, he was tallish, his nose was quite long, like mine she recalled. That had never seemed to be relevant before. He was tidy minded, like me but there the resemblance ended. Did he get confused as to who was who? Did the sisters play games with people and did this game go wrong? Or did he choose to have the best of both worlds? Was Bernice the victim of their deceit? Or was it, as the gypsy implied, a family cover-up. Was Bernice infertile? She never conceived, did she? Was that the problem? Did Bella agree to be surrogate and then changed her mind? Or was it all done behind her twin sister's back? Did he love both of them? Was Bella more giving and passionate, or was he just greedy?

He must have known how much I suffered, mustn't he? She asked herself. Why didn't he stop it? Did Bernice own everything? Did she blackmail him? Why was I so afraid – still afraid? Part of me has that anger. Is it a kind of madness? Is that why Bella is locked away? Is she locked away like the mad woman in *Jane Eyre,* imprisoned for life in the attic of this strange Crystal House? Or does she own Crystal House? Perhaps, she tried to kill him or me.

She allowed her imagination to colour her thoughts, visualising a quarrel. Bella announcing her pregnancy – accusing her brother-in-law. Bernice screaming and accusing. Two women identical in looks – were they identical in personality? Was her mother Bella as hateful as her sister? Did he share them because he was greedy or because he got a thrill or because Bella was the nice one? She imagined his reasoning. Bernice is a cow, but Bella? What a difference! You would never think they were identical twins…So, Caroline asked herself, did they get away with it? Did Bella pretend to be Bernice? Did they swop when outsiders were involved? Had they always played games?

Did their mother know? Of course, she did. Mothers always know the difference, Caroline thought. Some little thing like a mole or a different facial expression or a difference in nature – some little thing. So, who would know about this disgraceful pregnancy out of marriage? This future bastard. There must have been some give-away clues or was it a family secret, not spoken of outside of the family? Did those family members, who she had dismissed for so long as nothing to do with her, know her history? That one who said she looked like 'her mother' Bernice. Did she know? Was she rubbing some salt in the wound?

Like mother, like daughter. Bernice used to say that after they knew that April was on the way. She had supposed that she was being likened to the young woman who had left her on the doorstep of the Children's Home. But, of course, she was like her mother Bella. She had got herself into trouble, but what about him? Why was the 'he' never in trouble. Why was it always the 'she'?

She was rambling. Her heart was beating too fast. She could not take a deep breath. It was coming in gasps. Oh God! She jumped off the bed

Jenny came out of the bathroom and reached forward to steady her companion, guiding her back to the safety of the bed.

'I don't think I had better leave you. Are you still feeling sick? Shall I see if there is a doctor on call here? Oh Caroline! You must calm down. Now breathe slowly.'

'I'm fine now. I got up too fast. I think it's vertigo. Do you ever get that?

'Sometimes. All these mid-life problems! Are you all right now? Can I make you a cup of tea or something?'

'No thanks. I am all right. Like you said, mid-life!'

'I'll leave you to sleep, shall I? I'll have a session of bingo. You never know. I might win and that would upset Mrs Ernie. I'm sure she thinks I am loaded. Just close your eyes and don't answer the door to anybody. I'll take the key.'

Caroline listened for the click of the door and opened her eyes. Jenny's concern had blocked her thinking process. Now, with her mind free to wander more freely again, she sought out memories in her childhood, beginning to rationalise those times when she could not understand why she was being punished. She could see that she was used as a weapon by both her mother/aunt and her father. Punishments and rewards. Rewards and punishments. She had a sudden image of 'her' living in a strange house. Crystal House. Was it in the crystal ball? Did it actually exist? Did the gypsy see it? Was there a duplicate of her adoptive mother there? A living ghost? She threw the duvet over her head and drew her knees up to her chin. In the darkness under the cover, she cast her mind back to the photographs displayed on the wall of her 'mother's' bedroom. Suddenly, as though it had been illuminated in her brain, she saw the familiar face of a lady once described by someone as her grandmother and realised that it was familiar because she now recognised a strong resemblance to herself, as she was now. Skipped a generation. She had heard that said before. Was the lady, with her long grey hair, and strong features, her true ancestor? So, what had happened to those photographs? Did her mother Bella have family photographs? In the midst of all of this agonising, she began to feel the threads of belonging. But then what if the gypsy was making it all up, and she herself was making it all fit? She was good at doing that wasn't she?

Jenny requested a large brandy at the bar and looked around. The usual little cliques had gathered, coming early and bagging the best position as they described it. There was no need to seek out Mrs Ernie. Her raucous laughter pinpointed her position, seated at a table for six people along the back wall of the ballroom, as it was grandly named. Actually, there was very little space for dancing; a square of bare floorboards amongst the tables. However, it was quite adequate. Most people were content to drink, and chat after the bingo session, and the entertainer of the evening had plenty of space to set up his equipment.

Jenny had been looking forward to the evening. Occasionally, there was live music in her local, but mostly it was karaoke with some singer, with high aspirations, grabbing the mike after consuming enough alcohol to raise the confidence stakes. She had even had a go herself. Now, she was anticipating that this would be more enjoyable; more professional. The poster on the notice board promised guitar and a wide selection of country and western, played by the well-known performer Hank Brailsey. Jenny had never heard of him, but then she had never heard of a lot of people, she reasoned. He certainly looked good on the poster, in his blue denim jeans and shirt, his hair long on his shoulders and his guitar hugged close to his chest.

Her enthusiasm waned after two pages of bingo, when it seemed to her that she must be on a different game to everyone else. One of those nights, she thought, looking at the rows of uncrossed numbers and wondering how the machine could so unerringly miss her out.

'House!' There it was again. She sat back in her chair, staring dispassionately at the checker advancing on the winner of twenty pounds. Wow, she mouthed. She looked across to Mrs Ernie, who somehow had become her rival in these big stakes. She was throwing her head back and draining a pint of beer. Not a happy bunny, Jenny thought. That cheered her up, but then her mind was back on Caroline. If only she could drown her sorrows in drink.

'Final game, folks, so eyes down.'

Jenny was programmed to obey in spite of her growing indifference, and she stared at the numbers in front of her suddenly caught up again with the excitement, as, one after another, she crossed the squares with her marker pen.

'House.'

'Can't be.' That was Mrs Ernie's voice.

Jenny waited for her card to be checked, dreading a verdict of miss-call. She had done that once before and it was so embarrassing.

'All correct. Congratulations. Give her a clap everybody. She has won the jackpot of sixty pounds.'

'It's that one with that posh woman. What does she need with the money?'

Mrs Ernie's voice sounded loud and clear in the sudden hush. Jenny looked across and they were all giggling and putting their hands across their mouths.

She felt triumphant. Not only because she had won, but in the fact that she was labelled rich and superior in the eyes of Mrs Ernie and her cronies. She watched the bingo caller walking over with her prize and found herself grinning from ear to ear. He gave her fingers a squeeze, and she felt the colour rising in her cheeks. I'm not only rich but attractive with it, she decided.

She closed her fingers over the twenty-pound notes. If Sherry was here, she would have persuaded her mother to make a bee line for the bar, or cadged a tenner for a packet of cigarettes, she mused. So, what would she do with it? What would be her treat? Should she go back to the room and share her success with Caroline. She got up from her seat and walked slowly across to the door marked exit, aware of the comments coming from the table opposite. 'It always goes to them what have got it,' she heard Mrs Ernie say. If only they knew how little she had.

She stood in the foyer debating whether to disturb Caroline. She could be asleep. On the other hand, she might enjoy some music. But then she had got undressed and gone to bed. A glass cabinet caught her eye at the side of the staircase. It housed a variety of jewellery; an inducement to buy for a friend or relation or perhaps for oneself as a souvenir of the holiday. A pair of ear rings caught her attention. She gasped, 'Oh, how lovely!' They were what Sherry would call 'danglies'. Caroline liked danglies. She had once said that studs became obscured by her shoulder-length hair. These looked like blue sapphires set in silver rings and attached to the studs and pins with slim silver chains. Caroline would love them. Jenny knew that without a doubt. She turned to see the hotel receptionist watching her. 'Can I help dear?' she queried, returning her gaze to the page on trendy wear for the tropical beach.

'How much are the sapphire ear rings, please?'

'Not sapphire of course. Quite expensive I'm afraid. They are our mid-range. We do have cheaper. Would you like to see, or perhaps you would like to look at some others?'

'No. Just tell me how much.'

The woman sighed and reluctantly it seemed, got up from her stool, leaving her magazine with its fashion pages on the counter top. Jenny felt a return of the old irritation she experienced frequently. 'Do I have "benefits" written across my forehead?' she had once complained to her partner. He had laughed, she recalled, and made some derogatory comment.

The woman unlocked the cabinet. 'Ah, I was right. Twenty-five pounds. But then these on the next level are all under fifteen. Some are only a fiver but are a bit flimsy.'

'Could I see the sapphire ones, please? They are so lovely.'

The woman held them up, dangling them against the light. The blue glass shimmered, seeming to be detached from the studs with the fine silvery chains scarcely visible.

'Yes. I will take those, thank you. Do you have a box or some tissue? They are a gift.'

The receptionist opened a drawer in the base of the cabinet and pulled out some tissue paper.

Jenny wanted to say that if it was a full moon her face would stay in a frown. It was something Sherry would say, but she was too happy at that moment to linger on the negativity of other people.

She almost skipped back into the ballroom with the ear rings safely put away in the bottom of her handbag. She could not wait to give them to Caroline, but she wanted her to be wide awake. It would be such an exciting way to begin the next day.

The entertainer was already there, and Jenny returned to her table, putting her handbag down at her feet. She stared at the figure standing in the allotted floor space. He was hardly a heart throb, she thought. The photograph on the poster must be at least twenty years out of date. He still wore his hair long but it was thinning and lank now, and his shirt hung loosely over his jeans, concealing an unhealthy-looking bulge. His guitar hung from his shoulder, and his hands gesticulated as he recounted his anecdotes, obviously well-rehearsed and often repeated, pausing for the laughter and already targeting the table where Mrs Ernie and her cronies sat with their beer glasses and half-empty crisp packets.

However, he changed into a musician once his fingers took over his guitar, and he became true to himself. Jenny's anxiety was washed away in the tide of country and western music which filled the room, drowning out the raucous voices. She felt a rising admiration for this man whatever his real name was. She doubted that he was born with the name of Hank. Probably he had been a fan of the Shadows in the Beatles' era. Why should a man with so much talent, have to resort to entertaining the likes of Mrs Ernie? Why wasn't he famous?

'Any requests for a final vocal? I may be able to oblige.'

He was looking directly at Jenny, and she felt the colour rising in her cheeks.

'The Rising Sun,' she stammered. It was the first one that came into her head. It was a karaoke favourite.

'One of my favourites as well,' he said. 'What's your name?'

'Jenny,' she almost mouthed the sound, but he picked up on it, and walked towards her.

'OK then folks. For Jenny. "The House of the Rising Sun".'

He was serenading her it seemed. She had seen this in films where musicians played on request.

Everyone clapped when he reached the end of the song, and he bowed his head, looking under his eyebrows at Jenny and smiling.

She mouthed her thanks, her colour flushing in her cheeks. He was a Sir Lancelot, and yet it was Queen Caroline she loved. So, why did she have such butterflies in her stomach?

Mrs Ernie brushed past her on her way to the bar. 'Watch your sixty pounds, duck,' she commented with an exaggerated wink, jerking her head towards the entertainer.

However, it was not only Hank who had wind of the win. Harry had also witnessed Jenny's good fortune. He had watched her leave the bingo session, and was finishing his beer and contemplating his next plan of action, when she walked back in. What a sleaze that performer was, he thought. I could not have done it better myself. Jenny was flattered. He could see that. He had her down as damaged goods. Failed marriage and a need for sisterhood or more than that if she had the chance, he guessed, especially with Caroline and all her goodies.

Well, whatever? He shrugged. It was worth a few freebies wasn't it? He could write it in his report as time spent in investigating. That was what Carter wanted.

Jenny watched him approaching with a sense of relief. He was a familiar face and a fellow traveller in spite of her suspicions. She was aware of the entertainer glancing across at her as he packed up his equipment, and she was about to make an exit, although the thought of the dark room that housed her bed and suitcase was not particularly inviting. Somehow, the excitement of her win and the enjoyment of the music had given her an appetite for the late hours. Harry was known to her and there seemed to be safety in his continued presence in her life as a fellow traveller at least for the next few days.

'Are you ready for a drink? Not rushing back, are you?'

'No. I'll keep you company. I'll have a white wine and you get what you want. I'll treat you. I won at bingo amazingly!'

'Well done. Is Caroline poorly? She didn't seem very good at dinner. Was the day too much for her? These hills get you, don't they?' Harry glared at the entertainer who was making his way towards them.

'Thanks mate,' he called. 'We enjoyed the music, didn't we, Jenny? Have you got far to go?'

'It's been a long day. Thanks. See you around.'

Jenny felt the colour rising in her cheeks and looked away. She was cross with herself for betraying Caroline, and here she was defending herself by using Harry as some kind of shield.

They watched Hank leaving the ballroom and then made their way to the bar away from the noise of recorded music and the people still sitting at the tables.

'So, how is Caroline then? You didn't say.'

'I wish I knew. She went into that gypsy booth and had her hand read and whatever she told her, poor Caroline has not been the same since. She won't tell me anything so I have left her to sleep it off.'

'Perhaps tomorrow's trip will cheer her up. It is a long drive around, I think. Is it going up Snowdon on the train? I have never been to Snowdon, have you?'

'No, that's not tomorrow, but then you have been to Africa, haven't you? So, I guess this is all quite tame really.'

Jenny couldn't resist trapping him. She knew that he was all lies, but somehow, in this atmosphere of unreality, sitting here in a hotel with a glass of wine and money in her bag, she was enjoying the rivalry for Caroline's affection and a spot of male baiting.

Harry regarded her, guarding his tongue now, yet intent on furnishing Brad Carter with the information he seemed to require. What did he want? Obviously, he knew all about Caroline's finances. He himself was sure that she had no interest in her so-called housekeeper other than as a general kind of skivvy, but then the solicitor had paid for his holiday and supplied some spending money. He had to give something back, and then keep it going so that he could earn a bit more after their return. He resolved to spend some time with Caroline away from her 'keeper'. There was something troubling her and he meant to find out what it was. Whether he would share it with Carter was another matter, he decided. There could well be big stakes here and Carter's money could be peanuts in comparison.

Chapter Eleven

Caroline slept fitfully that night and Jenny was witness to the sound of her visits to the en-suite, observing the strip of light showing under the door separating the two rooms. She was in two minds whether to get up and make some tea, thinking that whatever was keeping her companion awake would surface into an enlightening conversation. She was nervous to attempt such an intrusion into Caroline's private life. There was still a huge social barrier between them. She was really like a personal assistant and carer rolled into one. This seemed to be her role. Her evening cleaning job with the crabby old woman, Mrs Bagley, often included making tea and sandwiches amidst the cleaning routine. More often than not she worked over the hour. Stupid, Sherry called her. She would be saying that now, wouldn't she, she mused? Still, she had enjoyed the evening. It was such a thrill to win the full house bingo prize, and she had enjoyed the entertainment and Harry's company, in spite of her opinions of him. She was experiencing a feeling of being protected and cared for rather than always being the carer.

She pressed her phone, illuminating the screen, and the date and time. Seven-fourteen and time to get up at last. Her body was stiff from the tension of insomnia during the last few hours, her attempts to sleep being disturbed by the flushing of the toilet and the restlessness of her companion. She struggled to free herself from the duvet, shivering in the chill of the autumn air. The hotel was not heated yet, and the light coming in through the small window high in the wall was dull, with all the indications of an overcast sky and the threatened rain.

She opened the door slowly and tip-toed past Caroline's bed. She decided to use the tea-making facilities and ease Caroline into the day. She suddenly felt comfortable in this role, re-establishing the employer/employee role that she had decried in her earlier reflections.

Caroline grunted her thanks for the proffered drink, and muttered, 'What time is it?'

'We've got just over half an hour before breakfast,' Jenny said in a bright voice. 'It's a bit dull at the moment, but it could clear up. In any case, we are on a tour today so we can sit back and enjoy the scenery through the rain drops. It's got to be better than working.'

Caroline grunted again, and pulled the duvet back over her shoulders, pushing her face into the pillow.

'Shall I use the shower first then? Give you a bit longer? We don't have to rush down for breakfast. The tour starts at half past nine. Plenty of time.'

Jenny jetted the hot water down her back, enjoying the warmth and the way that it seemed to clear the tension from her muscles. Normally, she did not enjoy this morning treat, having only a bath and no shower in her flat and limited hot water. They had done a lot of walking yesterday, she mused. Perhaps it had been too much for Caroline. She was not used to physical activity, using her car instead of walking and doing little hard work generally. But then she had been so full of enthusiasm walking in the fresh air on top of the Great Orme. It was all about the gypsy, wasn't it?

Harry, looking bright and refreshed, was attacking a full English breakfast, when they reached their table.

'There's an amazing choice,' he spluttered, through a mouthful of sausage.

Jenny grinned. 'That's one thing we Brits do well, isn't it? I don't suppose you got this in Africa. Are you going on the tour today? It looks a bit cloudy, but there's bound to be coffee stops and local shops where we can stretch our legs. To be honest, we neither of us have much energy after yesterday. It will be good to just sit back and watch the world go by, won't it, Caroline?'

Harry turned to Caroline sitting on his right. She nodded, and stirred her spoon in her coffee, staring at her dish of cereals.

Harry looked back at Jenny who gave a slight shrug of her shoulders and sighed.

The crowd of holiday makers, gathered in the foyer and waiting for the arrival of the coach, were all armed, it seemed, with that British stoicism; waterproofs at the ready, and bags bulging with snacks and bottles of water. At least no one was going to starve, whatever the gods might hurl their way weather-wise, or whatever wise. Mrs Ernie was cackling loudly over some comment that her bingo partner, a large woman in tight leggings and a strange woolly striped hat, had just made.

Jenny looked at Caroline, wanting to share her amusement, but her companion was staring across the esplanade at the grey sea, her lips pressed together and her eyes barely visible behind dark glasses. 'Pollen,' she had explained, when she had put them on after breakfast.

The windscreen wipers were mesmerising with their clicking motion, and the voice of Jim Reeves drifted down the length of the coach, inducing a coma-like state, and even sleep, for some of the holiday makers, who had had a restless night following the enthusiastic activities of the previous day.

'We shall soon be at Betws-y-Coed,' announced the driver. 'This is a charming place with lots of interesting little shops and places to eat. It is a pity that the rain has decided to follow us today but there is no need to get wet. Plenty to do. We will have two hours here and then continue our tour. Hopefully the rain will clear up soon.'

Twenty minutes later, buildings came into sight, and the coach swung round into a parking area and came to a stop. People began to shuffle along the central gangway of the coach. Caroline, Jenny and Harry were in no hurry to move. They peered through the raindrops running down the windows.

'Let's make for a coffee shop, shall we?' Harry nudged Jenny's shoulder.

'Do you want a coffee, Caroline?'

Caroline grunted, 'Whatever.'

Jenny looked at Harry and shrugged. 'Better than working for a living,' she muttered.

About ten minutes later they sank down on some straight-backed tubular metal chairs, sheltering from the rain under an awning along the front of a restaurant. The establishment were serving early lunches, and the waitress service was being stretched to its limits by the bad weather forcing holiday makers to seek cover.

'So, tell us about Africa then,' Jenny said, smiling at Harry. 'Did it rain much or were you burnt to a frizzle?'

Harry narrowed his eyes. He knew that Jenny was not impressed by his tales. She was from the same school in life. He wanted to laugh and make some comment about wishful thinking or 'in my dreams'. But he was there to make an impression on Caroline, and to win her trust. He had to keep up appearances. Instead, he trotted out a few facts he had found in a book about what life was like in South Africa and how there was still a lot of hardship. 'Even sitting here in the rain is good,' he said. 'We are so lucky.'

Caroline nodded. 'Life could certainly be worse,' she said.

Thank goodness, Jenny thought. Perhaps they could get back to enjoying this holiday in spite of the weather. As she nodded and smiled, the rain stopped falling and a shaft of sunlight shone out from the edge of the cloud.

Ten minutes later the atmosphere had changed from weary depression to enthusiasm, as people lowered their umbrellas and set off to explore the quaintness and picturesque scenery of this little town.

'We're the last of the big spenders,' Harry remarked as they wandered from one little gift area to another. Harry had taken photographs on his mobile phone, but Jenny had purchased postcards.

'No one will want to see my holiday pics,' she said. 'In any case, my phone is so old that nothing seems to come out well.'

'So, let's have a groupie, shall we.'

'Not me,' Caroline said, stepping to one side. 'I have no desire to be on this social networking as they call it. I am a private person.'

'Oh, come on then, Harry. I'll give you an excuse to do a selfie. But let me see it before you use it.' Jenny pressed nearer to Harry and smiled into his phone, seeing their two heads on the tiny screen as he clicked the control.

'There! That's brilliant!'

Jenny nodded in agreement. It was the best one she had seen of herself for a long time. In spite of the rain and Caroline's moods, she was happy. Harry was good company even though she regarded him as a lying, conniving male.

They recognised other fellow travellers heading towards the collection point in a corner of the car and coach park. In spite of the improvement in the weather, they were ready to move on. Their seat at the rear of the coach was like a sanctuary, familiar and warm, with their shopping bag containing their snacks and mineral water nestling down on the floor. Jenny had come well stocked with crisps, not normally favoured by Caroline, but away from her disciplined life, she enjoyed the easily eaten snack followed by a chocolate bar washed down by water drunk from the bottle.

Jenny was relieved to see her relaxing and they chatted about the scenery and the houses half hidden away along the sides of the narrow roads. The so-called ugly house was a listed stopping place, and they followed the holiday party as they wandered through the rooms, listening to the story of how it had been built by robbers overnight, with smoke coming out of the chimney the next morning. This incredible feat meant that the builders could lay claim to the land. There was no cement between the boulders that had been rolled down the hillside during the night; apparently, the weight of one on top of the other kept them stable and upright. The smell of the earth and of the wet stones hung in the air. There was barely time to absorb all the history of the place and Caroline was loath to leave so quickly, but as the driver explained, this was not a good place to park with a coach and the stopping time was limited, in fact frowned upon, with tourists travelling by car needing to have access to this popular, well publicised attraction, without blocking the narrow road.

Jenny was pleased to see that Caroline was becoming more like her old self. She knew that history was her thing, and that she was looking forward to a visit to Conway Castle before they returned home. Perhaps, she had stopped thinking about the gypsy, or perhaps, after all, she was suffering more from the high pollen, and had slept badly.

Caroline was doing her best not to think about the past. She could not possibly share her worries with Jenny. If only she could have known her daughter April beyond that first month. She would be thirty-four now. Whilst Jenny had been playing bingo on the previous night she had tried to take her mind off the encounter with the gypsy, watching a programme on the television about a woman tracing her son after she had been forced to give him up for adoption many years ago.

Perhaps she could talk to Jenny about that part of her life. She had not included April in her photograph pretence. She remembered watching a similar programme and Jenny had said that her brother was good at tracing people in the family tree. April was registered with her chosen name and her own surname of Pearson, but would it have got changed? That had been a complication for the woman trying to trace her son, but apparently earlier records were available. She did not care if it cost her thousands of pounds to employ someone to find her daughter. Had April been told that she was adopted? Had she been punished because of her bad mother? Did she have children of her own? Am I a grandmother? She smiled at the idea.

'A penny for them. Something is amusing you.'

Jenny's voice broke into her thoughts. She shook her head as if in denial.

What was she denying, Jenny wondered? Was she back with that wretched gypsy?

She continued to stare at her companion, and Caroline felt obliged to give her an answer.

'Do you remember that programme about that woman who traced her child who had been given up for adoption? I watched a similar one last night. It was about a woman searching for her son. It is amazing what they can find out these days. I don't like all the gossip but I must admit that the internet can do good things.'

'My brother Mike spends hours tracing the family tree. I remember him saying that one of our cousins, a few times removed, had been adopted. I think it used to be impossible to trace people but there are all sorts of links now.'

Harry strained his ears to hear Caroline's comments. There was something going on here. I can feel it in my water, he thought, quoting his old grandmother. Brad Carter had mentioned that she had bought a doll for a child and yet apparently, to his knowledge, there were no grandchildren, in fact no offspring from her relationship. Why this sudden interest in tracing a child on the internet? Whatever she did, she must not have anything to do with Jenny's brother he thought. He realised now who Jenny was. Why did her name not ring a bell before, he asked himself? Mike Alford was a well-known villain under the 'umbrella' of his car valeting business. Quite a wheeler and dealer of stolen goods and probably drugs. It was a wonder that Brad had not made the link, although he was not involved in that strata of the law; more with business affairs and divorces. How could he warn her without rousing suspicion that his interests were not merely those of a fellow traveller?

But at last he had something to report to Carter. His nose was itching; a sure sign that he was on to something. His expenses were justified and the future was brightening by the hour. He stared out of the coach window, through the raindrops running down the glass again. Everyone had sunk back into a kind of apathy, it seemed. The view of the dark hillsides was gloomy, the silence almost threatening, with an increasing sense of the passage of time; passing minutes already now part of history, no more relevant than the story of the Ugly House. One could hear a universal sigh, it seemed. All lost in thought.

The driver's voice broke into the silence.

'Well folks. You can all relax now and leave the work to me. We will be returning on the coastal road, with time to spend in Conway before heading back to our hotel and an hour or so to freshen up in time for dinner at six-thirty. You may have time to visit the castle, but most certainly plenty of time to wander around the shops and buy your souvenir stuff or pressies and enjoy a coffee break.'

Jenny knew that Caroline had expressed a desire to explore the castle. She herself was not too keen on old ruins as she described them, especially on wet days. The darkness of the stone in the wet gloom of a day like today depressed her, and she hoped that the shortness of time and the prohibitive charge for entry would be deciding factors in their plans. She fancied a sit-down in a cosy cafe with a plate of cream cakes and a large, steaming mug of tea.

Harry was having similar ideas and plans regarding Jenny. He knew that Caroline was intent on exploring the castle and guessed that it was not Jenny's idea of a good time. He decided to volunteer to escort Caroline as he had done at the copper mines, curious to find out more about her interest in adoption, and pretty sure that Jenny would be pleased to escape for a while. He was right as he had anticipated. As they waited to leave the coach, checking the proposed time of departure and of the viability of going far, Caroline decided that an hour would be long enough to see some of the castle if not all of it. Harry used Jenny's tightening of her mouth and raised eyebrows to prompt his response.

'I'll do the same, I think. You can have a coffee and a browse around the shops if you like, Jenny. I know castles are not your scene. You can get rid of that frown. I'll make sure Caroline doesn't get lost or locked in a dungeon.'

Jenny gave him a long stare. Caroline was standing up ready to join the queue of people in the gangway. Harry tipped his head to one side in a gesture of triumph, she thought. She wanted to comment, wanted to wipe the smirk off his face, but instead she nodded. 'What the hell,' she mouthed under her breath.

'Back here for three-thirty,' the driver reminded each cluster of people as they struggled down the steps.

'I am giving the castle a miss, Caroline,' Jenny said. 'I need some caffeine and dry air. You know how I get claustrophobic. I can't do with narrow stairs and passages. Harry is going to keep you company. I'll see you back here.'

Caroline was relieved to see her companion walking off in the opposite direction. This holiday had widened the difference between them. It was not just the bingo, and Jenny's idea of what compromised a good meal, but she had little sense of history. Obviously, Harry was well travelled and she welcomed his input.

Harry mounted the old worn steps of the castle, his arm placed lightly behind Caroline's back. 'This rain doesn't help, does it?' he muttered. 'Nearly there.'

Caroline grunted in acknowledgement. She found his attentions reassuring. She needed to be reassured; needed to have self-worth. She responded to his running commentary of the history of the castle from the guide book, nodding and stopping to look when he directed, but he could tell that her mind was wandering away from the present moment.

He clicked his fingers and she flinched at the sudden movement. 'Penny for them,' he said. 'You are miles away. Lost in time!'

'Sorry. I've got a lot on my mind at the moment.'

'I couldn't help hearing you talking about that programme on the television. I was adopted,' he lied, 'but I have never traced my birth mother. I never really wanted to. It certainly is interesting though.'

Caroline stared, her eyes widening. 'Were you really?' But what if she would like to trace you? I know someone who is trying to find her child. I really must help her if I can. I know it will cost her money but she is quite prepared to do that.'

'She really should get professional help. Those teams use all the experts to produce programmes. I am sure it is not easy.'

'It's worth a go and in any case, she would not like too much publicity. There must be countless people who just need a little guidance and a few facts and figures. Here we are then. Back where we started and with five minutes to spare. That was good timing. I can hear Mrs Ernie already.'

Jenny, approaching from the opposite direction witnessed the relaxed posture and the evidence of shared laughter. I should be part of that, she thought. This is like a cat and mouse game. Waiting for the pounce after the playtime. Caroline was the cat of course, with all of the advantages. Perhaps she did not mean to be cruel, but she was behaving in a high-handed way; totally selfish, Sherry would say. Sherry was right sometimes. She was a good judge of character but was Caroline just so unworldly that she behaved like a spoilt child? Perhaps I can win her confidence with this adoption business, she thought. It was obvious now that Caroline wanted to trace her own child. She did not have any bosom friends, did she? So, it had to be her child. She was certainly saving that doll for somebody. Was she hoping to find a long, lost granddaughter as well? Mike was the one who could help. She would get in touch as soon as they returned home after this holiday.

Brad Carter was pleased with the news from Harry Bainer. It had been a brief telephone call, but he was now alerted to the possible dangers to Caroline through future dealings with Jenny's brother. He was familiar with the man's name, but usually it was shortened to Mike the Fence or Mike the Car Wash. That rogue, like his kind, preferred to stay hidden away as much as possible behind an alias, but of course, he was an Alford. The last person Caroline should get involved with was the local con man. And what was that Jenny up to? He looked at his watch and across to the clock on the kitchen wall as he drew his brows together in a frown. She was Alford's flesh and blood at the end of the day, he reasoned. Same blood in her veins, perhaps even if it was one-sided. No doubt their family relationships were complicated. Their kind always had a variety of loyalties and love affairs. Caroline was so easily taken in by the flattery and fuss.

He had instructed Harry to 'hold fire'. The details were important if they were going to use this information. He checked his calendar. They would be back at the weekend. He would welcome her safe return with a phone call on Sunday, inviting himself around to discuss the sale of some large furniture and somehow broach the subject of adoption. Perhaps a comment on the apparent antiquity of that scruffy doll would prompt some past memories. She was obviously attached to it but why?

He walked into the hall and up the steep staircase, following that familiar route into his mother's bedroom, and standing looking at himself in 'her' dressing table mirror.

'We've got to get rid of that baggage haven't we, Mother? She is like all of her kind.'

He watched his reflection as his lips formed around the words, then turned to look at the photograph in the ornate gilded frame on the bedside table, seeing the familiar stare of those dark grey eyes trapping him into a life time of obedience and loyalty.

A cold shiver snaked up his spine, and he turned away, screwing up his eyes in an attempt to block her image. The grandfather clock in the hall struck seven times, and he checked his watch as he turned and left the room, almost tripping over the frayed edge of the carpet square by the door.

My God, how I need to escape, he thought. This room and all of the memories were haunting him. Possession of Caroline Thorston's inheritance, or at least some of it, was his only chance to restore this house to its former glories, guaranteeing a high sale price, and a chance to be released from its clutches.

The atmosphere was strained as the three of them shared the evening meal. Jenny had had no time for a, so-called, cosy one to one when they had returned to the hotel after the day's excursion. Caroline had stretched herself out on the bed and closed her eyes, and Jenny felt obliged to retire to the side room and look at the travel brochures and small purchases she had made in her solitary wanderings around the town whilst Caroline and Harry had visited the castle. She had bought some postcard views to show Sherry and a small print of a painting done by a local artist portraying the Swallow Falls; a local beauty spot she had wanted to visit, but apparently not part of the excursion owing to health and safety regulations. The print was destined to hang on her living-room wall as a good memory she did not really have. But Sherry would not know that, would she? Harry was good at pretending she thought. What other yarns was he spinning about his worldwide adventures.

Now, at the evening meal, he was being unusually quiet, she thought. He kept glancing at Caroline, suddenly sensing Jenny's hard stare, and giving her a cheeky grin, raising his eyebrows and tilting his head to one side in a triumphant or speculative way it seemed. He was up to no good. She knew his kind. She had grown up with his kind! Suddenly, she realised that, somehow, he was one step ahead. A sixth sense was prompting her. This holiday meeting with him was not a coincidence. It had been planned. She would bet her bottom dollar on that, she thought. She would give Caroline the ear-rings and get back into her confidence. She would have to tread carefully. He was an expert, it seemed, on worming his way in. But what were his motives? Surely, he was not intent on persuading Caroline to marry him. He was too much of a loose cannon for that, she thought. So, was he preparing a hard-luck story? Her ex-partner had woven many a one to paint a bad picture of his life and to persuade the woman behind the desk at the job centre that he was not fit to work and was entitled to benefits.

Her mind was dwelling on the past, and she was recalling the way the charm changed to violent abuse and how she locked her bedroom door and listened for sounds of his violence, hardly daring to venture out into the living room, even though she had heard the front door slam behind him. But then could this Harry behave like that? There must be some decent men around. He was a liar. He had never been to Africa, had he? It was pretty obvious that he was trying to impress Caroline. He knew, didn't he, that he was not impressing me, she thought. That was why he grinned at me. Wasn't it? Conniving bastard!

Caroline's voice broke into her thoughts.

'The entertainer tonight is supposed to be very good. Very classical apparently. Shall we give him a try? I might as well have a go at bingo as well, seeing as it is our last chance this holiday. Tomorrow is packing-up night, isn't it?'

'She won the jackpot,' Harry said, nodding his head in the direction of Jenny. 'Did she tell you?'

'Really! No, not a word. You dark horse! So, are you going to treat us to a book tonight?'

'No. I have spent it.'

Jenny glared at Harry. Now it would look like she was trying to curry favours if she gave Caroline the ear-rings, she reasoned. She would interpret it that way. I could always keep them for myself or give them to Sherry. No, perhaps not. She would put them on a selling site.

Caroline was getting to her feet.

'See you later then,' she said to Harry.

They watched the evening news, from the comfort of the double bed, staring dispassionately at the small screen as the latest threats from terrorist groups increased the depressive levels in their own relationship. It seemed to Jenny that this short break had degenerated into a 'me and you' situation, rather than the cosy union she had anticipated. But why, she asked herself? Was that chasm in their social status too entrenched? Was she herself destined to be of the lower class; always inferior? But then Caroline seemed to have struck a chord in her relationship with Harry Bainer, and he was as common as they come, she thought. So, was it a gender thing? Were either of them ready for a woman to woman relationship, she wondered. Or were they always going to be employer and employee? She cast her mind back to her daughter, Sherry, and her opinions of Caroline. She was pretty well on the ball, she thought. Crude yet shrewd was how she had once described her.

She cast a glance at her companion. She was staring at the screen, yet Jenny could tell by the way she was pursing her lips and fidgeting with her fingers that she was not giving the news items her total concentration.

'Are you OK?' she half whispered. 'You look miles away. This is so depressing. We need to let our hair down tonight. There's a quiz before the bingo session. That should be a giggle.'

Caroline grunted and then sighed. 'I suppose we had better make a move,' she muttered, easing herself forward from her pillow and stretching her legs sideways over the edge of the bed. 'Harry seems enthusiastic about the entertainer. Let's hope he is right.'

Oh well, back with Harry again, Jenny thought. She jumped up, suddenly responding to that surge of rebellion that punctuated her life. She might win at bingo again, and that would be one in the eye for everybody including Harry Bainer.

They squeezed into a corner table, not favoured by the bingo fanatics as Harry described them. The view of the caller was limited by a group of occupied chairs, but his voice over the amplifier was almost deafening, and Caroline shrank back from the harshness and the vulgarity of his expressions and the reactions of the Ernie gang, now over a dozen strong who obliged with the responses, the quacks, and the gestures.

'Like a load of kids,' Caroline sneered.

Jenny nodded. 'Soon be over.' She reached over to pat Caroline's hand, retreating back into silence as Caroline reacted impatiently, pulling the hand back, and reaching up to stroke a wisp of hair away from her face.

'Now for the jackpot. Astonishing, ladies and gentleman. Because we have so many players tonight, the final prize is seventy-five pounds. Wowee.'

Most of the players responded echoing his cry. He waved his hands in the air as though he was conducting an orchestra, Jenny thought. She stole a glance at Caroline. Her companion was now biting her lip and frowning. She was glad to see that Harry was entering into the spirit of it all. Caroline was becoming a real drag. Oh well, it was her loss. Sherry's words echoed in her mind. 'Miserable old bag.' That was always her response to the attitude of older people and for once Jenny was in full agreement. She would give the earrings to Sherry. After all, Caroline would expect real sapphires, wouldn't she?

The caller's voice became monotonous in its rhythm, the numbers appearing on either side of hers, and she found herself losing concentration; knowing that she had no hope of winning as the game dragged on. The silence, apart from the almost hypnotic pronouncement of the numbers bouncing around the room, was suddenly broken by the sound of that dreaded cry.

'House.'

The word seemed to echo through the silence and all eyes left the squared papers to focus on the caller. It was Mrs Ernie. There were some moans of disbelief and the usual post-mortem of who wanted what, as the caller checked the winning sheet.

'It could only be her, couldn't it?' Caroline said to Harry.

Mrs Ernie was looking across to them, now waving the handful of bank notes.

Jenny waved back and stuck up a thumb in acknowledgement. After all, she was one of her kind wasn't she, she thought. The salt of the earth.

The mood in the room changed as the entertainer regaled them with songs from the musicals, and some more upbeat music on his guitar, with all the up-to-date backup programming from his equipment. Jenny was pleased to see that Caroline was impressed, in spite of the fact that a short time earlier she had mentally washed her hands of her employer.

They returned to their rooms tired but lulled into a pleasant mood with the music.

However, Caroline seemed determined to dwell on negativity.

'It had to be that dreadful woman, didn't it? We'll never hear the end of it. I bet that will go straight down their throats, the two of them. Then they will be pleading poverty again,' she said, her face twisting into a scowl.

'Perhaps she has had a hard life,' Jenny muttered. 'It can't be much fun living with Ernie, and who knows what troubles she has had.'

'You are changing your tune. I thought she got right up your nose. We could all claim that we have had bad times. It doesn't mean that we have to go around being a pain to everyone else. Does it?'

Jenny frowned. 'I am going to get to bed,' she responded. 'It's a full day tomorrow. Snowdon. Let's hope the rain keeps away and we get a good view. Of course, it will be nothing to Harry, will it, with his adventures in Africa? I expect he has been up all of those mountains.'

She wanted Caroline to share in with her cynicism, but her response was merely a shrug of the shoulders, and a muffled, 'Who knows.'

Chapter Twelve

There was no sign of Harry the next morning at breakfast. Caroline had made little attempt to converse as they passed each other between the bathroom and their various sojourns into early morning toiletries, apart from a grunt in reply to Jenny's opinion that it was a 'jeans and sweater' day by the sound of the weather forecast.

They did not comment on Harry's absence, concentrating on the choice of egg preparation and whether to have tea or coffee as though either topics were a new innovation at the breakfast table, and Caroline's furtive glances towards the door at the far end of the dining room confirmed Jenny's conviction that her companion valued his company.

At last she broke the silence, watching Caroline's face for any signs of concern.

'I hope Harry is not ill after last night. He did have a lot to drink, didn't he?'

'Did he? I didn't notice. He may have gone for a walk. You know how keen he is on physical exercise.'

Jenny shrugged her shoulders in a gesture of disbelief and muttered, 'Really.'

They returned to their earlier silence, concentrating on buttering toast and deciding on tea or coffee when the waitress arrived to clear the plates.

'Excuse me, I am just going to check. He may be ill and need help.' Caroline approached the reception desk and Jenny could see her pointing up the stairs.

'Oh, I see,' she heard her say, as the woman checked the keys.

'Apparently, he had a restless night and has decided to give the Snowdon trip a miss. He went out during breakfast and has left his key, so perhaps he fancies a quiet day around here. I know how he feels. I am not relishing a ride up Snowdon. It seems to be a wet foggy day forecast, and the lady at the desk said that we will be lucky if the train runs today.' Caroline's comments accompanied her quick steps back to their room.

'Oh well. Like I said, he has been up so many mountains that Snowdon will be nothing to him. Just a hillock I suppose.' Jenny's voice was harsh in her criticism and she cleared her throat noisily as she struggled to keep up.

Two hours later, they alighted from the coach at the tail end of the queue, in no hurry to join the group jostling with waterproof coats and umbrellas. Mrs Ernie, was still bragging of her triumphant win at bingo, whilst she refastened Ernie's coat as though he was a child, Jenny thought as she waited in the next queue at the station. Apparently, he had mismatched the toggles and one side was lower than the other. Previously, she would have shared in the criticism, but today she was in sympathy with the underdogs of this world, standing behind Caroline like some kind of hanger-on, she mused. But then Harry was the hanger-on, wasn't he, she told herself. For goodness sake get a grip!

They sat in the cramped space on the train, their knees in close proximity to the people seated opposite and stared out through the mist at the steeply rising landscape. It was a 'bucket list' venture, Jenny decided. A cheat as well. Number five: 'Climb Snowdon'. She nearly expressed her thoughts out loud, but then changed her mind. Caroline would have no idea of a bucket list, she thought. She glanced sideways at her companion, noticing the closed eyes and drooping mouth. A sudden surge of compassion swept through her.

'Are you OK? You were right about the fog. Never mind. We can get a cup of coffee at the top and we can claim to have done it, can't we?'

Caroline opened her eyes and nodded, drawing her breath in at the same time. 'Harry doesn't know what he has missed, does he?

I suppose we can always pretend that it was amazing. He isn't the only one with an imagination.'

Jenny grinned. That sense of togetherness was back. Who needs men, she mouthed silently, as she stared at the thin bespectacled man in the opposite seat who was gazing fixedly at the steamed-up window.

A mind reader, if such a one existed, would have described the passage of thought in the three fellow travellers as identical, in as much as that Caroline, Jenny and Harry were all contemplating the methods of tracing an adopted child.

Harry was sitting in a restaurant in the shopping centre at Llandudno, a short distance from the hotel, staring at his mobile phone. Brad Carter was demanding more information about the private life of Caroline Thorston and he had little to report. He had to get her on her own and tempt her into more personal disclosures, before the holiday ended, and she was passed, via Jenny Alford, into the clutches of her brother Mike. He was sure that there was a lot of money at stake. If she had given up a child for adoption and was now trying to locate her, then a huge lump sum could pass into the hands of the Alford family. They were crooks. He had a nose for crookery and the trail was becoming stronger, but he liked Jenny, and would prefer to keep it that way, although she was an adversary in this game of cat and mouse. Perhaps she could be an ally, and they both could benefit from Brad Carter's legal skills. But firstly, Caroline had to verify the existence of a child; a daughter presumably, with the doll in mind, or was that part of another story; a fictitious, yet hoped for granddaughter?

Caroline was staring at the trickles of condensation on the window, the monotonous sound of the machinations of the train, dulling her mind. She felt imprisoned, trapped in her thoughts. Harry was an adventurer. She knew that. I am not stupid, she reasoned. But he had such a likeable quality, and his confession that he was adopted had somehow added to his likability. But then what would he know about tracing people? Jenny's brother Mike, was a better proposition. Her mind wandered briefly to her solicitor Brad. He would know all the legalities, wouldn't he? But then she did not trust him after that fiasco at his house. And what did he know about her own adoption? How much paperwork had survived after her parents' death? What did he know about this strange Crystal House? She shivered at the memory of her encounter with the gypsy. How the world had plotted against her. Perhaps she could find another clairvoyant who would know all of the answers. But then such a person would not be in a caravan on the sea front. With such powers she would be a world celebrity, possibly working on the internet. She sighed. Everything these days seemed to be on the web. Perhaps Jenny would know.

Jenny was aware of the warmth from Caroline's body. Contact in this train was so intimate in its lack of space, yet the apparent nearness of her friend exceeded that of the lady on the other side. She could feel her skin tingling under the leg of her jeans and wanted to press even closer. Suddenly it seemed, they were on the same side again. She had to keep the advantage. How could she return to discussing the television programme? How could she encourage Caroline to admit that the lost child was hers rather than that of a friend, and to convince her to share the details with brother Mike? She knew that he would be prepared to investigate. He would name his price, and it would not be cheap. She knew that of course! But then, money was not a problem for Caroline. How grateful she would be! Surely it could not be that hard to trace a missing person with all the records now available on the internet, she mused.

'I suppose we can say we have done it.'

They were back at the hotel, wearied by the long return journey in relentless rain.

Caroline took of her shoes and sank back onto the bed, folding her hands behind her head and closing her eyes.

Jenny nodded. 'We've got time for a bit of a rest before dinner. When does that programme come on again? You know. The one about tracing people. I must tell Mike about it. He is so keen on family history.'

Caroline opened her eyes. 'I have been thinking about it. Did you know that Harry was adopted? He told me the other day. He doesn't seem to care who his real folks were. Perhaps people don't want to know. Perhaps they don't even realise that they were adopted and finding out who they really are could cause a lot of upset.'

Jenny nodded again. That Harry was such a liar! What was he up to?

'I have always thought that it must be awful not to know who you really are,' she replied. 'My father was a bad man, but at least I know he was my father.'

'How can you be so sure?'

'He blamed me for getting stuck in a relationship. My mother was pregnant with me. It was a shotgun wedding as they used to say. I had a dreadful childhood.' Jenny's eyes filled with tears. She felt utterly tired now and the thought of returning to her everyday existence on the following day was now utmost in her mind. Caroline sat up and reached out her hand.

'Oh dear, Jenny. I had no idea. Here's me thinking that I have all the troubles in the world and you have such bad memories. You are right of course. We should know where we come from. I'll let you into a secret but keep it to yourself. Actually, the child I want to trace is my daughter April. I had such guilt about giving her up for adoption, but I had no choice, even though I was eighteen. I had been so controlled by everybody and was so immature. They made me give her up and I have regretted it ever since. But what if she is really happy with her adoptive parents? What if she hates me for abandoning her? These are the questions I ask myself over and over again. In any case, she will be thirty-four years old now, heading towards middle age and not wanting such an upheaval in her life. I was so young, but then old enough to know better, you might say. I was so innocent and trusting.' Her voice broke and she cleared her throat. 'Perhaps she is married with children who love their grandparents. I would be a stranger. How can I disrupt her life? Haven't I done enough harm already?'

'Yes, I know it must be hard, but what if she is not happy? What if she was adopted by bad people, and she longs to know who her real parents are, like that one in the programme? What if she is living in poverty; a single mother with no hope of bettering herself? That woman last week was searching for years. She was desperate to find her mother, and then it was too late, wasn't it? Her mother died during the previous year. Although she did discover that she had a sister. Well, a half-sister I suppose. But still related. You could always find out, and then decide what to do, couldn't you? That's what I would do. If nobody else knew, would it matter? She could have a big family and perhaps look like you. And perhaps have a little girl who reminds you of your mother in the photograph album. Who knows?'

Caroline moistened her lips and sighed. Her mind had moved away from her daughter and was back into her own troubled childhood. Would it have helped if she had known who her real mother was all those years ago? Probably not. She glanced at her companion. She wished she had not shown her that album. She wished she had not told so many lies.

Jenny rushed on, relieved that she was making an impression. 'Do you want me to ask my brother if he can help? I know he is pretty good at it. I can find out what it will involve. I know birth and death certificates are available at a price. That would be a start wouldn't it?'

Caroline nodded. 'We can always stop if we hit any snags, can't we?'

Jenny stood up. 'A nice cup of tea, I think before we freshen up for dinner. And let's see what that Harry has been up to. No doubt he will be full of himself.'

Harry Bainer watched the two friends entering the dining room. They looked relaxed and smiling; both attractive in their middle-aged way. He could quite fancy either of them, although Caroline was the best catch, with all that wealth and breeding. No wonder Brad Carter was panicking. It was pretty obvious what his game was, he thought. And here were two women becoming more than good friends, it seemed. But then he doubted that. Caroline needed some passion and his charms never failed. Even so-called lesbians were putty in his hands. As far as he was concerned, they were just frustrated females needing dominant males. After all, they had both had relationships with the opposite sex. Just because those relationships had failed, it did not make them lesbians. He was ready to accept that Jenny Alford could be as villainous as her brother; they had grown up together in a world of hard knocks, and he surmised that she would have no qualms in engaging in money-making schemes. Yet, at the same time he could not resist using his charms on her, whilst keeping up with his own level of deceit.

'So, did you nearly get drowned on Snowdon? I understand it was a wash-out.'

'It was amazing,' Jenny said.

Caroline hid a smile with her napkin and reached for the menu.

'What's the chef's choice tonight?' she asked. 'I have worked up such an appetite with all that fresh air.'

Harry shook his head. 'No idea,' he replied. 'I thought that you couldn't see a thing through the rain. Mrs Ernie never stopped moaning in the queue about the waste of money. Like you said, Caroline, I bet she has spent her winnings already.'

'Well, we enjoyed it, didn't we, Jenny? It was like being on another planet when we reached the top, and the coffee was very welcome.'

Jenny nodded and raised her eyebrows. Harry had the feeling that there was something he was not being told. They had joined forces, but it was not anything to do with mountain climbing.

'I had a rest this afternoon and caught up on my latest whodunnit,' he said. 'I could do with stretching my legs for a bit. Any offers of company?' He looked at Caroline.

Jenny cleared her throat and frowned. 'We have planned to pack and have an early night. We may listen to the music in the ballroom for a bit and have a farewell drink. But, quite honestly, we have had enough exercise for one day.'

'I'll see how I feel,' Caroline said quietly.

It was Harry's turn to raise his eyebrows, casting Jenny a sideways glance and smirking.

'Give me ten minutes.' Jenny heard Caroline say as they stood up having finished the meal. She did not give Harry the satisfaction of turning around. She could visualise his triumphant grin.

'I'll get on with packing, then we won't get in each other's way. I don't suppose you will be long. I'll catch up on the soaps,' Jenny muttered.

'That's a good idea,' Caroline responded. 'I just want to have one last look at the sea, and the esplanade looks so cheery now the lights are on. I shall miss this coast line.'

'We can always come again. It has been such a treat. I am so grateful, Caroline.'

'Of course. You are such a big help.'

Jenny pressed her lips together. Why did I have to say that, she thought? She was playing right into his hands, putting herself down. But then, she was grateful. It had been so wonderful to escape from the drudgery of her life and to have meals put in front of her. She wanted to stay here for ever and said as much to the lady at reception as she collected the key to their suite. That lady replied that it was cold and windy in the winter, and that she longed to escape.

Harry watched whilst Jenny disappeared through the door, then waited for Caroline to get into step with him. This was probably his last chance to get her on her own, and he did not want to waste it.

'I have been thinking about what you said yesterday, and I got the impression that you know someone who was adopted and wants to trace her real mother.'

'Well, not actually,' Caroline almost stumbled on an uneven paving slab, and Harry grabbed her arm.

'Steady on! I seem to have a bad effect on you. So, is it really you then? Are you looking for a lost mother? Or am I jumping to conclusions?'

'Oh no!' Caroline could feel the colour rushing to her cheeks. No one was to know about Crystal House. That was her big secret. That was put away in the back of her mind until this holiday was over. In fact, it was not as important as finding her daughter.

Harry waited, sure now that she would find the need to explain herself.

'Actually, I'm the missing mother. Perhaps someone is looking for me.'

'Ah. I get it. So, what happened to you then? It's good to get things off your chest.'

Caroline explained briefly that she was forced to give up her daughter, and never understood that she could seek her out, until she had watched that programme.

'I have no idea what happened to her,' she continued. 'Perhaps one day we can fill in the gaps with no bad feelings, but I would not want to cause unhappiness. Jenny says that it would not hurt to trace her birth registration, and possibly find out her whereabouts. What do you think?'

'I would get expert advice if I were you. Have you got a solicitor?'

'Yes, but he does not deal with missing persons. He is looking into my financial affairs after the death of my husband. Jenny's brother seems to be the one who knows about family trees. She is going to see what he can find out. Anyway, that is nothing for you to worry about. Let's take one last look at the lights before we start thinking about going home.'

'She has a daughter and is keen to get some info on her. The cleaner's brother is going to be involved, so it would be a good idea if you make contact, before he gets his hands on her money. She is very open to fraud.'

Harry re-read his text message to Brad Carter before he pressed send. He had been careful not to name anyone. He was of an age when the latest technology appeared to be complicated and threatening. He had no desire to have a Facebook profile and the words hashtags and trolls were in a language he did not embrace. His mobile phone was a 'pay as you go' model, with a minimum of functions. He preferred to just use the text messaging facility but it was amazing to him that he could take such clear photographs with his phone. He had struggled to use a conventional camera in the past, and more often than not half the film was wasted on poor light conditions or in the beheading of a vital witness in the current investigation. Of course,

Brad Carter was also of the old school, he thought, well up in legal matters but relying heavily on his secretary to do all the complicated stuff on the computer. No doubt Mike Alford would be one step ahead of everyone else. He would know how to use technology to his advantage, with the latest smart devices, and probably would come up with all of the answers at top speed, and at a price.

His phone buzzed. That was quick, he thought. Was he sitting on it? The message was brief.

'Good work. Delete.'

So, no further instructions. Fine, he thought. Just sit back now Harry, old chap, and watch the world go by.

Chapter Thirteen

The journey home on the following day was long and tedious, now that the excitement of a week's holiday was a distant sensation. It was as though the travellers had entered into a trance-like state; all communication dulled into a monosyllabic state or merely of grunted responses. The tape recording of music from the fifties and sixties droned on, barely distinguishable through the steady hum of the coach engine, and the rhythmic clicking of the windscreen wipers. It was a relief to stretch leg and back muscles in the queue for the toilets and to exchange the coach seats for the hard, upright chairs in the coffee shop.

The caffeine induced a rush of adrenalin to the brains, dissipating as the travellers returned, slumping back into their seats, and some soon drifting into an unnatural sleep state for this time of the day.

Jenny stared out of the window, no longer excited by the sight of the changing landscape. There was nothing to look forward to, it seemed. Soon, she would be Jenny the cleaner again, her life revolving around vacuum cleaners, lavatories and bleach. Caroline was snoring quietly, her mouth open and her head sunk down onto her chest. Jenny nudged her, and her companion jerked back into an upright position, commenting, somewhat hoarsely, on the raindrops running down the windows.

'Back to the grindstone,' came a voice from behind. Jenny half turned, then decided to ignore the remark. The only good thing about this return to everyday life was the parting with Harry Bainer. She knew his every motive regarding Caroline. He was of her strata in society. On the make, like her ex-partner, she thought, as the jealousy and resentment rose. Caroline had closed her eyes again, and Jenny pressed closer to her, wanting to shield her from the attentions of what her daughter had recently described as male predators. The description had stayed in her mind; the thought of being prey, vulnerable women trapped in a life of servitude and oppression both saddening and sickening her. She was not going back to that ever, she thought. She would fight for Caroline to the ends of the earth. That mental imaging both excited and empowered her, and suddenly she had a future away from the job description of domestic cleaner. Her first step was to contact her brother and set the ball rolling. Harry Bainer was merely a holiday acquaintance.

Time slipped slowly by, and passengers alighted at their home towns calling their goodbyes to the remaining travellers, their voices brightened by the relief of an end in sight and the kettle on the boil. Mrs Ernie and her spouse were sitting closer to the front of the coach. It was their stop next.

'Wake up, Caroline. We are next.' Jenny stood up reaching for the bags wedged in the overhead luggage space. Harry was standing behind her, his strong arms ready to take the strain. Jenny allowed him to pull the duffle bag down, grateful for his input, yet despising herself for her physical weakness. His wink and grin annoyed her. It was not an act of chivalry, she decided, but an acknowledgement of her inferior female status.

'Thanks Harry.' That was Caroline's voice. 'Whatever will we do without you?'

Harry recognised the patronage, as Jenny would have done before her devotion to Caroline had exceeded the mistress and maid status. The lady of the house was back into her own level of society. He would have to tread carefully from now on. His first step was to contact Brad Carter with more details of Jenny's plan to involve that crook of a brother of hers in tracing Caroline's daughter, he decided. He needed to keep Jenny in his sights. Perhaps it was time to alter his tactics. He waited for Jenny to reach for her bag, and gave her an exaggerated wink, pretending to pull at his hair and bow his head in response to Caroline's last words. 'You look after yourself, Jenny,' he muttered.

It was a natural point of separation. Jenny's apartment was within walking distance, and Caroline was heading towards the taxi rank, where a stationery black cab was sited, awaiting the next client. Mrs Ernie gave a desultory wave of her hand, her eyes focused on the back of her husband as he struggled with the large suitcase, Harry was now striding along in the direction of the high street. It was as though they had all become little more than strangers; a bursting of the bubble that had enclosed them for the last week.

Jenny turned her head in time to see Caroline climbing into the taxi, and a deadening sensation clamped down onto her chest, tightening her breathing. There had been no mention of future plans. Was it business as usual, she wondered. She suddenly felt overwhelmed by insecurity.

The short walk between the bus station and the block of flats loosened her stiff limbs, but she arrived at the street level door only to find that the lift was out of action, and the grey concrete steps with the trodden in chewing gum and cigarette ends seemed to be a depressing prelude to her future hours, as she trudged up the three flights. It was as though time had moved her back, she thought. It was like being in a game. But then what was the reality. 'This of course'. She answered herself out loud, ignoring the jeering grin of the youth who ran past her.

The key turned stiffly in the lock, and she pushed her case through beyond the half opened door into the narrow space she called the porch. The living-room door was open and the stuffy air, thick with cigarette smoke caught at her breath. Sherry had been there recently. She sank down into the armchair aware of its shabbiness and of the cooking odours persisting in the grease on the cooker top and in the washing up bowl. The cold tap was dripping; the sound like a ticking clock counting down her life.

Now, the holiday seemed like a dream; full of surprises and pleasures, the prepared meals, the new vistas. Yet in spite of all of that, she had been beset with insecurity; a deep apprehension of where she was in the great scheme of things; servant, companion, lover?

'Oh! Who am I kidding?' She threw the question out into the silence, startled by a squawk coming from the cage in the corner.

'Oh, goodness, you made me jump! Sorry, Polly, old thing. Did I scare you?'

She reached forward and pulled back the ragged piece of blanket that was draped over the bird-cage. The parrot put her head on one side, fixing her owner with a beady reproachful eye, or so it seemed to Jenny.

'Oh, my God, Polly! She hasn't done a thing has she, except to throw some seed in? And no water either.'

Jenny burst into tears, and Polly responded with, 'Give us a kiss. Give us a kiss.'

All of the pent-up love Jenny felt for Caroline, was released for her pet. In that moment, she identified with the creature. The parrot, like her, had all the bare necessities to survive, yet she too was enclosed; imprisoned in her circumstances.

Jenny opened the door of the cage. 'Come on, Polly,' she said. 'Stretch your wings while I clean out your cage.'

The bird put her head on one side and made no attempt to venture out.

She is traumatised, Jenny thought. Could a bird become traumatised? Was she herself traumatised by life? Was it too late to change even after the week's holiday? Could she spread her wings, or were they clipped so short that even the previous week of freedom would have no life-changing consequences?

Caroline handed the cab driver a five-pound note with a dismissive wave of her other hand.

The man touched his cap and grinned. 'Have a nice day,' he said.

She ignored the sarcasm in his voice and waited whilst he drove away before pulling her suitcase into the driveway.

The front paved area had taken on an air of neglect in her short absence of one week. She stared incredulously at the prolific growth of dandelions in the cracks, their yellow blossom heads bright against the grey slabs and their flat green leaves spreading into rosettes. He would have a fit, she thought, her mind leading guiltily back to the buried can of 'weed killer'.

The front door creaked as she pushed it open. That was new! The sound seemed to echo in the emptiness, and she had the strange sensation that she must tip-toe like an intruder. The lounge had an air of expectancy she felt, a kind of frozen in time feeling, waiting for company. No cat, of course. It was too late now. She would collect her from the cattery tomorrow. She made her way up the steep staircase struggling to carry the suitcase, unable now to take advantage of the wheels. The same feeling of desolation greeted her as she put the case on her bed and walked back onto the landing. Now she had the impression that she was a ghost, and for a moment or two enjoyed the fantasy, but then the feeling of loneliness was back. She recalled how she had always felt lonely after a holiday, even though life had returned to normal. Loneliness was her normality. But then did she want to share her life with Jenny and her family? Shared confessions of abuse were not a basis for the sharing of confidences. Apparently, Jenny's brother was good on the computer but then she did not know him. What about Harry? He was more with it, as they said. But then, according to Jenny, he had a run-of-the-mill kind of phone. Was that because he was unworldly or as Jenny implied, mean and cunning. Jenny did not like Harry. In fact, she made it quite clear that she did not trust him.

Suddenly Caroline felt threatened by the people who her parents and her late husband described as working class. In her mind they all became predators. But then she had described David, the father of her child, as a predator, a paedophile had she not? What difference did money and breeding make? But she had loved him. That was the difference! If, there was a knock on the door now, and he was standing on her doorstep, she would welcome him with open arms, open heart, open everything she thought. Her mental imaging invoked physical responses and her breasts tingled, the sensations travelling down her body. Perhaps he was waiting for her in the fullness of time. Was that eternity? That world of the spirit, where, free of physical encumbrances, she would have no fear of punishment. She could be how she chose to be. But then, perhaps her destiny was to be with him in the land of the living. After all, he was the father of their child. Perhaps he too was looking for April. Perhaps he was on his own now. Perhaps he was divorced or a widower. She pulled at her ear, as he used to do to signal his passionate desires and tried to recall the expression in his eyes. Were they grey or blue? Oh God, I can't remember, she inwardly moaned.

That emotive memory of the past and of her lover's possible role in her future, propelled her mind towards her earlier plans, and she walked quickly into the kitchen to fill the kettle in readiness for a cup of tea, comforted by this act of everyday normality. She decided to see what Jenny's brother could unearth using his family-tree skills, and she would find David, and confront him with his responsibilities of fatherhood.

'I don't care if I am rocking the boat,' she muttered.

Harry Bainer strode along without a backward glance. The coach overtook him on its continuing journey to the final drop-off point. The driver hooted, and Harry waved his hand and grinned broadly. He had shared some time at the bar with him, a short overweight man, typical, it seemed, of his sedentary occupation with hours spent travelling backwards and forwards trapped behind the steering wheel. He did his best, Harry mused. It was not easy to please everyone with his choice of recordings and his chat. His jokes were a bit on the crude side, raising cackles from the likes of Mrs Ernie, he recalled. Caroline was not amused. 'We are not amused.' Who said that? Some important woman. I bet he'll be glad to offload his last passengers. But then it could all begin again tomorrow. One man's meat is another man's poison. His mother used to say that. She was full of sayings. What would she say now about his dealings with Brad Carter?

He was close to the supermarket and in need of milk and bread before he settled down for the evening in his flat over the local barber's shop on the high street. Would it be a good move to knock on the solicitor's door, or would that blow his cover? He decided to give Carter a ring on his mobile phone.

He stepped into the doorway space of an empty shop, half turning away from passing shoppers, and cupping the phone against his ear, ready to converse.

'Brad Carter speaking.'

'Brad,' Harry's voice was hoarse; almost a whisper. 'I'm close to your house. Shall I pay you a call? I've got a space to bring us up to speed.'

There was a brief silence followed by a gruff 'OK.'

Harry smiled. He was skint and Carter owed him. The solicitor maintained that he paid on results. Well there were plenty of results this time, and plenty of action to come. Usually he was invaluable in digging up the dirt, so to speak, in divorce cases, but he knew that Carter's plans involved his personal relationship with Caroline Thorston and her wealth.

So, play your cards right, Harry old boy. Just be a little backward at coming forward. That was another of his mother's expressions, bless her! Don't worry. Mum's the word! He grinned at his cleverness as he raised the door knocker and allowed it to drop onto the metal plate with a thud. The net curtain twitched and he straightened his back in readiness to do battle and restore his battered resources.

Brad Carter said, 'Five minutes,' looking at his watch, and checking the time with the clock on his desk.

Harry followed his gaze, noting the neat array of stationery aids on the desk; a stapler, a paper hole punch, a small pair of scissors, and red and black ball point pens. Of course, he knew that his employer was precise in his methods, yet he was aware of that lack of surety showing in his nervous clearing of the throat, and his quick glances at his watch.

He decided to make the opening gambit, needing to impress Brad with his observations of his wealthy client Caroline Thorston, and his suspicions that she was about to throw herself into the grip of a local criminal. So far, he had merely alerted his employer to the dangers, dangling the information in brief text messaging. More details were worth more wages, and he was enjoying his unusual position of power. However, he was not prepared to divulge any more information verbally. He had not deleted the text messages as Brad had requested, and now he was in a strong bargaining position with the promise of a written report warranting further reward. He was determined to stand his ground. 'You stand your ground, my lad.' That was his mother again.

'I won't take up much of your time, because you will want a written report, but time is money for both of us, so I would like some money up front, and this is my expenses claim for time spent at venues involving entrance fees, and taxis, etc and goodwill towards gaining the lady's confidence.' He gave a wink and was pleased to see a frown appear behind the horn-rimmed glasses balanced on Brad Carter's nose.

The solicitor pulled open a drawer in his desk and took out a tin. The words 'Petty Cash' were written in bold black ink. Harry frowned and raised his eyebrows. Petty indeed. He would see about that. Brad Carter and his like charged a hundred pounds a letter. His information was worth at least fifty. However, he tempered greed with caution.

'I will need about twenty extra for my time spent putting everything on paper. I have only kept a rough diary. So, how about I do it later and pop it through your letter box tomorrow?'

Brad frowned and then nodded, carefully counting out fifty pounds for expenses and adding a twenty-pound note from his wallet.

Harry noticed the thick wad of notes left in the wallet, and the bitterness created by a life of constant hardship gnawed into his consciousness.

Brad Carter closed the heavy door, scarcely allowing the space and the time for his employee to exit the premises. He looked at his watch, checking the accuracy of the old grandfather clock in the hall, tutting at the difference of half of a minute. Five minutes, Harry had said, but in actual fact it had been seven. He quickened his steps into the drawing room in an attempt, it would seem, to challenge the passage of time.

He sank down into his favourite armchair, crossing one leg over the other and tightening his fingers into fists. During the week of Caroline's absence, he had sifted back through years of paperwork involving the Thorston family, some of it going back to when his father was the legal adviser and he was intrigued to find loose threads concerning the hasty marriage arrangements of his present client Mrs

Thorston. It would seem that there were secrets in her family, and her present interest in tracing a child was a strong link with the past.

He frowned at the thought of her putting her trust in the likes of Jenny Alford's family. Mike Alford was a slippery customer; well known in the antique trade for receiving and handling. He could not be allowed to get his hands on Caroline's money.

'Time must be on my side,' he muttered, looking at the clock on the wall, and then down at his watch. Harry was the ideal man to spy and according to his promised notes on the week spent in the company of Caroline and Jenny, it should be easy to keep one step ahead.

He went out into the garden where the darkness of late autumn was stealing the colours of the herbaceous border, creating deep shadows amongst the trees on the undulating boundary. He sighed, his mind as always back with Elizabeth and the lost ring. This nightly vigil gnawed at his soul but he had to do it, in the same way as he had to go into his mother's room each night before he went to bed, standing at the dressing table in front of the cut-glass vase containing her ashes.

Now, his steps lead him away from the garden, back through the French doors. He looked at the clock. The hour hand was pointing to nine, and the minute hand was edging its way to the ornate gold marker, signifying the completion of the hour. He reached for the bottle of wine, already uncorked in readiness for the evening ritual, and carefully poured out a measure into the waiting glass.

Chapter Fourteen

Monday morning arrived, damp and dreary with a forecast of more of the same to follow. Caroline had been awake since first daylight, listening to the radio, her mind wandering in and out of her memories of the previous week. It seemed like a nothing kind of time now, she mused, and yet so much had passed through her awareness. So, what was next in the great scheme of things? She smiled behind the tight edge of the duvet, her hands gripped across her stomach, and her feet stretched down the length of the bed. Bare necessities, of course. Food was a must, even though it was always way down on her priorities. But then could she eat on her own now? She was missing Jenny already, and she needed to collect the cat.

As she went through her daily ritual of showering and dressing, with a perfunctory effort to unpack her case in the process of returning to some kind of normality, she tried to prioritise her future actions. Yet the gypsy's words bounced around in her memory. Her mother was still alive in a place called Crystal House. Could it be true? How could she believe a gypsy at a seaside resort? But yet it would explain the family likeness between herself and the man she called Father, her actual father. It would explain her adoptive mother's comments and hatred, and the punishments she herself endured. She must ring Jenny, she decided, as she stirred the coffee granules into the steaming mug of milk. Of course, she knew that she needed help to continue with the organisation and disposal of the excesses of the house contents, and the question of her daughter hung like a gigantic question mark in her mind. So, do something about it then, her mind demanded.

She reached in her bag for her phone, carefully following the process of locating Jenny's number. Jenny had spent some time in educating her in modern ways, and she fumbled now, determined not to fall back into her old ways of relying on a landline. The purchase of a new, cordless system was on her list, according to Jenny.

It was ringing. 'Come on, Jenny,' she muttered.

'Hello Caroline. Are you OK?'

'Just having my coffee and wondering what to do with my day. We need to get back into routine, don't we? There is still a lot to do if you can get around here today or do you want to go back to your old work times?' Caroline heard the sharp intake of breath. 'Are you OK? Did you sleep well?' she asked. 'Oh, don't worry about my jobs. Let's meet up in the town. I really need to do some shopping but can't be bothered to cook. You know what I am like! To be quite honest I can't get that lost families programme out of my mind. Perhaps you could have a word with your brother when you have some spare time. Anyway, come here and we can decide what to do. See you later.'

'You're tarted up, Mother. So, what are you up to then?' Sherry had let herself in moments after Jenny had put her breakfast dishes to soak in the sink.

'Mind your own business. It's a good job I don't have to rely on you. Poor Polly was in a right state and no doubt old Mrs Bagley was abandoned. But then what can I expect. You have such a busy life.'

Jenny glared at her daughter and pushed past her to reach for her coat and bag.

'Now, if you don't mind,' she continued, 'I am going to meet Caroline for coffee, and you needn't light up. I don't want to smell like an ash tray, thank you.'

'Oh! Get you! Don't worry! And, for your information I did do the old bag. She was really happy and said that I was a damn sight better than you and she would be sorry to have you back again.' Sherry pushed past her mother and slammed the door behind her.

Jenny was immediately sorry for her comments. Sherry did not look well and at the end of the day, she thought, she was the only family she had. She was reminded that Caroline was desperate to trace her daughter. But then sometimes ignorance is bliss as her mother used to say. What if this April, or whatever she was known as now, was totally different to her mother? What if she was in an unhappy marriage or even, God forbid, was a drug addict or prostitute? What can of worms would Caroline be opening? A lot of investigation was necessary before she committed herself to a life-changing relationship. She was so naive in spite of the wealth and privileges. Jenny decided not to bring the subject up today or if necessary to change the subject. It was best to have business as usual, she thought. There was plenty to occupy them still, with more of Mr Thorston's family valuables to be cleaned and disposed of. And then there was the contents of the loft; a dusty job for someone. But not for me, she thought.

She hurried her steps to the bus stop, casting anxious glances back along the main road leading away from the town. She was missing her car already, even though it was a major source of worry during those last few weeks before the holiday. Still, it had done well and 'he' had paid for it, albeit little more than scrapyard value. Perhaps Caroline would lend her some money. A few hundred pounds would be nothing to her. Perhaps she would bring up the subject of April after all. Caroline would be so grateful.

The bus was almost empty, and she chose a seat halfway along, nodding greetings to a woman whose face looked familiar. She recognised so many people, yet was merely on nodding terms, she mused. But then did she care? The only person she wanted to be with was Caroline. She stared dispassionately at the rows of houses, being replaced by clusters of bungalows as they neared the town boundary. She was not familiar with the position of the bus stops and jumped to her feet with an exclamation of impatience as she saw Caroline's house disappearing out of view. She lurched along the gangway and the driver obligingly pulled up and allowed her to hurry down the steps. He gave her a cheery grin, and she was grateful for his act of chivalry, rare these days in her perceived world of male chauvinism.

However, such warmth of feeling towards the opposite sex was eroded by the sight of the solicitor's car in Caroline's driveway. So what did he want? Jenny pushed at her hair and straightened her back out of its weary posture. Let battle commence, she thought. Bring it on.

She went around to the back of the house and tapped on the door. Caroline's face appeared on the other side of the glass. She was grinning broadly and wagging her thumb in the direction of the lounge. It was a conspiratorial gesture, and Jenny giggled, her spirits lifting.

'Could you carry on as normal?' Caroline whispered. 'I have to listen to his latest plans to get a good market value, etc. I really don't care at the moment, but he will be out of our way and we can talk about you know what.' She disappeared back into the lounge, closing the door behind her.

Jenny resented the barrier of the door, but then accepted it as part of Caroline's plan to get the solicitor out of the house, rather than any secrecy on her part. In any case, the washer was on a long programme, and the sound of the motor masked any of the conversation taking place.

Brad Carter had settled himself into the armchair closest to the coffee table, spreading some papers down on the polished surface.

'Nearly there,' he said. 'These are the last lists and statements to be assessed, and you will soon be a woman of substance as they say, and all of the money accrued can be credited to your account. These things can go on and on. I have taken the opportunity whilst you have been away and progress has been halted on current matters, to look into your late husband's family history. My late father dealt with it. It all fascinates me, and money was paid over to be invested at the time of your marriage, by your mother's family it seems. It is now held in trust for you, and seems to be rather hidden away, so there is still plenty of paperwork. I expect you know about that though. Anyway, it will all be yours soon, and you will be free to move on.'

Caroline mouthed her thanks. She had no idea what he was talking about. Could it have been some kind of dowry, she wondered? Did Robert have to be bribed to take her on, damaged as she was, and why was it from her mother's family? She had always been led to believe that her father was the wealthy one. Her heart was thudding and she clutched the arm of the chair, her veins standing out on the backs of her hands. She wanted to ask if there was any reference to a Crystal House. Did such a place exist? But finding April must come first. In any case she wanted to keep the details of her own background out of the clutches of Brad Carter. He was becoming far too familiar, and she did not trust him with her personal affairs. As soon as he had completed all of the necessary legalities of her late husband's will she did not wish to continue the present relationship. It had gone beyond the bounds of business, and she had decided to engage a different legal adviser when everything was resolved.

She listened and nodded as he explained the lists of investments and whether he would advise selling or waiting. She had no idea what he was saying. She was desperate to get him out of the house and share a morning break with Jenny.

Brad looked at his watch. 'I must dash,' he said. 'I have another client at eleven.'

Jenny heard the slam of the front door, and moments later the sound of his car engine firing into action. At the same time, the washer buzzed at the end of its programme, and she opened the door to remove the contents, and put them into the basket ready for drying.

'Thank God he has gone. Now Jenny. Leave that and let's get some details down for your brother.' Caroline had come into the kitchen and was tugging at Jenny's arm. Jenny wanted to hug and kiss her, but obediently followed Caroline into the sitting room. She sat down in the armchair which Brad Carter had recently occupied, first plumping up the cushion, and stroking her hand across the seat.

Caroline laughed. 'You can't help it, can you? You always have to straighten cushions. Brad Carter can't help checking the time. I'm sure we all have little habits.'

'You pull at your ear when you are thinking about something.'

'Do I really? I wonder why.'

Jenny noticed how the colour flooded into her friend's cheeks and also wondered why.

'I must fetch my cat. She will think I have abandoned her,' Caroline announced.

'My Polly was miserable. Did I tell you I have got a parrot? Sherry was supposed to feed her but she was in such a mess, poor bird and had no water. She has hardly said a word except "Give us a kiss".'

Caroline laughed, and Jenny had to share in with her reaction, even though it was not really funny. Now, they were back in their holiday mood, it seemed, and Jenny moved the topic of conversation on to the internet and the tracing of lost people.

'So, are you going to give me some details of your daughter? All I know is that you call her April. I don't see much of my brother, but my daughter does. She would pass on the information about April's birthday and where she was registered. I think that is all you need.'

'That is what they do on that programme, but it depends on whether she has a new name, doesn't it?'

'Well, my brother does seem to be good at it. If he can't do it, then we will have to get some advice.'

'Brad might know.'

'Do you think so? He always seems to be agitated. He's got some funny ways. Look how he gave you too much to drink, and then put you in that weird bedroom. Anyway, I've brought a notepad. Was April her only name?'

'Yes. I wanted it to be Caroline in the middle, but my mother said that I was to distance myself from her. It was a family disgrace and not to be talked about by family or friends.'

'So, it was April Pearson, and father unknown? What date was it? April the what?'

'April the fifteenth 1983. I was eighteen on October the fifteenth. It seemed significant. We were sharing the same number.'

'Oh. That was nice. So, when was she adopted then?'

'She was nearly a month old. Wasn't that cruel? Although they only let me feed her, and she was taken away in between. My adoptive mother was very possessive I remember. Perhaps she wanted a baby of her own and had to adopt me instead. So, why did she hate me so much?'

Jenny stopped writing and leaned over to reach for Caroline's hand.

'Did she hate you? What makes you think that? You had more than I ever had. You were lucky.'

'I was punished constantly. Locked in a cupboard under the stairs for hours. I was so glad when she died.'

'But she looks so nice in the album, and you looked very happy.' Jenny hesitated. 'I had a terrible childhood. My mother allowed me to be abused. At least that didn't happen to you.'

Caroline pulled her hand away and sat back in her chair. The colour had flooded to her face. Jenny recognised the signs of embarrassment. She always did that, she thought. What other secrets was she hiding, like keeping the photograph album in the airing cupboard and the Great Majesto with the holes stabbed in his eyes? Was he her father or perhaps the abuser, she wondered?

'Only by him of course,' Caroline was saying. 'But I did not think of that as abuse at the time. I can see now that he took advantage of me, but I was so happy to be loved.'

Jenny returned her attention to the notepad.

'So, shall we say that she was adopted round about the middle of May 1983? Whatever you decide we have to keep to that, don't we?'

Caroline nodded. The secret strands in her memory being drawn out into the public domain were paining her dreadfully. This was the only time she had ever shared such details of her baby's birth. Could she allow it to pass into the hands of strangers, albeit Jenny's family? But it was too late now, wasn't it, she asked herself? The cat was well and truly out of the bag, as her mother had said when the pregnancy was confirmed.

'Have you got Mike's telephone number? I tried the one I have and it doesn't seem to connect.'

Jenny was back in her flat, listening to the usual list of daily disasters in her daughter's life, but with the time spent with Caroline uppermost in her mind.

'Oh, I expect he has got a new number. You know what he is like; ducking and diving. Anyway, knowing what you're like, the number you have is probably donkeys' years old.'

'Oh, don't exaggerate, for goodness sake!' Jenny frowned. 'We haven't had mobile phones for that long.'

'Really! Perhaps you haven't. Anyway, why this sudden interest in Uncle Mike? I thought you couldn't stand him. Have you taken my advice and collared some of the family silver? He would soon shift it. No questions asked.'

'I know he takes chances. But then he does have a legitimate business as well. He isn't a scrounger. I just want to see if he can trace someone. He gets on well with family history, doesn't he?'

'This wouldn't have something to do with your Mrs Thorston, would it?'

'If you must know it's about tracing her daughter.'

Sherry's face lighted up into a smile and then a wide grin.

'Is it really? This gets more like a soap every time I see you. So now what? Was she raped by the gardener and disgraced the family by giving birth to a council house brat? Oh, dear me, what a shame.'

'I have no idea of the circumstances. All I know is that she is trying to find her daughter who was adopted. She doesn't want to approach these television people who are doing a programme about adoption. Too much publicity I suppose. But I told her that it all seems easy to find out on the internet these days. Mike has gone back a long way, hasn't he? Last time I saw him he was talking about our family tree. Apparently, we have royal blood in our veins. Something to do with Scotland and a castle.'

'A fat lot of good that has done us. I must say. Obviously, we are the poor relations. But then I'm not sure whether it is a good idea for this Caroline to poke around even if she is loaded. What if this daughter doesn't want to be found? What if she doesn't know she was adopted?'

'I think Caroline just wants to know where April has ended up. It must be hard for her to confess her past secret life. Surely you can understand that. It was such a disgrace in the past. Abortions were dangerous. Lots of women died and many had to agree to adoption. Nowadays, young women don't seem to care as long as they get a house and benefits.'

'That's a bit harsh, Mother. Perhaps they actually prefer to stay single.'

'Anyway, the registration details are in this envelope. Date of birth and name at the time of adoption. She is willing to pay for the services and don't go spreading this about.'

'As if!'

✳

Harry Bainer sat at a table in the Black Swan, watching Mike Alford, who was standing at the bar. Harry could see a family resemblance. The features were an enlargement of Jenny's he decided: a largish nose, slightly hooked, and a pointed chin. His hair was receding and greying at the temples, and there the resemblance ended; Jenny's thick, bouncy curls having a reddish hue. He had ordered a pint of beer and was looking at his watch. At that moment a woman came in and looked around. Harry recognised her as Jenny's daughter, Sherry. He had seen photographs of her on Jenny's phone and since the holiday and his continued instructions from Brad. Carter to track Jenny's movements, he had watched her leaving her mother's flat on the previous day, and then by walking closely behind her, he had listened to her telephone conversation with her uncle. This job was not rocket science he had thought with a grin, as she made it apparent to all and sundry that she was speaking to her Uncle Mike. 'Black Swan tomorrow at twelve, Uncle Mike. See you then, Uncle Mike. No, I can't explain on the phone. It's to do with my mam, but it could put a bit your way, and me as well.'

Harry activated the voice recorder in his pocket and walked to the bar. Sherry was handing over a sheet of paper. 'These are the child's details,' she said. 'This woman will want some kind of proof of identity, won't she? It could be worth a few quid. She is loaded. I bet you could come up with something. Don't forget I want a share.'

'Now, I wonder where you get your cheek from? Tell your mother I'm on to the case. No, better not. She will panic. Tell her I am pleased to be able to help. Cheers.' He raised his glass with dregs of beer left in the bottom, pushing the piece of paper into his pocket.

'Don't I get a drink then?' Sherry grinned, changing the grin to a scowl as he turned to go.

'Another time, darling,' he said, also grinning and exposing nicotine-stained teeth behind a ragged growth of beard. 'I'll be in touch.'

An hour later, Brad Carter was listening for the second time to the brief recording of the conversation that had taken place in the public house.

Then he said, 'Mrs Thorston ought to be warned. How can she be so naive? I knew that woman was trouble from the moment I laid eyes on her. My mother had endless problems with domestics.'

'It's not going to be easy,' Harry said. 'I could blow my cover. At the moment Caroline trusts me. I am not sure of Jenny Alford. Actually, I think she is innocent in all of this. It's not greed motivating her. She would like to share more than money with Caroline Thorston, if you get what I'm saying.'

'What, she's gay, you mean? Do you think so? She's obviously had a relationship and a child, and there's no way that Caroline would entertain anything like that. Not that we have ever discussed such things, but you can tell, can't you?' The solicitor shifted on his chair and cleared his throat.

'Perhaps she was not allowed to be herself. It happens.' Harry stared at his employer. He had heard rumours about him, but he had dismissed them as idle gossip. Brad Carter was just eccentric, and his motives were obviously money-based; not greed, but ambition.

'Oh well. We shall just have to see how it goes. It's not easy to trace people with just the date of birth. Her name was changed no doubt and it becomes a closed book in many cases. I will try to steer her in another direction. Keep an eye on things. Payment on results as usual.' Brad opened the petty cash tin and took out a five-pound note.

'I'll take a cheque if you are short of the readies,' Harry said.

Brad grunted, and picked up the phone, waving his hand for Harry to leave.

'Miserable bastard,' Harry muttered. He should keep in touch with Jenny but he was not sure of a welcome. Caroline liked him. She was really in need of a shoulder to cry on, he decided. He knew where she lived. That had been easy. Her address had been on her luggage label on her case. He had made a note of it as soon as he could. Of course, Brad Carter had all of her personal details, but he wanted to avoid any entanglements. It was so easy to slip up, and he had to have his story word perfect. So, how to do it? That was the question. He had not the energy to hang around in her neck of the woods waiting for a chance meeting, he decided. He would have to box clever. Why would he have the need to knock on her door? It would have to be something they had in common. The holiday of course – a competition? What if, apparently, he had seen details of a competition based on comments about a holiday spent through the local travel agency and decided that Caroline could win? What if he told her that she was so clever with words that she ought to have a try? But then what if she investigated it and found that it was not true? No, he decided. She was not the kind of person who would go in for anything like that. Why would she with her wealth? So, it would be a reason to knock on her door, wouldn't it? She would be pleased to see him, because she would be flattered. He knew that she needed his brand of charm; a little bit of rough, and that she would be back on his radar, so to speak with the latest developments in the Alford family.

'Guess who came yesterday.'

'That Brad Carter?'

'No.'

'The window cleaner? The Queen?'

'Now you are being silly.'

'Well I don't know. I'm not a mind reader. Not like your gypsy.'

Jenny had taken off her coat and hung it on the coat stand next to Caroline's expensive suede jacket.

Caroline frowned and Jenny immediately regretted her reference to what she assumed was an unwelcome reminder of that incident in their holiday.

'Sorry. I am tired. Not a brilliant night's sleep last night. So, who was it then?'

'That Harry, whatever his name is.'

'Holiday Harry? Harry Bainer? What did he want and how does he know where you live?'

Caroline shrugged her shoulders and frowned.

Jenny tutted impatiently. Harry was not the kind of person to make social calls. She was sure that there was more on his agenda. In fact, his attachment to them on holiday had seemed to her to be more than a coincidence, and yet she could not fathom out why.

'It was something about a competition. A promotion run by the holiday company. He wondered if I was interested. I told him that it was not my kind of thing. He didn't stay long.'

'He's a chancer. Just watch out. I don't believe a word he says.'

Caroline grunted and stood up to look out of the kitchen window, her thoughts apparently moving on to the state of the garden, and how she would need some help this year in helping it into its winter state.

'Do you know a general gardener, Jenny? Have I asked you that before?'

'No and yes. Actually, to get back to now, I have some good news about tracing your daughter. My brother is willing to investigate on the site he uses for tracing family links. I have given him the dates, etc and he says he will do his best. He can't promise anything but something may turn up. Apparently, it is all a bit of a lottery. That reminds me. A friend of mine went to see a spiritualist. He was amazing, she reckoned. I saw a poster about some famous one coming to the community hall. Do you fancy going?'

Caroline shook her head. 'Not really,' she replied. Let the dead stay dead, she thought. There were too many horrors in her past. She wanted no contact with a medium or with fortune tellers. Suddenly, her thoughts were back with the gypsy and with Crystal House. Where was it, and what did it have to do with her mother now? Did she really want to know? Did she really want to know anything about anybody? Why not let the past stay buried like that husband of hers in the cemetery with the fancy headstone now marking his grave?

'Shall I come over on Tuesday as usual then?' Jenny asked.

Caroline nodded her head.

Chapter Fifteen

Caroline held the phone away from her ear. Jenny's voice was harsh with excitement.

'He's found her birth details, and you can apply for a certificate if you want one. It is a copy of course, but people mislay them and it is easy to get another one. If you write a request, he can do it for you. It has to be a next of kin, I think. So, that's a good start isn't it. I knew he would sort it. He is really switched on to the internet. By the way, there is a fee for this service of a hundred pounds. Can you make it payable to 'MA Valeting Services'? This is his only account and the same one he uses for his family tree sites apparently.'

Caroline was shaking with excitement as she put the phone down on the table. He had not found April. She realised that of course, but it would be so good to be able to see that proof of her birth; that significant day in her own history, when her child first saw the light of day, and she became a mother. They could never take that away from me, she thought. She was a mother, a title never truly held by her adoptive mother, who she now knew was, in reality, according to the gypsy, merely her aunt.

The sudden ringing tone of the phone made her jump. 'Jenny,' she gasped. 'Is it still OK? Gosh I'm all of a shake.'

'Caroline! It's only me. Are you all right. You sound as though you are having a fit or something. Shall I come round?'

'Oh Harry! Goodness me, you made me jump. I have just had such wonderful news from Jenny about April.'

'I am coming over. Just checking to see if you are at home. I've got some good news as well about that holiday competition. I'll see you in about ten minutes.'

Caroline half staggered to the chair, almost sitting on Marigold, and dislodging the doll's wayward shoe in the process. Her mind was racing. Did she want Harry to be here? Should she disclose her secrets to a comparative stranger? What exciting news should she tell him other than the discovery of the birth certificate? But then he knew that she was intent on finding April. It was no secret and certainly no crime.

Harry tapped out a message on his phone. 'MA made the first move. I am on my way to C's.'

'Over and out,' came the reply.

Harry shook his head and grinned. Carter thinks he is on a deadly mission, he thought. He would be checking on the time and expecting news within the hour no doubt. James Bond, Secret Agent! Who was he kidding?

As he waited for the arrival of the town bus, the cheeky grin left his face. Caroline was really getting into a dangerous situation with Mike Alford, he mused. That crook could fleece her. She set so much importance in protecting her privacy, yet here she was putting her faith in such a confidence trickster. And how could Jenny be so hoodwinked by her brother? But then she was besotted with Caroline and would do anything to keep in favour. Poor Jenny! She had endured a hard life and it was not likely to get any better in his opinion. She was well enmeshed in servitude whereas he, somewhat optimistically, fancied his chances on equal terms with Caroline Thorston, with a future of leisure to follow. 'Keep in there, kiddo,' he told himself. The best way forward was to play one off against the other until he was the only one left standing with Caroline and her fortune within his hands.

Caroline retrieved the felt shoe from the floor and pulled it back on the doll's foot. 'Naughty Marigold,' she mouthed.

The ringing of the doorbell brought her mind back from the past, where she had been briefly wandering into times still so indelibly printed in her memory, propelling her feet towards the sound.

She opened the door coming face to face with Harry's cheeky grin, such exuberance re-igniting the excitement she had experienced earlier, and she walked ahead of him back into the drawing room, with renewed vigour in her step, and the previous euphoria back in the place of that brief, negative sojourn into her past life.

'Come on, Marigold. Move yourself.' Caroline picked up the doll and pushed her behind the chair.

Harry did not comment, noticing how Caroline's cheeks were flushed, and contemplated his next move. 'Slowly, slowly, catchee monkey,' he said inwardly. His mother used to say that.

He waited whilst Caroline was sitting in the chair before he sank down on to the couch, repositioning a cushion, and resting one hand on the arm, smoothing the surface of the seat with his other hand as though he was removing dust.

'Make yourself at home!' Caroline exclaimed. 'Has Jenny missed a bit?'

'Oh no. That's a habit of mine. Sorry. I'm sure Jenny doesn't stint on her cleaning. She's done it for long enough, hasn't she? So, what's your good news then, or shouldn't I ask?'

'It's nothing so amazing really. It's just that Jenny's brother has traced April's birth certificate. Of course, I knew the birth was registered but I never saw the document so it is just proof that she exists.'

'The problem is going to be in identifying her now though, isn't it? Do you have any idea who adopted her?'

'No, not yet, but then one step at a time. I just want to be able to hold that birth certificate in my hand.'

'There will be a charge you know. I had to get a copy of my birth certificate once for a visa. My mother couldn't find mine anywhere,' Harry lied.

'Oh, obviously I know that. I'm not stupid, Harry.'

Harry recognised the impatience in her voice and decided not to enquire about the amount of the charge and to change the subject.

'So, for my good news. I told you didn't I, that I put our names down in this holiday competition? Well, apparently, I have been selected for a draw in a kind of raffle. The winner has a free four-day break in Blackpool. It is for a double room, so I wondered if you and Jenny would like it, if I win. But then it is all 'ifs' isn't it? Like winning the lottery.'

Caroline nodded. At the moment she was far too excited by Jenny's news to contemplate another holiday. The journey home had seemed an endless experience, and now she was enjoying the peace afforded to her by her solitary lifestyle.

'We will have to see,' she muttered. 'Well Harry. I don't want to rush you, but I have got a lot to do. My solicitor will be arriving shortly to tie up yet another bunch of loose ends. You can't believe how much is involved in sorting out my late husband's affairs.'

'Of course. I won't keep you. Just thought you would like to know my good news and you must let me know how things go. It would be wonderful for you to trace April. Like I told you I sometimes think that I would like to trace my mother, but then my adoptive mother was very good to me. Life can get complicated. Be careful, Caroline. I'll keep in touch about the holiday.'

Caroline watched him walking along the drive towards the gate. She liked him but detected something in his manner that did not ring true. Jenny did not trust him. She had made that clear, but then Jenny did not seem to trust anybody. She had been very doubting over the gypsy, hadn't she? And as for Brad Carter – another male out to get her! But then look how Jenny was pulling out all of the stops to help find April.

Chapter Sixteen

'Caroline! My brother has found her! Your April!'

It was two days since their last communication, and Caroline had taken to getting up late; watching television in her bedroom and not allowing her imagination to focus on the past or the future. It was close to lunch time now and she was still in her dressing gown, albeit having left her bedroom and reached the drawing room.

Jenny's voice was so high pitched with excitement that Caroline had to hold the receiver away from her ear.

'How does he know? Is she still called April? Where does she live?' Caroline also was yelling now, and her legs had become so weak that she sank down into the armchair, pinning Marigold against the cushion.

'I don't have any details,' Jenny continued. 'He is going to contact you and wanted your phone number. Is that all right to give him it and he is having to pay for registering with this search thing. I don't understand it but I know it is not a free service so he will need you to pay his expenses. Is that OK?'

'Of course! Give him my number and tell him to go ahead and I will settle up with him straightaway.'

The phone clicked to signal the end of the call, and Caroline sat staring at it, as though it was alive and would burst into life again at any moment. Her heart was beating so fast that it frightened her, and she tried to take in a deep breath. She became aware of a sharp pain in her back and struggled to free the doll compressed against the back of the chair.

'Oh, sorry Marigold,' she gasped. 'You are going to meet April at last. Perhaps she has a little girl who would like a doll.'

She sat Marigold on her knee and pulled her shoe back on, ruffling her orange tousled hair into shape. But that state of euphoria was being replaced with doubts. What if April did not like her? What if she did not want to know who her real mother was? What if she was happy with her adoptive parents? What if she hated her for giving her up for adoption? These questions were not new ones. She had asked them so many times in the past when she had acted out the fantasy. But now this fantasy had become reality, and she began to tremble with the threat of possible answers.

At that moment, the phone began to ring again, the sound seeming so loud and discordant that the trembling in her breathing passed into her fingers, and she fumbled to pick up the receiver. For a moment she assumed that the male voice was Brad Carter, but then realised that the tone and the accent were unknown to her.

'Am I speaking to Mrs Thorston? Caroline is it?'

'Yes. You are. How can I help you?'

'I am Jenny's brother Mike. Did she tell you that I have traced your daughter? It took me a long time as you can imagine with all the apps to wade through but I got there in the end. It wasn't cheap, but I know you will reimburse me. Jenny has assured me of that. So, for my time of at least ten hours and the cost of the programme I will need three hundred and thirty pounds if you can sort that for me and then I will arrange for you to meet. She is now called Amber, and she is looking forward to meeting you. So, if you can make out a cheque for my charge like you did before to MA Valeting Services and give it to Jenny next time you see her, I will make contact with Amber again. How does that sound to you?'

'That sounds amazing. Thank you so much. Was it complicated? It never seems easy on those television programmes.'

'It took a lot of effort, but then nothing is easy on a computer is it?'

Caroline shook her head, making a croaking sound of agreement. 'I would be hopeless,' she said. 'Everything amazes me these days. Of course, I will pay you your expenses. That sounds very reasonable to me. I will be seeing Jenny later on today I expect or would you like me to post it to you?'

'Give it to my sister again. That will be fine. I know that I can trust you from what Jenny has told me. So, I'll leave you to make plans and as soon as possible you can meet up with your daughter.'

The phone call ended with a click and a return to the dialling tone, and Caroline slowly replaced the receiver in its holder. Now that she was alone again with her thoughts, the contrasting silence felt like a blanket smothering her senses. She drew up her knees and clasped them with her hands. All her questions seemed to have been answered in that brief telephone call. They had changed her name, yet Amber was so close somehow; the same first letter, and to do with nature, she mused, obscure, unusual. It was as though the adoptive parents tried to respect my wishes, she thought and apparently Amber wanted to arrange a meeting. She was not opposed to it. She was not resentful.

She reached for her handbag, seeking out the shape of her cheque book in the bottom. It was surrounded with tourist information leaflets and supermarket till receipts, and she vowed to get rid of past paperwork and move on into this future she had envisioned for such a long time. She wrote MA Valeting Services on the relevant line on the blank cheque, as directed by Mike Alford, and then had a sudden impulse to make the payment into five hundred pounds, rather than three hundred and thirty as he had requested. Obviously, he was not a greedy man, and she was so grateful for his time and effort. He could be so helpful if she needed more information, she thought.

She signed her name with a flourish, and with a sense of purpose and success not often apparent in these days since her bereavement. She had always been used to having cash at her disposal. Robert had made her a generous allowance during their marriage, and she in return was expected to be there in whatever role he desired, albeit nurse and doormat during the last year of his life.

She experienced a huge surge of excitement as she slotted the cheque into an envelope and placed it carefully on the mantelpiece under one of a pair of heavy brass candlesticks each defining an end of the patterned marble slab.

She sank back into the chair, suddenly feeling extremely tired, and closed her eyes. Now in this retreat from the material views of her surroundings she allowed her brain to work out a timetable of future events. What would April want to know? What could she tell her? Would she be disgusted by the immorality of her father and of his age? What did the exploitation of a young woman tell anyone of his character? Should she say that he was a 'one night' stand, when they both got carried away in moments of passion and then she never saw him again? Would April accept that, as would a modern young woman, rather than the action of a man who could be described as a paedophile in the modern climate of female exploitation? She had never thought of him as being old, yet what would his age be now if he was still alive. She mentally added on thirty-four to thirty-eight. He would be seventy- two, wouldn't he? Not so old really. He had always seemed to be old. Anyone in their thirties was old from a teenager's point of view, and the knowledge that a man of his age was her father could seem very off-putting for Amber. Well, he was nearly forty at the time wasn't he, her mind reasoned; middle-aged, wasn't he? And she was so innocent; little more than a schoolgirl. Would Amber realise that, or would she be very critical? Would she understand the innocence of sheltered young women at that time; the fear of an unwanted pregnancy and yet the rushing of emotions and the newly found power of hormones?

She thought about the cheque. She had given the previous one to Jenny, so presumably that was still a safe arrangement. It suited her to be secretive about this. She had no idea where Mike Alford lived, or where his business premises were situated. She did not want to know. Somehow the general anonymity was part of her fantasy; part of the game she had played for a long time and her thoughts returned to the photograph album and her abandoned task of replacing more of the seemingly unimportant or faded ones with some of her own photographs. She turned her steps towards the staircase and the landing where the airing cupboard was still the hiding place of the old album.

She gasped at the sight of the pile of freshly laundered bedding on the shelf, remembering that Jenny had spent some time in tackling the ironing before they had gone on holiday. Did I leave the envelope here with the spare photographs in it, she wondered? Did Jenny have any suspicions about her stories of the past? She did seem to know the village church. What about the magician?

She found the envelope under some folded sheets, and opened it, drawing out the old photographs she had removed to make spaces for her own photographs. The Great Majesto stared out at her through damaged eyes, and she remembered the recent satisfaction she had gained from stabbing that hated face with the point of the compasses she had retrieved from the old pencil case. Then, her mind was back into her childhood to the photograph of her adoptive mother and the frenzy of stabbing it with a sharp knife.

'Lizzie Borden took an axe.'

Oh God that's back! Please leave me alone. Why do you haunt me? Her face twisted and she screwed up her eyes in an attempt to take away the image of the magician and her memories of that day when Marigold had been hidden away and the new doll had been produced from the top hat.

She pushed the sheets back over the album and the envelope containing the photographs. They could stay there for now. The link with her past was too painful, even though most of the images were of complete strangers. She would not use them to show her daughter as had been her original plan. It was a silly idea, she mused, especially as she now knew that her supposedly adoptive parents were her real father and her aunt, if the gypsy had got it right. That would be the next step, she decided. She had found her daughter, and now she must find her mother. The ancestors would be hers and not someone else's. Jenny and Brad Carter may wonder, and no doubt that Harry would be full of good advice if she said anything, so she would keep things to herself concerning Crystal House until she had met up with Amber. Hopefully, she would not be curious at first about her ancestors, although she must have wondered about them at times in her life. Did she also fantasise?

She went into her bedroom, catching sight of herself in the long mirror. The reflection of this wild-haired, pale-cheeked woman in her long nightgown and flimsy wrap could be her own ghost, she thought. Where did she belong in all of this fantasising and future realities? Magic Mirror on the wall. Was she Snow White ill-treated by the wicked stepmother as she used to believe, or was she the wicked daughter, who had made up magic spells and wished such bad things to happen in the past? Would Amber see her wickedness? Had she inherited it? Was she opening Pandora's Box?

'Oh, for goodness sake!' Her voice echoed around the bedroom, and she shivered, suddenly aware of the chilliness of the room, and her dishevelled state. Jenny would be coming for the cheque soon, and here she was, still looking as though she had just got out of bed. There was not time now for a shower, and she hastily chose jeans and a sweater, and brushed her hair, securing it into a pony tail with a hair band. That's the first thing I must do, she thought, regarding herself in the mirror. She considered that her thick hair was her greatest asset, and it was seriously in need of attention after the exposure to sea air on the holiday, and the hours of sleeplessness in recent nights tangling it into knots. A blond rinse would brighten it, she decided. Jenny would know.

There was a knock on the kitchen door. That's her, Caroline thought, hurrying down the stairs and almost tripping in her excitement. But then the atmosphere was strained, a strange moment or two as Jenny hung her anorak on the hall stand and waited for Caroline to speak. Neither of them it seemed were comfortable in these moments now. Was it lady of the house and servant again, or was it bosom friends? Jenny wanted to hug Caroline, noting with some disquiet, her pale cheeks and scraped-back hair. Caroline avoided eye contact, turning away and heading for the sanctuary and the comforting 'lady of the house' kind of status of the drawing room.

She sat down and waited for Jenny to speak, still not sure of the situation now. Had she come to work, or was she merely collecting the cheque? Jenny stood in the doorway waiting for instructions. Caroline reached forward and picked up the cheque. 'This is for your brother,' she said. 'He rang me earlier. I'll put it in an envelope if you don't mind giving him it. He said that it was best that way to keep it separate from his business post. So, are we back to our schedule? I will still need some help.'

Jenny sighed. 'Course we are, if you still need me. I certainly need to earn some money. Are you thinking of moving nearer to your daughter? I don't suppose she lives nearby. People move around a lot, don't they? Not like the old days. Of course, I will be glad to help. But you look tired. By the way I have booked tickets for the spiritual meeting I told you about, but if you haven't time now with all the news of your daughter, I will find someone else to go with me. In any case it is not until next month. Four weeks on Friday in fact.'

Caroline shrugged her shoulders and nodded, with little indication it seemed of her intentions. She had an overwhelming desire now to see her daughter in the flesh, and she could not contemplate any other future events. Who would she want to see from this so called 'other side'? The dead could stay dead. The ancestors could stay in the album. It was immaterial who they were. She had spent hours in the past, during sleepless nights, attempting to visualise her daughter's physical features; trying to recall his features, and combining them with images of herself both from the past and into more recent days. April had grown up, in my imaginings, to be like me, she mused. He did not come into it then, did he? Suddenly he had become part of the equation again. What if April had been looking for him? But then, how could she? He had been anonymous, hadn't he? And he would remain that way, so that was never going to be a problem.

She turned her attention back to Jenny.

'The bedrooms could do with a once-over, I think. Do those today Jenny, and we will sort out your hours before you go.'

Jenny stared, an uncomfortable flush of heat travelling up her back and infusing into her neck. Caroline had reverted to being her employer again.

'I will have to finish by four,' she said. 'Don't forget that I am having to use the bus now, since my car gave up the ghost.'

Caroline nodded. 'That will be three hours then. Plenty of time to change the bedding and give everywhere a good clean. The back bedroom will be comfortable for April or should I say Amber? She may want to meet here. I can't get used to that name, although I expect I will do in time. I think there are still some of your things in there from before the holiday, so perhaps you could sort them please. That book dealer is coming again tomorrow, so if you want me I shall be in the study. There is still so much to do and I need to get this place ready for selling. It is far too big for me, and like you said I may decide to move nearer to my daughter.'

Jenny sighed. 'Don't do too much,' she advised. 'You look like I feel. There's plenty of time, isn't there? I am sure you have waited this long, and a few more days is not going to make a huge difference. Anyway, I'll get that room sorted and then that's one less thing to worry about.'

Caroline nodded. 'Don't forget to take the cheque, will you? I'll let you know when I will need you. Probably Tuesday. We can get back to our normal timetable now the holiday is over.'

The books from the top shelf were piled up on the study table where they had been left since before the holiday. They were old and shabby, but perhaps of more value than those previously packed into boxes ready for the charity shop. Last time he was here, the book dealer had promised little return on them, and had picked out about a dozen of apparent value in the second-hand trade. Caroline was not prepared to haggle. Many of these old books had belonged to her husband or even to earlier relations in his past. She had sentimental connections with those of her childhood and later years and they were not included in the sale, or in those piles destined for the charity shop.

She closed the door behind her and reached forward to switch on the small radio on the window sill. She did not want to hear the sound of the vacuum cleaner. She needed her own space now. Jenny represented an intrusion somehow in spite of the fact that she was part of the story of tracing April. As she turned the volume knob on the radio, her guilty thoughts were drowned out by the familiar voice of the local radio announcer.

'Before our next selection, we have a guest who has news of his book-signing at Grant's bookshop on the high street in Canhead, on Monday. Let me pass you over to David. It's Dreighton, isn't it? Have I got that right? Fine! Now David, would you like to tell our listeners about your book?'

It seemed as though the house was holding its breath. Caroline's heartbeat quickened as the author began to speak. David Dreighton!

Was it him? She recognised the voice. It was slightly hesitant as though he was nervous, but it was him. He cleared his throat, giving a little cough. He always did that. She could visualise him doing it. He was talking about his book, but his words could well have been spoken in a foreign tongue. They were not important. The sounds were important. His voice became husky and her mind was back in the little bed and breakfast establishment where they had played out their fantasies and where April had been conceived. She tried to grasp what he was saying, but her heart was beating so fast that it hampered her senses. She heard the interviewer say that his book would be available to buy at the bookshop at two-thirty for the duration of two hours. So that gives you plenty of time folks to meet David Dreighton and his first book called *Ancient Buildings*. A collective history.' It looks fascinating. It must have taken a lot of research.'

'Can I just say that it is available on the internet if people can't make it to the book signing.' That was David again.

Caroline repeated the words in her mind. It was the kind of thing he would say. Informative, precise. She sank down into the fireside chair in the corner, no longer aware of the piles of dusty books and the half-emptied shelves. Even the thoughts of her future plans to meet her daughter had become overshadowed by the recall of his voice, so familiar, yet from so long in her past. She had often tried to bring it to mind but it was hard to visualise a sound. Sights were easier. She could still remember the shape of his head and features and the gestures he made. Yet the sense of sound and of smell are always elusive until the brain is reacquainted with them. That sweet smell of violets reawakened each spring, and that first yearly heady smell of a rose. Now the sound of his voice had wakened in her all the sweetness of her youthful emotions. It was the story before April. Before that second love story began. And of course, he was a crucial part of it. The passing years had almost negated that, but he was and would always be the father of her child. Should he know of her quest? Would he care? Would he be embarrassed or guilt ridden? He should be, she thought. He should feel as guilty as hell.

She stood up and stared out of the window across the side garden. She could still hear the buzz of the cleaner, reminding her of the day, the hour, the now of her life. I am middle-aged, she thought. He's old. But yet she still loved him. She had said that before many times, hadn't she? But then what about the times when she had said that she hated him? Had he ever wanted to know what had happened to April? Was she his love child, a precious reminder of their passion, or would he deny all connections to her? Had he denied it in the past? She did not know. She had never seen him again. She could insist on a test. She had thought about that on the rare occasions when she idly watched programmes on the television where feuding couples demanded proof of genetic links. There could be no dispute could there? He was the only man in her life at that time, but she had no proof of that. Should she seek him out? Was it worth all of the hassle? Was his wife still alive?

She began to inspect the books, arranging them into piles relating to chronology and condition or occasionally rarity. She did not profess to be an expert on the value, but it was giving her something to do, some comparative yardstick in the passing of the next two hours. For a time, the background noise of the vacuum cleaner persisted, but then the following silence became more of a disturbance than the noise, pushing her mind back into the space to dwell on the past. The conception of her child and the visual imagery of David Dreighton as part of that act was now tangling her mind and her emotions. The previous, supposedly simple act of tracing the whereabouts of her daughter, had now become an anguish, a pain, tearing at her emotions. She had regarded the role that she had played as the heroine, the princess, the soul in torment, part of a visualised past tragedy, as a fantasy; a story to be re-read whenever she wanted to escape from the boredom of her marriage. Now, it had intruded back into her life; into her reality. Should she ignore it? What if she had not clicked the switch on the radio? What if she had not decided to sort out the books? Was the very physicality of them a link with his book, whatever it was that he had written? Something about buildings, wasn't it? Was that how fate worked? Cryptic clues thrown out at specific times to point one in the direction the gods had decreed? Do I believe in fate, she asked herself? She nodded. One had to believe in fate. She had always believed that. Otherwise, nothing had any meaning; any significance. So, this was all planned and she had to follow the directions; join up the dots.

'So, how's the precious Caroline then, or shouldn't I ask?'

Sherry was back in her usual place in her mother's kitchen, smoking the inevitable cigarette.

Jenny was holding her cup of coffee in both her hands absorbing the heat and staring beyond her daughter at the shrouded bird cage.

'Well?'

'Sorry. I was miles away. Naturally she is excited about tracing her daughter. I expect your Uncle Mike has told you that he came up with details on the website. It is all a mystery to me, but he seems to know what he is doing. I have a cheque for him. Caroline is very grateful, I know, but I am worried that she is going to be disappointed. What if this woman is not what she expects? Caroline has a picture of someone of her social standing. Some nice respectable, well-educated woman like herself. She knows nothing about her daughter's life and of her adoptive parents.'

'Well, that's not your problem is it? I must say, I was surprised that Uncle Mike tracked her down so quickly, but he is pretty slick on the internet, and it seems that we can go back to William the Conqueror now on these sites, according to a mate of mine who is doing her family tree. Still, life is never that simple. How many people are who they really think they are?'

'That's a bit profound coming from you at this time of the morning. Anyway, this is for Mike. I won't be seeing Caroline until next Tuesday. We are back to our normal hours and you can take that "I told you so" look off your face. Actually, I am glad to have some time to myself. Keeping up appearances is not really my scene.'

Sherry raised her eyebrows and shook her head. 'If you say so. Whatever floats your boat. She is always going to need help. Those sort always do. So get what you can. I keep telling you that but it's like water off a duck's back. Anyway, what the hell? I had better go, and I will be meeting up with Uncle Mike at the darts tonight. He is a bit of a hero in the team. So, I will pass on the cheque. Have you had a look at it? I bet you haven't.'

'Just keep your nose out, Sherry. I sometimes wonder who you take after.'

'Oh, stop fretting, Mother. I'll play your little game. It's not the end of the world though, is it?'

Jenny waited for the slamming of the door and sighed. Sometimes, she thought, it did seem like the end of her dreams. Caroline was back in her own domain, and here I am back in mine, she thought. The memories of the holiday had receded into the past so rapidly that it was now more like a fantasy, and yet it was barely two weeks since they had returned.

Harry Bainer watched Sherry leaving the high-rise flats and walking towards the shopping centre. He dropped his tobacco roll-up on the pavement, pressing his foot hard down on it to extinguish the smouldering tip, and scuffing it into the gutter. He was tired of hanging around, having watched Jenny arriving, followed half an hour later by her daughter. He hurried to catch up with her. She was on the phone again, her voice penetrating the space between them.

'Just been to Mum's. Yes, I've got the money. A cheque again. She will be expecting to hear about her long-lost daughter soon. I'll see you tonight at the match. You bet. See you then.'

Harry needed no further instructions. He knew exactly what to do next, and Brad Carter was a sure bet for a coffee and a chance to spend some time away from the inevitable 'street corners and dustbin areas' of his life. Surely this was worth some more money from that so called petty cash tin, he thought. Should he exaggerate the time spent in sleuthing? Could he appeal to Carter's sense of fairness? Did he have one? It was worth a try. At least it was worth a cup of coffee and a rest in comfort. He settled for that. One day his ship would come home, as his mother used to say. Caroline was in need of a man. There was no way that her relationship with Jenny could ever extend beyond boss woman and servant, he decided. And Jenny needed a bloke, he mused. She really did. Could he be spoilt for choice?

Brad Carter chewed on his pen. He had returned to some rough notes pertaining to what, in his opinion, was a rather messy divorce. 'I'm sick to the back teeth with divorces,' he muttered. It was Saturday morning and life outside of his house was noisy with traffic in the supermarket car park, and the chatter of people walking along the footpath close to his back windows. As always, or as it seemed in recent months, he began the weekend with cursing his parents' decision to sell the land to the supermarket developers. He knew that it was the only way for them to remain in this house at the time, and that the large garden at the rear of the property was very attractive and an enviable possession in the eyes of most people, yet he hated the place more and more. Now Harry Bainer's recent disclosures regarding Caroline Thorston were weighing heavily on his mind. How much money had she parted with, and how much fraud was being committed by that con merchant Mike Alford? How could she believe that it was that easy to trace adopted children? He needed to see her. He reached for the telephone and dialled her number.

His heart quickened when he heard that familiar voice. His feelings were governed as always by his frustrated memories of Elizabeth. She was a shape he kept in a pocket of his mind; a symbol of womanhood likened to his memories of his mother like a lucky charm, a talisman of security in his life fraught with obsessive time-keeping and ritualistic eating patterns. He looked at the clock and then back at the watch on his wrist. It was nearing twelve o'clock and time for his midday sandwich and cup of coffee. He tapped his fingers on the desk impatiently and was about to press the exit button when she answered.

'Caroline. I must get over to see you. I have some information that is very important and I cannot discuss it on the phone. How about two o'clock this afternoon?'

There was a silence and he visualised Caroline gazing across at the window.

Then she said, 'OK,' and the telephone clicked, returning to the familiar buzzing signalling the end of the call.

He stared at the phone for a moment, surprised and somewhat taken aback by the brevity of her answer. That one almost truncated word alarmed him. She was withdrawing and such an action was threatening his links with her and her considerable wealth. This latest discovery he had made from his father's accounts, of a secret benefactor, had raised the stakes considerably. There was no time like the present to update her expectations and to increase her dependence on him as her legal advisor. He checked his watch again, visualising the midday sandwich and cursing Harry Bainer for his bad time-keeping. It was over half an hour since he rang. Such was the rising panic within him of the threatening nature of time that he was startled by the long buzz of the front door bell.

'All right all right. I'm coming,' he gasped.

Harry followed him into his office, a surge of optimism rising in his chest. This was a good time to increase his demands or threaten to withdraw his services, he thought. Carter was falling apart.

'OK, so she is paying that crook for his so-called services, is she? What is she getting in return?'

'Apparently her long-lost daughter, who was taken from her and adopted. She told me that a friend of hers was looking for her child but it was pretty obvious that she was talking about herself, and then Jenny has confirmed it. That daughter of hers, Sherry, she is called, has got a gob on her. I could hear her all over the street. She is meeting Mike Alford at the local tonight to give him a cheque from Caroline. He is in the darts match. Quite a local hero by the sounds of it. I will get some photographs. Everyone will be clicking away. That Sherry is not exactly the soul of discretion.'

'Big words for you. OK then off you go and come back tomorrow with the evidence.'

'You can't give me an advance, can you? I am skint and will have to buy a drink and merge with the crowd.'

Brad looked at his watch and turned his head to see beyond Harry to the clock on the wall. He jerked open the drawer in his desk and took out the petty cash tin, lifting the lid and extracting a ten-pound note.

'That should keep you going and one drink should do. You need your wits about you. You know I don't approve of drinking on the job. Now I must get my lunch and press on.'

Harry noticed the shine of perspiration on his forehead, and his anxious gaze at the clock. Boy, did this bloke have a problem, he thought. Should he demand more money? What about his wages? This tenner was for expenses. He cleared his throat to make his point, but then backed away as his employer flung open the door of his office and seized his arm.

'Just leave. I am ten minutes late for my lunch. This will never do. And close the door behind you.'

Harry stumbled into the passage way, half-turning to see Carter almost running into the kitchen. He fumbled for the latch, dragging open the heavy street door, that was reluctant to oblige, it seemed, and almost fell down the steps into the entrance to the car park. He stood, regaining his composure and balance. The man is cracking up, he thought. He was in control of Caroline's affairs and yet he was cracking up. He must warn Caroline. She was being ripped off by everyone, wasn't she? But then why should she trust him? He was just a holiday acquaintance to her, wasn't he? Perhaps he could tell Jenny, but how, without blowing his cover? She would mistrust him immediately if he admitted to spying on her family and on her beloved Caroline.

Caroline heard the sound of a car in the drive and recognised the classic shape of the solicitor's Rover. She sighed. She could do without him today. The book dealer had taken over an hour deliberating on his choices, rejecting many books as no longer of any value, and others of possible merit in the second-hand book trade. She had paid little attention, her mind still on the forthcoming book signing. She had studied the man's appearance when he first came into the house. Sixties, she had guessed. He looks antique, she had thought, a sliver of mischief rising above her dark thoughts. Then the picture of the father of her child was back in her mind and the word antique no longer amused her.

Now she recalled his comments. 'That's an interesting one. Gothic architecture. Did you hear that some local bookshops are hosting an author with his book on architecture? It could be a good read, although this one takes some beating. I understand that this new guy has won a prize with his book, but I have never come across him before.'

He left with a box of books and cash in hand for Caroline, assuring her that he had given her the best price he could pay in the present climate of the second-hand book market, and advising her to off-load the rest on a charity shop, or in some cases into a recycling bin.

Now Caroline turned her attention away from the recent past, giving her solicitor access through the front door. She was feeling somewhat triumphant with her independent actions and organisation, in spite of the fact that again she had been disappointed by the book valuation. At least, she was opening her own avenues, she thought, as she showed him into the sitting room.

'I got a good price from the book dealer,' she lied. 'Mind you, again there are a lot of books only suitable for the charity shop, according to him. I have piled them up on the bottom shelf. What a lot of dust! Still, that's another load done with. There aren't many more.'

'Actually, there is some paperwork that has somehow been overlooked in your husband's affairs. I have been tracing records back to my father's time in office. He dealt with your mother's family inheritance, and it seems that there was a large sum of money held in trust for you, which for some reason has not been released. Did your mother ever speak of a place called Crystal House?'

Caroline stared, and breathed in hard. Those two words were in her story. The words of the gypsy. Yet could it be possible? Could she accept the words of a gypsy? Some fantastical mystery that had invaded her mind, filling it with hobgoblins. Twins, spiteful, revengeful, stealing from each other and filling their space with hate. Lizzie Borden took an axe. She was part of it. Part of the hate. Locked in the cupboard. Was Bella locked in a cupboard? That thought had haunted her, but it did not exist, did it? It was only in her imagination and in the crystal ball of the gypsy. But now, he was talking about a Crystal House.

She stared blankly at him, not wishing to share her thoughts; not wishing for him to invade the privacy of her imaginings.

'Do you want me to investigate this, Caroline? It has nothing to do with the estate of your husband. I can continue to complete that paperwork and we can perhaps allow time to let all of this come to light, but I do think that you should be aware of it. It does seem to all be securely invested but is in trust for you when the right circumstances arrive. I would advise you not to discuss this with anyone until I have delved into it. The law is so incredibly complicated, and my father was a stickler for the details. Crossing every "t" and dotting every "i", as they say.'

'OK. That's fine. I am sure you know what you are doing. Anyway, I must get on with packing up these books. That will be another trip to the charity shop.'

Caroline walked to the door leading into the hall, and he reluctantly followed her, half-turning to look into the sitting room. The strange doll stared back at him from the armchair positioned close to the fireplace, and a shiver snaked up his spine. There was something going on, yet he could not place it. Caroline had frowned when he mentioned Crystal House. He was expecting questions or answers, but she had changed the subject. Now she was ushering him out through the front door, and he was no nearer to broaching the subject of her lost daughter and her dealings with the Alford family. He had no alternative but to continue to employ Harry Bainer. He checked the time with his watch, and again with the digital numbers on his dash panel of his car as he settled into the driving seat. The jackals are circling in, he thought, carefully steering through the exit of her driveway onto the busy road leading back into the town. He did not include himself in that category. In his mind he was the knight in shining armour. Elizabeth had been his fair lady and now Caroline was the lady of the lake holding up the sword that could empower him and free him from the grip of his house and all of its problems. The promise of more wealth at her disposal gnawed into his ambitions. Crystal House and its location were on his immediate agenda. Time, time, time. The word chanted repeatedly in his brain. He must find the time before it was too late.

Chapter Seventeen

Caroline needed companionship, but not in the flesh. There was too much going on in her mind to give her any freedom to be sociable, and she settled for the comfort of the armchair in front of the television, taking in the so-called omnibus of her favourite 'soap', critical of its content as usual, yet mesmerised by its relentless tunnelling into her brain with its social issues and cliff-hanger scenarios. The commercial breaks gave her space to either re-top her coffee mug, to stretch her legs and walk in the direction of the downstairs cloakroom or to sit back in her chair and close her eyes. She could not allow her mind to wander away again into the past, instead, concentrating on her future plan to attend the book signing on the following day. The remainder of the day seemed to pass by slowly, and she opted for an early night in her bed as an alternative to her cramped position in front of the television.

However, hours of sleep and then waking so early was not a good way for her to begin the next day. She did not need all this space to think, but her dream state had allowed such confusion and fear; elements of the past mixing with random happenings for no apparent reason, that she had been glad to leave it behind and anticipate instead a day of uncertainty and possible future heartache. There were at least seven hours ahead of her before she set off in the direction of Canhead. It was a town not familiar to her in its location or its geography, so she would allow plenty of time to get there, she mused. She could perhaps make a day of it, exploring the shops and possible tourist attractions. She extracted the large road atlas from the bottom bookshelf at the side of the chimney breast and turned to the index, discovering that it was on a page well used for location and directions in the past. Her husband's past, she argued with herself. She had never had to drive far beyond her immediate locality, and the suggestion of motorways on route promoted feelings of fear. Her answer as usual was the avoidance of any confrontation. So, I will follow the country roads, she thought. It is a nice day and why get stressed? Her finger followed a possible route on the map and she guessed that it was about thirty-five miles to Canhead avoiding the busy major roads.

It seemed that putting her plan to paper was a useful way of occupying herself, and when Jenny telephoned, she was halfway through accomplishing her set task. She almost told Jenny what she was doing, being quite caught up with her own sense of adventure but stopped in time realising that Jenny would offer to go with her and be her navigator. She could hardly explain that she was on the trail of the father of her child. This had to be a secret mission, and instead she cleared her throat and pleaded that she had not slept and was going to try to catch up.

When she heard Jenny's bright voice level down into disappointment after her initial enthusiasm, she felt guilty at such deception.

'Oh, I'm sorry you are not good,' she was saying. 'It's nothing pressing. Just to let you know that your cheque has been passed on and it shouldn't be long before you can meet up with your daughter. I can't wait for it to happen for you.'

'Me too. Thank you, Jenny. I'll see you on Tuesday.' She hung up, aware of the seeming lack of excitement. How could she explain that she had somehow stored her daughter away now to make room for this latest emotional roller coaster.

She agonised over the next few hours with changes of clothes and shoes and rearranging her hair into styles portraying the casualness of youth; curly and falling around her face, or the more severe mature woman look; drawn back away from her face or piled high on her head. What would he expect? Well, he was not expecting anything, was he? Well then, what would he remember?

241

She recalled a photograph of herself that she had slotted into a space in the album of pretend ancestors still hidden away in the airing cupboard. That was how he would remember her with her hair falling in curls on her shoulders and a side parting. She did not need to look at it. It had always been her favourite likeness, and one she associated with his description of her as a secret princess. But then she preferred to cover her forehead with a fringe these days to hide the lines appearing in her skin. So why worry? She would keep the fringe and he would not remember details like that after all the years since she had last seen him. She could still have the loose curls. He did like to run his fingers through them. Should she wear a dress, or something more casual; jeans for example and a zip-up fleece, as though it was all a big surprise and not an occasion? He was always formally dressed, wasn't he? But then that was his job and those were the times of more formality. 'I'm going back thirty-four years,' she muttered. He could be trying to portray a youthful look. Hardly ripped jeans – she giggled at the idea. He was in his early seventies. But he could have abandoned his tie and be trendy and casual. Or, on the other hand he could be trying to portray a Bohemian look, but then architecture was hardly arts and crafts, was it?

By eleven o'clock she had reached her ultimate verdict; a long sleeved, floral patterned blouse, together with close fitting leggings in a powder blue and a denim waistcoat. Her sandals were in a deeper shade of blue and she carefully painted her toenails with a cerise coloured varnish to match the flowers in the blouse. She regarded herself in the chaise longue in her bedroom, twisting and turning and practising her smile of recognition. It would not be a look of surprise, would it? Obviously, she would know who he was. His would be the look of surprise.

Inevitably, she lost her way on her rambling route across country. It was as though fate was trying to intervene, and after making the third wrong decision and finding herself in a dead-end road leading to a mud track across the fields, she began to wonder whether she should abandon this connection with her past. But then curiosity once more overcame her doubts, and she reversed, a sudden feeling of wildness seeming to correspond with the roaring of the engine as her foot pressed on to the accelerator, and mud sprayed sideways onto the grass verge.

At last, with a sigh of relief, she reached the outskirts of the town, and followed the road into the centre. She had no idea where the bookshop was sited, but as her mother-stroke-aunt, as she inwardly referred to her these days, had always advised, 'You have a tongue in your head, well use it then.' Wise words, she recalled but even so they were said impatiently. There never seemed to be kindness. But now, she must not allow such bitter feelings to mar this reunion. This was her special time, however it happened. Indeed, this was their special time, she reasoned. An act of new beginnings or could it be of final closure? Did she need to end one story to enable another one to begin? She turned the car into an area designated as a long stay park, pulling into a space and looking around for the ticket machine. She read the instructions and inserted the money required for a four-hour stay, feeling reassured that she would have plenty of time. It was just after two o'clock now, so no time for hanging about she thought. Hopefully the shop was in a central position and there was not far to walk.

Use your tongue. That was her aunt's voice echoing in her brain once more.

'Excuse me.'

'Yes, love. Are you lost?'

'I am looking for the bookshop. Grant's is it or is there more than one?'

The old lady let go of her shopping trolley with her right hand and pointed across the car park to a cluster of buildings. 'It's over there, dear. We've only got one. Such a shame when shops close down. It's all charity shops and estate agents these days unless you want a supermarket. There seem to be plenty of those. I'm surprised Grant's is still with us. Get your skates on. It could close down before you get there.'

Caroline mouthed her thanks and set off across the carpark, dodging the pot-holes filled with water from a recent heavy shower. Would there be a queue or would the apparently unsettled weather have put people off? The old woman gave a depressing description of the shopping centre. Still, our high street is no better, she mused. What if she was the only one at the book signing? How embarrassing could that be! Just me and him.

She looked at her watch. She was early after all that panicking. She could see the shop on the other side of the road from the alley way leading from the carpark. There was no sign of a queue yet, but then he was not a super-star, was he? A coffee house along the street had an inviting appearance; tables on the pavement with groups of people relaxing now that the sun was shining once again. Caroline moistened her lips. The journey here had stressed her and she was in need of caffeine. In any case it would be a good vantage point. She may even see him arriving. Her heart was beginning to thump and she took a deep breath before she used a gap in the flow of traffic to cross over the road.

The coffee was amazingly good for such a small establishment and quickly revived her flagging spirits. She checked the time on her wristwatch and patted her hair. Two people had entered the bookshop, and another couple were approaching the doorway with the obvious intention of going in. She did not want to wait long. Her courage was beginning to leave her again in spite of the stimulation of the caffeine. She stood up, scraping the legs of the chair against the roughness of the paving, and smoothed her hand down her leggings.

The shop was quite small and she could just identify, at the end of the gangway and squeezed in the corner, a small table partially obscured by a small gathering of people waiting their turn to be handed a book and to have it signed by the author.

'It looks like we pay on the way out,' said a man waiting in the queue in front of her. 'It's good to actually meet the author.'

Caroline did not try to look beyond him. She had caught a glimpse of a seated figure but had ducked back behind the man in front suddenly afraid of being identified. Her heart was beating quickly now and she was aware of the perspiration on her forehead and in her eye sockets. People were squeezing past the short queue intent on normal shopping and pushing against her. A board showing details of the book; title, author, and price no doubt encouraged them to avoid the author, Caroline thought. At twenty pounds a copy, it certainly was not cheap compared to an everyday paperback, and the title *Ancient Buildings. A Collective History*, was not on many people's 'must have' list she guessed. She opened her bag and drew out a twenty-pound note.

She could see him. She regarded the familiar shape of his head, and the strongly defined features. She followed the movement of his lips although the words he spoke were not yet distinguishable, merely sounds, yet she could well recall the shapes of the vowels and the consonants in his refined, educated accent. Then she heard the huskiness still there and she could detect that slight suggestion of a northern accent that had always fascinated her.

Now, she stood there looking at the top of his head and noticing a bald patch on the crown, as he reached for another book from the pile, placing it in front of him. She waited for him to look up, shaking inside and suddenly fearful of making eye contact.

But he did not look up. 'Would you like a dedication?' he asked.

'Yes please. To Caroline.'

She saw his sudden confusion. She heard his quick intake of breath before he raised his eyes and they were both back in the time of that shared intimacy. She wanted to giggle and to pull at her ear lobe. Surges of emotion first caught at her breath, and then travelled down her body, fluttering in her abdomen and weakening the muscles in her legs. She recalled later how time seemed to hang there in a strange silence, like a bubble enclosing the two of them and excluding everything and everyone around them.

He reached for a notepad and scribbled quickly on the first page. She read the words: 'Coffee in a couple of hours?' He had drawn an arrow pointing to his left to indicate the coffee shop where she had recently waited and she knew exactly what he meant.

She nodded. He was playing the role as though they were still part of that fantasy, she thought, her heart thumping. Little messages and eye contact. He signed her name in the front cover, slotting the note in and closing the book. She moved making space for the next customer and slowly walked along the other gangway hardly noticing the array of books and magazines on the racks at either side. In such a short space of time they were back in that bubble, she thought. Back into the past as though all of the years that had passed by were of no consequence. She paid for the book at the till, nodding vaguely as the shopkeeper promised her a 'good read', then she wandered along the street, staring into shop windows at displays of clothes and assorted second-hand ornaments and bric-a-brac in the wide selection of charity shops. Three estate agents displayed properties for sale or for rent, and she carefully read the details, and compared the prices, as though her main interest in life was choosing a place to live in the area. She checked the time. Six o'clock was her deadline for parking. She would not need that long, she reasoned. What could she say to him that would take up that amount of time? She was hardly going to tell him her life story, was she? What about April? Would he have known what happened to his child? Would he care? She could always go home without seeing him. He had looked very confused.

She had walked along both sides of the high street and once more was close to the book shop and the cafe. Her feet were beginning to ache in the blue sandals, and she needed to sit down. The sign indicated that the place closed at five. That would give them half an hour, she reasoned and then she could make her escape. She collected her coffee from the counter and chose a seat close to the front window, pushing her bag under the table, and brushing her hand down her leggings.

'Sorry. I got held up. A very earnest woman needed to tell me the history of her house. So, dear Caroline. How are you? You look very good. I would have known you anywhere. I'll just grab a coffee. Don't go away.'

Caroline smiled, that familiar tremble catching her breath. How could she be angry? He was old now, but still her kindred spirit. None of their years apart could alter that, she thought. She watched him returning to the table with his coffee. He had a slight limp, she noticed.

She answered his question, briefly deciding not to mention worries over a sick husband and her more recent sleepless nights.

'I am very well, thank you,' she said. 'You look well. Older and wiser I think. And how is your wife?'

'We divorced a long time ago. How's your husband? '

'He died.'

He stared at her as if expecting further details, and the silence between them became an embarrassment prompting them both to pick up their mugs of coffee.

She studied him, noticing the lines in his brow and the frown mark between his eyes. He seemed to have an anxious look, a permanent worry marring his features. Did she cause his divorce? Did he still love her, or was it always a big game with him? He could have looked for her, couldn't he? She frowned at the memory of his disappearance. She had decided to ask him about April as she had passed the time in staring into the high street shops. Did he know that they had a daughter? Did he know that April was given away for adoption? But now she decided not to burst the bubble. This was enough. Just the recognition of their past connection was enough. April, or Amber as she now was known, was all hers. No man was going to organise her life ever again.

'Well David, it was nice to catch up but I expect you have to get home. I hope it was worth it for you. Good luck with your sales. I will have a good read when I have time.' Caroline heard her voice somewhat shrill and breathless. She stood up, scraping the chair legs on the laminated wood floor. 'I must rescue my car before I get a ticket, and I have quite a long journey home.'

'Oh, that's a shame that you have to dash off. Can we keep in touch? Here's my card. Can I have a contact number or are you planning on moving?'

'Oh yes. I am pretty busy. Here let me write down my phone number for you.'

She opened her handbag her fingers locating a till receipt resting in the bottom underneath her purse and her mobile phone. She smoothed the paper with her finger before scribbling her mobile number. You can always leave a message. I will try to get back to you.'

She wanted to say that she would always have time for him. That she wanted to meet again and share in his dreams, his fantasies. But she could not risk rejection a second time. He had abandoned her and his child. He must have known that she was pregnant, and now April needed her. In the same instant the distrust of men, forged by their abuse of her in her past, hardened her emotions. He had made no attempt to find her, had he? So what had changed?

She drove back following the reverse of the route she had taken earlier. Journeys always seemed to be easier on the way home, she mused. It was like some homing instinct; a need to return to one's roots. But then, were they her roots? Had she ever had a sense of belonging? She decided that she would put the house on the market as soon as she had made contact with her daughter, wherever she was. It would be so good to sever the other links with her past. But then what about Crystal House? What about her mother Bella? What did Bradleigh Carter know about Crystal House?

David Dreighton had watched Caroline walking away, seemingly out of his life again. What a coward I am, he thought. Why didn't I tell her that I have never stopped loving her? They had been such a formidable gang, those Greenways, he thought. First Bella pushed into some kind of imprisonment, and then her daughter Caroline. Over the years since the enforced separation, he had observed her from afar, gleaning information from the gossip on the grapevine, or the social gatherings linked to the business dealings of Robert Thorston. Once, at a large public gathering to celebrate the opening of a new shopping centre, he had watched her dutifully accompanying her husband, and wanted to go over and speak to her, but he feared the consequences of such an action. He consoled himself in those very early years that he had been paid for his co-operation and had been given custody of their daughter April. Poor little girl, he mused, she was a burden, a shame to the family name, but he had the joy of her for two short years. He could barely cast his mind back to that fateful day when she had developed sepsis and had died. In spite of the bitter-sweet memories, it had all ruined his life. Jean could not wait for a divorce. Their marriage had already become a sham; a front of respectability.

'For God's sake,' he muttered bringing his hand hard down on the steering wheel. 'What the hell does it all matter?' The family name, the family jewels. It was like some kind of throwback to the Doomsday book; the Dark Ages. The faces of both Caroline and their child haunted him in both daytime and night-time dreams. His daughter's death, when she had just reached her second birthday had sent him over the edge into a black despair, and into thoughts of suicide.

He had read Robert Thorston's obituary in the county newspaper with mixed feelings; hate, pleasure and hope. He asked himself whether he could ever become part of Caroline's life again. Would he have the courage to make contact? Did she know what had happened to April? Would she blame him? Did she have children? There was no mention of family in his obituary. It merely said 'Beloved wife Caroline'. He grunted, turning the steering wheel hard round and pulling up into the small parking area in front of his house. He decided to leave the boxes of books in the boot until he had had something to eat. It was all hardly worth the effort, he thought. He'd sold a dozen or so copies. But then he had seen Caroline, hadn't he? That must be worth a million copies.

He walked slowly up the pathway to the front of his eighteenth-century cottage, where he had lived for the last twenty years. His hip was aching and he was developing a headache. A patch of stinging nettles was reaching across the doorway, and he sighed, suddenly feeling the threat of old age and of encroaching inadequacies. It had been all that he could afford. Jean had demanded the four-bedroomed modern house and a large amount of cash in settlement at the time of their divorce, and he had not put up a fight. He pushed open the door and went in, noticing again, the slight smell of mustiness and the shabbiness of the fireside chairs. He could not bring Caroline here. This was not a fairy-tale cottage where dreams could come true. Yet he loved its antiquity. They had told each other such stories, hadn't they? But then Caroline Thorston was a wealthy woman, used to having everything she wanted. Should he make further contact? There was definitely a spark there, he mused. But then what about Crystal House? How much did she know?

Caroline put David's book on the top of a row of other books on the bookshelf by the chimney breast, happy for it to remain there with her favourite books until she had the time to study it. The hard cover was in a deep russet brown, and the title in gold lettering presented a classical look, corresponding in style to the volume of 'H G Wells Notable Novels' that she had rescued from the pile of books and was waiting to be read, when she had the time. Now, the bleep of the answerphone could not be ignored. She was expecting a message from Mike Alford. She was not disappointed, and all thoughts of her encounter with her ex-lover left her mind.

'Good news, Mrs Thorston,' he said. 'I will call you later in the evening with details of contact.'

She played the message over again several times, not with any doubt in her mind, but purely to enjoy its content. He was a man of few words, she mused. Her mind went back to the earlier events of the day. David had been a man of few words. She smiled at the memory of their secret codes under the noses of his wife and her parents. Today had had the same feeling of secrecy with his eye contact and cryptic note hidden away in the first pages of the book. Now she had the urge to read it again, to relive that delicious feeling of shared secrecy.

She retrieved the book from the shelf, opening it and regarding his note. She recalled the hand writing. It had not changed, but why would it? He was in his late thirties then. She had kept all of those messages he had written, in an old school history folder. She had no idea what happened to it. Probably it had been disposed of together with all of her other shameful secrets; magicked away like Marigold. She folded the note in two, concealing his written words and put it in the front partition in her purse, separate from coins and bank notes. She was not curious about the content of the book, merely tracing her finger into the shape of his name on the cover, and then returning it to the bookshelf.

This day had seemed endless and she watched the hands of the clock moving slowly on to past seven o'clock. The ringing of the phone jolted her out of a sudden surrender to sleep.

'Hello,' she gasped. 'Caroline Thorston. Can I help you?'

'Are you able to travel to Thanfield and meet with your daughter? She has suggested the station buffet there as a good place for her to reach at two o'clock on Wednesday. I know it is some distance for you, but she has to fit it around her job and she has a half-day mid-week.'

'Of course, I can. It is Mr Alford isn't it?'

A grunt encouraged her to continue. Her voice was shaking now. 'How will we recognise each other?' she asked.

'Wear a blue scarf and carry an umbrella and she will do the same. Sounds crazy I know, but she seems to think that it is unlikely for anyone else to be standing near the entrance to the buffet at two o'clock like that. She will wait for half an hour.'

Caroline giggled. David would have given her the same kind of message. April must be like her father.

'Tell April I'll be there. I can't wait to see her again.'

'Don't forget it's Amber now.'

'Of course not. Thank you so much, Mr Alford.'

The phone clicked and she was left in the silence of her thoughts. She was trembling now. What a day it had been; the past linking up with the present twice! That was significant, wasn't it?

Chapter Eighteen

Jenny struggled with the release mechanism on the vacuum cleaner, emptying the fluff and dust into the dustbin. She sighed, already tired of the morning tasks. She knew that her brother Mike had been in contact. He had left a message on her phone late on the previous day, but Caroline was avoiding eye contact it seemed. She decided to broach the subject over coffee.

'So, it's good news then about your daughter. Mike tells me that you are going to meet her. I bet you can't wait after all this time.'

Caroline nodded, and sipped at her coffee.

Jenny waited for her to speak, staring expectantly across at her.

'Is she local then? You may have met her already and had no idea who she was. Although you didn't used to live in this area, did you? Still stranger things happen, don't they? That happened in one of those programmes about missing children. The son had been living in the next street all the time and she never knew.'

'No. She lives near Thanfield.' Caroline pushed the chair back and stood up, rinsing the dregs of coffee out of her cup into the sink, and staring out of the window. 'It looks like rain. I hope the weather is not going to change,' she said.

'Oh. Are you going to meet her in Thanfield then or is she coming here? I would love to be introduced after you get to know her, of course. Do you need company? It's a long way to drive.' Jenny saw Caroline's shoulders shrug and recognised the gesture. It was a sign that her employer was not in the mood to communicate.

She continued with her Tuesday work schedule, upset by this display of secrecy. After all, she fumed, if it had not been for me, she would not have known anything about her long-lost daughter. She emptied the clothes dryer, folding the duvet cover and the pillow cases and pushing the tea towels into the kitchen drawer. The clean bedding could finish airing in the cupboard. She trod wearily up the steep stairs noticing that the cupboard door was slightly open. The clean bedding was ruffled and she could see the edge of the old photograph album. Would Caroline show it to her daughter, she wondered? Why had the Great Majesto been removed and why had someone stabbed holes in his eyes?

There was no sign of her pay packet on the kitchen work-top. She was still owed for last week. She could hear her employer talking to someone, and she looked around the door into the sitting room. Caroline was making a phone call on her new cordless phone.

'I need to reach Thanfield before two tomorrow afternoon,' she was saying. 'So, that's twelve midday arrives at one-forty. That will be fine, thank you.'

Jenny ducked out of sight and was back in the kitchen before Caroline came in with her wages in the envelope. 'Sorry I forgot on Friday. You must remind me, you know. I just haven't got back into routine.'

It had started to rain as Jenny made her way to the bus stop. She was surprised to see Harry Bainer walking along ahead of her.

'What are you doing in these parts?' she called.

He spun around. 'I could say the same about you, but of course you work for Caroline Thorston, don't you?'

He knows I do, she thought. What was his game?

'I have been to see an old friend,' he continued. 'We had a good chat about Wales. It seems like weeks ago since we were there, doesn't it? So, has she found her daughter yet? That seemed to be all she could talk about last time I saw her. Did she tell you that I am likely to win a prize with that holiday company? Five days half board for two. I asked her if she would like it if I won. Maybe for both of you.'

Jenny shook her head. 'I don't think she can focus on anything but her daughter. She is going on the train to Thanfield to meet her tomorrow, but she is not telling me anything, after all I have done. But there you go. We don't count, do we?'

'Thanfield? That's a long way! I expect she will have to make an early start.'

'She's catching the morning train. Midday I think. Ah, the bus is on time for once.' She climbed up the steps ahead of him and squeezed into the first available seat, next to a large lady. 'Whatever am I doing telling him about Caroline's plans?' she asked herself? 'Why is he snooping around?'

Harry watched Jenny alight at the bus stop across the road from the block of flats. He felt sorry for her. She looked tired. Did she realise just how crooked her brother was, he wondered? She must know that he had been in prison. He continued to stare out of the window at the afternoon shoppers on the high street, as the bus approached the terminus at the supermarket. This latest information regarding the affairs of Caroline Thorston no doubt would be seized upon by his employer, he thought triumphantly. Five minutes later he was at the steps of the solicitor's house using the tarnished brass door-knocker to attract attention.

The net curtain twitched and seconds later the door creaked open and Brad Carter's face appeared. He led the way into his office, checking the time with his watch, and Harry was reminded of the white rabbit in a recent advertisement for something that had now slipped his mind. 'I'm late, I'm late,' The words chanted in his head.

He recounted his conversation with Jenny, adding that he had been on the case since nine watching the house and being in the right place at the right time.

'She's what? Oh my God. How can she be so stupid?' Brad banged his fist down on the desk.

Harry shook his head.

'So, what is she going to do then? Come on! Is that all you have to tell me?'

Harry nodded. 'I could always get the same train in the morning and follow her. I don't suppose I will be able to eavesdrop. It depends on where they go, but I may manage a photo or two. But then she may be the daughter. We don't really know, do we?'

Brad shook his head. 'No way,' he said. 'It is not that easy. I know from experience. This is a big con if ever I saw one. God knows how much he has cheated her out of so far. Yes. Be on that train tomorrow. Cover up well and don't let her see you and don't lose her. Still you know the score.'

Harry held out his hand, and his employer carefully opened his cash tin and counted out some notes.

Caroline pulled out a blue scarf from the drawer in the bottom of the wardrobe. It was her favourite accessory colour. April's as well, she guessed. The umbrella did not match but then she was not endeavouring to look fashionable, was she? She looked in the mirror and ran her fingers through her hair. It was still curly, and the streaks of blond from her pre-holiday session at the hairdressers caught the light from the late afternoon sunshine streaming in through the bedroom window. Would her daughter approve of her? Would she forgive her for giving her away for adoption? She smiled, pursing her lips, and saying, 'Darling I have thought about you, every day of my life.' That was what the mother had said to her daughter in the last episode of the television series. It was not true, but it sounded good. Who did her daughter look like? Herself or did she resemble her father, David? Caroline could visualise him so readily now since her recent encounter. Would April want to know what he looked like? How much did she know of her true ancestry?

She awoke early the next morning with bright sunshine streaming in through the gap in between the bedroom curtains. She had been to Thanfield once with her husband Robert. It was famous for secondhand book festivals and she remembered that the small town was busy with traders and customers. She had no recollection of a railway station, but then why would she? He had made the journey a few times on his own in his pursuit of first editions, those copies now in the hands of the dealer whom she had done business with on the previous Saturday. She had accompanied him once in what seemed like an age ago. Still, she mused, none of the geography or character of the place was important. A railway station buffet was somehow isolated from the life of a small town. It would be merely a collection of tables and chairs set possibly amongst a dirty cream and green background. Her thoughts turned to the film *Brief Encounter* she had viewed recently during a nostalgic trip into past cinema on the television. That buffet was dreary, yet the meeting of the two characters was charged with high emotions. She imagined her daughter wearing a blue scarf, and pretty as a picture, sitting opposite her, stirring her coffee. It was almost an identical scene to the last episode of the television programme about tracing lost children; even to the venue. That had been at a railway station. Somehow, the repeated scenario seemed significant; obligatory. Mrs Thorston meets her long-lost daughter at Thanfield. It even sounded like a scene in a drama. She giggled.

The train was on time, and she found a seat quite quickly in the first carriage facing forward with a table in front to house her bag, and to give her some privacy. She hated travelling backwards, as she described it, and consequently was unaware of a fellow traveller now seated at the far end of the carriage. Harry Bainer was in disguise in as much as he had on a hooded jacket and dark glasses and he had chosen to sit with his back to her. He had a newspaper opened at the ready, in case she walked past him.

The train was due in at one forty-five and Caroline stared out of the carriage window, hardly noticing the landscape as it slipped by her vision. She checked the time. How could it pass by so slowly, she wondered? When it was scarce, at times of panic, it seemed that it leapt ahead, or was gobbled up. Yet now, waiting for it to pass, was like torture. Her thoughts were back into her childhood, when she was locked in the cupboard and with the hatred she felt for her adoptive mother or aunt, as she really was according to the gypsy. Had her real mother ever longed to see her? Was April dreading this meeting?

She closed her eyes and tried to visualise a younger version of herself or would their daughter have a likeness to David? Should she have told him her plans?

A man's voice came over on the speaker system announcing the imminent arrival at Thanfield and advising all passengers to check their luggage before alighting at the station.

It was a popular day in the calendar for the small market town. A book fair was advertised on the bill board, and the main flow of pedestrians was out into the town through the exit barrier. Caroline looked around her. She could see a sign for Ladies, but there was no indication of a buffet and no sign of a woman wearing a blue scarf. Had she got it wrong? She knew that she had not. Ask a porter. She nodded in agreement with herself. Would that man know? No, he was strange-looking in that hooded jacket. Ah, she exclaimed to herself there's one. The porter did not speak; merely pointing to the adjacent platform and leaving Caroline feeling inadequate and irritated by his obvious contempt. No men were necessary, she decided. Keep away, David Dreighton.

She needed to spend a few minutes in the room marked Ladies, and spent some time at the wash basin, rinsing her hands and checking her make-up and hair. It was dark and gloomy in this area of the station, the Victorian frosted windows letting in little light and the single bulb in the middle of the room casting a yellow haze over everything, including her face. She stared anxiously at her reflection, and then checked the time. Two o'clock! Goodness! It was two o'clock and April would be waiting!

She almost tripped in her haste to return to the other platform and the buffet sign. She was there. A young woman, wearing jeans and a denim jacket with a bright blue scarf hung loosely around her neck, and an umbrella attached to the handle of her canvas bag, was looking along the platform. Caroline waved excitedly, almost tripping over.

'April. I'm here. I mean Amber of course.'

The young woman waved in return and turned to go into the buffet room. She walked across to a table in the corner and pulled out a chair. Caroline followed behind, suddenly feeling inadequate, overwhelmed by the apparent surety of this stranger.

'It's been such a long time. I expect you had given up on me.' She almost whispered the words she had rehearsed so many times on the train journey.

'I have been looking for you as well, but it cost money and I didn't have enough. I could do with a coffee, could you?' Her voice was high pitched with a strong Midland accent.

Caroline nodded, and reached in her bag for her purse. 'I certainly could. And what about a bite to eat. Are you ready for a cake or something?' She handed a twenty-pound note to the young woman and watched as she pushed back her chair and walked across to the counter.

She was plumper than she expected. She had visualised a slender young woman; long-legged, graceful. She turned her head, and Caroline noticed a tattoo on the side of her neck, disappearing down beyond the scarf. Her hair had red and purple streaks in amongst the long unevenly cut strands, and as she offered the note in payment for the coffee and cakes, Caroline could see that her nails were painted in colours to match her hair. One thing was apparent. She had a healthy appetite. She was piling up the plates with filled bread rolls and cakes, and now had reached the beverages. She turned, mouthing 'tea' or 'coffee'. Caroline said, 'Coffee please.' Moments later Amber was back at the table, barely seated before she was pulling the wrapper away from the bread roll and sinking her teeth into the crusty bread.

'Goodness me, you are hungry,' Caroline exclaimed.

'First thing I've had today,' the young woman said.

'So Amber. We don't have much time but can we talk about you? Are you happy with your family? I don't want to upset anybody you know. I just want to know that you are all right.'

The young woman bit hard into the bread roll again and mumbled, 'They threw me out. I left home years ago.'

Caroline was shocked, waiting to hear an explanation. She reached forward to grasp her hand. 'That's dreadful,' she stammered. 'Why did they do that? If only I had known. I would have looked after you.'

'Would you? What, even though I was pregnant. Still you know all about that, don't you? The way you were treated.'

Caroline felt her colour rising. The guilt was back. She owed her daughter so much, yet it seemed to be too late.

'Well, I am here now, so I can help you. Did your child get put into care?'

'No. I wouldn't have that. He is ten now, nearly eleven, and going to grammar school if I can afford the uniform. It costs a fortune and I don't get paid much.'

Caroline tried to visualise a ten-year-old grandson. She had dreamed of a granddaughter, who would care for Marigold like she did but not be punished. She wanted to right all of the wrongs somehow; turn back the clock.

'That's nice,' she said. 'What's his name?'

'David Paul.'

Caroline' heart skipped a beat. 'Why did you choose David?' she asked. 'Is that after his father?'

'No. I just like it. I have no idea who his father is. I was date raped. You know drink spiked and ill for days. I don't remember much about it. I was totally shocked at being pregnant and then they threw me out. Anyway, I have managed without them. I am a qualified hairdresser so I can get by.'

'Oh April. If only I had known. Anyway, I am here now so I can help you. Is there anything you need at the moment?' Caroline was shocked by her graphic descriptions.

'I would be grateful for some cash to get David's uniform. He has got into grammar school and the list seems endless.'

'Of course. Have this and then I can put some money into your account.'

Caroline opened her handbag and took out her purse. 'About five hundred there, darling. That should cover his requirements.'

Amber pushed the notes into her bag. 'I don't have an account,' she said. 'I would prefer cash if you can help me. I have got a big gas bill to pay, and I have got laid off from work.'

'Let's get to the bank then. I have got about two hours before my train ride home.'

'That will be so good. I can't tell you how happy I am. There's some good shops along the high street. Perhaps you can treat yourself as well. You deserve it.'

Caroline climbed up the step onto the train feeling happier than she had been for a long time. Amber was such a lovely young woman. She looked transformed in those rig-outs she had tried on. And her joy was reward enough.

As the train picked up speed, already she was planning her next visit. She had offered Amber a home with her, but she had declined the offer, explaining that David would not like a change of school. They had giggled in the changing rooms, and she had felt like the teenager she had always wanted to be. Her April would want for nothing now. The thousand pounds cash she had withdrawn from the bank would help until she could transfer a larger sum into a bank account for her.

'So, what have you got to report then?'

Harry had pulled down his hood and returned his dark glasses to his pocket after leaving the station and walking to the supermarket car park at the rear of Brad. Carter's house and being given entrance through the old back door.

'She's spent plenty on this woman whoever she is. A bit of a tart by the look of her.'

'Did you actually see them spending money? How do you know that it was Mrs Thorston's?'

'Well, by the state of her, she's not got two pennies to rub together as my mum used to say. They went into the bank and made a withdrawal. I did see Caroline hand over a wad of notes, and they both had a few bags of shopping; clothes and shoes I think. There was not a lot of time, and I was dodging around. I did take some pics.'

He produced his mobile phone and clicked onto photos. He had quite a clear image of them coming out of the bank. 'Neither of them was aware of being observed,' he explained. 'They were both intent on fastening up their bags.'

'She reminds me of someone.'

'Yes, me too. But these girls all look alike with their dyed hair and piercings. Anyway, you can pay me my wages for the day while I am here, and I can grab something for my tea from next door.'

'I gave you some cash yesterday. Have you spent it already?'

'Yes. Have you travelled on the trains lately? Here's my ticket and what I had to eat. I could work for someone else. Following rich people for a pittance is not exactly fun you know, although working for Mrs Thorston could be good. She needs a gardener and odd job man.'

Brad Carter grunted and looked at his watch. He had to see Caroline before she made any more arrangements. It was too late now. She would be suspicious of evening visits after the fiasco last time. He decided to contact her and make an appointment to see her on the following day to discuss this mysterious account involving someone at Crystal House. She seriously needed advice.

Chapter Nineteen

Caroline took off her shoes and sank down into the armchair next to the fireplace. It was Marigold's chair, but she would have to squash in. Her grandson David would prefer something different. What did eleven-year-old boys like? She had no idea. Perhaps Jenny would know. She couldn't wait to show her the photograph. She clicked the buttons on her mobile phone, and the photograph of Amber was there again. There was something so familiar about her face. Could it be a resemblance to David's side? Should she send it to him and ask him?

She wanted the excitement to continue. She decided to text message him and include the photograph of Amber. She could tell him that he had a grandson called David. That would please him. She tapped out the message, 'This is our daughter April. Met her today. She has a son called David.'

Moments later her mobile phone buzzed. It was a message back from David Dreighton.

'I must see you. Hold all of your plans. I will explain.'

What was there to explain, Caroline wondered? Did he know about April all of this time? Had April knowingly named her son after her real father? Was everyone plotting against her?

She shivered, pulling Marigold towards her. The hatred was back. What did she really know about David Dreighton? She stood up and went to the bookshelf, retrieving the copy of his book. His photograph was on the back of the cover. It was not a recent one. He looked handsome; more or less as she remembered him. She tried to visualise the face of his book-signing session. His hairline was receding now and his skin was showing his age. His eyes crinkled at the corners.

She opened the book, scanning the contents listed on the first page. 'Crystal House page 23.' She gasped. She could not believe it. It was no coincidence, was it? Just one big secret separating her from the reality of her life. They had all known that her mother was Bella. David had known. Robert had known. Now Brad Carter was pointing in that direction. How else could this Crystal House appear so suddenly? It was like a board game, she thought. She was one of the counters, not a player. She was being pushed around, not allowed to know the next throw of the dice. But then, it seemed, the gypsy had broken the rules.

The mobile phone buzzed again. 'Coming over early tomorrow. It can't be left. David,' she read.

She sat staring at the words. She did not tell him where she lived, did she? She knew that she had been very guarded that day. So how could he drive over to see her and what was so urgent?

She slept fitfully, her legs cramping in spasms reflecting the tension in her whole being. There was no dreaming state where she could escape from reality, merely a restless revisiting of the day's happenings and of her re-acquaintance with David Dreighton.

Eventually, she gave up on the whole business of sleeping, and found herself heading towards the kitchen.

He arrived earlier than she expected and she glanced at herself in the hall mirror as she hurried to the door. She could see his outline against the frosted glass. The memory of his physical shape had never left her, merely been reawakened by her recent contact with him. He strode in, almost pushing against her and not speaking. She turned, catching sight of herself again in the mirror, her face devoid of makeup and her hair tangled.

'Coffee?' she queried.

He shook his head.

'Let's just get down to why I am here, Caroline.'

'How did you know where I live?'

'Oh, I'll sort that out later. The main thing is your contact with this young woman, whoever she is. I can tell you quite definitely that she is not our daughter April.'

Caroline stared at him. He was agitated, almost angry it seemed. She did not speak, waiting for the explanation. He took a deep breath before he made his next pronouncement.

'April died in early childhood,' he said.

Caroline felt her arms stiffening, and her fists clenching with the shock of hearing his words. She stared at his face, now already so familiar, trusting him, yet not able to accept his words without further explanation.

He reached forward to comfort her and she backed away.

'Can I explain? Can we sit down somewhere that's more comfortable and I will try to fill in all the blanks in your life? I can't believe that you have never been told.'

Caroline nodded. She had moved back into that space where she obeyed; accepting her role of the subservient girl, the fantasy lover, the obedient wife.

He followed her into the sitting room and she sank down into her chair opposite to the television set, putting Marigold on the floor. He glanced around, choosing to sit on the edge of the sofa and leaning forward towards her.

'Why didn't you tell me the other day?' Caroline broke the silence before he could begin.

'We had so little time and I honestly thought that you knew. Can I explain now? After April was a month old, I took charge of her. I did not want her to be with strangers, but your parents were determined that your life should not be ruined by the disgrace of it all and were in favour of putting April into care. I arranged for her to be looked after by a woman I knew and could trust. By this time, my wife had thrown me out and was demanding a divorce and everything she could claim. I wanted to keep April safe until I could marry you.'

Caroline grunted, and shook her head. 'Really. Then why didn't you?'

'They wouldn't let me contact you, and the next thing I heard was that you were engaged to Robert Thorston. What could I offer you as good as that? I had to make a big divorce settlement and I was living in a flat with hardly space to swing a cat, never mind having a wife and a child there.'

Caroline shrugged. 'So, what happened to April then? How did she die?'

'She was lovely, fair hair and blue eyes. She looked like you. She got meningitis and it all happened so quickly. It was no one's fault. It was like losing you all over again. Caroline, you must believe me. I rang up your parents and told them. Your father was always such a close friend but he was not in charge. He was always being punished.'

'That made two of us then. But what had we done?'

David sighed. 'Oh, my dear Caroline. You have been so wronged. There is so much explaining to do. I think it is best if I start from the beginning.'

For the next hour, Caroline learnt how he had known Anthony, her father, from their university days. He was training to be an architect and Anthony was a budding civil engineer. They were close friends. He was best man at Anthony's and Bernice's wedding but he had known Bernice and her identical twin sister Isabelle, or Bella as she was known, for over a year.

Caroline nodded. 'They shared everything didn't they?' she said.

David nodded. 'So, you knew about her then, did you?'

She explained about her encounter with the gypsy.

'She was like the other side of the same coin. Bernice was so serious and strait-laced, whereas Bella was wild and constantly in trouble. Anthony was so attracted to Bella, and it seemed to me that it was a mutual agreement between the three of them for Bella to provide a child. Kind of surrogate. I don't know whether Bernice couldn't conceive. But then she turned against Bella and she, in turn, left with you to live on her own.'

'So, he was my true father. The gypsy said that. I didn't know what to believe but he still betrayed me, didn't he? So where did you come into this then? Did you have a relationship with my mother as well? Was I second-best? Does this get worse?'

David sighed. 'I must admit that we were all infatuated with Bella at one stage. By all, I mean our university friends. She was so alive and vibrant, but she was frowned upon by your father's family and the marriage was arranged with Bernice together with her half of the large family fortune that eventually the twins would inherit. I knew that he was in love with Bella. I was not surprised when I heard on the grapevine that she was pregnant and that there was a big cover-up.'

'So was I adopted by them? He was my father anyway. But was she legally my mother? What happened to my original birth certificate? She told me that I was found on a doorstep. That I was a bastard.'

David frowned. 'As always in these families, like I said, it was a big cover-up. Bella was becoming wilder and she was leaving you on your own and making accusations about your father. I think neighbours reported her for neglect and so, apparently, the family stepped in. I met up with your father again years later and was invited around as you know. He told me how he was in a bad relationship and I could see how unhappy you were as well. There was something about you that reminded me of your mother. I don't know what it was. You were more like your father in looks. I think you were so unhappy and living in a dream world. Whatever. You bewitched me and then gave me the daughter I had longed for. I was not going to be robbed of that.'

Caroline was sitting very still. She had not spoken for some time and he leaned forward in silent communication, a question unsaid on his face.

She recognised the expression. It was a look he had used a lifetime ago, she thought. April's lifetime ago. Nothing could ever change the fact that he was the father of her child and the love of her life. She began to cry and he left the sofa and sat on the floor beside her, patting her knee.

'Would you like to see some photographs of April? I have brought her album. I know it cannot make up for the two years that were stolen from you but it will put some good pictures in your mind. I'll fetch it, shall I? It is in the car.'

Caroline nodded. It was all coming together like a jigsaw puzzle. She would know what April looked like. She could dream about her. She had been returned to her like her precious Marigold. She would have no need of pretend relations now in that old album. She had only invented them to show to her daughter. She knew now with certainty who she was, but then did she want to know her mother? Was she at Crystal House as the gypsy said? Had David seen her when he did his research? Is that why there was a chapter in the book?

The sound of the door opening and David's footsteps in the hall brought her thoughts back to April, and she spent the next hour sitting with him on the settee, studying each image of her daughter as the child had grown from early babyhood into a two-year-old toddler. Now, she could visualise her again at her birth. It had been so hard to bring that image back with no other reference than her memory of that first meeting, and those treasured times when she was brought to her for feeding.

She closed the album and drew in a long, sighing breath.

'Do you believe in predestination David? Was April destined to have such a short life? Am I destined to meet my mother?'

David looked up, his eyes questioning.

'The gypsy told me to look for Crystal House, and you have written about it. Is she still there, and why? Is it a retirement home?'

'She has been there for a long time. I haven't told you very much about her life in recent years because I thought it would be too much for you, but she is your mother and you have a right to know. One of her accomplishments was her ability to play the piano. As children they both had lessons. She was a great performer and Bernice was just the opposite. Consequently, Bernice would not have a piano in the house. I can remember you talking about wanting to learn. You did have a guitar, didn't you?'

Caroline nodded. 'It's still around. He threatened to put it in the bin so I hid it.'

'Who did?'

'Robert, my husband. That would make him turn in his grave if I started playing again. She, my aunt, hated it as well. So, what happened to my mother then? Don't stop.'

'I suppose you have to know. She tried to kill someone with a knife. She was found to be suffering from a kind of madness and was locked away in a mental institution for many years. Eventually she was allowed to spend the rest of her life in Crystal House where she is cared for by a group of nuns, at a price of course.'

Caroline's eyes widened and a shiver snaked up her spine. 'Lizzie Borden took an axe.' The words were jumping about in her head and then the face of the magician was there staring out at her with his pierced eyes. My God, my God, her mind exclaimed. 'Like mother, like daughter.' Her mother-aunt used to say that. The photograph of her that she had stabbed with a knife when she was a child. Had it been found in the dustbin? She knew, didn't she? Like mother like daughter! So, they did not lock her up like her mother. But they imprisoned her in a loveless marriage. How much did they pay him? She continued to be trapped in fear of punishment, like being shut up in the cupboard, she thought. But then she had got rid of him, hadn't she? Oh yes, she certainly had.

David put the album on the floor and put his arm around her.

'I'm sorry, Caroline. You really did not need to know that. I was upset when I saw her, but she is just an elderly lady now, old before her time really, and living in a world of her own.'

The gypsy told me to go and see her. I really do need to know my own mother, don't I? Can you tell me where Crystal House is?'

'I'll do better than that. I will take you there. Leave it with me and I will organise it with the nuns who run the place. I must go now. I have got another book signing, but I will be in touch. Don't get up. I can see myself out.'

Chapter Twenty

Caroline watched through the front window as he climbed into his car, and moments later the solitude was back. She opened the album again, staring at each image, seeing her child appearing across the pages in those precious days of her short life. She picked up Marigold, holding her to face the photographs.

'Wasn't she pretty?' she asked. 'She would have loved you, but they stole you away. They stole both of you away.'

The sound of the phone startled her and Marigold fell to the floor.

'Mrs Thorston? Mike Alford here. So, how did it go? You met up with Amber then?'

'Yes. But she was not my daughter. My daughter died when she was two years old. You got it very wrong, didn't you Mr Alford? I shall be consulting my solicitor.'

'Wait a minute! Are you threatening me? I have heard on the grapevine that you couldn't wait to bury your old man. They could always dig him up. What would they find?'

Caroline did not answer. She returned the phone to its holder, her heart beating fast.

He knows. He knows. He knows. That last desperate day when she overdosed him. When he finally broke her spirit; turning the knife in all the wounds he had inflicted over those long years.

'Caroline. Are you upstairs or downstairs?' That was Jenny's voice.

'I'm in here.' Caroline rubbed her eyes, the tears of anguish wet on her cheeks.

Jenny ran forward to embrace her and Caroline sank down into the armchair, turning her face away. 'I thought you would be so happy. I've been imagining you meeting her.'

'Did you really think that brother of yours could do anything good? You must have known. He deserves to be put in prison or killed off.'

'Why? What's he done?'

'Don't tell me you didn't know.'

Jenny's breathing was uneven. 'I don't know what you are talking about,' she gasped. 'Didn't you meet April then? Wasn't she there?'

'This is her, look. A common little tart.' Caroline scrolled down to the photograph on her mobile phone.

'Oh goodness! That's my niece Kay,' Jenny stammered.

'Your niece? What, his daughter?'

'Yes. I don't really know much about her, but I have seen photos. Honestly, I had no idea. How could he do this? How did you know?'

Caroline had calmed down and picking up the album she began to turn the pages, explaining that April had died not long after the photographs were taken.

Jenny waited in silence, but her mind was racing. Another album she thought. So, what was this all about?'

'He rang me. Your brother. He rang me about ten minutes ago. He is not a nice man, is he? He has cheated me, but I am not going to the police. I can't really prove anything. Just stupid. That's me. I would prefer it if you keep this to yourself.'

'I believed him as well. But how did you find out that April had died? Do you want to explain or just tell me to mind my own business?'

Caroline told her about David and their relationship and of how she had met up with him at the book signing. 'We did not talk about April. I was keeping it to myself, but then last night I sent him the photograph I took on my phone of Amber, or Kay is it, and he drove over this morning in a panic to explain. He had not allowed April to be adopted when she was taken away from me, and he arranged for child care whilst he was at work. He was waiting for a divorce so that he could marry me but sadly, she became ill just after these last photographs were taken and died. I was never told and they had married me off. So now the search is over.'

Jenny sighed and reached across to clasp Caroline's hand. 'Bastards, all of them,' she muttered.

'Anyway, I now know who my real mother is.'

'What? The one in the old album?'

'No. I was pretending. I don't know who they were. That album was in the box from the auction. David has told me everything. That gypsy was right. She said that my real mother is Bella, the twin sister of the woman I called mother, who hated me. Bella is still alive and living in a kind of residential home called Crystal House. David has written about it in his book. I went to his book-signing. I told you, didn't I?'

Jenny shook her head. 'Hang on a minute,' she said. 'Do you mean that gypsy on holiday. I knew that she had upset you. God, Caroline! Why didn't you tell me? I thought that I had offended you.'

Caroline struggled to her feet. 'Let's read the chapter in his book together. I don't seem to be able to function these days on my own.'

She went into the study and returned with the handsomely bound copy of David Dreighton's book.

'It's a lovely book,' Jenny commented. 'Smells nice. Not like those other musty ones in there.'

'So, Crystal House, page twenty-three. Here we are.' Caroline began to read out loud.

''Crystal House was once an imposing Victorian Gothic red-brick mansion, the home of the Peasgood family, nouveau riche mine owners, with its unusual feature of a glass dome rising up in the centre of the roof line.

'The architect, William Stoarte as a young boy had been impressed by the Crystal Palace in the Great Exhibition of 1851, and the design of Crystal House in later life fulfilled a childhood dream.

'Today, the original building remains largely the same, but now functions as a retirement home accommodating a small number of elderly residents in the charge of several nuns.

'A wide gravelled driveway winds along to the side of the house taking up most of what perhaps was a large box hedged garden, now limited to a small area on the left-hand side and enters between rusting wrought-iron gates supported on either side by red brick pillars and by thick layers of ivy reaching out from the garden behind. Indeed, the ivy has the gates so firmly in its grip that they no longer are able to be closed, defeating their purpose of offering security to the residents of this strange house.

'A black and white mosaic tiled path leading up to the front door, is flanked on either side by black rope border stones once defining the flower beds that now show neglect, weeds growing apace in the sour earth.

'Conifer trees, planted many years ago, crowd into the building, their heavy branches shading the bay windows, cutting out the light for the tenants and concealing the shabbiness and decay; the moss and layers of dust and dirt.

'The porch offers refuge from the chill north-easterly winds that sweep across from the Arctic Circle in bleak winters, but few people linger there, seeking sanctuary beyond the heavy panelled door that opens into a spacious entrance hall. The stained-glass sections of this once splendid door now represent a weakness rather than an artistic asset, threatening the security of the building against intruders, with the crumbling lead and the encroaching dirt and decay.

'Author's comment. It is sad to see the decline in this splendid example of Gothic architecture in all of its red-bricked splendour. The crystal dome is unique and deserves to be preserved as a national treasure.'

Caroline smiled. 'David is so clever,' she said.

Jenny grunted. There was nothing clever about the way he had abandoned Caroline, she thought. Flesh and blood matter more than bricks and mortar every time.

'So that is where my mother is cared for by nuns. I can't wait to meet her.'

'What does she know about you? She must have wanted to see you. Do you think she was told to keep away?'

Caroline shrugged her shoulders, and stood up, leaving the book open on the table. 'I expect she will remember David. They were both students. But perhaps she hasn't seen me since I was a toddler.'

'Is she an invalid or what? Do you know why she is there?

'I don't know. She may have had a breakdown.'

Jenny recognised that sudden withdrawal. Whatever her employer knew, she was not telling. 'So, are you going to see her? Do you want me to come with you? I don't mind you know. I am so sorry about my brother. I will never speak to him again.'

'No. I am going with David. She knew him from their student days. You can get on with your jobs now. I need to be on my own.'

Chapter Twenty-One

It was early afternoon before they turned through the gates onto the driveway leading up to Crystal House. David's description in his book was accurate in its detail, yet it had not prepared Caroline for that initial impression of mystery and decay. It seemed to her that the house was looking at them; watching their slow progress along the pot-holed, muddy driveway. Rows of windows, black oblongs; sightless it seemed, yet who was behind that dark glass watching these approaching intruders? She shivered.

David patted her on the knee. 'The crystal dome, look. Isn't it magnificent?'

Caroline nodded. The afternoon sun high in the cloudless sky was reflected so brightly in the glass, drawing the eye away from the shabbiness of the red brickwork and the blackness of the window panes. The car swung around in the gravelled driveway, and they came to a halt opposite to the front entrance. Caroline, her back stiffened from the long journey, struggled to get out of the car and stepped onto the tiled pathway, recalling David's description of it and remarking on the ornate edging now barely visible amongst the prolific growth of dandelions and couch grass.

'They could do with a gardener,' she remarked.

'That's the least of their problems,' David replied, shaking his head.

A cold gust of wind suddenly blew against the backs of her legs making her gasp and she reached for the support of his arm as they made their way to the door and rang the bell.

Moments later, they were being invited in by a young girl and Caroline was left on her own in the entrance hall, waiting for David to sign the visitors' book. 'Fire regs,' he muttered. She nodded. To be truthful she was in no hurry to meet her mother. What had seemed to be so exciting after all of her fantasising now filled her with a kind of dread. Her mind drifted back to the previous night when she was unable to sleep, remembering her school days when she had studied Charlotte Bronte's *Jane Eyre* and had shivered at the fearful description of the mad woman in the attic. Was her mother locked in somewhere beyond that ornate staircase at the far end of this hallway? Or was she in an attic room? Would she attack them?

David had returned accompanied by a stern-faced nun who then led the way, seeming to glide strangely along in front of them as though she was on wheels, Caroline thought. They climbed the stairs, and her eyes were drawn upwards to the crystal glass dome through which the light entered the centre of the building, illuminating a circular gallery and the hallway below. She tried to visualise how spectacular it once must have been. Now years of grime and moss had accumulated to such an extent that the rays of the sun could scarcely penetrate the glass panes. What a big task to clean it, she mused. It would need a team of experts. Hardly a job for the nuns. Here and there, shafts of light allowed glimpses of ornate carvings and other works of art lined up along the gallery walls, and as they reached the top of the staircase, Caroline could identify them as religious artefacts and paintings depicting scenes from the Bible.

'The Light of the World,' David whispered. 'Holman Hunt. Not the original of course. That is in St Paul's.'

Caroline nodded. This was a Catholic establishment of course. Was her mother religious?

A large crucifix was fastened to the wall in a space in between two other religious paintings. Caroline could glimpse, on passing, that it was carved from wood with inlaid silver glinting in the light. She shivered, then said out loud the words her aunt had so readily quoted in the past. 'Someone just walked over my grave.'

'That's a strange expression,' David whispered, pulling at her arm. 'I know what you mean though. It is getting to me as well. Ah. Apparently, this is it.'

The nun had stopped outside of a door and was selecting a key from amongst the bunch fastened to a belt around her waist. She slotted it into the keyhole and turned it.

'She may be asleep,' she said in a hoarse whisper. 'Do not attempt to wake her. She has few visitors and is very nervous. You can only stay for half an hour, as I have other jobs to do. Rap on the door when you wish to leave and I will unlock it and let you out.'

Caroline shivered, and the feeling of panic was back. She was about to meet her mother after all the years of deception, but who was she? What would she remember?

They felt obliged to tiptoe into the room, David leading the way, and Caroline following. The curtains were drawn to and very little light was penetrating through the heavy velvet fabric, but they were immediately aware of a large four-poster bed with muslin drapes at the corners and of the shape of a sleeping figure.

David put his finger to his lips.

Caroline sighed and walked slowly across to the bed, leaning forward for a moment or two to study the elderly lady who was her mother Bella. White hair framed a face heavily lined with the wear and tear of life, yet, she mused, with a certain serenity in her sleeping state belying her diminished circumstances. She relaxed now and looked around. Like everywhere else, it seemed, this room had seen better days.

It was quite large, with long elegant windows, the gaps in the curtains revealing ornate stained glass in the transits. The curtains themselves, deep Prussian blue velvet, hung in tatters here and there, and the remains of the crystal beading which edged the pelmets now swayed sadly in the draughts penetrating the rotting window frames.

A scratching sound startled Caroline. 'Mice?' she mouthed.

David shook his head. 'Trees against the glass,' he whispered.

Caroline remembered how the old conifers were crowding in on the building, adding to the gloom.

The floor creaked under her feet and she looked down at the shabby carpet, stained with spillages, the original red and gold pattern beginning to fade. As her eyes became accustomed to the gloom, she became aware of a painting on the opposite wall. It portrayed a young woman sitting at a piano.

David had followed her gaze and said 'That's Bella your mother. She was an amazing pianist.'

Caroline shivered. Ghost from the past, she thought.

'That's her piano, look. I remember it. A baby grand. I doubt she ever plays it now.'

'It's so cold in here, David,' she whispered. 'They could have a big fire burning in this wonderful old fireplace. What beautiful tiles.'

'Dutch by the look of them. I think they have fires in the winter. No central heating. Looks like it has never been cleaned since the winter.'

'More like years. All that ash and dust. It can't be good. Even the clock on the mantelpiece has stopped. I can remember brass candlesticks like that when I was a child. Surely there are electric lights.'

'There look! We can hardly see them for the dust.' David pointed to the glass chandeliers suspended from the ceiling and shrugged his shoulders.

Caroline visualised spiders and wondered if her mother had nightmares like she did.

As if such a fear had suddenly penetrated her sleep, Bella suddenly called out and pushed back the covers. Now Caroline could fully see the pale face and the white hair reaching her shoulders. Her eyes seemed hollow and staring. Somehow timeless she thought, yet with signs of advanced senility although she was only in her early seventies. She looked back at David, suddenly afraid to speak.

'Dementia,' David whispered. 'Poor Bella. She is in a world of her own.'

Bella appeared to be startled by their voices. 'Is it that time again?' she said. 'I don't want soup. Take it away. I hate soup.'

Caroline stared at this strange old lady who apparently it seemed was her mother; her appearance conflicting with the memories of the woman she had called her mother for most of her life. Yet they were identical twins. Would Bernice have ended up like this if she had not been killed in the car crash? It's the inside that counts, she thought.

She leaned forward and patted Bella on the arm. 'Not soup. We have come to see you. I am Caroline, your daughter.'

'No. You are not Caroline. This is Caroline.'

Bella pointed at a photograph frame on the bedside table. 'Caroline and Marigold,' she said. 'That's my Caroline.'

It was an image of a little fair-haired child with a doll.

Caroline gasped. So that's why I love Marigold, she thought, and that's why Bernice hated her and got rid of her at the birthday party. Bella has no idea of how time has passed by. But then I believed that imposter Kay was my daughter because I had little memory of April, and now my mother only remembers me as an image in a frame. But she remembers Marigold.

'Did you buy Marigold for Caroline?' she asked.

Bella smiled. 'I certainly did. Caroline loves her, don't you, Caroline?'

'You play the piano don't you, Bella.' That was David's voice now.

Bella looked at him and smiled. 'Hello David,' she said. '*Moonlight Sonata*. That was your favourite, wasn't it? Would you like to hear it? They have just made a recording.'

She pointed to a small set of drawers positioned at the side of the piano.

David recognised it as a storage place for sheet music, each drawer having a hinged front. He sighed. This should be cleaned and treasured he thought to himself. Now, apparently, the drawers housed tapes of recordings.

'All your recordings?' he asked.

Bella nodded, her eyes shining now. 'Play Moonlight,' she said, and pointed to an old tape player and recorder on the chest of drawers.

'It's a long time since I worked one of these,' David said, grinning.

'Don't believe him. He's always kidding.'

Caroline had a sudden sense of not belonging. I am not in their world. I'm in the future, she thought. But then Beethoven's *Moonlight Sonata* took over, leaving no space for conversation. In fact, she thought, music transcended everything; past and future. Just this was enough. 'It's beautiful, Mother,' she whispered. 'I shall never forget this time with you.'

For a brief moment they made eye contact and then Bella said, 'Thank you, Caroline.'

As the last sounds of the piano recording left the room, a new sound drew their attention. The key was being turned in the lock, and moments later the head of the nun appeared around the edge of the door.

'Time for her soup,' she said. 'She must calm down or we will have problems. Come along. I will show you out.'

Caroline saw David putting the tape recording into his pocket and looked at Bella, but there was no indication of acknowledgement or protest. It seemed that her mother had returned into her own world, fearing soup and nuns and recalling only the past.

Caroline left Crystal House without a backward look. She had no need to refresh her memory. The sight and sounds of that brief reunion were printed forever on her mind, and yet mixed up with it all were the words of the gypsy. 'Twins share everything.' Would her Aunt Bernice have developed this kind of insanity? Or was she always insane? Were they both unbalanced from childhood? Could she forgive her for something which was not her fault? And what about me, she mused? Have I inherited the same genes? 'Lizzie Borden' chanted her brain.

She hardly spoke on the way home. The rain fell steadily and for a while the rhythmic clicking of the wipers dulled her mind into sleep.

They stopped for coffee and stretched their legs looking with little interest at the goods on offer in the retail outlets at the service station yet looking all the same. After half an hour spent in these futile wanderings, they returned to the car, now ready to resume the journey.

David squeezed her arm. 'It will soon be dark,' he said. 'And it looks set to rain all day.'

Caroline nodded, although her inner voice silently added 'Does it matter if it rains forever?'

David seemed to pick up on her thoughts. 'It was not your fault, you know. You mustn't take any of the blame. It would probably have been the same outcome for her if she had not had you.'

She could not accept that. What was he saying? Was he saying that her life was immaterial? 'You could say the same about April, couldn't you, but my life was changed forever. I would not have been married off to that monster and I may have had a career. Done something worthwhile. Bella must have been unhappy when I was taken away from her. Look how she keeps that photograph at her bedside. She has never forgotten me and it must have affected her life.'

David did not answer, braking hard as a car pulled out in front of him and cursing under his breath. 'Brilliant pianist,' he said instead. 'I've kept that tape for you. I will get it put onto a CD. I would like to rescue all of them, but that nun was a bit like a prison warder.'

'She wouldn't let me have piano lessons. She was such a cow.'

David sucked in his breath. 'You mean Bernice,' he said. 'That's a bit strong for you.'

'I used to enjoy playing the guitar. I've still got it hidden away. He hated it. I think I will get back to it.'

David patted her knee. 'That would be good,' he said. 'Take your mind off things.'

His platitudes irritated her. No, she thought. That was not the point of music. It was not a distraction. In any case music did not need a point. It is what it is, she reasoned, like the moon and stars in the sky, like the flowers and the birds, like the beating of the heart, like magic.

'That place is up for sale,' David suddenly said, sensing her hostility and changing the subject.

'What, Crystal House? What will happen to the residents? Are there many there? We didn't see any, did we, but you mentioned it in your book? What about my mother?'

David shrugged. 'I don't suppose it will make much difference, unless it is bought by a big concern as some kind of national treasure, then it would have to be empty, and restoration work done. Somebody could spend some money on it even if it was just on the dome. It is a crying shame the way it has become so run down. An old people's home has no need of history after all, does it?'

Caroline frowned. 'You will be old one day,' she muttered. 'Where will they put you, I wonder?'

A little seed of ambition was growing in her mind. What if she bought Crystal House and looked after her mother? She liked the idea of living there instead of in the ghastly modern house where she had spent so many unhappy years.

Chapter Twenty-Two

Caroline could scarcely contain her excitement now as the idea of buying Crystal House became rooted in her brain. David stayed only long enough to see her safely back in her house, to her relief, declining refreshments and promising to be in touch.

She went into the sitting room and waved at Marigold who was still reclining in the armchair where she had left her the night before. 'I have seen a photograph of you, all bright and new,' she said. 'Fancy, my mother bought you for me and I never knew, did I?'

Was it a trick of the light, or did Marigold smile? She giggled at the idea. I'm going crazy, she thought.

The sound of the telephone ringing startled her back into the reality of the day. It was Brad Carter.

'Just the man I need,' she said. 'For some advice,' she added.

He cleared his throat noisily and she could just imagine him checking the time with his watch. 'I understand that you have been to Crystal House,' he said. 'I did have a brief chat with David Dreighton, the architect. I remember my father talking about him. I told you recently, didn't I, that I had been going into a lot of my father's paperwork. Did you know that Bella Greenway is your mother and that she owns Crystal House? You are her next of kin. You were never legally adopted by your aunt, because her husband Anthony Pearson was truly your father and it was left like that. You will inherit Crystal House and a large life insurance when she dies. You will be very wealthy, Caroline.'

'I did know that I am her daughter. David Dreighton has told me everything. It is all a long story, but then he did not know that my mother owned Crystal House. He knew that it was likely to be sold. I think the head nun, or whatever she is called must have told him, but my mother is in no fit state to make decisions. It was difficult to converse with her.'

'Well, Caroline, perhaps David doesn't know all of the facts or is deceiving you somehow. But I am telling you that it will all be yours one day, although apparently it is in a bad state. It may be a huge white elephant as they say, but you can rely on me to investigate all the legal side of it when the time comes.'

'Thank you,' Caroline's voice was disappearing, almost becoming a whisper. She felt that she was back in a fantasy world again, but also, she was beginning to realise that she had been isolated in ignorance of all of the arrangements that had been made by the family. The thought began to creep across her mind that David had known that she would inherit Crystal House. He certainly knew more than he was saying, and when had he contacted Brad Carter? What did all of them know?

Time began to move quickly it seemed through the next few weeks. Then on one day she had a mother, and on the next day she was mourning the departure of her sole relative. She had a sudden feeling of great loss, even though their relationship had been so fleeting. She was determined that her mother's memory would be honoured and ordered Brad to make the necessary arrangements. With the help of the sister in charge, her mother was laid to rest in the garden at Crystal House, and an ornate gravestone was erected, with the words

Bella Greenway

Loving Mother of Caroline

carved into the granite. Caroline had toyed with the idea of including Marigold, but then changed her mind. Marigold would have to wait.

She had forgiven Jenny for her brother's crime. His threats had alarmed her. She could still see the look on her husband's face as she had administered the overdose that had ended his life. But that criminal Mike Alford had got it wrong, hadn't he? He said that they could exhume the body, but she guessed that he had too much to lose and what policeman was going to listen to the likes of him? She needed friends not enemies. Besides, she had become very fond of Jenny, and needed her to organise the packing-up of her present home leading to the sale, and later the cleaning of the many rooms in Crystal House. Harry Bainer had happened to come by one day still talking about a holiday competition, and she asked him if he could help Jenny with the heavy jobs. She felt safe with them both. They belonged in the part of her past where everything had become meaningful; a sudden blossoming of her life.

The weeks and months passed by. David now stayed at Crystal House most of the time, supervising the renovation work. Harry continued in his employment as gardener and handyman, his friendship with Jenny deepening. Whilst Brad Carter made frequent visits, noticing with some satisfaction how David Dreighton was aging; this rival for Caroline's affections preferring to spend his time with his computer in the library. Besides, Caroline was paying him well to organise her large income, he reasoned, and he had not given up on selling his house and moving in with her on a more permanent basis.

One December day, a few months later, Caroline was practising her guitar in the ornate drawing room. Jenny had lit candles and was busily filling some vases with holly. They were expecting the arrival of Brad Carter, and David had spent the morning researching the whereabouts of a well in the grounds. Harry was involved in this. He had been ordered to clear an area in the corner of an overgrown plot, that could be concealing the well cover.

'That's sounding good,' Jenny commented, leaving her holly arranging and glancing across to Caroline. '"Somewhere Over the Rainbow." That reminds me of when I was a little kid and going to see *The Wizard of Oz*. There was the Lion, and the Tin Man and the Scarecrow wasn't there? Are we going to have a concert at Christmas?'

'Yes. I've been thinking about the story and the characters. You know David is the Lion, needing courage. He didn't have the courage to stand up to my family, and then The Tin Man. What did he need?'

'A heart,' Jenny said. 'And the Scarecrow needed a brain.'

'So, Brad can be the Tin Man, no heart, just a big ticking clock, and Harry is not exactly Brain of Britain, is he? So, he can be the Scarecrow needing a brain.'

Jenny grinned broadly. 'What about me then?' she asked.

'You can be To-To the dog, my faithful friend.'

'What do you mean? General dog's body?' Jenny laughed. 'And you are Dorothy, I suppose.'

'No, Marigold is Dorothy. I could be The Wicked Witch of the West, but really I think I am the pot of gold.' Caroline gave a strange laugh and propped the guitar up in its stand. She pulled Marigold on to her knee and a large knife clattered to the floor.

'Caroline! What are you doing with that knife?'

'What knife? Oh dear!' she said, shaking the doll. 'Better put her in the cupboard, Jenny.

Naughty Marigold!'

Epilogue

What dramas were yet to unfold? I leave that, readers, to your imagination, for we are all storytellers. Yet, I am persuaded to make one last stab into the future.

Twenty years had passed by and Crystal House was once more unoccupied. The on-line details of the sale had caught the attention of a young architect and his bride to be. Good fortune had smiled on them; indeed, laughed loudly, as they were still recovering from the shock of winning the jackpot in a popular weekly lottery. For the young woman, brought up on an estate on the outskirts of Manchester, living in such a dwelling was beyond her wildest dreams and was a daunting prospect. Nevertheless, she agreed to go on a viewing of the property with her fiancée.

'Wow! What a place!' he exclaimed, as they pulled to a halt outside of the front entrance and saw the carefully cultivated gardens to either side and the pathway leading to the ornate porch. The crystal dome sparkled in the afternoon sunshine and for a few moments they were mesmerised by its splendour.

'Apparently it belonged to an eccentric woman,' the estate agent said. 'She was loaded, and spent a great deal of money having it restored. There was a lot of gossip over the years from people who were employed there; casual work, you know. Mostly, it seemed, she was looked after by a group of friends. They were all a bit eccentric like her, but then you know how people talk.'

It was love at first sight for the young architect, and a few months later after their wedding, and all the purchasing legalities were in place, they moved in with their worldly possessions and the excitement of making future purchases to fill the empty rooms.

As they wandered through the entrance hall he pointed to a panelled door in the shadow of the ornate staircase. 'Is that a cupboard, do you think?' he asked. 'I don't remember noticing that before.' He turned the knob and opened the door. The hinges creaked. 'You could hide in that!' he exclaimed. 'Did you ever play that game, where we all had to hide? Sardines, was it?' He used his phone to illuminate the murky, dusty depths. 'Oh look. I think there's something in there. At the back. Can you see?'

His wife peered in. 'Lots of cobwebs. Hang on. It looks like an old doll.'

She stepped inside and reached out into the dusty corner. 'It is a doll,' she said. 'Nobody mentioned children here, did they? I wonder how old it is. Oh bless. Poor thing. Look, it's got orange hair.'

He shuddered. 'Ugh, weird,' he said. 'I bet it could tell some tales if it could speak. It's filthy. Just bin it.'

'No, I'll clean her up. She was here first. She reminds me of a marigold with that orange hair.'

Lightning Source UK Ltd.
Milton Keynes UK
UKHW021809100419
340803UK00003B/215/P